A Lady's Lesson
in Scandal

Meredith
Duran

More "luscious" (Liz Carlyle)
historical romance from

MEREDITH DURAN

Read her powerful, passionate novels
of scandal and seduction in
nineteenth-century London . . .

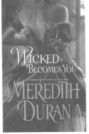
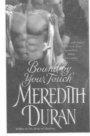

And her stunning, critically
acclaimed debut novel

THE DUKE OF SHADOWS

All available from Pocket Books

ALSO BY MEREDITH DURAN

A Lady's Lesson in Scandal

Meredith Duran

POCKET STAR BOOKS

New York   London   Toronto   Sydney

Pocket Star Books
A Division of Simon & Schuster, Inc.
1230 Avenue of the Americas
New York, NY 10020

This book is a work of fiction. Names, characters, places, and incidents either are products of the author's imagination or are used fictitiously. Any resemblance to actual events or locales or persons, living or dead, is entirely coincidental.

First Pocket Star Books paperback edition July 2011

POCKET STAR BOOKS and colophon are registered trademarks of Simon & Schuster, Inc.

For information about special discounts for bulk purchases, please contact Simon & Schuster Special Sales at 1-866-506-1949 or business@simonandschuster.com.

The Simon & Schuster Speakers Bureau can bring authors to your live event. For more information or to book an event contact the Simon & Schuster Speakers Bureau at 1-866-248-3049 or visit our website at www.simonspeakers.com.

Designed by Esther Paradelo
Cover illustration by Gene Mollica
Hand lettering by Dave Gatti

Manufactured in the United States of America

10 9 8 7 6 5 4 3 2 1

ISBN 978-1-4516-0693-5
ISBN 978-1-4516-0699-7 (ebook)

*To my critique partner, Janine Ballard,
for her brilliant insights, steadfast friendship,
and the thoughtful elegance of her prose,
which never fails to inspire me.*

Acknowledgments

My thanks to the usual suspects who so graciously endure the vicissitudes of my writing process: my wonderful and ever-supportive family; the archaeologist who never says no to Brussels sprouts; the lovely lawyer-to-be currently marooned in the village. I am particularly grateful to Janine Ballard and S. J. Kincaid for their feedback on various drafts, and to Courtney Milan for kindly offering clarification on a nineteenth-century legal treatise that had begun to give me a migraine. (Any inadvertent misinterpretations are without a doubt my own.)

A LADY'S LESSON IN SCANDAL

By the time the whistle finished shrilling, Nell was already out the door. She knew she shouldn't push; once or twice there'd been a stampede and somebody had gotten hurt, broken a leg or arm. But she couldn't slow down. Ever since Mum had taken to wheezing, Nell was finding it harder to breathe, too. No longer could she ignore the thick stink of the workrooms or how often she had to cough as she rolled the cigars. By the end of the day there barely seemed air enough to fill her lungs.

Outside, in the dimming twilight, the damp breeze smelled sour from the coal smoke, but there was enough of it, and that was what mattered. She wove through the milling crowd, girls pausing to tuck their shawls down over their hair, to toss saucy remarks to the lads, chattering like they hadn't got better places to be than this infernal, stinking factory, and maybe they didn't, at that.

Finally she reached a stretch of open pavement. Relief hit her, and with it, a lifting of spirits. Nice thing about working at the factory: every day had a happy ending. She found a wall to lean on and settled against it just as a hand grabbed her elbow.

She ripped free and came face to face with Hannah. "You scared the life out of me!" she gasped.

Hannah's pale, freckled face was alight with excitement. "That's because you're a goose, Nellie. What's your take for the week?"

Nell looked around for eavesdroppers. "Nineteen shillings." Her neck was cramped from hunching over the worktable and the ache in her knuckles would keep her awake tonight, but nineteen shillings was the best she'd ever done.

Of course, it would sink to ten after her stepbrother, Michael, took his share. That wasn't enough to tempt a good doctor to the flat and eat next week besides.

Hannah pulled a face. "Only fifteen for me." Usually she beat Nell by a crown; her fingers were cleverer. "Was yesterday that did me in. I was going gorgeously but then the labor-mistress took a temper and made me unroll half the pile. Ah, well." She wiped a strand of honey blond hair from her eyes, then waggled the fingers of her uplifted hand. "D'ye like my gloves? Found 'em at Brennan's dollyshop. Cost me two days' wages, but they're genuine kidskin, he said."

"Oh, they're lovely." In fact, the knuckles were cracked, and the white leather had long since grown dingy with use. In her friend's place, Nell could have found better uses for a crown. Good tough wool, for instance. A new kettle. Some fresh fruit—Lord alive, her mouth watered for a crisp country apple.

Then again, she had chilblains, and Hannah didn't. So who was the wiser?

She took Hannah's arm and pulled her into step along the pavement. "You won't let your father see them." If Garod Crowley found out that his daughter was keeping a bit of coin to herself, there'd be an awful row.

Hannah laughed. "I'm no fool!"

A passing lad made eyes in their direction. Nell didn't recognize him, so she frowned to send him on his way. He winked at her before turning onward, but despite her blush, she wasn't fooled: he'd been admiring Hannah. With her heart-shaped face and big, velvet brown eyes, Han had grown dangerously pretty in the last two years.

"Oh, say, Nellie—are you coming to the GFS?"

Nell had forgotten there was a meeting tonight. The ladies who ran the Girls' Friendship Society had a tendency to lecture and a provoking way of trying to pry into a girl's private affairs, but they also kept a brilliant collection of books that they'd lend to any girl who joined. "I wish I could go," she said. But Mum was too sick now to leave alone. That last quack's potions had only made her worse.

"You've got to come! They're having a tea for us!"

"I know. How lovely." She would have enjoyed a proper cup. What with how hard she was saving, she couldn't afford aught but bohea tea these days.

The thought dimmed her mood. She could save all she liked, but it was a slow effort. Meanwhile, Mum grew worse almost by the hour.

"—to give us gifts as well," Hannah was chattering. "You can't miss the meeting!"

"I've no choice. Suzie's got a shift at Mott's tonight, and Mum can't be alone."

Hannah cast her a sharp glance. "Let Michael look after your mum for once!"

Nell almost laughed. *That* would be the day. Ever since Mum had taken too ill to work, Michael wanted nothing to do with her. Suddenly he remembered he was only a stepson. "I expect he'll want to keep company with Suzie." He enjoyed the fast atmosphere of the supper club where his wife kept bar—and the fine liquor Suzie slipped him when she was working there.

He enjoyed Suzie's wages, too. Didn't let a penny slip past for his wife to keep. Nell couldn't count on her to help.

What she needed was a moneylender. They scrupled at loaning to a woman, but somebody probably would agree to lend to Michael in her stead.

Would Michael hand over the money once he had it, though? He'd never been one to share. Last year, he'd come into a handsome windfall somehow but he'd put every penny of it toward his political club. Now he'd washed his hands of politics, but gambling and gin kept his pockets empty. If he took a loan and refused to share it . . . Nell couldn't think what she would do.

Or rather, she could. She knew exactly how to solve her difficulties. Michael would be more than willing to help on *that* point. But she couldn't do it. The very idea made her bones go cold and the gorge rise in her throat. *Milk once spoiled is naught but rubbish,* Mum always said.

Then again, Mum told her all they needed was prayer. It didn't make a girl a heathen to know that wasn't true.

Miserable, she glanced toward Hannah. They'd lived in the same building as children, walked to school together, spent Sunday evenings making mischief in the road. They'd kept nothing from each other while growing up. But lately that had changed. Things were happening that Nell couldn't manage to speak about for shame. *My stepbrother wants to whore me*: how did a girl bring herself to say that? And what use in doing so? Hannah had naught but sympathy to give.

Still, a bit of sympathy sounded so lovely right now. Nell gathered her courage. "Han, I've got to tell you—"

"Oh, would you look at that!" Hannah dropped her arm to fly toward a shopfront. The gas lamps burning in the window illuminated a row of photographic prints.

Nell exhaled. She was relieved, really. She could manage it on her own.

Still, to her surprise, she had to blink hard a couple of times against the urge to cry. "I'm in a hurry."

"Oh, come on—just for a moment!"

With a sigh, Nell walked over to the window. This was the new craze, to buy pictures of society beauties. Michael had a couple pinned to the wall at home, flash ladies in evening gowns and tiaras. Sometimes when Nell was frying haddock at the fire, she caught herself staring at them. They looked like dolls, their waists so tiny, their hair so smoothly rolled. Impossible to believe that as she stood there choking on the smell of fish, they were living in the very same world, the same moment in time, not a handful of miles distant. As unreal as they seemed to her, they might have been living on the moon.

"I know about this one!" Hannah pressed a finger to the glass to indicate a handsome girl wearing a dark brocade gown trimmed with silk roses. "Lady Jennie Churchill, does that say?"

Beneath the photograph sat a fancy placard covered in cursive. Nell gave it a quick look. "Aye, right enough."

"She's the American one what married the Duke of Marlborough's son. He's got a case of the glim, they say!"

Nell shrugged. "Lie down with dogs, rise up with fleas."

"No, these toffs don't visit any threepenny uprights, Nell. They keep their molls high class! Set up a girl with a flash place in St. John's Wood and her own coach and driver, even."

"And how would *you* be knowing it?"

"People talk, don't they?"

The conversation was making Nell's stomach tighten. They did talk. They accused her mum of putting airs into her, educating her above her station. If she took the path Michael was pushing on her, they would gloat till the cows came home. "They talk a whole lot of rubbish, all right."

"Oh, don't be sour! A proper gentleman isn't the same as a man off the street. No, I expect it's just talk about his lordship." Hannah frowned, her finger tapping the glass. "Still, poor girl. Hope he don't make her sick."

"Nothing poor about her," Nell muttered. "Those diamonds at her throat could feed and house us both for five years."

"Well." Hannah fell silent, studying the rest of the pictures. She pointed to a photograph farther down the row. "Look there. She's a lovely one, ain't she?"

"La-di-da. Give me a fortune and I'd look lovely, too." Nell cast an anxious glance down the street. The crowd was already starting to thin. Once everybody cleared out, it wouldn't be safe.

"Well—and hey! I'd say she does look a good bit like you! Really, Nell, have a look at that!"

Did that group of lads coming toward them have specific intentions, or were they just making their way on down the road? "God save me from looking like a wax doll!"

Hannah giggled. "Oh, you're just jealous because Dick Jackson was walking around with a print of this one t'other day."

She recognized one of the boys, a good, churchgoing fellow. Relaxing, she turned back to Hannah. "I've got no business with Dickie Jackson, and I'll not say it again. He spends more time in the lushery than he does at his work, and that's enough to finish him for me."

"Well, what is it then? D'you truly not fancy her beautiful? You've got to admit the resemblance!"

Nell sighed. It was cold out, and not everybody here had gloves. But there was a look on Hannah's face, a sort of wistful awe, that made her feel small hearted. If looking at these silly pictures tickled Hannah's fancy, then she could stand here a bit longer.

She cupped her hands to her mouth and blew, the heat of her breath stinging her chilblains. "Right you are, then. She's a jemmy lass."

"Oh, leastways *look* at her before you say it! Tell me who she is."

With a roll of her eyes, Nell turned her attention to the placard beneath the photograph. "Lady Katherine Aubyn, daughter of Earl Rushden." She glanced up and felt a shock. "Why . . ."

"Lady Katherine," Hannah repeated softly. "Queer how much she looks like you."

Nell's hand shook a little as she touched her own chin. Katherine Aubyn had a cleft there, too. Her jaw made the same stark square. Her nose was as long and thin, her eyes as widely spaced.

A prickle moved down Nell's spine. The girl looked just like her. How was that possible? She knew she wasn't handsome, but this girl with her face looked perfect, not a single wrinkle or blemish to prove that she was real. The photograph was like a magic mirror—a view into a different life where she was born to riches, where maids wove silk ribbons through her brown hair and fastened a fortune in pearls around her neck before she sat down to pose for a portrait.

Lady Katherine wore a faint smile. It seemed to deepen as Nell stared. *My pearls could buy a thousand visits from a thousand doctors,* that smile said.

Gooseflesh rose on her arms. Hannah asked, "How do you reckon you look so much alike?"

She drew her shawl tighter. Witchery! This girl had stolen Nell's face and was getting far better use from it. "Boring," she said sharply. "She's boring, that's what. Not a line on her face—you think she ever farts, or does she have the maids do that for her, too?"

Hannah laughed. "Well, with *that* much chink, who needs to be interesting?"

Nell forced out her own laugh. "True. Her daddy'll buy her a husband if she can't find one on her own."

The picture made her feel sick somehow. She linked her arm through Hannah's and pulled her away.

Her friend cast a forlorn glance back at the shop window. "Can you imagine, Nell? What it'd be like to have your face up there? To have the blokes paying for your picture?"

"Lord, no, and I'm glad of it!" Her voice sounded firm enough. "Don't think I'd want *my* face in Dickie Jackson's pocket."

Hannah's laughter started out surprised but trailed off into sad. "Oh, Nell. Truly, though, *don't* you wonder? Piles on piles of chink. Not a care in the world."

She couldn't imagine it. But she'd seen what trouble lay in trying. "They don't go hand in hand, love. Rich women have got cares of their own." She had to believe that. Wasn't anybody in the world without a heart and a worry to burden it.

"Ha! I could use some cares like that!" Hannah

slid her arm out from Nell's to do a little twirl over the pavement. "Shall I wear the diamond or the emerald tiara tonight, milord? The silk dress or the satin?" She batted her big brown eyes and sketched a mock curtsy. "Oh, you wish to give me even *more* money? However will I make do?"

Nell still felt dizzy, like that bleeding photograph had leapt out and slapped her. "Oh, you've brought back the rotting disease from one of your whores?" she retorted. "Too kind of ye, milord!"

Hannah planted her fists on her hips. "That was just patter! Anyway, I'm serious. You *must* wonder. Say you do."

Nell felt herself frowning. "You shouldn't waste your time hankering after what you can't have. That's no road to happiness."

"Happiness?" The other girl's lips crooked in a sneer. "Aye, and I'm happy right now, ain't I? With my ding gloves that some fine lady probably gave to her maid. Who probably gave 'em to the scullery girl before they ended up at Brennan's!"

Nell felt a moment's shock: the outburst was so unlike Hannah. But why not? Hannah mightn't have *her* worries, but neither of them had a future full of pearls and comforts. Meanwhile, the fog was coming on thick, lowering in dirty, sullen clouds to the uneven cobblestones. All around, light and sound were dimming, and the wet chill in the air warned of rain. Somewhere in this city, Lady Katherine was warm and snug, but out here, it promised a nasty night, the sort in which an unhappy spirit could find more than enough trouble to suit it.

God save us both.

She pulled her shawl over her head and then held

out one hand, exposing cracked red knuckles. "If you're going to toss those gloves, I've got a use for 'em."

Hannah stared. Her lips tightened around some emotion that Nell didn't want to guess at. "I'm sorry, Nellie. I don't know what's got into me."

"Oh, but I do," Nell said softly. "Aye, Hannah, of course I think about it." God above, she thought about it far too often lately. She barely could sleep at night for the thoughts in her head. "But it's stupid to dwell on it. It only hurts."

That photograph seemed such a bad omen. There was only so much good fortune to go around, and another girl with her face had already claimed her share.

Superstitious rubbish, she told herself. Aloud, she said, "Try to focus on the bright things, love."

Hannah took a deep breath, then gave her a determined smile. "Aye, you're right, of course." She looped her arm back through Nell's. "Well, come on, then, ducky. We'd best make tracks; it looks to be heading for a pea souper."

Hannah's fingers were saying something different from her smile. They dug into Nell's arm hard enough to hurt. Hard enough to give her a new worry when she already had too many to bear.

She opened her mouth, then thought better of it. *I think about it constantly,* she might have said. *It's a stone in my chest, a hot, fiery stone, the injustice of it.*

But what good would it do for Hannah to know that? She needed a different sort of example—one that showed her how to accept what she couldn't change. You *had* to accept it; otherwise the fire in your chest would spread and burn you, inside out. Nell felt it happening to herself. She'd seen it happen to her stepbrother. Last autumn Michael had been ranting, raging, ready to change the world. He'd joined the Socialists, helped them gather over a thousand men. They'd gone marching through Hyde Park screaming slogans, demanding justice.

And what had they won? The wrath of the police. Broken ribs and shattered noses. A couple of days' notice in the newspapers . . . and then it had been over, and the toffs had gone back to their tea parties, and Michael had turned to gin.

No. Best to forget such things.

"I will," Hannah said, giving Nell a start. She hadn't realized she'd spoken aloud. But it had been the right thing to say, for Hannah's grip gentled, and she gave Nell a real smile this time, then launched into a popular ballad making the rounds on the street. Nell joined in, and together they set a brisk pace for home.

Nell woke that night to the sound of footsteps stopping next to her head. Her eyes opened on a silhouette looming over her. Not an arm's reach away, Mum loosed a wet, choked breath.

"She's done for," said Michael from above. "Death rattle."

That made the hundredth time he'd said the same. She could smell the gin on him. The floorboards creaked under his feet; his balance was failing.

She pushed herself up on an elbow. "Where's Suzie?" she whispered.

"Where's Suzie," he mocked. "Where in bloody hell do you think?"

To her right, she heard her mother murmur something. *Don't speak*, Nell willed silently. *Keep sleeping.* She'd seen Suzie's state earlier this evening—eye blackened, face red and puffy from weeping. Michael could go days without the drink, but none of them rejoiced when he did. His abstinence invariably ended in a glut that lasted for days.

If he wanted a fight, he could have it in the back room. Mum needed her sleep.

Nell pushed aside the blanket and got up. The back of her neck prickled as he fell in step behind her.

A thin sheet separated the two rooms. On the other side, a kerosene lamp sat on the small table beside the hearth. Thinking to light it, she felt for the matches.

His sudden grip on her wrist pulled her around. Hot, moist, his hand was twice the size of hers. "Don't," he said. "Leave it dark. I don't want to have to look on your ugly face."

"All right," she said on a breath. Mum said he had a demon in him that fed on the drink. Nell rarely paid her much mind when she took to raving of devils, but nights like these, it was easy to believe such things.

With her free hand, she felt behind her for the long iron fork she used to grill sausages over the fire. It fit nicely into her palm, a solid weight, reassuring. She'd sharpened the tines a week ago. "Where's Suzie?" she asked again. *Not dead, pray God.* Once a man took to using his fists, he rarely stopped. One day, she feared, Michael would hit one of them too hard.

"Mott's." His laugh was low and nasty. "Knee-deep in the lads, wouldn't you know. Made me sick to watch her."

She wished that she could see his face. He took after her stepfather, brown in his coloring as dirt, but he was well built, a boxer, handsome and proud of it: he didn't let himself sneer or twitch unless he'd given over to his temper. If she could see the line of his mouth, she'd have clearer intentions about this fork in her hand. "It's part of her job, Michael. She makes good money there."

"Don't she? I wonder how she manages so much. Maybe I know."

"I know she loves you." Pathetic but true. Suzie had been a properly pretty girl with a dozen suitors. Most of them would have treated her better than Michael did. Like countless women before her, she'd thrown her fortune into the slops by following her foolish heart. When Nell married, she'd choose a man for better reasons: kindness, decency, a solid roof to shelter her. A lad who loved her more than she did him: that was the safest way to happiness.

"Sure and she loves me." Michael's voice was starting to slur, but his grip on her wrist didn't slacken. "Awfully worried for Suzie, ain't you? I'd worry for myself instead."

"I will, when there's reason for it." As far as she could tell, she was the only one in this flat that kept her wits about her.

"I'd say there is. I heard about that little talk you had with the labor-mistress. You've got a powerful wealth of ideas, don't you?"

She caught her breath. Were people speaking of that? All she'd asked was for Mrs. Plimpton to speak with the master about a few windows for the work-rooms. Much good it had done—the woman had fallen apart with laughter. *You're not paid to breathe,* she'd said. *Back to work with you.*

"Didn't do any harm," she whispered. "Just a brief chat."

"You're a fool. You think they give a damn about your comfort? They look at you, they see one of us. Just another rat for the slaughter."

The bitterness in his voice struck at her. She heard his whole history in it, and it made her soften a little. Before jail, he'd had ideas of his own about what workers deserved. He'd put his money toward the cause of reform and all he'd gotten for it was misery and abuse. She could understand if he thought her a fool for following in those footsteps.

"I won't say anything more," she said. "But I'm right, Michael. It was the air in the factory that made Mum sick. And they could change it so easily—"

His nails dug into her. "Am I meant to care?"

She tightened her grip on the fork. If he made her stick him, it'd be a long and ugly night. "No."

"You get sacked and I'll care. I'll be fixing you up with Dickie, no matter your thoughts."

"All right," she said evenly.

"He was asking after you in the street tonight. Two crowns, he had in his hand. Said he'd be as glad to spend them on you as on another girl."

The darkness felt like a hand pressing over her mouth, stopping her breath. Damn Dickie Jackson. He knew very well what he was doing with such remarks. Like waving a flag in front of a bull: he thought himself so clever in baiting Michael. Thought it was only a matter of time before her stepbrother forced her to it.

From the other room came the sound of a strangled cough. *Oh, God, don't let her get up. Let her be too weak to get up.* "I brought in twice that amount this week." Her voice sounded hoarse. Her wrist was starting to throb.

"Or you could make two crowns in a quarter hour. You think you're too good for it? Fancy yourself better than the rest of us, maybe? Somebody *special*?"

She swallowed. Sometimes lately she asked herself the same. So many girls she'd known had earned a quick coin up against the wall. Why should it be different for her? Aye, she could read and write and she'd worked hard to educate herself, but that didn't make her special. Everybody starved the same way. In the end, everybody died.

Two crowns for a quarter hour. It would be a handsome profit.

But not for her. Wasn't logic or reason that drove her, but something gut deep, hard as diamond: she could consider such a turn, but she'd never agree to it. There was another way. She'd find it, somehow. If not the moneylender, she'd go thieving before she laid down for Dickie bloody Jackson. "I earn my keep here—"

"Ha! Mason down the street says I could have twelve a week for the space you take up—"

The anger leapt up from nowhere. "Your father promised we could stay here!"

His grip fell away. "Your bloody *mum,* not you. And she's *dying,* do you hear that?"

"You're drinking away the coin that could save her!"

The blow came out of the darkness. Agony like lightning knifed through her jaw. The floorboards slammed into her. She opened her eyes, hearing her own strangled gasp, the rough wood burning beneath her cheek.

In the background, Mama called out. "Cornelia! Are you . . . quite fine?"

"Are you quite fine?" Michael mimicked. "The bloody queen in there!"

Nell held still. Her brain seemed to be rattling in its casing, but her jaw still worked when she wiggled it. He'd used the back of his hand, not his fist, thank God.

"One good kick," Michael said softly. "That's all it would take, you uppity bitch."

Anger swamped the pain. This stupid, useless fork she still clenched in her hand—she should have stuck him when she'd had the chance.

"But you've got money to earn," he continued. "So get used to lying on your back."

I'll kill you first, she thought.

She saw the broad shape of his shoulders silhouetted against the curtain before he pushed it aside. The cloth ripped and fell. His footsteps clomped across the floorboards, setting them to shuddering. Hinges squeaked. The front door slammed.

A quavering voice called from the next room. "Cornelia? Cor—"

The cough that punctuated that call roused Nell to sit up. The room was spinning around her. She wiped blood from her nose. Rage tasted bitter as bile. She hated him. She hated Dickie Jackson. Hate, hate, dizzy, hot; she hurled the useless fork aside.

Cloth rustled in the next room: Mum was trying to sit up.

Nell took a large breath. "I'm all right," she said, forcing herself to her feet, hurrying past the torn curtain, crossing the distance to the pallet. "Shh, Mum, lie back. I'm all right."

"No," Mum said. Her graying hair was a pale nimbus around her shadowed face. "God save you. God spare you. God keep us all . . ." She turned her head aside to cough.

Nell laid a hand to her back, supporting her into easing back down to the floor. "It's all right, Mum. Go back to sleep."

"You must ask . . . for help. He is wicked but he will help."

"All right," Nell murmured. She brushed her hand

over her mother's hot, dry cheek. The fevers always got higher in the evenings.

Mum turned her head away, fretful. "Listen," she said. "Write to him. I hoped . . . I did it for you, Cornelia. His lust, he was a devil. Lewder, more prideful even than Michael. Lust and lewdness . . ."

Brilliant. The last thing Mum needed right now was the exertion of one of her fits. "Calm down. Just lie quietly."

"No." Bony fingers caught Nell's arm and dug for attention. "Gird yourself. Ask God to protect you. But tell him who you are. Tell him . . . I thought to save you. Part of him for my own. To *save* a part of him." A hack took Mum, wet and violent. The effort to breathe wracked her thin frame.

"All right. I'll tell him." *Damn* Michael. Damn the Malloys upstairs, too, who'd taken it into their heads that Mum was a minor saint. They encouraged her talk of demons and angels; they asked her to intercede for them. "Mum, you need to sleep."

"I'm lucid." For a startling second, Mum sounded as firm and sharp as she once had, back in the days when she'd boxed Michael's ears for taking the Lord's name in vain and forced him onto his knees beside the rest of them for three hours every Sunday. "You can go back now, Cornelia. I forgive you."

"I'll go back. Just calm."

"You must go to your father. Lord Rushden is waiting."

Nell froze. Lord Rushden? The father of that girl in the photograph?

The coincidence lifted the hairs on her nape. "Mum, what do you mean?"

"Oh, the devil," her mother said, sighing. "But I forgive you."

"Forgive me for what?" Nell whispered.

"You must speak to your father." Mum's voice sounded peculiar, suddenly—queer and girlish. "You must speak to his lordship."

Her *father*? "Mum." She barely dared to breathe. "What are you saying? You can't mean that Lord Rushden . . ."

"Never let him tempt you," Mum murmured. "Resist sin."

"You're raving." Nell's throat closed on a hard swallow. "Donald Miller is my father." Mum had talked of him. A nice, respectable gentleman farmer from Leicestershire, who'd died of the cholera when Nell had been a babe in arms.

"Never," Mum said, still in that wispy, dreamy voice. "A lie. Only Lord Rushden, Cornelia. Long ago, before. He *will* help you. I took you for your sake. But I can help no longer. Only write to him."

Her heart was pounding in her throat. Impossible to think it, but she could find no other interpretation: her saintly mum was admitting she was a bastard. The bastard of a lord.

No wonder she looked like that girl in the photograph.

She leaned forward, gripping her mother's hand hard. "Would he pay for a doctor for you?"

"Oh, Cornelia . . ." Her mother's high laugh sent a chill down her spine. "The devil will do far more than that."

2

$\mathcal{F}$ew pastimes were so tedious as a party thrown to prove the host's depravity. Colton's rout was no exception. The walls had been covered in dark velvet, the electricity shut off. The only light came from iron candelabras positioned throughout the room. A miserable-looking string quartet sat in the corner, sawing out what Simon belatedly recognized as *Te Deum* played backward. Over their heads, an upside-down cross dangled on a chain from a darkened chandelier. The hired girls in the room—those who still wore clothing, at any rate—were dressed as nuns.

Simon laughed under his breath as he stepped inside. Why this enduring fixation on nuns? The faces in the raucous crowd were largely familiar to him, and as usual, he did not see a Catholic among them. He could only conclude that something in the Anglican tradition cultivated fantasies of popish defilement.

At least he saw no black mass under way. Small mercy, that.

As notice of him spread, greetings came right and left—an MP leaving off with a half-naked woman to sketch him a bow; three city magnates toasting him so enthusiastically that most of their whisky landed on the carpet. He replied with cordial nods as he looked through the crowd for his quarry. A babble of excited speculation reached his ears, mentions of his sins both real and imagined. Mostly imagined, of course.

He felt his lips twist. Old Rushden had never

understood that. He'd believed everything he'd heard of his heir, and even now, Simon could not regret that he'd never tried to convince the bastard otherwise. Even tonight, on the precipice of final ruin, Simon could not see how it might have gone differently. His guardian had judged and damned him from the get-go; he'd never had a chance.

"Rushden!" Harcourt approached, skirting a pair of half-dressed dukes who were directing a girl's gyrations atop a banqueting table. She looked no older than fifteen, still able to smile enthusiastically on idiocy. "You came!"

"And so did you," Simon replied, his gaze lingering on the girl. As one of the lordlings made an open-handed grab for her breast, he sighed. Very tempting to offer her a coin to fund her escape, only she wouldn't take it. This gathering presented the best business opportunity she'd ever receive.

He turned his attention to Harcourt. "And why are you here?" He was the last man to scruple at drunken revelry, but this lot wasn't reveling as much as showing off for each other. Harcourt generally kept better company.

"I know, a sad scene." Harcourt drove an unsteady hand through his ginger hair, causing a curl to flop across his eye. "But the night is slow. And I thought you'd be at Swanby's soiree! Wasn't your newest pet performing there tonight?"

Simon nodded. "It ended an hour ago." He'd instructed Andreasson, the Swedish pianist whose talents he currently sponsored, to bang out several discordant pieces. Lady Swanby's guests had pretended to enjoy the music and would be sure to report enthusiastically on it tomorrow, the better to advertise their attendance to those who'd not been invited. "Made quite a stir."

Despite his efforts, the blackness of his mood must have showed in his voice, for Harcourt narrowed his eyes and stepped closer. "Never say it went poorly!"

The idea surprised Simon into a laugh. "Of course not." His discoveries were always en vogue. To disagree with the Earl of Rushden's artistic opinions was to risk being thought a bumpkin.

Of course, that might change once it became known that he was all but broke.

"Then what ails you?" Harcourt asked.

He shrugged and took a drink from a passing servant's tray. The liquor's burn felt noxiously chemical. He didn't see much point in keeping silent on the court ruling; the newspapers tomorrow would trumpet it across the nation.

But as he lowered the emptied glass, he found he did not want to speak of it just yet. His disbelief still felt too large to put into words. Never mind that his predecessor, the ninth Earl of Rushden, had been insane. Never mind that only a madman would have commanded his fortune to be divided between a living daughter and a dead one; that only a madman would have designed a legacy that left the next earl penniless, the family estates to rot and crumble, the retainers to be sacked, and the lands to go to seed.

Never mind all this. The court had decided to uphold old Rushden's will anyway.

Somewhere in hell, the bastard was enjoying his revenge.

Simon let go of a long breath. No, he would waste no further effort on this nonsense. Let the journalists struggle to explain it. "Nothing ails me," he said, and felt relatively certain, after a moment, that he meant it. Life was a great, big, ludicrous joke. Anyone who took it seriously was a fool.

Harcourt still looked doubtful. Simon pulled up a smile for good measure. "Have you seen Dalziel hereabouts?" It hadn't been a good day, but it still could end well.

"Oh ho!" Harcourt broke into a grin. "Never say he's still hiding the book from you? I can help you with that." This offer was punctuated with an ostentatious cracking of Harcourt's knuckles. Since retiring from the Fusiliers, he was at loose ends, and nothing cheered him more rapidly than the prospect of violence.

Simon hadn't anticipated needing to go to such lengths. But why not? That Dalziel had taken the money and failed to surrender the manuscript seemed, after this very long and inexpressibly irksome day, deserving of bloodshed. "By all means," he said with a shrug.

He started forward into the crowd, Harcourt at his elbow. Hail-fellow-well-met thumps buffeted his shoulders; waggling brows and slurred encouragements trailed in his wake. As he sidestepped a knot of men who'd gathered to watch the finance minister rip the habit off a brunette, he found himself suddenly, darkly amused. The middling classes prated so earnestly in magazines about the rewards of hard work, ingenuity, learning, right living. A look around this room would serve them the most effective rebuttal imaginable. Their nation was governed by horny, overgrown schoolboys.

"Colton will be beside himself to find you here," Harcourt remarked. "Was asking after you earlier. Said he hadn't seen you in weeks."

Colton was the host of this event. Intent on proving

his credentials as a man-about-town, he'd been court-ing friendship from any half-notorious gentleman he could locate. Avoiding him grew tedious; encouraging him was a deadly mistake. "I'll tell him I went off to find God," Simon said dryly. "That should quell his interest."

As the remark echoed in his ears, it began to sound less ludicrous than portentous. The court ruling left him little choice but to hunt for a wealthy bride. Alas, rakes excelled on the marriage market only when in a state of reform.

The crowd parted and he spotted Dalziel. The man was standing a short distance away, behind a long table atop which an unclothed woman was serving as the platter for canapés. When anxious, Dalziel ate; at pres-ent, he was plucking up cheese and grapes with speed and enthusiasm.

His animal sense registered danger: he glanced up and did a comical double-take as his eyes met Simon's.

"You," he gasped, then stumbled as the woman playing the part of the table slapped his clumsy hand away from her eye. Regaining his balance, he wheeled to flee.

"Hold there!" In three long strides, Harcourt caught Dalziel and turned him around by the shoulder, slamming him up against the wall with enough force to make a nearby candelabra rattle.

"Don't hurt me!" Dalziel squeaked as Simon strolled up. The lovely lady on the table gave Simon a smile and reached out to take his empty glass.

"My thanks," he said to her.

"Shut your face," Harcourt was bellowing at Dal-ziel. "You're lucky if I don't gut you. What do you say, Rushden? A facer to start?"

Dalziel whimpered. "No, no—for God's sake! Please . . ."

Putting his hands in his pockets, Simon looked Dalziel up and down. The man was generally quite florid, but just now his puffy face had gone as pale as Italian cheese. He'd clearly been enjoying himself this evening; his waistcoat was improperly buttoned and his cuffs gaped open. Was there such a thing as poor form at an orgy? Simon put the question aside for later consideration. "You have something of mine," he said.

Dalziel's mouth worked. He had the wide-eyed, startled look of a small creature trapped in sudden bright lights. "Please, I—I want no trouble."

"Pathetic," Harcourt commented.

"No trouble is required," Simon said. "Simply hand over the book."

"I've not got it!"

"But feisty," Harcourt said in impressed tones.

Simon cut his friend a silencing look, then leaned toward Dalziel. "This game bores me. You're not clever enough to play it, and you won't like how it ends."

The color rushed back into Dalziel's face. "It's no game," he squeaked. "You—you didn't honor the terms!"

"Terms? You named the price. I accepted it." The manuscript was not particularly valuable; no true collector would have coveted it. But Simon did, and Dalziel, knowing this, had asked for an undeservedly high price. "Don't tell me," Simon added with open scorn, "that a hundred pounds did not satisfy you?"

"Zero," Dalziel whispered.

"I beg your pardon?"

"Zero," Dalziel said through his teeth.

"Cheek," growled Harcourt. He tightened his hand around the man's neck, his knuckles turning white as Dalziel loosed a gasp of pain.

"Zero!" Dalziel screamed—then flushed a violent red, as though mortified by his own outburst.

Simon laughed in astonishment. The man was a caricature. "Zero is a number," he said. "Not an explanation. Do try again."

Dalziel's gaze cut between them. "I tried to cash your check," he said rapidly. "It was refused!"

"A mistake," said Harcourt. "You should have asked to speak with Rushden's banker!"

"Morris, yes. I did speak with him." Dalziel swallowed. "Ain't a mistake. Morris said—he said your account's been frozen!" He shrank into himself with a little gasp and crammed shut his eyes.

The reaction, and the remark that had preceded it, seemed so bizarre that Simon wondered if the man was having an attack of some sort. "What's wrong with you?"

Dalziel cracked open one eye. "Don't hit me!"

Simon took a step backward. "I have no plans for it." He wouldn't hit a man who showed no intention of defending himself. It seemed a bit much, though, to inform Dalziel of his own effeminacy.

Harcourt was staring, wide-eyed. "*I* would hit him. That's a deuced nasty rumor, Rushden. People will think—they'll think—well, I don't know what!"

That I'm pockets to let.

Good God. Could Grimston have acted so quickly?

Simon turned away to disguise his reaction in a survey of the crowd. Yes, of course Grimston would have acted at once. He was guardian to old Rushden's remaining daughter; what money went to her, passed through his hands first. He'd coveted every penny of the estate, and would no doubt help himself to a good many of them before Kitty attained her majority.

He drove his hand through his hair as he turned back—pausing midturn as he caught his reflection in one of the pier glasses set around the room to show the guests their wicked antics. In the mirror, he saw a man, more than averagely handsome, more than averagely tall, resplendently fashionable in evening blacks, with an expression on his face of ill-concealed shock.

The man now smiled faintly. What a clever turn out. He was the very picture of a buffoon as sketched by some cartoonist in *Punch*. The caption beneath his portrait would read: *The wandering rakehell faces his destitution manfully, in the finest French fashions.*

He released a long breath. The coroneted bankrupt: not very original. He had some small funds tucked away, though. Enough to buy this book, certainly.

Perhaps he should be more concerned with paying his creditors.

Comical thought. Who in London actually paid his creditors?

Simon laughed. It was a strange sound and he watched its effect on his reflection, trying to hold on to that peculiar sensation of looking at himself as a stranger would. It was far more comforting to fathom bad news about oneself when seeing clearly what an ass one was. Then it did not feel so much like bad news as it did a rare piece of justice.

He turned back to Dalziel, who flinched. "I'll have the money to you tomorrow morning," he said. "You will be at home, waiting for me."

"Yes, yes," Dalziel said quickly, gratefully. "I'll be waiting."

Simon swept out a mocking hand. Dalziel shoved off the wall and bolted into the crowd.

Harcourt looked after him. "Is it true?" he asked quietly. "Are you hard up?"

"Suffice it to say that I'm in the market for marriage." He shrugged at Harcourt's marveling look. He had no objection to the institution. He'd been engaged once, in love not only with the woman but with the idea of becoming a husband to her.

Of course, in the aftermath of old Rushden's interference, his tolerance for courtship had eroded. He would not take well to explaining and excusing and proving himself to some wide-eyed debutante.

The thought actually made him weary. The French probably would diagnose him with a bad case of ennui, but he rather thought that what ailed him was a case of adulthood.

Harcourt was shaking his head. "Bad timing here."

"Indeed." The season was almost at an end. He'd have to follow the likely prospects north and waste his summer grouse hunting in Scotland.

Simon laughed softly. He could not believe it had come to this.

"If you'll excuse me," Harcourt said thoughtfully. "I think I'd still like to plant a facer on Dalziel. Meet you outside afterward?"

Simon remembered with a start his promise to return to Lady Swanby before dawn. It had seemed a fair reward for her good taste in showcasing Andreasson. Her husband, she claimed, was a very sound sleeper. "Not tonight. Possibly tomorrow." Although most of his day would probably be spent in conference with panicked accountants, solicitors, secretaries, stewards . . . Sometimes he felt as though half the world

depended on the fullness of Lord Rushden's bank accounts.

"I live in hope," Harcourt said. With a clap to
Simon's back, he departed.

A low, sultry voice came from the direction of the
table: "Did you scare them off, then?"

"Hmm?" Simon glanced down at the woman. Her
mons veneris and upper thighs were blanketed in nuts.
At least she looked to be out of her teens. "No," he said
with a smile, "I'm afraid they got the best of me." His
smile turned into a laugh as he considered the assortment of food laid across her. "Darling, I'll admit it: I
have never felt so envious of confections." He plucked
a walnut from her navel.

"Don't stop there," she purred. She had pretty, dark
eyes, tilted like a cat's. "You can have them all, you
can. And maybe something else for dessert."

"Charming," he murmured. Alas, he didn't play
with the help. And now—he laughed again—he
couldn't afford to do so anyway. "Some other time,
perhaps." He lifted her hand for a kiss, then turned on
his heel for the exit.

As he passed into the hallway, a nearby clock began
to chime the midnight hour, and a startled bellow came
from below.

It seemed Harcourt had caught up with Dalziel.

His laughter welled up again from nowhere, suddenly, and with such startling force that he had to stop
and lean against the wall. He had no idea what set
him off, but the hilarity expanded to encompass more
and more, to encompass it all: Dalziel shrieking below;
old Rushden selling off manuscripts like a merchant;
grouse hunting, for God's sake, and little debutantes
in white dresses, demanding repentance; Simon's

mother's disgust when she heard all these tidings from her comfortable summer home in Nice; and the intensity of his own delusions, his *grand musical talents,* a youth misspent pursuing them, all for nothing, now, as the clock rang so insistently, though it made no bloody difference whether or not anyone knew the time, not really; it kept on moving whether one was informed of it or not.

He wiped tears from his eyes. As his mirth ebbed he became conscious of a curious sensation in his stomach. It felt like an ache, not a pressure as much as a sort of hollowness, expanding, cold, like the dull blue deepening of twilight.

Alone in this hallway, he suddenly felt . . . like the only person in the world.

Lady Swanby was waiting. The thought made him draw a long breath and push off the wall. Yes, God forbid he keep Lady Swanby waiting for him. What an inconvenience it would pose her to have to find someone else with whom to pass the night.

Like billiard balls bashing around the table, he thought. How randomly we smash into and away from each other.

He shook his head at himself. Heard Harcourt below and put a smile on his face. As he started down the stairs, he threw in a salute to the clock for good measure. "Time waits for no man," he murmured.

But every day, it certainly ran out for someone.

A girl got to thinking after her mother died. Some people were born saintlike, and Nell's mum had been one of them: righteous, holy, with a pale, thin voice made for muttering prayers in some hushed alcove where nobody could overhear. At the wake, people had said she'd been beautiful once, but Nell couldn't imagine it. Beauty was a broad grin, a loud laugh, the water beating up on the Ramsgate sands—things that would be here tomorrow, that didn't give a damn.

Mum had always given a damn. Anxious, worn by it. Even her silences had offered reproach. *Did you? Would you? Will you? Oh, devil's child, what am I to do with you?* Furrows in her forehead, bruises beneath her eyes, trembling hands permanently stained by the tobacco she'd handled—Jane Whitby had been anything but lovely, and Nell wouldn't think of her.

Nor would she cry again, blast it. She was done with weeping. Mourning was a luxury for the rich, a duty for the righteous poor. Nell was neither. *Self*-righteous, maybe. Poor, without doubt. But there it ended. No need for tears.

She forced a smile onto her face in the darkness. Oh yes, she knew her faults very well. No grace in her. No forgiveness. What modesty she had came of shame. And in her heart no piety swelled, no compassion or patience. Resentment was what fueled her now. *Rage.*

She was the one who belonged in jail, not Hannah. Hannah's only fault had lain in the company she'd kept. But the ladies at GFS hadn't cared for the truth. *I am very sorry for your friend*, Mrs. Watson had said. *But we cannot condone thievery. You must trust in the fairness of the law.*

Oh, aye, the *fairness of the law*. Much fairness it had been to haul Hannah away—Hannah, whose only fault had been to pick up Nell's purse the moment before the bobbies had swept in to search them. Hannah hadn't taken that brooch from Mrs. Watson, or the money, either.

Nell had confessed it but nobody had paid her heed. *Where do you think I got the money for my mum's wake?* she'd yelled. *Or for the medicine that came before it? I'm the thief!*

It hadn't made a difference for Hannah, but somebody had carried word of Nell's speech out the door. It had traveled to Michael, who'd knocked her down the stairs in his rage that she'd not shared the profits; it had reached all the way to the factory, where the foreman, already troubled by her talk of windows and the right to leave the workroom for lunch, had called her a troublemaker and sacked her.

No justice in Bethnal Green. So she'd find a bit of it right here in Mayfair.

"Oh, Cornelia, I fear for you. Wickedness is in your blood."

"Right you were, Mum," Nell whispered. Dressed as a lad and set on bloody revenge: to become any more wicked, she'd need Lucifer's own instruction.

Ten pounds was what she'd asked of Lord Rushden. Had he sent it, she'd never have needed to steal a thing. But he'd never bothered to reply. He was about to find out that he'd sold his life cheaply.

She pulled back the hammer. Heard the hollow click of the chamber falling into place. Irons, now *they* were lovely. The one in her hand had been polished to a fine, gleaming shine. Brennan's doing. The pawnshop owner had laughed when she asked for it, but a few coins had sobered him up. Hadn't even tried to thieve them. That wasn't Brennan's way. "You've got guts, Nell," was what he'd said when he brought out the pistol. "Let me spiff it up for you. Make it a first-class affair."

Oh, she'd thought it very first class—the pistol, the

hansom cab she'd hired to get here. No omnibuses for her, not tonight!

But now that she was inside, the taste of humiliation was back in her mouth, stale and bitter like old beer. *First class,* she thought with scorn. For all it meant to her kind, it might as well be a phrase from some foreign language. First-class cab? The residents of these parts owned too many coaches to count. Wasn't anything first class about a chariot that stank of someone else's vomit. Remembering it, she drew a deep, steadying breath—and then scowled.

The air in this dark hallway smelled better than she ever had. Not a trace of gas, and no smoke, coal or candle or otherwise. Fresh flowers and wax, the barest trace of some exotic cologne, mingled into a perfume that made her feel as if she was dreaming. Wealth: there was even a scent to it.

And a feel. It had never been hers, but Mum had described it so often that she'd known what it would be like; she felt it now, beneath her. The carpet was so thick that her feet sank deeper with each step, growing more and more difficult to lift. And the sound—no babies screaming for feeding, no kids shrieking in the stairwell. An immensity of silence filled the long corridor. The gentle ticking of a clock lulled her breath into calm rhythms. *Be at peace,* the house invited her. *Feel . . . smell . . . rest.*

Ha. No rest for her. Her grip tightened as she prowled forward, counting off the doors to her right. She'd watched for hours from the shadows of the trees in the square: as the lights had started to shut off, this area was where the activity had concentrated. The fifth door seemed about the right spot.

The crystal knob was cold, smooth beneath her

fingers. Alas for Lord High and Mighty, his servants were proper workers; the door opened without a squeak.

A snore rattled through the room. Jesus, Mary, and Joseph! If she hadn't just eased off the trigger, she would've shot herself in the foot just then. How typical *that* would have been. Obviously God had no sense of irony, a mercy for which she paused to give quick, heartfelt thanks.

Three cautious steps carried her into the center of the room. Her eyes found the source of the noise, a portly, balding man asleep on a cot in the corner. Valet, that would be, and if she wasn't mistaken, she smelled gin even from here. With a roll of her eyes, she moved lightly past him to the next door, which also opened soundlessly. She shut it behind her with a small click.

She turned, and as she beheld the canopied bed at the far end of the room, a sharp breath escaped her. So. She was here, then. End of the road. She swallowed against a welter of emotions too tangled to separate. Grief. Bitterness. Fury.

Not fear. That would be stupid.

Nevertheless, she paused for a moment to draw a few steadying breaths, to *orient* herself. Big room. Desk, dresser, standard assortment of furniture— glossy, thanks to some maid's aching wrists. The curtains were drawn; through the open window came the rustling of wind in the leaves, the minute scurrying of some night creature through the garden. The moon was riding high in a bank of clouds, loosing a shaft of light that illuminated the rosettes on the dark Oriental carpet.

A grim smile twisted her mouth. She had enough of

the stage in her to appreciate nature's invitation. She moved into the center of the moonbeam and leveled her gun at the canopy.

"My lord," she said quietly. "It's Nell come to visit. Best awake and face your death like a man."

3

ℒike a man?" The lazy voice came from her right. She whirled, fingers tight around the barker. "Is there some template for a manly death?" the voice continued from the darkness. "Because I was preparing to weep and cringe. Is that off the table?"

She stared hard into the shadows. She couldn't see Rushden's face but his low, amused voice was enough to make her think he wouldn't be weeping anytime soon unless she made him. "Step forward," she said.

"So you can take better aim? That seems unwise."

She hesitated. This was not the neat murder she'd envisioned. Also, Rushden sounded a small bit young to have tupped her mother some twenty-three years ago.

But Mum had called him the devil, hadn't she? And devils didn't age. "Here's a tip," she said sharply. "A man don't cower in the dark."

A soft laugh answered her. "Fair enough."

He stepped forward into the square of moonlight.

Her heart leapt into her throat and pounded like it wanted out. If this man was the work of the devil, it was a wonder more men didn't sell their souls. He was tall, broad-shouldered, lean. Black hair. Full, hard lips. Mocking eyes.

Naked as the day he'd been born.

The man's laugh matched the look in his eyes, low and unkind. The moonlight showed his fine white teeth, as straight as rails. Nice to be him, nice to be raised on fresh meat at every meal.

"I wouldn't be laughing if I were you," Nell said.

"Yes, well, you'll permit me that much. Otherwise, as you see, you have me at a slight disadvantage."

She glanced down. No, she wouldn't call it *slight*. Small mercy that the light probably kept him from seeing the blush on her face.

"Do you like what you see?" he murmured.

Maybe there was light enough, after all. Was this man enjoying himself, buck naked with a gun pointed at his pretty face? "Trying to distract me, are you?"

"Undoubtedly," he replied.

She nodded. She could see how he thought his body might prove useful in that regard. What nobs she'd seen from a distance generally looked soft and doughy to her. Not this one.

He also didn't look near to Mum's age.

A memory sifted upward. *Lord Rushden was never one for sporting,* her mother had said that one and only time she'd spoken of it. *He spent much of his time indoors. He took little interest in the work of his estates. I suppose that accounted for the sin in him; the devil loves nothing more than a pair of idle hands . . .*

Her throat tightened. Mum had never been a hand with descriptions; she very well might have neglected to mention that her lover was a class-A looker with the body of a boxer. Still, trying to square Mum's description with *this* body took more imagination than Nell possessed.

Bloody hell.

This couldn't be the right lord.

He tilted his head slightly. It was the posture of a man considering something. She hoisted the pistol higher. "Don't try it," she warned.

"Oh, never," he said easily. "You'll find I rarely try."

This one talked a lot of nonsense in his fancy, drawling voice. "Who are you?" And what the hell was she to do with him? Couldn't exactly admit her mistake and go waltzing back out.

His dark brows lifted. "My dear. Are you telling me you didn't bother to learn my name before deciding to shoot me?" He laughed again. "This day grows better and better."

Weren't many men in the world who could condescend with a pistol in their faces, but she should have known that they'd congregate right here in Mayfair. "You're not very bright, are you? Seems to me that since I'm the one with the iron, *you* should be the one smiling and scraping."

"Scraping?"

Blimey! Suddenly he was closer than he'd been before. She leapt back. "Don't move!"

He lifted his hands, palms out. "All right," he said. "I'm a statue."

"Statues don't move," she said tersely, and his hands stopped climbing. "That's better. Also, you keep in mind that I heard a great many fancy statues lack for heads."

A faint smile curved his lips. "Yes. I'll keep it in mind."

She took a long breath. "You ain't Lord Rushden."

His hesitation was slight, but she noticed it. "In fact, I am."

"You aren't old enough!"

"Ah. Perhaps it's my predecessor you're seeking."

At least Mum's lessons were proving good for something. Most folks in Bethnal Green would not have understood this bloke. Had it not been for all those nights spent with books they could ill afford,

Nell wouldn't have understood him, either. "You mean to say that you're the *new* Earl of Rushden."

"Yes."

She held very still, waiting for the implications to hit her. They struck hard, like a wallop from Michael's fist, and they had just about the same effect, for the first sting was followed by a wave of hopelessness so black that she felt her grip on the pistol tremble. "When?"

"Eight months ago," he said.

Eight months. Her body took a sharper breath, alarming her; it felt too close to a sob. There'd never been any hope, then. She was too late even for revenge.

"I see this is bad news for you."

The man's comment cleared her head. It wasn't bad news that old Rushden was dead, save it meant that she'd now go to the gallows for nothing. For pulling a gun on a man who was nothing to her. Unless . . . "You're his son?" she demanded. Mum hadn't said she had a brother. Maybe a brother would take an interest in helping her.

"Third cousin," he said.

"Oh." They were barely kin, then. She couldn't hope for aught from him.

"What's your grudge against the man?" he asked.

She narrowed her eyes. "Why do you care?"

"My dear, you're aiming a pistol at my face. I'll care about anything that concerns you."

The smooth answer made her instincts bristle. He was being slippery with it. He had an idea in his brain that concerned her motives.

"You seem . . . undecided," he said.

Wasn't he the sharp-eyed one. She'd been ready to die if it meant taking her father with her. Justice for her mum: she'd gladly see it through. But she didn't fancy sacrificing herself to make a stranger pay for his peculiar pauses.

The gun was growing heavy. She adjusted her grip and saw him take note of it. He was going to do something in a minute. He talked lazy as a lord, but he hadn't earned those muscles by lying on his arse all day.

"I don't want to shoot you," she told him. "I had only one killing in mind, and you're not it. But if you leap at me, I'll reconsider."

"I don't want to be shot," he said. "So I won't leap."

She nodded once. "How do you suggest we conclude this little rendezvous?"

"What an interesting way you have with words. Sometimes you sound as if you were raised in a hovel. And sometimes . . . Wherever did you learn such vocabulary?"

"None of your business!"

"And it occurs to me that you look familiar."

"That's your imagination."

"I find myself wondering how old you are, Nell."

She didn't like the way he said her name. The interest in his voice felt too personal.

"Let me guess," the man said. "Twenty-two, thereabouts?"

Lucky guess. Or maybe he'd kept tabs on the old earl's bastards—though she couldn't think of a reason for him to do so.

In itself, that seemed a bad sign.

"What's your full name?" he asked.

"Perdition," she said flatly. "And I've been thinking on it, and maybe I'll shoot you anyway. Seems to me that the fewer Aubyns in this world, the better for the rest of us."

"I've often thought the same." He directed her a bizarre, pleased smile. "Really, we're remarkably in accord." He paused. "I haven't introduced myself. My name is Simon. Not Aubyn, you'll be glad to know. Simon St. Maur, at your service." With a flourish of his hand that made her flinch, he sketched her a bow. A *naked* bow.

He had muscles in places she'd never even known could flex.

She cleared her throat. "Lunatic relation, are you?"

"I've often been called so. And let me guess." His eyes were sharp on her face. "Nell is short for . . . Cornelia."

No reason to be alarmed, she told herself. Nell wasn't short for much else. "Wrong," she said. "It's Penelope."

"Tell me." His voice was thoughtful. "Were you really going to kill your own father?"

When he put it that way, it sounded biblically wicked. Wicked enough to distract her just for a moment, and that was all he needed. He lunged forward and before she could fire, he'd smacked the gun out of her hand.

The next second there was a tremendous bang and he had her wrists clamped together and twisted up behind her back as he held her pinned against him. She wrestled as good as she was able and heard him grunt once or twice; her cap came off and she spat hair out of her face as she thrashed.

"Jesus bloody—" The rest of his words were lost in a gasp as she managed to twist and take a bite of his bare shoulder. Solid and hot and salty.

He spat a curse and a door banged open behind her.

"—the police!" somebody shouted, somebody else, probably the foxed valet, and she thrust up a knee. St. Maur did a sharp swivel that caused her to lose her mouthful along with her balance, at which point he had her. She squirmed to confirm it: yes, she was pinned like a butterfly to a board, and soon to be just as dead.

"No police," St. Maur said. "Have the blue bedroom readied."

"The blue bedroom!" came the scandalized reply. "Sir, surely the garret—"

"But the blue bedroom has a lock." Glancing back to her, St. Maur added, "On the outside."

The door thumped shut again. St. Maur's free hand hooked into her hair and yanked her head back so they were looking at each other. Her addled brain once again pointed out that he was a fine-looking specimen: his eyes were some muddled shade between green and gray, and every bone in his face was sharp and straight, ruthlessly perfect.

"You'd best let go of me," she said—or croaked, more like; it was a bad angle for making threats.

One black brow arched. "I think you're finished giving orders for the night."

She put a sneer on her own lips as some new evidence made itself known. "Bit of a pervert, aren't you?" He was hard as a fire iron against her.

The shameless boor did not pretend to miss her meaning, giving her a slow smile that made her throat tighten and blood sting into her cheeks. "Absolutely," he said. "And what of you?"

"Me *what*?"

"What am I to think of you?"

"Nothing," she spat. "I'm nobody."

"Oh, never that," he countered. "A confused little girl, no doubt." He let go of her hair; his knuckles brushed down her cheek, the lightest touch ever to raise the hairs at her nape. "A miracle . . . perhaps." His voice dropped. "A figment of a desperate man's imagination? Possibly."

"You're spoony," she whispered. Mad as a bloody hatter.

"Hmm. Again: possibly." His hand moved down her throat. Gently skimmed the line of her collarbone. That hand wasn't showing any sign of stopping. "Or possibly just very insightful." His touch lingered at her shoulder, his thumb delivering a firm, massaging pressure. She stiffened against it. She'd rake his eyes out.

"Come into a man's bedchamber at night," he said in a low voice, "and he might mistake you for his dream."

A jolt of dread shot through her. "Take your hand off me."

"Oh, I would. But the day I've had . . . After such a day, such a miserable defeat arranged at someone else's hands, it's very difficult to take orders. Fancy it, if you can: having your life turned upside down by a villain. So many expectations crushed. And then the villain's daughter appears, intent on blowing your brains out."

He meant her. He meant her father as the villain. "I never knew him," she said quickly. "Never. I've nothing to do with him—"

His finger pressed across her mouth. Hot, rough. Her stomach fluttered. "Shh," he said, soft and comforting, as though she were a babe. "No matter. You're still the answer to the riddle. And you called me perverse. I wouldn't like to disappoint you."

In astonishment she watched him lean down to kiss her. *Brilliant*: an opportunity to knee him in the balls.

But his hand planted itself back into her hair. He retook his grip and held her immobile as his lips touched hers.

She snapped at him.

He drew his head back a little, laughing. "Feisty."

"I'll bite your tongue out," she warned him.

"Will you?" He looked diverted. "Shouldn't you properly be begging for mercy? From the police, etcetera?"

She froze. Was that an offer? Had he just asked for her body in exchange for her freedom?

His smile slipped into a knowing angle. "Here's your chance," he said, and leaned in again.

She tried to hold still as his tongue slipped between her lips. Tried to endure it. Only a fool would refuse such a bargain.

But his mouth was . . . warm. Not as she'd expected. His lips were gentle as they molded against hers. She felt dizzy, suddenly. This wasn't right. He should be mauling her. She'd been kissed before, hurried gropes she'd beaten off or smacked away, but never like this.

He pulled back a little, his heated breath covering her mouth. "How are we doing?"

"Sod off," she muttered.

With a little laugh, he applied himself again.

She hesitated only briefly. He would call the coppers or he wouldn't, but maybe he meant what he'd said: maybe she could sweeten him up and leave him kindly disposed. She opened her mouth and kissed him back.

In reply, an interested little noise came from him. *Mmm.* His hard body came all the way up against hers. He was taller by a head, but her neck didn't hurt: he'd slouched down to meet her. And he was licking into her like a child after the last traces of pudding in a bowl, and his mouth tasted like brandy, hot and rich and dark and clever. His hands, long fingers, felt down her spine, pressing, testing, against her lower back, finding the ache there, rubbing it out. She felt a surge of heat, animal-like, this strong, naked man rubbing against her as his mouth devoured her. Why not? What choice did she have?

The quiver in her belly strengthened. She would give herself to him. Let this long, strong body do what it liked with hers.

Lay the terms, a cold voice instructed.

She broke free, not to fight, but to say, breathlessly, "If I do it with you, you promise you'll let me go."

His mouth had found her ear, but at these words, he stilled. She had the curious impression that she'd startled him somehow.

He pulled away. The moonlight reflected in his gray-green eyes. Thick, dark lashes framed those eyes, which studied her so narrowly that her intuition strengthened: yes, she'd surprised him. And he didn't like it. He started to frown.

"Alas," he said. "We've had a misunderstanding. I want a different arrangement entirely."

Nell woke up the next morning spitting mad. She was mad at the fact that the door was still locked. That nobody came when she pounded on it. That she hadn't just shot the man straight off last night. She was done with being bullied like a dog. He seemed a right arrogant bastard and was a pervert by his own action and admission; she could have done the world a favor by ending him.

She was mad, most of all, at the way she'd slept. One might expect after being mauled by a blackguard to toss and turn a bit. But the bed was like a dream, a soft, fluffy, sinner's paradise, its pillows stuffed with feathers, the mattress so quiet that even bouncing on it couldn't draw out a creak. She'd slept like a baby—or, worse yet, like a woman without a brain in her head. The *stupidity* of it sent cold waves of horror through her. The lock was on the outside of the door! As she'd slept, St. Maur could have come in and done anything!

Now she paced the perimeter of the bedroom, her temper growing worse with each pass. Not ten minutes away, people were suffering, starving—good people, girls who worked from sunup to sundown, babies who'd not asked to be born. But here there were houses full of *stuff,* fancy sheets woven with silk floss as soft as a baby's bum; fancy washstands carved of dark wood that glowed like cherries where the light hit it; curtains the shade of the summer sky, heavy and glossy and smooth to the touch. The velvet-flocked wallpaper was so soft beneath her fingertips that had her eyes been closed, she might have thought she was brushing the belly of a rabbit.

And the stool in the corner! One wouldn't imagine you'd get too fancy with such a piece, but this stool was covered with embroidery so fine that her knuckles ached just looking at the stitches. Unbelievable. The rich even spoiled their arses!

Given a knife, Nell would have cut out that embroidery—some goofy-looking, underfed girl with a unicorn lying next to her, his head in her lap—and sold it for five quid, easy.

But she no longer had a knife. Last night, a couple of thuggish footmen had held her by the arms while a pug-nosed, sour-faced maid had searched her up and down, going straight for the blade Nell kept in her boot.

Why St. Maur was keeping her instead of handing her over to the police was a question Nell didn't want to entertain. There were a lot of things she didn't think about as she paced—like, so what if he knew her name? Folks in Bethnal Green didn't talk to strangers; he'd be hard-pressed to track her down once she escaped. No, she had better things to think about—like what she would manage to steal. A good deal, she hoped. She deserved it for sparing Mr. bloody St. Maur his wretched, dog-eaten life.

She started with the book on the table by the bed. Gilt-edged pages and a cover of patterned red leather. She'd read a good many books in her life, but this was the handsomest she'd ever seen. The story inside looked ripping, too—some yarn about a magical, cursed stone. Mum would have loved it—as long as she wasn't in one of her moods where only the Bible would serve.

The thought brought a lump into Nell's throat. She swallowed it down as she traced the grooved design on the cover. She'd not read anything since Mum had passed. Her fury had been too thick for words to penetrate.

Indeed, she rather felt like she'd woken up this morning from a long, mindless binge on gin. The numbness was gone. Her senses seemed sharpened, startling at everything. Even the play of sunlight on the carpet, the moving shadows of leaves, made her flinch.

She loosed a long breath. The book would fetch a good price. She tucked it under the mattress and cast her eye around for more.

By the time she heard footsteps in the hall, she'd picked out several likely pieces: a scrap of lace that had been sitting beneath a vase on the little round table by the bed; a china figurine of a dopey-eyed milkmaid; two silver candlestick holders. She slid them underneath the mattress alongside the book, then sat down atop them as the door opened.

"La-di-da," she cooed as St. Maur walked in—a fine gold watch in his fob, his tie crisp and as white as a baby's first diaper. His black hair was brushed back in thick, rippling waves from the sharp bones of his face. "A far finer sight with your clothes on," she said, and there was a lie she'd tell again and again even if he tortured her. "Me eyes was right sore from the abuse they endured last night."

His easy smile looked genuine. It made a dimple pop out in his right cheek, proof that preachers lied when they said God was just. Wasn't any fairness in giving a man with money the sort of face this one was sporting. "Now, now, my dear," he said as he took up a position against the wall by the door. Didn't cross his arms or cock his knee or take any measures to look intimidating; rather, he slung his hands in his pockets and tipped his head as casually as a street Arab aiming for an open-eyed nap. "Let's not begin our discussion dishonestly. I'm a lovely sight with my clothes off, and we both know it."

Whatever reply she'd been expecting, it had not been *that*. She'd known some peacocks in her time but it took downright cheek to reply to insults with self-praise. "Big head on you," she said, unwillingly impressed.

"Doubtless," he replied.

Silence fell as they studied each other. He had an

excellent poker face. Probably made a killing at the card table, and she didn't doubt he played. He had the mouth of a sinner, his upper lip sharply bowed, his lower full and wide. That mouth had done expert things to her own last night. He knew how to use it.

The thought made her itchy. She looked away for the space of a breath, then back. His growing smile lent him a wicked, sensual air. He looked too comfortable with himself to be a man who cared for Sunday manners.

"You seem cheerful," he said.

Did she? Then she had a brilliant poker face, too. "I feel cheerful," she lied. Like a cat forced into water. "A little West End holiday, like a free night in a fine hotel. Leaves me fresh for the coppers, no doubt."

He lifted his brows in a look of surprise. She got the feeling he was putting it on for show. "Forgive me; I thought I'd made this clear last night. I don't intend to call the police. I hope that fear didn't trouble your sleep."

Why it hadn't made one good question. Why he wasn't calling the police made another, but she was hardly going to press her luck by asking. "Kind of you. But if it's not the blockhouse for me, then I'd best be going."

"Have somewhere to be, do you?"

She maintained her smile by an effort. She had the pawnshop to visit, in fact. "Sure, and I can't be missing work, now, can I?"

"And where do you work?" he asked.

She laughed, though it wasn't funny. "Wouldn't you like to find out!"

"Indeed, I would."

The intensity of his interest suggested an irksome

possibility. "Don't tell me you're one of those do-gooders."

She was done with them. Blooming hypocrites! Come to Bethnal Green with concerned little frowns, luring girls with promises, when all they had to offer was snobbery and those bleeding blankets. God help her if she ever laid eyes on another one—all the same, dull gray wool stamped with Lady So-and-So's Relief Fund, because heaven forbid a girl should try to pawn it, and buy herself something a little more sightly than an ugly rag that screamed her poverty to anyone with eyes. "Look elsewhere if you want to save somebody," she said. "I'm not interested in do-gooders' charity."

His expression did not change. "While I sincerely doubt that I fit the description, you'll have to elaborate for me: what on earth is a do-gooder?"

She eyed him skeptically. "I'm sure you know some."

"Tell me and I'll think on it."

"Oh, they're a strange breed." She spoke slowly but her thoughts were scrambling. Why so much talk? If he didn't mean to call the police, why had he kept her here? "One sort is looking to bring you to the Lord. The other is more *your* lot, people with lives so comfortable that they get bored. Come into the Green to find out how we live. Tell us what's wrong with us, then go back to their fancy houses and do nothing at all."

He lifted a brow. "Charity workers, you mean."

Ha. "I've never seen them working, but I expect they lie and say they do. Aye."

His laughter sounded startled. She allowed herself a small, sly smile in reply.

His own smile faded. He frowned at her, giving her a look more searching and genuine than any he'd worn to date. She gathered that it had just dawned on him she was as human as he, with wits in her head and a mind to direct them. "My dear Lady Cornelia," he said, "you—"

"Nell is just fine." What was he on about with this fancy talk? "And as I said—it's Penelope."

"Hmm." He considered her in silence. At length, he said, "You seem to have inherited your father's . . . unusual . . . brand of charm. Ornery," he added with a smile.

Hearing something good about her father—even indirectly, even as a jibe in disguise—seemed wrong, like nature reversing itself, the sky landing and the earth going up. On the other hand, her father was dead, so it wasn't like she could resent St. Maur for praising him. People were beholden to praise the dead, even the bad ones. It was the living who were the pains in the arse.

"Thanks," she said. "Glad to hear it. Maybe I'll just try to charm my way out of here, then, because I wasn't joking. Some of us have to earn our bread."

He gave a visible start. "Bread! Good God, you must be starving." He leaned over to yank on a rope hanging out of the wall. Bellpull, probably. They'd installed some at the factory in case of emergencies. They were useless, though; the time she'd pulled one, the hydraulic pump hadn't stopped for five long minutes. In the interim, it had pressed more than tobacco. A woman had died.

The memory made her stomach judder.

"Do you take coffee, or tea, or both?" he asked.

"I'll take an omnibus." She put the full force of her will into the glare she gave him. "Or I'll take a quid, if you want to pay me the week's wages I'm sure to lose when I don't make an appearance at my job."

"Done," he said, so immediately that she felt a small shock. So casually he offered up that much money?

But of course he did. To him, twenty shillings was dust on the floor.

She felt sick. She could have asked for more. Twenty-five. Thirty, even.

But it still wouldn't be enough without the loot under the mattress. She'd need a proper fortune to spring Hannah.

A mobcapped maid ducked her head inside the door. It wasn't the sour-faced, scrawny one from last night, but a pale, plump thing that darted Nell a scared look. Nell bit her tongue against the urge to shout *boo*.

"A tray for the lady," St. Maur told the goose. "Coffee and tea, if you will. And perhaps . . ." Nell caught his amused glance. "Chocolate, too," he said. "Along with the usual breakfast assortment."

The girl's eyes widened. "Very good, my lord." She ducked a curtsy before fleeing.

Nell stared after her. Something of her thoughts must have shown in her face, for St. Maur said, "What is it? She offends you?"

"No, of course not." But it made her spine crawl to see a girl duck her head and bob like a slave. "Just can't understand why anyone would go into service."

"Why not?"

"Having to bow to the likes of *you*, for starters." She hesitated, suddenly uncertain of why she felt so hostile toward him. In all fairness, he was being pretty kind about the fact that she'd broken into his house and threatened to shoot him. He was even going to give her a quid.

That was what made her bristle. He was offering

kindness that she didn't deserve, which meant he wanted something. What could a man like this possibly want from *her*?

"Oh, I don't know," he said easily. "Three meals a day, a comfortable lodging, safety, security—surely these things are worth the occasional curtsy?"

"I guess it all depends," she muttered.

"Depends on what?"

"On how much your pride is worth to you."

He pushed away from the wall, a languid, easy move. She leapt off the bed and positioned herself in reach of the candlestand. He had a long, clever mouth, but if he tried to put it on her again, she'd brain him.

St. Maur walked on by her, momentarily examining the mattress. Her heart leapt into her throat. But if he noticed the lumps, he didn't remark on them. Turning, he said only, "You value your pride, I take it?"

That struck a nerve. She'd lowered herself to thieving for her mum's sake, which made it all right—so she'd told herself.

But in the end, the doctor hadn't been able to do a thing. Now Mum was dead and Hannah was rotting in prison.

"Pride's the only thing nobody can take away from you," she said. You could handily destroy it yourself, though.

He lifted a brow. "I didn't figure a woman with a black eye to be so naïve."

She'd forgotten about that. She reached up to touch the bruise. Michael had been out of his right mind yesterday. Had she not managed to escape, he probably would have killed her.

The look coming over St. Maur's face made her flush. She didn't need his pity. "You can figure me however you like," she said. "Why, did somebody steal your pride sometime?"

"Not mine." He sat down on the bed, and the smile that edged onto his lips made her heart sink. He knew there was something under the sheets that shouldn't be there. "But the last earl was a different matter," he continued. "Somebody did steal his pride—or, to risk sentimentality, his pride and joy, as it were."

She supposed she was meant to find his pause suspenseful. "Spit it out," she said.

"They stole *you*."

A snort escaped her. Not hard to steal a bastard nobody had wanted. But she didn't speak the thought. St. Maur was clearly trying to trick her into something. Until she figured out his goal, it was better to keep herself to herself.

He seemed to see through her silence. "You have a great deal of discipline," he murmured. "Not many manners, but self-possession in spades."

There was something new in his regard, now—something canny and assessing that made her skin crawl. "What am I, a horse for auction? Would you like a look at my teeth?"

"No," he said with a slow smile. "Indeed, Miss Nell-not-Cornelia, it's your lucky day, for I want you just as you are."

She tensed. Here it came. Whatever he was after, he was about to announce it.

But he didn't. He simply continued to look at her, his striking eyes—more gray than green at present—wandering up and down her figure. It was his eyelashes, maybe, that made him so handsome; they were so thick and dark that they framed his eyes like whore's kohl.

But no whore had ever given anyone such a look.

His inspection was calculating. He wasn't figuring out how much to bid for her. He was deciding whether to bid at all, or whether to skip the bid and simply take whatever it was he wanted.

The realization set her heart to hammering, the heavy, solid knocks urging her to get up and get ready. He was a long, muscled man, too light on his feet for his height; it wasn't going to be easy to get away from him. But if it was going to end in violence, she'd rather get on with it. "All right," she said. "What do you want me for?"

His gaze lifted to hers. "What do you think of this house?"

She blinked. "It's nice," she said warily.

"Would you like one of your own?"

A startled laugh slipped out of her. He didn't so much as crack a smile.

Good God, did he expect a proper answer to this piece of nonsense? "Why not?" she said. "I'd keep the pawnshops busy for a few months, I reckon."

He looked thoughtful. "Stripping it, do you mean? No, you wouldn't require money in this scenario. You'd be wealthy in your own right."

Oh ho! His deck was definitely missing a few cards. "Sounds lovely," she said carefully. "Why don't you give me a taste now? Five pounds, say, just to test out how I feel about it."

"That can be arranged," he said. "But it would require an agreement between us."

Of course it would. "Let me guess. This arrangement involves me lifting my skirts."

"Indeed not," he said gently. "My dear girl, I only wish to restore you to your rightful place. To your true inheritance."

"Inheritance," she said flatly.

"Just so," he said.

He made no sense. "And what would that be?"

"First, ask who. There's your twin sister, for one—Lady Katherine Aubyn."

Her jaw dropped. That girl in the photograph she'd seen in the shopfront? Half sister, yes, but a twin? That would mean . . .

A smile crept over her mouth. "Didn't expect you to have a sense of humor."

"How shortsighted of you," he said, not sounding offended. "But I'm not joking."

No, she saw, he wasn't joking. He had rats in his upper story. He was *cracked*.

4

After she was done laughing so hard that her throat began to ache, she settled down to the best breakfast of her life. He did start to explain, but she knew well enough how tiresome these loonies could be when encouraged to enlarge on their fancies—she'd been raised by Mum, after all—so she waved him off and concentrated on her food.

Food? No, that was too ordinary a word for what they'd brought her. Folks in the Green would call it relishing, but she found herself thinking of words she'd never had the chance to use, words from the books she'd used to read to Mum: *ambrosial, delectable, nectarous*. She didn't waste any time admiring it; the point was to get it into her stomach before St. Maur decided he'd like a bite himself.

Not a hard task, that. She started with the gooseberry scones, heaping them with clotted cream; moved on to toast points with butter and strawberry jam; then to the boiled eggs and a sausage seasoned with something grassy smelling and delicious. The coffee she drank down straightaway, the tea she sipped as she went, and the chocolate—oh heavenly mother, the chocolate she put down after a single mouthful. She knew an unwise idea when she tasted one.

All through this feast, she ignored St. Maur. And all through it, he sat there watching her as though she hadn't just called him a madman and told him to hush. She'd seen cats with such patience, biding their time by the mouse hole, occasionally licking themselves to keep their pretty coats clean. But his expression took on a darker edge as the meal drew on. She began to sense that his fancy manners were only a mask—one a girl would be wise to leave undisturbed.

Finally, when not a crumb remained to occupy her, she wiped off her fingers and folded up the napkin— real embroidered linen, but with him watching, she could hardly pocket it—and took a deep breath. "Well. I may have to roll myself home, but I'll go with a smile."

"You didn't like the chocolate?" The darkness edged his voice now, too. Something had displeased him. She wouldn't bother to guess at what.

She lifted her chin. "No, I didn't." The chocolate tasted of heaven and if she finished it, she'd memorize that taste and then spend the rest of her life hungering for more. She didn't like wanting what she couldn't have, but she couldn't want what she didn't know about.

Which was why, she thought as she rose, it was best to be leaving as soon as possible. She just needed to get him out of the room a minute so she could collect her—well, more accurately *his*—things. "I'll be going," she said, "after a quick"—she cleared her throat—"visit with a chamber pot."

He stood as well. "Certainly. But before you go, I hope you'll permit me the chance to show you the house."

He spoke as courteously as though he were dealing with a lady of his own kind. It got annoying, after a while, since it was so clearly a show. "I can tell you exactly what your house looks like," she said. "I broke into it last night, and I'll warn you, the lock on your garden gate is as shoddy as cheap tin. The rest seemed nice enough to feed a few counties for the summer, and that's all there is to it."

He nodded. "One thing, then. I'd like to show you one thing before you go."

She hoped it wasn't a weapon. "You're not one of those *dangerous* lunatics, like?"

His mouth quirked as though he were biting back a smile. "I do hope not. If I returned your knife to you, would you feel safer?"

"And the gun," she said promptly. She needed to get that back to Brennan.

But no: "I'll save the pistol for your next visit," he said and turned on his heel. "Two minutes, Nell. I'll be waiting outside."

He shut the door behind him. She raced back to the mattress and hauled out the lace. By an inch, the book didn't fit in the inner pocket of her jacket, the candlesticks, either. Bloody hell. She put them back in their proper places and turned on her heel to snatch the linen napkin from the table—and the fork and knife, too; they felt heavy enough to be silver. A precious minute was wasted as she tested the knife on the embroidered stool, but the cloth proved too thick to cut.

The tour of the house: she'd be able to snatch up a few things along the way. Stuffing the cutlery into her pocket, she hurried out into the hall.

He was standing a few paces down the way, idly examining a stone bust of some ugly, big-nosed man in a wig. "Looks just like you," she said as she caught up to him.

"You're very kind," he said dryly, walking onward.

After a brief hesitation, she followed. He moved smoothly as a tomcat, a sort of easy prowl, his hands in his pockets, the most glossy, expensive gentleman she'd ever seen in the flesh. Somebody should take *his* photograph. He'd certainly sell well to the ladies.

He glanced over his shoulder and caught her staring. She scowled and looked away—then peered harder around her.

For all her bluster, she'd been too panicked last night to absorb her surroundings in detail. The corridor was just . . . infamously nice. The wood paneling had a carved trim. The carpet was a fine weave of gold flowers on a background of auburn and navy. Brass sconces gleamed. The air held a mix of waxes and lemony balms, and it smelled more than clean; it smelled like something you'd want to buy, a scent to lull you to sleep on nights when worries had you tossing.

No wonder he walked so lazily. Probably he'd never known a moment's worry.

To her irritation, she saw nothing small enough to be pocketed. "What's this thing you want to show me?"

"A letter or two."

"A letter?" She slanted him a glance. "I'd hoped for something a touch more exciting." Or valuable.

He shrugged. "You'll find them interesting."

"I doubt it."

He came to a stop, evidently struck by a thought. "I do beg your pardon. If you can't read—"

"I can read," she cut in. "And I'll tell you why I learned—so nobody would *read* me something that wasn't on the page. So don't think to be pulling *that* trick."

He gave her the sort of smile she saw on tired mums with crabby infants: there was no real feeling behind it. "I'm chastened," he said, and resumed his stroll.

Rolling her eyes, she followed.

They turned a corner and the hall opened into a

broad balcony appended on either side by flights of stairs that curved down toward each other. That door down there was probably the exit. "There's my stop," she said, making for the stairs.

His hand on her arm halted her. Had he squeezed or tugged, she would have shaken him off and maybe given him a sock in the gut for good measure: she was ready for it. But he didn't even take proper hold of her. His fingers laid themselves on the spot right above her elbow, a steady, warm touch that somehow stopped her dead.

Queer thought: he had a magic touch to him. She'd bet she wasn't the first lady he'd caught with two fingers.

"Please," he said.

She turned back, eyeing him. It had been a long time since somebody had spoken that word to her. She liked the irony that *he* should be the one to speak it. He looked exactly as the master of this house should—richly dressed, too handsome by half, and radiant with that indefinable air that all rich people seemed to have: a sense of being comfortable, completely at ease, not afraid of anybody or anything.

And why would he be afraid? The world would see in one glance that he mattered.

She had to swallow hard to get the lump out of her throat. Stupid, but he made her feel bittersweet. He probably had chances and possibilities that she didn't even know existed. He took them for granted, while a girl like her would need to sell her soul to get even a glimpse of them.

"What's your angle?" she said on a deep breath. "Why are you so interested in the old earl's bastard? And don't give me any nonsense."

He lifted a brow. "Evidently I didn't make myself clear," he said. "Nell, you aren't a bastard."

Looking at the girl gave Simon a headache. Or perhaps *vertigo* was the more accurate term. Each time he glanced into her thin, sullen face, he felt his brain waver under the strain of processing the message delivered by his eyes. She was remarkably similar to Lady Katherine—minus a few stone, a few hundred pounds in fashionable clothing and jewelry, and twenty-two years of tender rearing.

To say nothing of the black eye she was sporting. He'd find out who had done that.

He wondered how Kitty would like the knowledge that her twin was a guttersnipe from Bethnal Green. Nell was living proof that cosmetics and high fashion were not required for an Aubyn to be striking. But she also illustrated how very much Kitty's looks owed to pampering. Both sisters' eyes were a pleasing dark blue, but they required a complementary color to tip into violet, and Nell's current outfit—a ridiculously oversized jacket and sagging breeches—suggested that dirty gray was not among these colors. Her spareness emphasized the cheekbones for which Kitty was so admired, but also brought into prominence the cleft chin and square jaw which Kitty so often hid behind her fan.

He could not wait to introduce them to each other. Kitty had been very persuasive when contesting Simon's bid to have Lady Cornelia declared dead. It had been part of a strategy to strengthen his contestation of the will, and Kitty had been ardent in her opposition. *I feel in my heart that she is alive,* she'd wept to the judge.

How surprised she would be to learn that she'd been right.

Of course, it remained possible that this girl was an imposter, some by-blow of Rushden's with the luck to resemble Katherine and the wits to adopt the missing heiress's name. God knew Cornelia's disappearance had been very public news sixteen years ago.

On the other hand, did it matter? She looked close enough to Katherine to be her twin, and she certainly could be coached to recite the right memories. Once she was plumped up and put into a Worth or Doucet, nobody with eyes would deny that she was an Aubyn.

At least, not until she opened her mouth.

"Where are you taking me?" she asked him, although it came out rather shrilly, and more along the lines of *Ware-yuh takin' mee.*

Well, no one would expect the elocution skills of a six-year-old to have endured hard treatment. And this girl had been treated hard. That was clear enough in the way her eyes darted left and right, as though the hall might disgorge a bandit intent on mischief. He gathered that he might fall into that category, since she also took care to keep a remarkably constant distance from him—a length, he finally realized, just longer than an arm's reach. She took care to be impossible to grab.

"The library," he answered. He pondered the wisdom of informing her that she could be calm; he had no intentions of grabbing her at present. Indeed, he was still amazed by the effect she'd had on him last night. Granted, he'd been in a state of undress, which did tend to cast a man's mind into erotic directions. And she'd squirmed most enthusiastically. But apart from the fact that she smelled like a sewer and was more bones than curves, she was his predecessor's spawn and looked almost exactly like Kitty. These twin facts should have proved more effective than an ice bucket in chilling his interest.

Yet the attraction thrived. It flourished like a plant in some hot, tropical jungle. He could not quite believe he'd put his mouth to anything so filthy; in the strong morning light, a patch of dirt appeared ingrained on her neck. But there you had it: his interest was not only strategic, but prurient. He felt obscenely curious about her—and about himself, in her presence. Like a man drawn to the edge of a cliff by a suicidal curiosity, he tested himself now: did he want her because she was the heaven-sent answer to a dilemma? Or simply because he could have her—right now, if he liked, in any fashion he chose?

Yesterday he'd thought he'd learned what it meant to be powerless: to be robbed and defeated, comprehensively, by a dead man. The frustration, the humiliation of helplessness, had kept him up long enough to hear the smallest click of an opening door, and the soft fall of a footstep aiming for silence.

Had he wanted comfort; had he desired reassurance; had he required evidence that he was not powerless, after all—he could not have asked for better proof than her. *She* was a lesson in true vulnerability. She had broken into his home with a revolver so antiquated that only luck had prevented it from discharging accidentally. If, in retaliation, he decided to keep her locked in a room until his servants worked up the courage to object—which would take days, possibly weeks—he still would have nothing to fear.

Let the police be summoned. He would only need to inform them of the circumstances of her entry into his home, and she'd be off to prison in an instant. She was nobody—not yet—and he was the Earl of Rushden.

His predecessor had not managed to deny him all the perquisites of the title, after all. Even near to penniless, he'd still enjoy the privileges of his name, while she—well, she would be truly helpless.

Yet she seemed wholly unaware of her sad state. Not one plea for forgiveness had issued from her mouth. Not even, now that he thought on it, a *please*.

Come to think of it, *he* was the only one who'd spoken that word to date.

He laughed under his breath. Of course he was attracted to her—he'd always admired brazen gall.

He stepped ahead of her to open the library door. This gentlemanly reflex earned him a sharp look. She sidled past him into the room, then came to an abrupt stop. "Coo," he heard her whisper.

So, at least the library impressed her. Long and narrow, it lacked windows thanks to some cheap ancestor who'd feared the window tax. Halfway down its length, twin staircases spiraled up either wall to a narrow walk that ran the length of the room and supported additional bookcases. He supposed it *was* impressive.

"Here's a lot of books," she murmured.

Not as many as there should be. At odd moments, old Rushden's petty cruelty in selling his wife's books still astonished Simon. The old bastard had all but given them away simply to make a point—simply to spite the one person who had loved them as much as the countess had.

"I've become something of a collector recently," Simon said. Each and every of the countess's volumes would one day reside on these shelves again, even if it took a lifetime to regather them.

"You must spend all your time reading," said the girl.

He laughed. She cut him a peculiar look. "That's not quite the point," he said.

"They're books," she said flatly. "What other point is there?"

He paused. Actually, it wasn't a bad question. He might have asked the same, as a boy. He'd lost countless hours to reading, enamored in discovering that the forgotten things—odd, curious facts for which the world no longer had any use—could be wondrous, worthy of attention and care. He'd felt very clever for appreciating them, for pointing out things that even the countess had missed. She'd been generous in her praise. *I never thought of it that way. What a brilliant idea, Simon.*

Memories of his boyish gratification made him smile now. "I favor the unique," he said. "Literally. Many of these manuscripts are too rare and delicate to be read." He deliberately paused. "Although rough handling does have its pleasures."

She stared blankly. "So you're keeping them safe for somebody to ruin later?"

Had she missed his innuendo, or was she having him on? The latter possibility intrigued him. One didn't often think of the poor as having a rich inner world, much less a sense of humor. Their sullen eyes and sallow faces seemed to mask only a well-founded resentment and perhaps—if one believed the nervous talk at dinner parties—visions of the slit throats of their betters.

Come to think of it, humor wasn't an asset

commonly ascribed to anybody outside the beau monde.
Even the middling classes appeared from a distance to
be dull and despicably moral.

He eyed her as she crossed her arms and looked
around. A grubby little thing with keen wits and a
sharp tongue. Not at all what he'd expect of a slum rat.
She was slighter than Kitty, a touch shorter, narrower
through the shoulders—the best a body could do when
raised on gruel and water, no doubt. But her throat
was long, beautifully slim. The square angle of her jaw
looked sharp enough to hurt a finger that pressed too
recklessly upon it. Perhaps he should test that theory.
She was ignoring him with irritating ease, looking up
now at the skylights old Rushden had installed, and
her expression—

Her expression stopped his breath. She wore a look
of wonder so vivid and alive that he glanced up himself,
wanting to see the miracle.

But there were only the skylights, which remained
unremarkable.

Absurd to feel disappointed.

He glanced back to her face. Perhaps to her the skylights *were* miraculous. She hailed, no doubt, from one
of those dark and crowded devil's acres where glass
was broken and the sky was hemmed by overhanging
hovels. This world must seem entirely foreign. Everything clean, shining, immaculate: all of it strange and
new, remaining to be discovered by her.

A curious feeling twisted in his gut. He didn't
quite like it. How absurd that he should be envious,
even if only for a moment. Awed by glass and as-
tounded by architecture, she was the simplest explanation of how cathedrals had conned generations into
religious sentiments that justified their suffering. She

was a naïf whose requirements for awe were pitifully low.

He cleared his throat. "Just glass," he said. But he could not remove his eyes from her. Strangest thought: he wanted her to look at *him* with that brightness on her face. If he could not feel it himself, then he wanted to stare into it for a while, until it ceased to hurt him.

Her chin came down. She gave a pull of her mouth as though to mock herself, but he caught the lingering effect of her amazement in the smile that she could not bite back. "I've never seen such a thing," she said.

For the space of those six words, she sounded almost well spoken.

This was the second time she'd given him that impression. He considered her narrowly, wondering if she didn't remember more of the Queen's English than she let on.

"This whole place is so . . ." She turned full circle, her bony hands clenching in her shirt. Her fingers were a sallow, sickly shade, her knuckles white, as if she didn't have enough blood to fill her body. "It's beautiful," she said—roughly, quickly, as if the idea embarrassed her.

Which seemed peculiar in itself. To call the room beautiful was only to observe a fact. A great deal of money had been spent in making it so The fine oak paneling on the walls, the carved bookcases, the carpets of French tapestry, the porcelain and objets d'art scattered on the low tables, had been acquired (and, alas, entailed) at great expense by his various predecessors. He knew this for a certainty, since he'd spent the last few days negotiating with an underground antique dealer about how much these items might fetch were they suddenly "lost" into that man's possession.

He supposed there was no need to lose them now. The thought was bracing. Best get on with it. "As to the letters—"

"Where is that?"

"Pardon?" He followed her look toward a painting hanging over the door. *That* was the most irritatingly expensive estate with which he'd been saddled. Crumbling old pile, prison of his miserable youth. Somebody should have had the bollocks to knock it down a century ago, long before this whole entail nonsense began—

"Is it real?" she asked.

Puzzled, he turned back to her. "Yes. Paton Park."

"Where is it?"

"Some godforsaken pocket of Hertfordshire. Why do you ask?"

She visibly hesitated. "It's . . ."

He waited a moment longer, but she shrugged and seemed to lose interest. Looking down to her feet, she gave the floor a little kick. "Here's some fancy."

The exposed patch of floor was covered in painted tile—Spanish, from the looks of it. Was she going to remark on every feature of the room? "Yes, very nice."

She smiled faintly. "Nice enough to serve, I reckon."

Did a note of dryness infect the lady's voice? He gave her a smile in return, a fine, rueful blend of self-deprecation and deliberate charm. It would go easier for them both if she took a liking to him. "I confess, I normally reserve my attention for the books, not the room in which they're housed."

She ran an eye down the bookcases. "You must have a lot of attention, then."

The reply that leapt to mind gave him pause: it was

wholly sexual and thoroughly inappropriate. Nearly he laughed. She was a ragamuffin with holes in her sleeves. Putting his body to hers would be as hygienic as bathing in a wallow.

Perhaps that was part of her charm, though. A .aste of primitive perversions.

The other part, naturally, would be the sweet, dark justice of defiling his predecessor's daughter.

The notion filled him with a warm glow that did not bode well for his chances in the afterlife.

She backed up and dropped into an upholstered reading chair. He felt his brow climb. The violence of her movement and the violent effect it wreaked on her anatomy left no doubt that she was not wearing a corset.

Oh, good God. She wore lad's breeches; she smelled like tobacco and fish and onions. Of course she wasn't wearing a corset.

He realized he'd laughed to himself when she gave him another of those looks—wide-eyed, slightly pitying. She really did think him a lunatic. He couldn't blame her for it. It seemed his brain was going soft.

"So what's this letter, then?" she squawked.

"Right." He crossed the room, extracting a copy of Homer's *Odyssey* from the shelf. The first of the letters tucked inside was worn soft with time and the repetitive stroke of fingers. The old man had grown increasingly short of attention over the years, but he'd never lost grasp of his twin obsessions: thwarting Simon and finding Cornelia.

Simon had a quick internal debate as he returned to her. If she couldn't read well, she probably wouldn't admit it; she'd already made clear that she valued her pride. Yet if she didn't understand the letters, he'd no doubt that he'd lose her. Her concern for money was matched if not outstripped by her suspicions of him; she'd walk out today without a backward glance and tell herself later that leaving him had been the best way to keep out of prison.

Losing her was not an acceptable outcome. Holding her against her will would be problematic in regard to his larger goal.

He ignored the impatient hand she extended and settled against the edge of a heavy reading table. "The first is from Jane Lovell," he said.

"Who?"

The light from above was falling across her face at an angle that erased the freckles and the worry line between her brows. She looked girlish. Innocent. He supposed she *was* innocent in every way that mattered to this moment—which he suddenly sensed was going to be more delicate than he'd imagined.

This brief pang of compassion irritated him. He'd spent sleepless hours last night marveling at his good fortune. She had dropped into his lap like a gift from the gods, and nothing—least of all her—would convince him to waste the opportunity she presented. Compassion was not only unnecessary, then, it was entirely hypocritical.

"I assume she was the woman who raised you," he said. "But to begin with, she was your mother's maid. Lady's maid to the Countess of Rushden."

"Go on."

Her face might have been a mask for how little it revealed. He studied her as he continued, alert and ready for the slightest crack in her composure. "She stole you from the nursery. It seems she had an affair with your father—or perhaps not so much an affair as an encounter. By his account, it was not a long-standing arrangement."

She made a small and indelicate noise, generated in her nose. When her lip twisted, he recognized the noise as contempt. "Encounter," she said. "I suppose that's your fancy word for rape."

"No," he said. "I've never heard it described as such."

"Sure and you haven't."

Her words had the flavor and lilt of a jeer. He smiled in sudden recognition: this situation held a unique, gorgeous irony. Defenseless women were his least favorite type, but if word escaped that he'd held an urchin in his house overnight, nobody would be surprised. Titillated, yes; amazed, no. *Up to his old tricks again,* society would say, shaking their heads even as they blithely issued invitations to him for dinner.

Cornelia's own father, in spreading tales of Simon's exploits, had guaranteed that none of his peers would take Simon to task for misbehaving with her.

The idea inexplicably unnerved him. "Regardless of which word you use, the result was the same," he said. "In the aftermath, the old earl lost interest in her, and Jane Lovell did not take it well. Indeed, she seems to have lost her wits. For revenge, she took one of the earl's daughters when she fled. That daughter was named Cornelia."

She still had him fixed in that flat, unspeaking look. "Not the rarest name."

"You have a twin sister," he said. "The resemblance is . . . extraordinary."

Not the least of that resemblance lay in the long, haughty nose Nell now stared down. The last flicker

of Simon's doubt winked out. For three seasons, Kitty
Aubyn had frightened scores of her fellow debutantes
with this look. On Nell's face, it might have caused a
grown man to think twice.

"So," she said. "You think I was the girl this lady
kidnapped."

"Yes." He paused, because now wonder was ripping through *him,* and it was a heady sensation, novel
enough that he wanted to savor it.

Cornelia bloody Aubyn. For sixteen years, old Rushden had ripped apart the country in search of her. And
now, here she sat.

He cleared his throat. "She did not take you to ran-
som, I should add. She simply . . . took you." He lifted
the letter. "This is the note she left behind. It reads,
'To His Lordship—'"

"I *can* read," she said. "Hand it over." Leaning forward, she plucked it from his grip. As she considered
the note, some expression fleeted across her face—
surprise, confusion, he couldn't say. It did not show
in her voice as she began to read, slowly but clearly.
"'I have taken a payment for what you took from me.
You reviled me for a low woman; now your daughter
will live as the low women do. As for her sister, she
will have to look to you for providing her comfort. I
hope you prove better to her than you were to me.'"

She shrugged and handed the letter back. "Whole
lot of nonsense, sounds like."

"The ravings of a madwoman," he agreed. "But you
see what it means."

"Can't say I do."

"Then you're not attending. *You* are the daughter
she took. You're the legitimate child of Lord Rushden
and his lawful wife. You—"

"I'm listening," she said sharply. "And I'm not deaf, so you'd best keep your voice down."

Simon paused. "I wasn't yelling."

Now the girl looked uncomfortable. Glancing down to her hands, she lifted her shoulders in a jerky movement. "Guess you weren't."

Somebody yelled at her, Simon gathered, and on regular occasions. An alarming possibility occurred to him. "Good God. Are you married?"

Her eyes narrowed. "Eight times," she said. "Twice this week. What's it to you?"

A good deal, in fact. But he didn't think this was the right moment to explain himself. "Curiosity. Humor me."

Her lips thinned. "Not my job," she said. "You can hire someone for that."

"Touché." She had a fresh brand of cleverness about her. It occurred to him, too, that her concern this morning had been for the wages she'd miss, not for the husband who would be alarmed by her failure to return home.

No, he thought, she wasn't married.

He smiled down at the letter. Even had he been a praying man, he would never have thought to pray for Cornelia Aubyn's return. But this heiress extraordinaire, the former fixation of a shocked and anxious nation, had turned up *in his bloody bedroom*—and in the guise of a grimy, half-educated factory girl with no idea of her entitlements. No idea that she had the right to demand anything.

I could tell her whatever I liked, he realized.

The temptation was so dark and powerful that he actually felt the hairs lift at his nape.

Anything at all.

Old Rushden must be *writhing* in his grave. For years, he'd reviled Simon as a black-hearted bastard. Now his own precious daughter had reappeared, desperately poor, desperately needy, with a waiting fortune of a million bloody pounds.

The world had curious ways of balancing the scales.

He exhaled. "This other letter," he said with remarkable calmness, "would be one of the many that the earl received in the years before his death. First, though, I should say that your father did look for you—searched the entirety of Britain, in fact. Articles in the newspapers, sketches of you and Jane Lovell posted in the train stations, all of that."

Judging by the depth of the line between her brows, frowning was a customary expression for Nell Aubyn. "How do you know all this?"

"I'm thirty last January," he said. "I remember it. And I have cause to know the details. The late earl became my guardian two years before you disappeared."

Old Rushden had wanted to groom his protégé. Simon's parents hadn't even protested. Dazzled at the prospect of their son becoming an earl, they simply had handed him over. Simon supposed his mother might have wept, once or twice.

"Oh ho," said Nell, "so I *should* have shot you, then. You're practically him!"

Simon gave her a half smile. "There is no one on this earth whom your father would consider to be *less* like him than I." Rushden had nursed great pride over his lineage. He hadn't liked having to draw from the shabbier side of the family tree. It had fed and combined with his larger fury against the unjust fate that had deprived him of sons and a daughter besides.

That daughter now smirked. "You're trying to talk your way out of a bullet."

"Not at all," he said politely. "I already confiscated your pistol."

She cast a hopeful look around the room. "Could brain you with a fire iron."

"I don't allow fires to be lighted in the library. All that ancient paper."

"Where's that knife?"

"Patience," he murmured. "You can gut me later. For now, the matter at hand. The key thing is, he looked for you everywhere. But nobody saw hide or hair of you, although every lunatic in Britain had a theory of your whereabouts. The flood of letters did slow, eventually, but even in the last month of his life, one or two arrived that claimed to know where you were."

He'd said something very wrong. Her whole body shuddered as though she'd touched an electrical wire, then stiffened to a rigidity other women achieved only with a corset. "You get his letters, do you?"

Simon quickly wracked his brain for possible missteps. "No, he had a secretary for that." His oldest, closest friend, now Kitty's guardian. Grimston had always thought too highly of himself to admit he served as an amanuensis in exchange for the money Rushden "lent" him, but he'd handled Rushden's correspondence for as long as Simon could remember.

He noticed that Nell was going very white. "And the letters that came after he kicked the bucket?" she asked.

His instincts reminded him that discretion was the better part of valor. "The executor for the estate would deal with those." Grimston, also.

"What's his name?" she asked flatly.

"Later," he said, for it was clear she found the information important, and he would collect any bargaining chip available.

She nodded once, grimly. "Well," she said. "Let me see this letter, then, that his lordship's secretary thought worth reading." She stuck out her hand.

He handed over the letter, which was only a copy; the original was in Grimston's possession, having been submitted by his solicitors to the court to support the idea that Cornelia might still live. The irony was enjoyable, but Nell's peculiar remark distracted Simon from dwelling on it. She could mean only one thing by her questioning. "Did you write to him?" If Grimston had gotten letters from her and chosen to destroy them . . . well, that complicated matters. It meant this would be quite the bloody battle ahead.

He felt an anticipatory thrill at the very prospect. He'd lost once to Grimston and Kitty. He would not lose again.

"Hush," she said curtly. "I'm reading."

This time, she read silently. At one point, her lashes flickered as though in startled recognition, but when she handed it back to him, she said only, "That's a lot of money someone wanted."

"Yes." He supposed fifty pounds would seem like a fortune to her.

"Did he pay it?"

He nodded.

"Just to find out where I was?"

The question sounded awed, which stirred in him an odd, itching urge to wince. "It isn't that much money, Nell." He'd spent more on tips to the dealers at Monte Carlo.

"Maybe not to you," she snapped.

This was a pointless line of argument. "Of course he paid it. He wanted very much to find you."

"I guess they never told him where I was, though?"

That she sounded uncertain struck him as interesting. He'd always assumed the letter was nothing more than an extortion attempt, or a clever forgery fashioned under Grimston's direction to support Kitty's case. Certainly the wretched penmanship and mangled spelling had seemed too overdone to be real. "Do you think the writer actually knows you?"

She did not answer that. "To pay that much to a stranger . . . Those are some very deep pockets."

He bit his tongue. Old Rushden easily had spent five hundred times that amount on his various investigators and advertisements. "Your father was a very wealthy man," he said. "And he left all of it to his daughters." Every goddamned penny, and every single property for which he'd managed to break the entail. In the months before his death, he'd set men onto the estates like vultures onto a corpse. They'd liquidated what assets they could, then bound up the profits in a trust for the girls.

"You said I was one of those daughters," she said softly.

Finally, greed won the day. Simon smiled encouragement. "Indeed, I am convinced of it."

A cynical little smirk crossed her face. "So I suppose you *will* give me that ten pounds, then."

Christ, could her brain not budge from these trifling amounts? Five, ten, fifty—what matter? *Look around you,* he wanted to say, but he restrained himself, for this was the crucial moment. "You'll receive a great deal more money than that, provided you can prove that you're Cornelia Aubyn."

"Ha." It was little more than an exhalation of breath, but she suddenly looked weary. "Figures. I've no way to prove anything." She gave him a quick little sideways look. "Ten pounds would do me just fine, though."

He recognized that look. It was the quick calculation of a street dog that had spotted a bun dangling from a careless hand.

Perhaps the analogy was too apt. It called to mind, vividly, the fervor with which she'd—*eaten* was not the right word. *Attacked the food* more accurately captured it. The unsettling sensation he'd felt while watching her now resurfaced, a sort of revolted discomfort he recognized, belatedly, as his conscience.

He easily silenced that long-disused organ. It wasn't as if he were lying. Even if Kitty surprised him by uncovering a strain of sisterly feeling—or, more unlikely yet, an urge for fair play—her guardian would not prove so angelic. Simon had long suspected that Grimston had an eye to marrying Kitty himself, and was only waiting to determine how to accomplish this feat without producing a scandal. At any rate, he would do everything in his power to prevent his ward's fortune from being halved—particularly by an unknown guttersnipe of uncertain allegiances.

To secure her rightful share, Cornelia would need Simon's help.

"I'd be willing to assist you," he said. "There are ways to go about this sort of thing. Of course, it takes a legal fight, and that requires money in itself. But I could fund your efforts." He still had a few accounts tucked away, yet to be drained.

She gave him a sly little smile, crooked and slightly toothy. Bizarrely attractive. "But you won't help for free."

Ah, yes, he hadn't mistaken it: this was a *carnivorous*

smile she was offering. One alligator's congratulation to another: *I see what you're doing here.*

Perhaps she did see. Perhaps she saw him more clearly than most people did.

Or maybe she didn't see him clearly at all, for suddenly he wondered if he would have helped her, regardless, out of sheer, libidinal curiosity. Such pluck she had. What would it take to make her tremble?

"Perhaps I'd help you only for the pleasure of it," he murmured. "What do you think?"

She came closer. Simon put his elbow on his thigh and leaned in to meet her. Her father would have died several years sooner, no doubt of apoplexy, if only he'd foreseen this moment: his despised heir and long-lost daughter inclining toward each other like lovers. "Can't cozen a cozener," she said.

Her self-possession was a gorgeous thing. A dare he had no intention of resisting. "Rarely," he said. "But it's always fun to try."

One slim brow lifted. "Maybe you should just give it to me straight."

He felt his smile widen. He would give it to her straight anywhere she liked. On a whim, he reached out to touch her face.

She went still. Those magnificent blue eyes locked on his as he stroked her cheek. No, not magnificent: they were too much like Kitty's eyes. Yet beneath the grime, her skin was as soft as new velvet, and the discovery made his own skin prickle. A peculiar pleasure flooded through him, sharp edged, greedy, curiously prideful. It was a feeling he associated with the discovery of a rare genius, some talent that others had overlooked—a pirate's triumph, really: the thrill of finding and seizing buried treasure.

All for me, he thought.

"Take your hand away," she said, "or I'll knock your teeth in."

He almost invited her to try. She fenced so well with her wits. It might be entertaining to see what she could do with her fists.

But their surroundings called for a gentler seduction. He had a good many books on his desk too fragile to bear her weight if he were to push her down atop them.

He withdrew the reluctant hand to his thigh, where it dug into his quadriceps in the effort to behave itself. What would she look like once he'd cleaned her up? *Like Kitty,* his mind insisted, but his intuition spoke differently. The light in her eyes seemed too militant and keen now to be confused with her sister's.

"Honestly, then." He paused to clear the hoarseness from his voice. Had he ever had a woman quite like her? He didn't go trawling in the East End for bed sport, of course. But this bizarre attraction seemed to have less to do with her dirt than with her demeanor.

Due to the circumstances, his lust also contained an element of possessiveness. Quite novel, this covetous feeling. But natural. For his plans to succeed, nobody else must have this girl. Only him.

Indeed, she might well have been fashioned just for him. No family to placate. No tiresome expectations of romance and chivalry. No expectations whatsoever.

It dawned on him that her mood had changed. She had scooted forward to the very edge of her seat and now rested her weight on the balls of her feet, poised to spring up and flee.

He forced himself to sit back and cross his legs, creating the picture of a man at ease. It wasn't that he wouldn't enjoy catching her. But it always worked better when a woman wanted to be caught.

His posture communicated the desired message. She eased back in her chair.

He gave her a pleasant smile and borrowed her language. "To tell it to you straight, then: I inherited the earldom and a few crumbling and unprofitable estates. Your father took great pains to see that I inherited nothing else."

She watched him expressionlessly. "Why?"

He shrugged. "He thought very highly of the Aubyn lineage. My conduct . . . failed to satisfy him. At any rate, all the true wealth went to his daughters—at this point, to Katherine. As a result, everything left to me stands at risk. The estates are going to seed. I've no money to support or improve them, and this is widely known, or will be, soon enough. Paired with certain other considerations"—chiefly, his reputation—"this prevents me from finding a quick solution to my financial difficulties, such as—"

"Marrying an American," Nell said. "Somebody with money, like that Churchill bint."

"Yes, like that Churchill bint." Such marvelous language she used. "So, you see, I am—"

"Well screwed."

Her words—their hot, immediate effect—caught him off guard. He pressed his lips together, eyeing her up and down. "Hmm." So many possible replies. Such restraint on his part.

"Precisely," he said on his exhale. "Yet your miraculous reappearance offers . . ." He smiled. "Another route. I can help you reclaim your true place in the world, Nell. But I will have to ask you to make it worth my while."

"And how would I do that?"

Curious that he couldn't yet manage to read her tone or expression. He was accustomed to understanding people. Often he understood them even better than they did themselves.

He might have taken her inscrutability to mean there was no depth to her, but even their short acquaintance proved otherwise. Conversely, she might be opaque because her depths were so foreign, so purely lower class, that he simply had no hope for getting a grip on them without prolonged exposure.

Well. It seemed he'd turned into a snob, which made this next bit all the more ironic.

"You'll do it very simply," he said. "Marry me."

5

The world looked different from behind glass. Nell pressed her forehead to the window, felt the tickle and brush of the gold tassels that hung from the upraised shade. Puddles lined the road, the work of last night's rain, and they reflected back her passage, her pale face peering out from a vehicle large and black like a monster, lacquered to a high gloss, pulled by four strong horses with hides of steel gray.

She slid a palm up the polished wood paneling and took hold of a hand strap wrapped in velvet. They were flying through the street. She felt weightless. Released from earth, adrift in the scents of oiled leather and polished wood and something woodsy and male: St. Maur, sitting across from her, smelled as she'd always imagined a forest might. Nottingham, say. Or high Scottish mountains. Dark and a touch wild.

Possibilities, possibilities. They spiraled in her brain no matter how she tried to fix her wits on the goal.

She couldn't even feel hopeful. She was dazed. This couldn't be real, any of it.

"Almost there," said St. Maur. She sat back into her seat, her hand closing now on a button sewn into the maroon leather cushion beneath her, holding herself down. He was real enough. Beneath the brim of his silk top hat, his thick hair waved down his temples, disorderly, black as ink. With one arm stretched out along the back of his seat, his long legs casually crossed, he looked at her. He had a smiling mouth and watchful eyes. A bad combination to win a girl's trust.

He said she was an earl's true-born daughter.

Madness.

Yet what cause had he to lie?

The idea was like a firecracker, exploding again and again in her brain. She shook her head at herself and looked back out the window.

People looked smaller from this height. The swift passage blurred their faces into generalities: open mouths, upturned eyes. Gawking at the grand coach barreling past. Leaping back to save their feet or their necks.

She was used to being the one who nearly got run over. She knew that fists were lifting in the wake of this carriage, angry, hopeless insults offered silently. Nobody in these fine vehicles ever noticed them.

"You could slow down," she said.

"I thought you were in a hurry."

She was. Once he'd said he could get Hannah free for her, her amazement, her skepticism, had collapsed. Next to that offer, doubt seemed irrelevant, questions only a waste of time. "I am in a hurry," she said. "Makes no difference. You could slow a little."

He eyed her for a moment. Then leaned toward her—causing her to suck in a breath. The slight curve of his mouth acknowledged how she tipped away, ever so slightly, as he lifted his knuckles and rapped on the window behind her. She felt the warmth of him as he hovered near. Her pulse kicked up a notch; she found herself holding her breath as a face appeared at the window: one of the footmen.

A little pane in the glass popped open. "Your lordship?"

"A touch slower," said his lordship, and sat back, slowly and smoothly, like the coiling retreat of a snake. His eyes met hers. He lifted an expectant brow.

She set her jaw and kept mum. It was common decency to slow down. He didn't deserve thanks for it. His story made no sense, either. The letters weren't proof of anything. One of them had been from Michael, the greatest liar on the earth. Now she knew how he'd gotten that windfall last year: he'd conned the old earl of fifty pounds.

But the other letter? Maybe the penmanship had born a slight resemblance to Mum's, but nothing decisive. Anyway, it couldn't be true. If not her mother, then who had Jane Whitby been? Certainly not the sort of woman who stole someone else's baby.

The coach turned under an archway into a small courtyard bounded by stone walls. Gravel crunched as the vehicle rocked to a halt. The door opened, a man in dull green livery letting down the narrow stair.

St. Maur rose, a large man in a small space. She drew her legs tight to the bench, but the adjustment proved unnecessary: an easy duck, a twist, and he was stepping down onto the ground, the watery sunlight gleaming off his hat brim, casting his eyes into deep shade.

He ran a quick thumb and forefinger over the brim, straightening it. The footman stepped forward to brush down his long black coat. He tipped his head back until his eyes found hers.

"This won't take long," he said. "You'll wait in the coach."

Suddenly a hundred possible problems occurred to her. Anxiety brought her off the bench. "But how will you know that it's her?"

"Sit back down," he said, and then stepped back, watching, waiting for obedience.

She gritted her teeth and took her seat again, stiff with resentment. He wasn't *her* master. She'd make that clear as soon as circumstances allowed it.

"Hannah Crowley," St. Maur said calmly—while one hand checked the other for the fit of his glove, smoothing, tugging, as the footman continued to hunch at his heels, brushing the jacket, *thwip thwip thwip*. "Do I have that right?"

"Yes, but they may try to trick you into freeing somebody else. Say they've got a friend of their own inside. They might try—"

"They won't," he said. No boasting in his voice: just a simple statement of fact. Nobody would dare to play tricks on him.

The footman straightened and backed away, leaving St. Maur alone, framed by the doorway against the ugly gray face of the prison. He tilted his head in question. "All right?"

Slowly she nodded.

He gave her a faint smile. "Have a bit of faith," he said. He turned on his heel—nodding as he mounted the steps to someone out of sight.

The door thumped shut in her face.

She sat back. *Have a bit of faith.* The instruction seemed more comical the longer she dwelled on it. Faith in him? Why? Why in God's name should she have a drop of faith in a man like him? The clothing he wore probably cost a year's salary at the factory. He'd just walked into a prison as lightly as though to a dance. Ordinary fears had no purchase on him. He probably thought her quaint for worrying.

Have a bit of faith. Was it so easy to trust in his

world? Could it be that he simply had no concept of a situation in which wariness would profit him? When life was easy, when the floors lay even and carpets softened them, you didn't even have to watch where you stepped.

His voice lingered with her in the silent compartment. Gorgeous. Low, smooth, posh—his vowels so clipped they might have been chipped from diamonds. Mum had spoken like that. People had laughed at her for it. Said she nursed too many airs for the pennies in her pocket.

A scrap of fabric lay on the opposite bench. It gleamed in the low light of the side lamp. She plucked it up. Slippery-soft, the color of a summer sky. Fine white embroidery at the edges. *SR* picked out in the corner.

She slipped the scrap into her pocket. Just in case, she told herself.

Her head fell back against the bench. In case *what*? Did she really mean to humor this lunatic?

I took you, Mum had said.

Mum had refused to speak of Rushden after that night. Soon, she'd not been lucid enough to speak at all. But—*I took you,* she'd whispered. *I thought it for the best.*

Mum had always been a touch mad. But what would it make her to have stolen someone else's baby?

To have stolen me.

Nell swallowed. Too strange, almost sickening, to think that that girl in the photograph might be more than her half sister. If St. Maur was right, they'd shared a womb.

But Nell had known a pair of twins, the Miller

girls down the road. Inseparable, those two. Finished each other's sentences. Cared for each other before even their husbands. Such a bond as that—could a girl forget it? She'd looked into Katherine Aubyn's photograph and seen nothing that spoke to her heart—only to the blackest parts of her, envy and bitterness and anger.

But even if St. Maur's story wasn't true . . . She cast a look around the interior. This little space was finer than any she'd ever called her own. Ha! Finer than any she'd ever seen before last night. Cut-glass lamps fixed in brass, panels of polished wood, tapestry rugs rolled up at her feet—a girl could live in this coach.

Marry me, he'd said.

She reached into her pocket and felt past the handkerchief for the ten-pound note he'd given her to show his promises were good. She'd handled a bill, once or twice, but this one felt different, maybe because it was so clean. Crisp and crackling, like it had just come from the bank.

Did it matter who she was? St. Maur said people would believe it, regardless. And why not? She *did* look just like that girl.

She closed her eyes and took a breath through a throat that felt as dry as bone. If he came back with Hannah, maybe . . . Maybe she'd decide to give him a bit of trust. Just a *bit,* mind. She'd see where this led, at least.

Minutes passed. The vehicle trembled as others trundled by. Footsteps cracked toward the vehicle; three hard strikes made the door rattle. Now came an angry voice, demanding that the door be opened, the coach be moved; bloody cheek, blocking the entrance! Just as quick, two strident voices tumbled over each other to demand an apology. Lord Rushden's carriage; special business; respect your betters.

And in reply, a flustered apology. Humbly begging his lordship's forgiveness, etcetera.

She sat frozen as the footsteps moved off. So it really *did* work like that. She'd never witnessed such craven groveling, but then, nobody in Bethnal Green got the opportunity for it, did they? Not many lords would see a cause to visit Peacock Alley.

More footsteps approached. A muttered exchange between the erstwhile defenders of his lordship's right to park himself where he pleased. Her heart fluttering in her throat, she sat up. The door shuddered, then swung open.

Hannah's tearful face peered up at her. "Oh, Nell!" she cried, and then burst into tears.

"So he wants me to come back and marry him," Nell concluded. She spoke in low tones, aware of St. Maur waiting outside. His coach was set to take Hannah home, but by the terms of their agreement, she'd stay here in Mayfair with him. He obviously meant to hold her to the fine details, too: he'd not even gone inside his house, but was lingering on the front step. "Can you *believe* this tale?"

Hannah licked her lips. "No."

"It's a bit much, ain't it?" Nell reached out to take her hand. "Poor duck. You look exhausted."

Hannah nodded, looking down to her lap, to the fist in which she held the crumpled blue handkerchief Nell had lent her when she'd started to weep on the way to Grosvenor Square. St. Maur had noted the new ownership with a lift of his brow and a slight but pointed smile.

Now I know, that smile had said.

Yes, now he knew. She was a thief as well as a would-be murderess.

She didn't like to think how tight her throat would feel in a noose. She focused instead on Hannah, whose hand was trembling beneath hers. "You're all right, now," she said, giving the girl a proper squeeze. "And Hannah . . ." Why not dream big? "Think of it. This means I could be rich. Rich beyond all belief!"

A moment of silence passed. Hannah looked up to show a frown. "But you're not that girl, Nell."

"Maybe I'm not. But . . ." She hesitated, then spoke in a rush: "There's this painting in St. Maur's library and I swear to you that I've seen the place before." She'd been thinking about it. "I recognized the house in it. And you were the one who said I looked like that girl in the photograph."

"True, but you say—" Hannah cast a quick glance toward the door, which still stood closed. "You say you're her father's bastard," she whispered. "So maybe you saw the house as a babe." She wrinkled her nose. "Though I can't credit that you kept that secret from me! All these years, and you never breathed a word!"

"But Mum never told me of Rushden till she got sick." Why hadn't she told? Nell felt her stomach tighten. "And if this bloke is right, she had cause to keep quiet, didn't she?"

Hannah made a sharp noise and pulled free of her grip. "I can't credit my ears. You think your mum could do such a thing? Aye, Mrs. Whitby was a small bit daft, but it takes a bedlamite for sure to steal another woman's babe!"

Nell flushed. The words too closely echoed her own thoughts. "I'm not saying she was a bedlamite! But if she did it—" She took a breath. "Well, maybe she had cause. Maybe she worried for me. Maybe I wasn't safe, somehow, or . . ." She trailed off. Hannah was looking at her like she was blaspheming on a Sunday.

"Here," Hannah said tartly, thrusting the handkerchief out. "Take this back. If you're going off to whore, I want no part of the payment!"

Nell shook her head. A sinking feeling was overtaking her. "He talked of marriage, not a poke."

Hannah let out a snort. "You didn't used to be a fool."

Nell stared at the fine handkerchief, clenched so tightly in Hannah's freckled, work-worn fingers. "You're right to worry," she said quietly. "You're right about Mum, too. Of course she wouldn't have done that."

"No, she wouldn't." Hannah's jaw squared. "But I see how you were taken in," she offered. "He's a right handsome beast, and I'm grateful that you made him free me. But what a bounder to try to trick you like that! If he wants you for a moll, he might be honest, at least!"

Here was the catch. "I don't think he's lying." Nell shrugged. "What's he to gain by trickery? Men like him, they think they can buy any girl they like. And to want to buy me?" She made a face. "I'm no eyesore, but it's a bit of a stretch to think he'd go to so much trouble for *me*, don't you think?"

Hannah's mouth pursed. "You're pretty, Nellie. Dickie Jackson always—"

"Oh, piffle to Dickie! You twig what I mean. I'm not *you*. Maybe if it were *you*, I'd believe he'd make up lies to have you. But—let's be frank, Han."

"I don't know . . ."

"Forget the question of Mum," Nell said hastily. "Just consider this: no matter what's true, he believes his story. Either way, then, I've naught to lose by going back to him." Besides, St. Maur had too much on her for her to dare refuse his offer. But she wouldn't worry Hannah with that point.

"Oh, aye, I'd wager he *will* believe this story," Hannah said, her tone ominous. "Until the day comes when he's supposed to wed you! *Then* you see what he believes! You'll be left high and dry without a penny to show for it!"

Nell made an impatient noise. "No, but listen: he *did* promise to set me up, Hannah—a whole wardrobe of new clothes, he said, to introduce me to his kind. Now, imagine what I could do with three or four dresses—not the cheap sort, but silk and satin, the kinds you see in the photographs."

She paused, cheered by the thought. It was a lowering thing to consider his offer only because he could have her arrested if she refused it. But this plan was *flash*. Even if she'd felt certain of being able to refuse him without consequences, she would have considered this road. "No matter if he changes his mind about marrying me, I'll still have the dresses. Imagine how much Brennan would pay for just one of them!"

Hannah drummed her fingers against the leather bench. "I don't know. Aye, they'd fetch a handsome price," she said softly. "But what if he set the police on you for taking them?"

"But he could do that right now if he wanted." Of course, right now he thought he had a use for her. Once that changed, he might throw her to the dogs for fun. "It's a risk," Nell admitted. "But no greater than the one I'm running already."

Hannah pressed her hands together at her mouth, a prayerful posture that caused her lips to whiten. Nell went still, recognizing it as the preparation to a verdict.

"You said he wants your money," Hannah said finally. "He wants to *marry* you. If he's not having you on, then . . . then he'll really want to marry you." She blinked very rapidly, then crossed herself. "Begging your mum's forgiveness . . . you could be a countess, Nell." Her eyes got wide. "A *countess*."

Nell opened her mouth but words failed her. A *countess*. Her laugh felt slightly hysterical. "What a mad idea. If you'd only seen the inside of this place . . ." Or him in it. St. Maur's indifference to the luxury in which he lived—the impatience with which he'd glanced around his library, as though seeing nothing to hold his interest—*that* was what it meant to belong in his world.

She'd never manage that.

"He's a looker," Hannah murmured. She was eyeing Nell queerly. "Do you like him, then? Would you want to be marrying him?"

Nell leaned back. The leather seat felt like a warm, steady hand against her back, holding her up as all the butterflies came back to life in her stomach. "He's . . . clever," she said. "Slippery." More than that, of course. Sorcerer's eyes, the devil's mouth. Smiles that came and went like quicksilver.

He'd kissed her. If she agreed to this plan, he'd want more.

"It wouldn't come to marriage," she said.

Hannah tipped her head, looking doubtful. "He doesn't seem mean, at least."

"No. I don't know." He hadn't threatened her, but

she supposed a man of his ilk would have subtler ways of bullying. "I suppose I'll find out."

Hannah didn't like that. "If he's mean, you'd leave the dresses and run!"

Nell gave a pull of her mouth. Easy to say for Hannah, with a family who loved her and would support her through aught. "Not the dresses," she said wryly.

They met each other's eyes and laughed.

"A purple one," Hannah said after a moment, wistfully. "Oh, do try for a purple one—like we saw in Brennan's that time."

That dress had been ripping, though far too dear even to touch. "Aye," Nell said. "And a pair of white gloves, never worn."

"Never worn," Hannah breathed.

"And silk stockings. Why not? And a new petticoat—" Nell came to a stop. "I *have* to do this. It's a chance, isn't it? I have to take it."

Hannah looked down at the handkerchief. "Even if you only managed another ten of these . . ."

"Keep it."

"Oh, I couldn't!"

Nell gave her a crooked smile. "Yes, you can." She reached into her jacket and plucked out the ten-pound note from one pocket and the fork and knife from the other. "Keep these for me, too. If I'm not back in two weeks, they're yours."

"Good Lord." Hannah's hand trembled as she took the loot. "This is—this is a fortune! And these—are they silver?"

"Aye, I think so."

"How . . . I can't take all this, Nell!"

Nell drew a long breath. "If I'm lucky," she said, "I'll be coming back with loot worth a hundred times that amount or more." The idea boggled her. "A hundred times' worth," she whispered. "Plus the dresses."

She and Hannah stared at each other in amazed silence. *A hundred times, plus the dresses.* After such words were spoken, there wasn't much left to say.

6

The rooms he gave her were double the size of the flat in Bethnal Green.

Nell stood in the middle of the bedroom, beside a long, armless sofa that pressed lengthwise against the foot of the bed. It was eerie how quiet this place was. There was nothing to hear but the distant tick of the clock in the hall.

She turned a half circle. The mattress was big enough for four people. An embroidered coverlet of pale gray-green silk stretched over it. Pretty color. It almost matched his high-and-mighty lordship's eyes.

The thought made her stomach tighten. She didn't want to admire a thing in him, but she owed him a debt for Hannah's freedom and he knew it. He'd stood below, watching as she'd mounted the stairs in the company of his housekeeper, and his smile had looked something more than pleased: it had looked *smug*.

She didn't know what he had in mind for her. She couldn't begin to guess at what transpired in a rich man's brain. But she knew a handful of handsome lads, and when they got those smiles on their faces, a girl needed to watch out.

She wrapped her arms around herself. Better not to think about him right now. Instead she admired the pillowcases, whiter than clouds, with embroidery to match—a wondrous touch, a beauty meant to be enjoyed only by the head that lay on them. White was everywhere in this place, lace doilies and sheets and

St. Maur's necktie, which she wouldn't be surprised to learn glowed in the dark.

Maybe he favored white just to show how well his staff could keep it clean. Heaven knew that by comparison, what the rest of London called white was actually gray.

She took a step toward the window seat. The carpet was so soft under her feet!

She knelt down to touch it. Then pressed her palms against it. It was *springy*. She thought about getting down on all fours and clambering across it, but she was afraid somebody would come in and catch her. The older lady who'd shown her up here, Mrs. Collins, the housekeeper, had said somebody else would be up shortly to wait on her.

To *wait* on her!

She straightened too quickly. Not amazing if she felt dizzy. Through the open door to the left she could see the *sitting room,* where a person went if she wanted to sit. Apparently the armchair in here was just for show or something. Beyond it lay a proper, mechanized water closet as well as the *dressing room*— because this great bedroom, with its hulking wardrobe and toilet table, didn't contain enough space for a body to dress.

A laugh bubbled out of her. She covered her mouth with her hand—then frowned and lifted her fingers to her nose. A light trace of perfume lingered on them.

She looked down in amazement. They perfumed the carpets!

The door opened. She spun in time to see a girl enter from the hall—that sour-faced maid who'd taken her knife yesterday. The girl carried a basket in her arms, a heap of clothing folded atop aught else; she kept her eyes downcast and her balance perfect as she paused in the doorway to curtsy.

She certainly hadn't curtsied last night.

Nell eyed her, then the basket. She didn't feel too charitable. "What's that for?"

Light brown eyes flashed briefly up at her. "Night rail and wrapper; fresh clothes and the things for your bath, miss."

Oh ho, so she was *miss* today, was she? "So what's your name, then?"

"Polly."

"Well, Polly, maybe I don't want a bath."

The girl shifted her weight. "His lordship instructed me to draw one for you."

For all Nell knew, his lordship wanted her to strip naked so he could bound in and kiss her again. He'd try it in vain. She'd resolved with Hannah not to allow any nonsense until he made good on his promise of marriage. The fastest road to ruin would be to get herself with child. "I'm too tired for it. Is there a wash-basin here?" Generally she made do with a pitcher of water and a cloth.

"His lordship called for a bath," Polly said.

Nell hesitated. Judging by the smoothness of Polly's blond bun, the girl hadn't been doing much hard labor. "You going to haul the buckets?"

A small, disbelieving noise escaped the girl. "We've plumbing, miss."

"Bully for you," said Nell. But a great many stairs stood between this room and the ground floor, and fatigue was catching up to her. "I'm in no mood to wait. The washbasin will serve."

The girl gave her a peculiar look, then proceeded briskly past Nell into the boudoir. There she paused to lay down the fresh clothing before slipping out of sight.

Curious, Nell trailed after her and discovered that yet another room existed, its door having been cleverly concealed by a cover of wallpaper. White tile paved the floor inside, and a layer of varnish glistened over the pale blue paper on the walls. In the center of the room, beneath a small skylight of stained glass, two wooden steps led up to a handsome, mahogany surround that enclosed a large enamel tub, into which was aimed a bunch of copper pipes. The water came up *here*?

The maid had set her basket atop a small brass trolley, and now knelt to take hold of one of the knobs. "It—sticks," she said on a grunt, and then the knob gave way and she fell back onto her bum. A hollow knocking sounded, and then a bang like a hammer clanging.

"That's an ungodly racket," Nell said. "And I've no interest in an ice bath, mind you!"

"Only another moment." Polly righted her cap and climbed back onto her feet.

Suddenly water gushed out of one of the pipes, splashing into the tub.

Nell found herself gripping the door frame so hard that her knuckles protested. The water was *steaming*.

"It's *warm*?" she asked.

"Aye," the maid said with a sigh. "Too warm, at that. Once there's enough of it, I've to shut off the pipe and spill in some cold for you." She darted Nell a glance that said some people weren't worth such fuss, then smoothed her hand across the towel in the basket. "His lordship is very modern," she said stiffly.

"I can see that." Magical would have been the word

Nell chose. She couldn't remove her eyes from the gushing tap. It flowed like a river! The standpipe in the yard outside her flat in Bethnal Green carried water only twice or thrice a week, and not on any predictable schedule. What water it yielded came in a weak brown stream. If a body wanted to bathe, it meant hours lost to labor—collecting the pails; hauling them up the stairs; heating a bucket over the fire lest one freeze to death in the wetting.

Here, all you needed to do was turn a knob.

When the hot water was about three inches deep, the maid shut it off and switched on the cold. "You can start unrobing, miss."

Nell cleared her throat. "In front of you?"

"Aye, and who else?" the girl asked tartly. "I'm here to draw your bath, am I not?"

"I reckon I can wash myself," Nell shot back.

The maid turned, hands on hips. "That's not how you're meant to do it. There's soaps and lotions and the whatnot that I'm meant to apply."

Nell gaped at her. "Stars above, girl, have you no self-regard? I knew girls in service would do just about anything, but you mean to tell me you'll even scrub a lady's bits for her?"

The girl's jaw dropped. "I do beg your pardon!"

"You can beg whatever you like—and I'm sure you do, at that! But elsewhere, if you please, for I can bathe myself!"

"Sure and you don't smell like you can," the girl retorted.

"Oh, that's rich! I'd rather smell like onions than be a rich man's sukey. Haven't you any pride? What took you into service, anyway? Slaving for your keep— that can't be your idea of living!"

The girl sucked in a breath. "You'll note, *miss,* that *I* am not the one who reeks of onions and sausage!"

Nell paused. She couldn't argue with that. "Bit feisty, aren't you?" The revelation had her feeling a bit more warmly disposed to the girl. "Pity you're not allowed a mind of your own in this line. Best keep that sharp tongue hidden lest they cut it out for you."

The maid's laugh sounded incredulous. "Right-o. Don't think I don't know what you sort say about girls in service. Think we're dogs, don't you? While you sleep eight to a room in your dirty little hovels, scraping together pennies to spend on gin so the cold don't bother you! Aye, it's well and good to congratulate yourself on your *liberty* when you've holes in your clothes and live as dirty as rats in a warren!"

What a sad lot of misinformation. "You've been listening too hard to rich people's sermons, love. It ain't so bad as that."

The girl reached into the basket and snatched up one of the bottles. When she uncorked it and tipped a bit of the clear liquid into the water, a wave of heavenly scent wafted into the air—some sweet, cunning flower that brought to mind moonlight and a warm summer breeze. "At least you'll smell sweeter the next time I have to *slave* for you," she muttered. But when she turned, her eyes moved slowly down Nell's figure, and she got a frown on her face that Nell didn't like at all. "I'll wager I could count your ribs."

Nell fought the urge to fold her arms over her waist. "What of it?"

"So, you've not a spare ounce of flesh on your bones. If that's liberty, I'll take my lot instead. I eat better and I sleep better, and I never worry that tomorrow will bring a turn for the worse. Say what you like about me, but don't pretend you and your friends wouldn't wish for my comforts."

She hiked her chin and strode past Nell out the door. But she didn't slam it as would a proper woman in a temper. Being trained to *service,* she shut it nice and gentle.

That quiet click was somewhat lowering, though Nell had no idea why it should bother her. She didn't give tuppence for what some groveling girl in service had to say.

The tap was still running. She turned it off on the first try, which made her feel better. Sure and she didn't need a maid to do such things for her.

A quick touch proved that the water's temperature was toastier than a summer's night. Torn, she looked from the tub to the door and back again. Wasteful not to use this water for fear that St. Maur might appear. Cowardly, even.

Heart drumming, she stripped off her clothes and stepped into the water.

Jesus, Mary, and Joseph. The heat melted straight into her bones. As she sat, she felt muscles start to unwind that she hadn't even known she possessed. The tub was large enough for her to stretch out her legs and lean back, deep enough almost to float.

The ceiling was tiled, too. Each square looked to be painted with a different design, scrolling dark blue curlicues against a periwinkle background.

That right there was the color of heaven.

She stared up, her brain as quiet and pleased as her body. What had that girl dumped into the water? If there was a flower that smelled like this, she wanted to know the name.

After an absentminded while, she sat up and

reached for the basket. The little bottles had different colored liquids in them, and each smelled better than the next—this one of almonds, that one of strawberries, the next of roses. She tipped some of the rose-scented stuff into her hands and rubbed it up into a lather, then smoothed it down her arms and chest, scrubbing at the darker spots.

When she got to her ribs, she took a breath. The maid was right. She was bonier than she'd been the last time she'd bathed. Beneath the shelf of her rib cage, her belly caved in like an old woman's cheek. She ran her hand down the concave flesh, a queer little shock buzzing through her bones. It felt like the shakes she'd gotten after narrow escapes at the factory, during the old days when she'd still worked on the cutting machine that trimmed the cigars. The shock of realizing she'd nearly chopped off her finger had left her jittery for hours afterward.

"Well," she said softly. She'd just have to eat, was all. She'd eat every bite put in front of her here, and maybe ask for more besides. No matter what happened with St. Maur's plan, at least she'd have a fuller belly to show for her stay.

She swallowed the lump that was rising in her throat.

One bright spot here: no use worrying in how to fend off St. Maur's advances. It seemed a safe bet that he'd manufactured an interest with the idea that she might be charmed by it. He couldn't be wanting a woman whom even the maid called a bag of bones.

She slid down all the way under, submerging her face and her hair, giving her scalp a proper scrub. When she resurfaced, her deep breath made her grimace. There *was* a ripe stink in here.

She twisted around in the tub, sloshing water up over the edges, and then laughed when she realized what it was. Now that she was cleaner, she could finally smell her clothes.

That was how *she* smelled normally.

The laughter died. God in heaven. How could St. Maur hope to convince anybody that she was born to this world?

He was stupider than he seemed if he thought she'd ever manage to pass for a lady.

Simon gathered that most of his peers dreaded appointments with their stewards and men of business. Thirty years ago, when land had still been the staple of wealth, these meetings had probably carried a nice deal of pomp and circumstance. But since the collapse of crop prices, discussions of seeds and harvests and new machinery tended to the depressing side. How hard one needed to work to keep one's head above water, even and perhaps especially with a hundred thousand acres to one's name!

For all that, Simon looked forward to these conversations. Even the distraction of the guttersnipe above did not cause him to cancel the scheduled appointment. Talk of soil quality and rainfall gratified some obscure, old-fashioned corner of his soul. How good it was to own entire pieces of the world! He even liked to compose the solicitous letters that accompanied his stewards' donations to tenant families fallen on hard times.

As he signed one of these now, five men looking silently on, he reflected that his predecessor, too, had gloried in being the earl. But old Rushden's main joy had seemed to come from his ability to act without justification and owe no explanations for it. For himself, Simon had discovered a different way. He did not flatter himself as to the cause for it: he simply liked to play the hero. It took a humbler man than he to abjure an opportunity to win the undying admiration of a family whose salvation lay in his gift of fifty pounds.

His secretary retrieved the letter, and one of his accountants, glancing over the secretary's shoulder into the contents of the note, made a strangled sound. "My lord—we had agreed—such beneficence, while most noble—"

"I do recall that," said Simon. Tempting to announce that his financial troubles would soon be at an end, but until he spoke to his solicitors, he knew better. "Send it anyway. It won't be fifty pounds that puts us into the red."

After seeing the men out, he made his way upstairs through a house more hushed than a tomb. The silence felt edged, anticipatory, like the hitch in a sharply drawn breath. A maid, crossing the corridor ten paces ahead, started at the sight of him and bobbed a quick curtsy before ducking into the servants' passage.

It wouldn't be silent down below. In the kitchens, in the scullery, speculation would be running rife as to his guest's identity. His housekeeper had all but choked when he'd told her to put Nell in the countess's quarters.

He found himself drawing to a halt outside the very chambers so soon to become a fixture of town gossip. The closed door seemed undeservedly interesting. Had she turned the dead bolt?

He did not like the idea that she might have chosen to erect a barrier between them. He laid a contemplative hand on the knob, tempted to test the possibility.

A noise from down the hall made him turn. One of the maids, Holly, Molly, something or other, was approaching with a tray. As she caught sight of him, her footsteps slowed and she bowed her head to make an examination of the floor.

He'd imagined timidity a quality born of social distance. Certainly it went hand in hand with deference. But it occurred to him now that he might be a more unkind master than he'd fancied himself. His staff crept around him like cringing mice, yet there was nothing timid in Nell.

"Is that for Lady Cornelia?" he asked.

The maid jerked as though he'd struck her. Ah, now he'd done it: he'd accorded his guest her proper honors. By tomorrow evening or the day after, word would begin to spread through the West End. A Lady Cornelia in the Countess of Rushden's chambers. Who was she? No chaperone? What sort of lady could she be? And *Cornelia*? A peculiar coincidence, no? Surely it couldn't be . . . no, of course not.

"Yes, your lordship," answered the maid. "Mrs. Collins said—for her eye—"

"Arnica," he guessed. The tray bore a folded cloth and a bowl of steaming, clear liquid, fragrant and minty.

"I—yes, your lordship."

He smiled. What a lovely opportunity. Without hesitation, he lifted his hand to knock on the door—just as it opened.

Magic: Nell Aubyn stood on the threshold, her startled expression matching the small gasp from the maid. She wore a loose night rail, short sleeved, the neck cut low enough to show collarbones starkly defined.

The sight briefly threw him off guard. Her

gauntness paired with the bruise on her face made a disturbing picture.

By all objective measures, he was doing this girl a good turn. Why, then, did he suddenly feel villainous?

He pushed aside the notion. "Good evening," he said, taking the tray from the limp hands of the maid before stepping inside. "That will be all," he threw over his shoulder, and stood solidly in place, blocking entry.

The door thumped shut, closing him in with his future bride —who took a step back, clearly unprepared for cozy intimacy. For all that she looked tired and thin, the bath had brought her innate prettiness into sharper clarity. Her mink-brown hair contained copperish streaks that the dirt had obscured. It tumbled in wet waves past her pointed elbows, the ends curling by her waist. She smelled like roses.

The scent cleared his wits. Coming here had been a turn of good fortune for her. She would not be ill treated. "Did no one bring you a dressing robe?" he asked.

Her jaw jutted forward in concert with her scowl. Not a pretty effect, but riveting, somehow. Everything about her seemed overstated—as if she were slightly more alive than anyone he knew.

"It was itchy," she said.

"Ah. That will never do. We'll have a modiste in tomorrow. Also, someone will go to Markham's and bring you some ready-mades to tide you over."

She nodded warily, gathering up the neckline of her thin gown, hiking it up. As her fists tightened, a delicious shock ran through him. She had *muscles* in her arms: small, perfectly formed biceps that flexed distinctly as her knuckles turned white.

He stared openly, very willing to let her see his interest. He'd never beheld true muscles in a woman. Smooth, pale, and rounded were the natural feminine qualities. Yielding, cushioning. The musculature of Nell's arms seemed fundamentally obscene. Unwholesome. Fascinating. Proof of a reality to which he was not privy, a history he did not know and had no ability to imagine: this other life of hers, as a girl who worked for a living, sufficient unto herself, laboring for the coins with which she bought bread.

He lifted his gaze and felt a momentary, ice-water shock: he looked into a face that belonged to Kitty Aubyn.

Kitty would have shrieked to be discovered in this state of undress. Nell squared her shoulders and lifted her chin. Once again he saw the unique force of her will, the vivid, vigorous *animation* of her. Even her soggy hair seemed to quiver with life as she glared at him.

She was not unsettled by him in the least.

He wanted to unsettle her.

He wanted to take her biceps between his teeth, very gently, and lick away the roses until all that was left was the scent of her flesh.

He smiled at her: he simply couldn't help himself. He was *so* glad she'd wandered into his house to kill him.

"I didn't make a joke," she said. "No call to look comical."

He answered with a shrug. "I'm the joke, I fear." His attraction to her was inevitable, of course, scripted by the circumstances. Still, his basic nature played a role of its own. He wanted her not despite her muscles but because of them.

How on earth had she formed such strength? "What sort of work did you do?" he asked, even as she opened her mouth and said in a rush:

"I only opened the door to make sure it wasn't locked from the outside." She caught her breath, then blew it out. "Not to find company, not to chat with you."

He paused. "That door doesn't lock from the outside."

"I work at a tobacco factory."

He laughed—not at her answer, but at this strange little conversation, dizzying in its twists. "Worked," he said. "You work there no longer."

She frowned as if this news were suspect. "That's right."

Oh, but she would set London on its ear. And he saw suddenly why she intrigued him: she was one of a kind. Unique. The missing heiress turned factory girl. She appealed to the patron in him, he supposed—the seeker of hidden potentials, the cultivator of odd and rare talents. That she should be here in his house had so much potential in so many regards. For his bank accounts. For his personal convenience and enjoyment. For his amusement at Kitty and Grimston's expense. For his belated revenge on a dead man.

He realized suddenly that she was blushing, a delicate pink stain spreading down her throat. He watched it spread, curious to know how far it would travel, struck by the idea that a woman with muscles might blush at all. "Do you blush all over?" he asked.

She jerked her head toward the door. "Leave."

Now she was trying to order him about. Ill advised. This was his house now. He would do as he liked in it.

But at the last moment, her swollen eye checked

his sharp response. Somebody else had tried to put her in her place recently, and Simon suddenly felt certain that the attempt had failed. Nell Aubyn was nothing if not resilient—a quality he very much admired.

"In fact, I've come on a mission," he said. He tilted his head to indicate the tray in his hands. "Believe it or not, I rarely play the maid. But your eye wants treatment."

The swelling was not so bad that it prevented her from narrowing both eyes in skepticism. "It's just a bruise," she said.

The remark, the idea behind it—that she might consider such injuries negligible—did not agree with him. He spoke rather more curtly than he'd intended. "You're a valuable commodity. As I've explained, worth a great deal of money. You'll have to allow me to tend to you."

She hesitated before giving him a single, grudging nod. It seemed that he'd struck exactly the right note: as long as she considered his ministrations part of the larger, economic transaction, she'd allow them.

That the notion irked him struck him as absurd. His care *was* part of the larger, economic transaction. That he planned to enjoy putting his hands on her fresh, glowing skin was only a small bonus.

"Shall we remain here in your sitting room?" he asked. "Or would the bedroom suit you better?"

A small, disgusted noise came from her throat: *hmmph*. She turned on her heel and led him to the fireplace, where two leather wing chairs faced the low-burning flames. To the left lay a discreet door that opened into his apartments. He hoped she hadn't figured that out yet.

She lowered herself stiffly into one of the seats. He

laid the tray atop the small table by her feet—whimsical pleasure in behaving so domestically—and took up the towel, hooking it over his fingers into neat thirds before dipping it into the bowl.

When he knelt before her and reached for her face, she drew back, clearly startled. "I can do it myself."

"Yes," he said. "You could."

He did not wait for argument before laying the cloth against her cheek. She needed to learn her place in this partnership. Even a purely financial alliance tended to favor one contractor's vision. Casually, he asked, "Who did this to you?"

"None of your business," Nell muttered. The damp heat felt blissful, but letting him come so close didn't seem wise. When she closed her eyes to block out the sight of him, she grew aware of his arm pressing against hers, solid and warm. Some foolish part of her wanted to lean into it. She'd never been so spoiled in her life, and it was rotting her brain.

"Leaving aside my business," he murmured, "I'd still like to know. Who was it?"

His touch was so light on her cheek. He handled her as though she were fragile, special. A lady.

What a laugh *that* idea was.

She tried to shift away from his body—not so much that he would notice, just enough to spare herself his warmth. She was the classic fool, no doubt: the fly drawn to Lord Spider. What a luxurious parlor you keep, sir. Oh yes, I'll sleep in your web. Clever, handsome, an earl . . . he could grind her beneath his boot if he wished it.

Not to say she wouldn't make it hard for him. She was made of stronger stuff than glass.

"Well?" he asked.

Even his *breath* smelled expensive. He'd been drinking brandy by the smell of it. She fixed her attention on his hands, tanned, like those of a man who worked in the sun. Of course, the thick gold ring on his index finger dispelled such notions. No farmer had ever worn such.

She spoke from curiosity alone. "What would you do if I told you?"

"I'd make him regret it."

Her eyes flew to his. He blinked, as though he was as startled by himself as she was. Then he smiled, a whimsical little curve. "Behold: am I not husbandly already?"

She couldn't help a small smile in reply. "Judging by what I've seen, it might be equally husbandly to deliver the blow."

His smile faded. "That's a sad fact, if true."

"And that's a handsome offer you make," she said. Maybe he wasn't so bad, this one. "But it's not necessary."

"It's a basic service," he said flatly.

She snorted. "Then you must stay very busy, St. Maur. Today alone, I know a dozen women who'd have need of you."

His pinkie hooked the underside of her chin, raising her face so she looked into his. From this proximity his irises explained themselves: a narrow ring of charcoal encircled strands of green and palest gray, which faded, around his pupils, into a band of gold. Gorgeous eyes. His brows, bold slashes as black as ink, gathered in a deeper frown. "Are you regularly among that number?" he asked.

She loosed a breath through her nose. His pity

would probably work to her advantage, but she couldn't bear it. "No," she said. "I can look out for myself."

He looked at her a moment longer, but if he had doubts, he kept them to himself. Releasing her chin, he returned his attention to her cheek. As the cloth moved down toward her jaw, she stiffened. It felt too much like a caress. It reminded her of how he'd touched her this morning—and how he'd kissed her last night. More fool she not to mind it. Like a drunk at the scent of gin, she felt every particle of herself coming alive.

Curious how bodies could want each other from the start. Unlike the mind and spirit, the flesh decided instantly—which made the mind, Nell thought, all the more important. She snatched the cloth out of his hand. "You go over there," she said, flapping her hand at the other chair. In deliberately broad accents, she added, "I can manage me eye on me own."

He put two fingers to his brow in a mocking salute and did as she bade him. She took a long, steadying breath. Make Michael regret it, would he? She'd flirted with enough Irishmen down the pub to know blarney when she heard it. It must be his face, making her so stupid. His jaw was firm and square, his cheekbones sharp, that bump in his nose the only thing that saved him from pretty—and not by much. Long-legged, broad-shouldered, flat-bellied . . . he was too lovely to be believed.

And so was this whole affair.

"Something's rotten here," she said. "A man like you, I can't reckon you'd have a hard time finding a bride. What's your real reason for undertaking this stunt?"

He leaned back in his chair, propping his heels atop a stool that sat in front of the fire screen. He had a powerful flex to his thighs. She had a brief flash of what he'd looked like in the flesh: tall and leanly muscled, like an animal built to hunt.

"I've told you only the truth," he said, his tone contemplative. "Of course, it strikes me as noteworthy that you agreed to the plan even as you doubted my intentions. Perhaps you felt you had no choice, though. Who blackened your eye?"

A noise escaped her, pure irritation. "It's none of your business!"

He considered her a moment, a smile growing on his lips. "Hmm." He removed his boots from the stool. Put them flat to the ground as he leaned toward her, bracing his elbows on his thighs. The deliberateness of his movement, the slow encroachment on her space, made her pulse stutter. "Everything about you is my business now. It became so the moment you set foot in this house. Isn't that delightful?"

He looked *too* sure of himself, as if he knew something she didn't. She laid down the cloth, feeling the need to keep her hands free. "I never agreed to let you muck about in my life."

"You agreed to marry me, did you not? As my future wife, your concerns are mine. Quite straightforward, really."

What a load of rot. Every wife she knew kept more secrets from her husband than she shared with him. "And your concerns?" she asked, letting her skepticism sharpen her voice. "Do they become mine as well?"

"You may ask anything you like."

That wasn't quite an answer. "All right," she said, aiming to test him. "You're a fine-looking devil. You've got fancy manners and a title and a house to boot. Why couldn't you find a rich girl to marry you?"

"But I've found one," he said lightly. "She's sitting across from me, looking quite fetching in her night rail. God bless fabrics that itch."

To her disbelief, she felt a blush steal over her face. What nonsense was this? She wasn't coy or prudish, either. "Don't mock me."

"You don't think you're fetching?"

His eyes were sticky. A girl could get trapped in them. "I'm not a lady." But that didn't sound right, did it? She frowned, troubled by the suspicion that she'd just been unfair to herself. With an awkward shrug, she added, "Not your kind, at any rate. A . . . proper one, I mean."

"Ah, that." He sighed and glanced toward the fire. "Most proper ladies are very tiresome—full of demands I've no interest in meeting. Their fathers also pose a problem, tending as they do to frown upon my reputation."

He hadn't mentioned the reputation. "Why? What's the matter with it?"

"I had a rather wild youth."

It had to have been pretty bloody wild if it scared people off a titled bloke. "Did you kill someone?"

"No."

She'd caught his brief hesitation. "*Did* you, then?"

He looked squarely back at her. "I rarely see a point in lying, Nell."

He was more evasive than a thief with a copper. "But sometimes you do?"

He gave her a wry smile. "All right. Let's have it out then. The worst rumors that you'll hear." He sat back, eyeing her. "I'm a drunkard. Not true: I'm fond of my drink, but rarely drunk. A rake and a voluptuary: by some measures, perhaps, but not indiscriminately. Invitation only, as they say. A gambler: yes, but I have never played beyond my means." He paused, black humor sharpening his expression. "Though it would be quite easy to do, in my current situation. Generally, however, I gamble only for the pleasure of removing other people's money from them. What else? Ah— wicked perversions. Well, I suppose it depends on your definition of wicked. Some people seem terribly fearful of creativity. Substances less licit than drink: yes, occasionally. But I'm devoted to none of them." He paused. "Anarchism, worshipping of Lucifer, both false . . . is there anything else? Give me a moment to think on it."

She stared, dumbfounded. "Surely there can't be more."

"A few small trivia, certainly." He gave her a cheerful smile.

The mismatch between his tone and his admissions unnerved her. He seemed utterly unruffled by his recitation. "It doesn't bother you?"

"What?"

"That people lie about you?"

He tipped his head slightly. "Why should it? Apart from the inconvenience, of course, when it comes to wooing a wealthy bride."

"A care for the truth?" In his shoes, she'd be hard-pressed not to rake her nails across lying mouths.

His dimple popped out. "The truth is far more tedious," he said. "And people require entertainment. I provide that." He paused, looking diverted by this train of thought. "I suppose that everyone at heart is a storyteller. And I tend to inspire their stories. In that regard, you may think of me as . . ." He laughed suddenly. "A muse to the bored upper crust."

"A muse."

"Ancient Greek spirits. Provided inspiration to—"

"Poets and artists and whatnot," she finished. "I thought they were women."

"They were." He leaned forward, scrutinizing her. "So you *do* read."

She rolled her eyes. "Maybe the fifth time I tell you I'm up to dictionary, you'll believe me."

He made an amused noise, a breath pushed through his nose. "I didn't think board schools provided Greek literature to their students."

God in heaven. "Folks who can't afford books use lending libraries." Most of them were terrible, but the GFS had a tremendous collection. It was the only reason she'd joined the club.

"Of course." He eyed her. "You must think me a terrible snob."

"I know you're a snob." All his ilk were. "Why? Do you imagine you aren't?"

"No. I'll admit to it."

She grinned. "Seems like you're willing to admit to a lot of things that other people might prefer to deny."

His smile began slowly, then widened all at once. "You're not slow witted."

"Nobody ever said I was." How peculiar that he'd even think it. It stung her foolish vanity. "Perhaps you're misled by the fact that I'm still sitting here," she said. "No doubt a smart woman would leave. By your own confession, you're bad company."

"Ah. No," he said, his dimple flashing again. "You misunderstood me, Nell. I'm the best of company: I can promise that you'll never be bored."

She snorted. "It's not boredom I'm worried about."

"Then you're a very lucky woman."

What claptrap. He spoke like a child. "You're the lucky one. Otherwise you'd know there's a pleasure to be had from boredom. The best kind of pleasure: it means you've got nothing to worry about."

He leaned forward so abruptly she didn't have time to draw back. His fingers skated across her bruised cheek; his thumb settled at the corner of her mouth. "You needn't worry about me," he murmured. "I've never hurt a woman in my life."

A tremor ran through her at the feel of his thumb so close to her lips. It felt like the first shudder of a too-tight lid as it finally began to loosen.

Her body liked his. It happened sometimes. Didn't mean she needed to pay attention to it.

She cleared her throat. "You don't need to be touching me to make your point."

"But I like touching you." He studied her a moment. "Can't you tell?"

She saw his intention to kiss her. His grip wasn't firm. She could have pulled away. But sometimes when you pulled away they thought it meant you were afraid of them. And once they thought so, they did all sorts of things to see if it was true.

Slowly he lowered his head. His lips brushed over hers once, twice, so lightly that she barely felt the contact. Maybe she'd misread him, after all. These kisses didn't seem like lust so much as a token to solemnize his promise.

He drew back a little. His face not two inches from hers, he looked into her eyes. "Will you participate?"

It was a queer question, the more alarming because it showed insight. He'd seen her decision to steel herself. She didn't like how sharply he saw her. She pitched her voice low and hard. "I didn't come into this house to whore for you."

"No," he agreed. "We'll save that for the marriage bed. But in the meantime: a kiss."

"Which I just gave you last night," she said. "One's enough."

His mouth lifted at one corner, a wicked little smile. "If that's your opinion, then it was a very bad kiss, and I must be allowed the opportunity to atone for it."

"No." She knew where this road ran. She'd seen a dozen girls ruined by lads with a gift for sweet talk. "I won't be bearing your bastard, St. Maur."

He eyed her. "We'll need to have a talk," he said, "if you imagine that kissing leads to children."

"I know exactly what leads to children, and I'm *not* doing it."

"Then a simple kiss should be all right with you, sterile as it is."

She opened her mouth and found herself speechless. "You've a twisty way with words," she said at last.

He grinned. "I think I'll insist," he said, and came toward her again, only this time he slid off his chair onto his knees in front of her, and his hand pushed into her hair as he brought his lips back to hers.

Ah, he felt good. Hot and strong. His tongue traced the shape of her lower lip and her thoughts tangled. He followed her gasp into her mouth as his grip tightened in her hair. Heat kindled in her, loosening her stomach, warming the backs of her knees.

No. She struggled to keep track of her wits. *Stupid, stupid.* A man intent on his own pleasures was mindless, helpless, and an easy mark. But once the woman started wanting it herself, what power did she have?

But St. Maur was an expert, all right. He kissed her like the kiss was all there was, sufficient to itself, no rush or hurry or greater goal to it. His mouth moved deliberately, leisurely. He made a low noise as though he tasted something delicious; then she felt his thumb beneath her mouth, stroking a languorous line across her skin, as though to underscore what he was doing to her.

Doing to her. He shouldn't be doing *anything*.

As she stiffened, he murmured a protest. Such a small noise, so peculiar from a man: vulnerable, somehow. His grip gentled: she could pull away if she liked. But his knuckles brushed down her cheek, reluctant to leave her; then farther down yet, a quick skim of warmth along her throat, a lazy pressure along her collarbone. Not pushing, not grabbing. Only coaxing. *Asking*.

Her body lit up. The tips of her breasts, between her legs. Revelation unrolled through her, melting, then contracting: these places that men liked to involve also had their own role in it. When he asked, her body answered.

Her palm found his upper arm. It felt solid and hot beneath the thin lawn of his shirt, dense and thick, powerful. His hard abdomen pressed into her knees. He was coming closer to her, leaning over her; his height was in his long legs, so he was tall even when kneeling. Her free hand found his hair. It was softer and thicker than any hair she'd ever touched. A rich man's hair, born of a lifetime of feasting.

The thought snapped his spell. She pushed him

hard. He withdrew immediately, rolling his weight onto his heels in a fluid move, making no move to come after her. He simply crouched there, breathing hard. His hair was disheveled, his necktie coming loose. Had she done that?

He exhaled, pushing a hand through that mess of black, glossy hair. He was as beautiful as a summer night and twice as expensive as the moon; as she met his witchy hazel eyes, he licked his lips—tasting her, she realized.

She went hotter, a blush so fierce that her face probably caught fire.

His smile was lazy. "I *am* glad you decided to stay," he said.

She shot to her feet, ignoring how her knees still trembled. "If you want to stay glad," she said unsteadily, "then you'll get out right now. Otherwise—"

But he was already rising. With an easy, amenable bow, he turned for the door.

As she watched it close behind him, a shiver ran through her—the sort that announced a near escape. *But not from him,* she thought.

She wrapped her arms around herself, horrified by the notion that in his arms, her greatest threat might come from herself.

7

This is a case in which simple greed will have spared us a good deal of trouble." Daughtry spoke dryly, his eyes on his breakfast plate. He was a spare, silver-haired man whose sharply arched brows and dark, heavy-lidded eyes lent him a questioning and skeptical look no matter the object of his contemplation: as, for instance, the rasher he now forked up.

Simon often wondered if Daughtry's face was not the key to his success. Surely there was nothing so comforting in a lawyer as pessimism. "You mean," he said, picking up his coffee, "that Grimston and his charge did not have Cornelia presumed dead."

"Indeed." Daughtry paused to chew, then to dab his serviette at his lips, precisely covering the wrinkled expanse. He even ate his breakfast like a solicitor, slowly and methodically.

"It made sense, of course," Daughtry continued. He retrieved his fork, aiming it precisely at the quivering eye of his half-cooked egg, appearing to consider the best angle of attack on the yolk; and then, to Simon's mild disappointment, abdicated the decision by returning the fork to his plate. "By the terms of the trust, Katherine and Cornelia will not have full access to their wealth until they marry or attain the age of twenty-five. In the interim, Sir Grimston receives an annual sum allotted for their maintenance and education. Had we succeeded in our motion for a presumption of death, this sum would have been halved—leaving

Grimston, and by extension, Lady Katherine, substantially poorer."

Simon nodded. "But Cornelia's reappearance would do the same."

"Yes."

"So we should be prepared for a fight."

Daughtry cleared his throat. "For caution's sake, let us assume so."

"I'll enjoy seeing how they deny it. She's Kitty's spitting image." Simon hesitated. The remark left a bad taste in his mouth. It recast in comical colors the long hour he had lain awake last night. While he was glad to entertain himself with plans to strip and seduce Nell, he felt quite differently about Kitty. "They're twins," he added. "Obviously they look alike. I don't mean to say the resemblance goes any deeper than the skin."

Daughtry mistook his meaning. "Yes, I suppose that's the difficulty. Even if her resemblance to Lady Katherine is so extraordinary as you say, it will fall on us to prove that she *is* the Lady Cornelia, and not some natural child of his lordship. The childhood nurse can be interviewed as to the question of birthmarks and the whatnot. Determining the identity of the woman who raised Lady Cornelia will also be of import. If I may, I would recommend the firm of Shepherd and Sons for that purpose." He turned to bend an instructional look on the bespectacled secretary seated near the sideboard. This undersized minion nodded and made a note. "A very discreet trio," Daughtry continued. "And they know their way about the rougher areas. I've been very pleased with their investigative services."

"Excellent." Simon didn't care who did it, as long as it got done. "What else?"

"Ah . . . yes." Daughtry cleared his throat and set a

finger to his lips—some sort of sign, it seemed, for the secretary popped off his seat and bowed low, begging to be excused.

"Marvelous," Simon said when the door shut behind the lad. "Have them trained to hand signals, do you?"

Daughtry's lips sketched the barest and most fleeting intimation of a curve. "Discretion is my watchword, particularly in matters of . . ." One steel gray brow lifted. "Love?"

Simon laughed. "My God, Daughtry. Have you been hiding a sense of humor all these years?"

"Never," Daughtry said. "However, assuming you intend to shelter the lady . . ."

"I do." He wouldn't risk losing track of her in some rat warren in the slums. "What of it?"

"You must realize that her miraculous recovery will become a matter of public interest. If Lady Katherine and Sir Grimston prove obstinate, it may require an examination at the Law Institution."

"I'd expected as much." Her disappearance had filled the newspapers sixteen years ago. Her reappearance would prove no less notorious.

"There will be a great deal of speculation about her whereabouts prior to her reappearance. If you could find a less remarkable place to lodge her . . . perhaps with Lady St. Maur . . . ?"

Simon loosed a snort. "My mother?" She would want to dip Nell in lye and then boil her for good measure. Of all people, she'd be the last to believe that Cornelia might turn up in the guise of a waif from the slums. She'd always had great difficulty with the idea that the truth might be a separate quantity from the appearance. "Absolutely not. Besides, she's in Nice until the end of the summer."

"I see. But if her ladyship is to be lodged in your custody . . ." Daughtry paused. "Forgive me, but you must understand how it will appear to others."

"Quite scandalous, no doubt. What matter? No need for her to go courting. I'll make a satisfactory husband, I believe."

"You intend to marry her at once, then?"

"Once it seems clear that the inheritance will be hers, yes. Without delay."

Lips pursing, Daughtry nodded, then turned his attention to smoothing the edge of his cuff.

From a man usually no less rigid than a five-day corpse, this distracted gesture presented an extraordinarily loud statement of doubt. "Speak your mind," Simon said.

"As your legal advisor, I must contemplate all possible outcomes." Daughtry shrugged. "Once she's acknowledged as Lady Cornelia, her care will fall to Sir Grimston, and he will no doubt prove eager to . . . discharge his duties, as it were."

To profit from her, more precisely. She was only twenty-two; Grimston would enjoy three years of controlling her not-inconsiderable allowance, provided she remained unwed. "He'll do his best to remove her," Simon said.

A dark vision arose before him: having invested a good deal of money in facilitating Lady Cornelia's resurrection, he might succeed only to watch Nell be swept from his grasp. Grimston would want to postpone her marriage as long as possible. Encourage her to debut, perhaps.

"And if I marry her at once?" he asked. "Before, say, she is introduced to society?"

"That would aid our case," Daughtry said

immediately. "Should it come down to the courts, you can imagine that a judge would find it easier to acknowledge the noble birth of a countess than a woman of uncertain repute, found to be living in questionable circumstances with . . . a gentleman."

With a man of your reputation, he did not say, but Simon heard him clearly all the same.

"And yet if something were to go awry," Simon replied, "I would find myself a bankrupt lord saddled with a penniless guttersnipe for a wife. Hardly ideal, is it?"

"Oh, no." Daughtry looked surprised. "Indeed you would not. Should she be found to be other than Lady Cornelia, you would have no choice, I think, but to petition for an annulment."

Caught reaching for his coffee, Simon froze. "Would it be granted?"

"If her fraudulent self-representation was deliberate, it would vitiate your consent to the marriage. This is one of the most dependable grounds for annulment. I can't think but you would find the court in full sympathy with your plight."

Simon laughed under his breath. "But that's . . . thoroughly wicked of you, Daughtry."

The solicitor offered up a sly smile. A man didn't need a sense of humor to be a smug, gloating bastard. "It would be unfortunate," he allowed. "Nevertheless, it would be entirely within the law."

"The law is an ass," Simon murmured. Who'd written that? Shakespeare. He took a long drink. More accurate to say that the law was an *upper-class* ass. Who else had any hope of using it to his advantage? "She'll never have a chance."

Daughtry smiled again. "No, she won't."

Simon looked away toward the window. Pretty day, the early sun shining cheerfully through the glossy leaves.

Toying with the rag-and-tatters set wasn't his usual style. One didn't play with those who didn't know the rules or weren't equipped to abide by them.

But the prospect rarely carried such a dazzling reward—and not simply for him. Nell would profit, too. In most views, she stood to profit far more than he did. The money would allow him to maintain his accustomed life, but it would give her the chance to create a far, far better one. She would be able to live as she pleased: Simon had no intention of demanding anything from her but a share of the inheritance.

And if this bid failed? A few months spent living here wouldn't harm her. She'd leave his house well fed and well clothed. A happy holiday from hard labor, he thought. If she liked, she could take a few more pieces of silverware upon her departure.

"Put the investigators to work at once," he said. "I expect the key will lie in proving that the woman who raised her was Jane Lovell. Lady Cornelia called herself Nell Whitby, but she admitted that she took the surname from a stepfather. If Jane's marriage was legitimate, the parish registers would be the place to start."

"Very good. And shall I arrange a visit to Faculty Hall?"

For a special license, Daughtry meant.

"Go ahead," Simon said. "Nothing to lose, apparently." And everything to gain.

The door opened. His future wife entered the room—dressed, he saw in astonishment, in something very near to rags.

"Good heavens," he heard Daughtry mutter.

Long-ingrained manners overcame his amazement. He rose, as did Daughtry.

"Morning," she said brightly, dividing a chipper smile between them.

"Good morning to you," he replied. The sight of her put a rude period to the heady enthusiasm raised by plotting strategy. He'd forgotten how very much she did *not* look like a missing heiress. There was the issue of her boniness. And then, mysteriously, the trappings she'd somehow located: a drab, dark skirt, uneven at the hem; a long black jacket whose sleeves ended above her knobby wrists; a bowler hat. For God's sake, where had she gotten a *bowler* hat?

Amid the quiet luxury of his drawing room, she looked like the point to a joke. Or, better yet, an exclamation point: her eyes had found the breakfast dishes on the sideboard, and every line of her body strained toward it.

He took a breath and got hold of his anger. "Help yourself," he said.

She nodded and strode forward.

He sat slowly into his seat. Across the table, Daughtry managed an impassive look that should have won him an award. Silverware clattered against china; a tuneless hum reached his ears. In very high spirits, Nell was shoveling food onto her plate.

Silence held until she sat down at the table.

"Where did you get those clothes?" he asked.

She lifted her brows. "One of your sukeys brought them. Thanks much."

He bit his tongue. Apparently she was blithely unaware that she'd just become the butt of a cruel joke.

Daughtry sent him an unreadable look. He felt his anger sharpen, lent a new edge by embarrassment. Someone was going to be sacked before the morning was out. He had no tolerance for petty rebellions in his servants, much less their ridiculous little snobberies.

With an effort, he retrieved his fork and set to his sausage.

A wet splat drew his attention upward. A quarter of an egg now lay by Nell's place.

Her table manners would need . . . improvement.

She certainly did not lack for appetite, though.

Daughtry laid down his fork and commenced a close study of the tablecloth. Simon didn't blame him. It felt almost obscene to witness Nell eating. She hunched over her plate as though to guard it while she forked up the contents in a rapid, continuous motion. As she chewed, she flicked narrow looks toward the both of them—monitoring their intake, he realized with shock: adjudging if they would require more food from the sideboard, or, more precisely, how much food would be left for her once her own plate was emptied.

Through the opening door, one of the footmen appeared to gauge that very question. Nell startled at the entrance, then visibly relaxed when the man left without taking what dishes remained.

Pity, Simon thought, felt like an illness, a growing malignancy, the sort of painful cancer that made a patient welcome the cut of the scalpel that would remove it forever.

He looked away from her, toward the paintings along the wall. Old Rushden glowered down from the far corner, stiff as the corpse he'd become, but smug, somehow—his lips frozen in that slight curve that was not so much a smile as a sneering smirk. It had rarely left his lips: in his eyes, most of the world had been his inferior.

Perhaps his daughter was lucky that he'd not lived to discover her. Simon had no faith that the old man would have looked on her kindly.

The thought increased his discomfort. *He* was not looking on her too kindly. He, who had just decided to fire a servant for mocking her.

The door opened again: more food being delivered. Nell turned in her seat, obviously riveted by the sight of baked mushrooms, mutton chops, fried perch, and boiled tomatoes. As the servant placed these dishes onto the sideboard, she sat back, took a deep breath and, for the first time since commencing, laid down her fork.

He cleared his throat. "There is always more. And if you long for something in particular, you need only ask for it."

She gave him an intent, measuring look. "I will ask," she said, and the words seemed edged with some note of challenge. Did she think the offer false?

"Ask," he said. "What would you like?"

She took up her fork again, twirling it as she considered the matter. "Let me think on it," she said. A strange smile crept over her mouth as she returned her attention to the food.

No: she began to *commune* with the food.

First her bites slowed. The next French roll took all of a minute to disappear.

Then came the small noises from her throat as she moved on to a dish of berries and fresh cream.

Finishing these, she paused to lick her fingers.

And then she sighed, a full-bodied sound, breasts lifting and falling. The corner of her tongue came out to delicately lick a spot of cream from the corner of her mouth.

Another French roll started the cycle over again.

He sat very still, once again feeling the fool—albeit distantly, dimly, in a distracted kind of way. She did not notice his regard. Why should she? She was being seduced by strawberries. Ravished by rolls, overcome by Devonshire double cream. Every inch of her was rosy and vibrant with epicurean passions. She had no energy to spare on him.

Which was well and good, he thought, because he had no idea what his face might have revealed had she bothered to look into it. His pity had dissipated—vanished all at once—into something far less spiritual.

He darted a sideways glance toward Daughtry. The man looked appalled.

Which, absurdly, made him smile. Ah, well. Daughtry was an upright sort. But he was not.

Yet it wasn't simply lust that gripped him. This growing sensation felt like revelation. He'd never seen someone . . . *enjoy* herself so. And over what? Breakfast.

She picked up a cup, sniffed, and smiled. His enterprising cook had remembered his request that she be brought chocolate for her breakfast. Nell showed no hesitation to drink it now: she lifted the cup and the pure, white arc of her throat as she swallowed all but begged the brush of the back of his hand.

When she set down the cup, it was empty.

He felt—he felt as if his revelation somehow concerned envy. Chocolate might be uncommon in Bethnal Green, but bread and berries could not be novel to her. Bizarre, but he envied her the delight she took from them. It was no small talent to know how to immerse oneself in mundane pleasures. It had been a very long time since he'd experienced the feeling that he saw on her face.

Curious to consider that he might have something to learn from her. Years, perhaps, since he'd found a novelty able to keep all his senses occupied.

Perhaps she was such a novelty in herself.

Her eyes met his. "You're staring," she said.

"Am I?" He couldn't feel too concerned.

She reached up and brushed off her mouth, then glanced down, following the path of the crumb she'd dislodged. A flush bloomed on her cheeks: it wasn't just the one crumb in her lap, he suspected, but several.

But if she was gathering now how sorely she'd abused etiquette, it didn't stifle her. She looked back up to meet his eyes. Hiked her chin and glared down her nose at him. Down *Kitty's* nose.

He felt a small shock. God above, she looked so much like Katherine Aubyn.

"You must see the likeness," he said to Daughtry. It made his head ache. One moment he managed to forget it; the next, it slapped him in the face.

The solicitor darted her a reluctant glance, as if frightened of what he'd see. "There is a remarkable similarity. I can credit that they are twins. However, I will say that the unsuspecting eye *might* be forgiven for . . ."

"Overlooking it, yes." Asking the courts to recognize this woman as the legitimate daughter of an earl would test every polite sensibility. Justice would require a touch of persuasion, a small sleight of hand. A proper corset, Simon thought, and a good deal of starch. "We'll have to groom her, of course. Modistes, a proper lady's maid, perhaps someone to school her in deportment—I've started to make the arrangements."

"Very good," Daughtry said in tones of relief.

Nell reached toward her ear and snapped her fingers. "No, not deaf," she said. "Just invisible, I take it."

"Indeed not," Simon said instantly. "Forgive us. In fact, Mr. Daughtry here will be coordinating our efforts to see you restored to your birthright. And as for today . . ." He trailed off, observing suddenly the rather . . . jaundiced flavor of her regard. She did not look friendly.

Perhaps he shouldn't have kissed her again. Seduction might muddy an otherwise straightforward arrangement.

She hadn't seem offended by it, though. No note of maidenly modesty had colored her reaction. Her expression after breaking the kiss had looked more like . . . amazement.

He smiled, amused by his own vanity. Well, but she was his future wife: could not wooing her be considered a wise, even chivalrous course of action?

But first, he had a piece of business to settle: a servant to sack. "We'll start today," he said, "by introducing you to the staff."

There were over two dozen of them.

As the underlings lined up before her in the great domed entry hall, Nell actually found herself counting. She'd reached nine by the time the "upstairs staff" had finished making their bobs and curtsies. Fourteen more from "belowstairs."

She gritted her teeth as the introductions dragged on. She didn't like being bobbed to. Without intending

it, she kept inching backward, and the damned staff
kept inching toward her, a line of advancing toadies,
implacable in their witless obedience to their lord and
master.

St. Maur found her retreat comical; he actually
laughed at one point and asked if she'd like a chair.
She didn't bother to reply, but her look took the smile
off his face. He didn't even know their names! It took
the housekeeper and the walking cadaver of a butler,
Hankins, to call out their names.

When everybody's name had been announced,
St. Maur murmured in Hankins's ear, and Hankins
motioned the upstairs maids forward again, a line of
girls in identical black dresses, identical lace aprons,
each wearing the mobcap that marked her choice in
life. Six automatons in all.

Here, St. Maur suddenly recalled that these were
his employees, not simply players in a penny gaffe held
for his bored perusal. He took an *interest*. "A question
for you," he said to Nell, his voice ringing through the
echoing space. "Which of these women brought you
the clothes you're wearing?"

She opened her mouth, an indrawn breath away
from replying—and something tipped her off. The
silence deepened: the trained circus before her had
stopped breathing. Her eyes found Polly and the pallor
of the girl's face had her gaze skipping onward, sliding
down the line, landing on the housekeeper.

Oh, ho. Nell recognized the jut of that woman's jaw.
Here was the very picture of a labor-mistress sensing
danger. The foreman's displeasure had communicated
itself. Looking now for the source of it, for somebody to
punish so she might spare herself trouble, Mrs. Collins
crossed those forearms like hams beneath the mighty

prow of her righteous breast and swept a pugnacious inspection down the line of slaveys.

Whose eyes all latched onto Nell.

Nell cleared her throat. "I don't remember."

A brief pause. Nobody dared breathe yet. She didn't look toward Polly, although she wouldn't lie to herself; she would have enjoyed the gratification of a grateful look from that sour little creature.

She turned away from temptation, putting her attention squarely on the master of the house, whose displeasure with her looked mild but definite. Oh, but wasn't it *terrible* when the underlings stepped out of line! Wasn't it vexing beyond belief when the poor proved they weren't deserving or much *grateful,* either!

"Look again," he said, and had she not been listening for the faint note of frustrated interest, she'd have missed it entirely. She was ruining his fun. He hadn't expected his entertainment to be snatched from him. Poor lad. How on earth would he occupy himself now?

"All right," she said: easy, pliable, too thick-witted to guess at such complex operations as a master at work on the trail of an impudent rebel. She made a show of surveying the girls. Polly stared straight ahead, blank-eyed, only her folded lips a giveaway to the nerves that must be screaming in her stomach.

Nell pinched up a bit of her skirt. It was nice wool, soft to the touch. But apparently it wasn't as fine as she'd thought.

She shook her head, then manufactured a regretful look for his lordship's sake. "No, sorry. I can't recall."

She saw the moment he caught on. Not a stupid man, more was the pity. His eyes narrowed. Instantly he thought better of his suspicions: she wouldn't lie to him, would she? Over this trifling matter? Of course not. Or . . . would she? He frowned a little. Gave her that searching look that betokened a new idea. Why, *yes*—yes, she *would* lie. But why?

She smiled at him. *Go look in the mirror,* she thought. *Go look at your handsome, smooth face and your wide, strong shoulders and your straight, white teeth and your eyes that have never missed a single night's sleep for worry of how to feed yourself.*

He blinked. He made an abortive move, as though to step back from her. Caught himself and then—contrary to all her expectations—he smiled: slowly at first, and then, all at once, gave her a lopsided grin. It took her breath away. Such an open, unabashed concession, this smile! For a moment of pure stupidity she felt dazzled, knocked sideways, amazed.

Here was a man who could lose with good humor. Whose temper reserved itself for more important things. Who laughed now, a low, smooth laugh that acknowledged his own defeat and her cleverness, too; he seemed to enjoy her cleverness, even.

The breath went from her, a *hoo* that would have made her cringe were she not so wrapped up in the sound of his laughter, which rubbed around her like fur, made gooseflesh prickle on her arms. "Fair enough," he said, low, amused. "Fair enough, Nell." He glanced over her head. "Dismiss them," he said to Hankins, and then, to underline his point, flicked his hand: *Away. Shoo.*

Which handily snapped her out of her lunatic daze. She discovered a sudden, powerful urge to knock his teeth in. People weren't flies and this wasn't a game. Somebody here had almost lost her livelihood over his desire to demonstrate the dangers of having a *spine*.

The servants marched off, little soldiers, disciplined

in their single-file line. God knew where they'd scatter out of formation: around the corner, she'd wager, anywhere as long as it was out of sight. A show of proper obedience. She suspected, she hoped, they would grin to themselves as soon as they rounded the corner.

St. Maur spoke from her side. "You interest me," he said, and his tone suggested this fact itself surprised him, meant something more to him than perhaps it should: a man surprised by being interested was living a piss-poor facsimile of life, in her view.

She eyed him with a touch of impatience. "You don't interest me." Not now. Not after this scene.

This, too, startled him. He tipped his head slightly, as if to see her better. She noticed his brief glance past her—checking to make sure the butler and housekeeper weren't listening, she'd wager. God forbid he speak too frankly in front of the underlings.

"I've upset you?" he asked. "I didn't want to mention it earlier, but your dress is absolutely—"

"*Serviceable*," she said. "The first I've worn in a long while without a single hole in it. How does that strike you?"

He stared at her. It struck him dumb. Good. She crossed her arms and enjoyed the sight of him rendered speechless, if only briefly.

Because he recovered bloody quick. "Then you'll be glad to hear that there are several more upstairs," he said. "Straight from the shops. Delivered not an hour ago."

"Good." She hoped one of them was purple. "But this one will do me for today." For all the Queen's gold she wouldn't have put off this dress now. She smiled at him.

He blinked. Puzzled by her intransigence. "All right,

if that's what you wish. But you must understand that appearances are important." He frowned. "In this effort, I mean. I don't hold with the general notion." He gave a pull of his mouth, a sideways grimace: acknowledging that he didn't expect her to be convinced, not now, not after the show he'd just organized. "For the purpose of claiming your identity," he said, "it would help if you looked the part. That's all I mean."

She nodded. Made sense. "Is there a call to look the part today?"

He hesitated. "No. That is—I've arranged for the modiste's visit; she'll take your measurements for some more au courant fashions than Markham's provides. And a woman recommended by Daughtry, a sort of tutor in deportment, will be paying a call. But—" He seemed to come to the end of his breath, and also his enthusiasm for the effort of persuading her. "No one of import."

She wondered, with a sarcastic little smirk to herself, whom he might consider to be of import. Not any of the twenty-five or more people in his household. Not anyone who had a real skill or service to offer him. And by definition, she thought, that group included her: she was nothing more than a bundle of money to him. She'd be wise to remember that his courtesies were empty. His charm was only a business strategy.

"Brilliant," she said. "Let me know when those folk arrive." She turned on her heel and started across the hall.

"Ah—where are you going?"

She turned back. He had a hand planted in his hair. Poor, pretty lad. He looked flustered and irritated by her. Hard position to find himself in: he probably had no idea how to deal with a human being who hadn't been trained to his orders.

"I'm going to your library," she said. She was clear on the brightest side of this whole arrangement: she now had a thousand books at her disposal, and unlike him, she didn't mean to save them for later. "I expect that's all right with you. Unless you'd prefer to put me to work?"

He lowered his hand slowly. "No," he said. "The library is fine."

The floor-length coat was a pale blue wool trimmed in yellow braid, the wide lapels a fashion so new it hadn't shown up yet in the pawnshops. The coat fell open in front to display a short bodice of blush-pink silk and an underskirt that matched. The wide blue sash that banded Nell's waist gleamed like water. Satin, no doubt.

As she studied her reflection, Nell began to grin. She looked like somebody in a painting. Even the setting was perfect: behind her, late morning light beamed through the tall window, glimmering along the gold brocade of the curtains. Past the glass, green oak leaves waved in the breeze, pieces of blue sky glowing between them. What a glorious morning. *Focus on the bright things:* that had always been her rule. She wouldn't think of Mum right now, or let anything grieve her; she'd make herself enjoy this moment.

"Might be the handsomest one yet," she said to Polly. Nine other dresses lay discarded on the sofa at the foot of the bed. She supposed she'd said the same of each of them, but—"I really mean it this time. This one's the best."

"I reckon it might be." Polly edged back into the reflection. She'd been fussing over Nell's hair for half an hour, and now angled to give it another go.

Nell batted her hands away. "I'm looking at myself, aren't I?" She turned a full circle, cranking her head to see all the angles. It was coming clear why St. Maur hadn't thought much of yesterday's black gown.

Nobody in Bethnal Green would recognize her like this. Only a rich girl could afford to buy this pale, prissy shade without fear of the dirt that would show on it.

"The blue suits me," she said softly.

"Oh, aye, so it does."

Polly's agreement counted for naught but toadying. Still, Nell couldn't doubt her own opinion. The jacket made her eyes look bluer. Her cheeks picked up the pink of her bodice. Her waist had a nice curve to it, displayed to advantage by the fine cut of the coat. She looked *pretty*. She, Nell Whitby!

The devil's lures, Mum snapped in her mind.

Aye, and what of it? Already in the devil's clutches, she felt entitled to enjoy a lure or two. "I couldn't wear a better color," she said defiantly.

"I expect not," Polly said. "At least—it would be a very close call between this one and the violet tea gown."

"Oh, I'm saving the purple dress." That was for Hannah. "That one I won't wear."

The maid crept back into the reflection. She was twisting her wrists at her waist, nervous as a mouse in open territory. "I should redress your hair, if you'll permit it."

Nell looked blankly toward her bangs, which Polly had curled with a hot iron into ringlets at the top of her brow. "It's nice as it is," she said. A style for ladies who never left the house. One foot into the damp and these curls would melt away.

The thought made her grin. "These clothes are for ladies who never do anything useful." The edges of this open jacket would catch on corners. The tight sleeves would constrict her from lifting a basket onto a worktable. Clothes designed for doing nothing: the idea delighted her.

"I reckon so," Polly said hesitantly. "But they do suit you, milady."

Milady! Nell turned away from the mirror to cut the girl a wry look. "Orders given belowstairs this morning?"

Polly blushed and looked to the floor: she knew she hadn't pulled off that address.

"If we're to rub along," Nell said more gently, "you'll call me by my proper name—and never lie, either."

"I—I'd get in trouble if I called you such now."

Nell studied the blank crown of her mobcapped head. "Aye, right," she said grudgingly. "Call me what you must, then."

Polly looked up, her round eyes earnest. "But I wasn't lying. You *do* look lovely. It's naught to do with the gown. But if you don't like this one, we can try the others again—"

"And spend another two hours at it?" Imagine that: having so many gowns that it took two hours to try them all! St. Maur had ordered a heap of silk petticoats to boot, as well as stockings in gay, vivid shades, hats and mantuas, and *ten* woolen combinations. The pile of clothing atop the sofa towered almost three feet high.

As Nell cast another look over the upended boxes, an uneasy feeling snaked through her. Easy to feel that she'd awoken into a fairy tale. But this was real life. Happy endings were rare. She couldn't think of any she'd witnessed firsthand.

A wise woman wouldn't permit herself to get

comfortable in this place. She'd never take for granted that her good fortune would last. She'd stay sharp and continue to look for advantages, knowing that what came so easily could be taken away in an instant. That stash of lace and silver she was building beneath the mattress—she'd keep adding to it.

Didn't mean she couldn't enjoy the dresses, though.

She smiled down at herself, at the unbelievable sight of her own rough hands against the fine silk underskirt, drawing it up to permit her a quick stride. "I should go," she said. His high-and-mighty lordship was waiting downstairs to introduce her to some lady who meant to teach her manners. He'd spoken of a dancing master and a tutor for her speech as well.

"Aye," Polly said softly. "I—" She pushed out a gusty breath. "I have to thank you, milady, I can't say what devil possessed me to play such an awful trick yesterday—"

"It's all right." Nell winked at her. "We'd had words, so I reckon you owed me a bit of what for. Just so long as we're square now."

"Oh, aye, we're square," the maid said fervently. "More than square, milady. Almost—a circle, I'd say!"

Nell surprised herself with a laugh. "You're a mad one. Show me the way to the morning room, then, ducky."

"Not quite right." Simon ran his fingers across the piano keys, lightly plucking out the problematic passage. "Don't be afraid to exaggerate here. You're hiding the F-sharp in the middle of the phrase."

When the expected reply did not come, he glanced up to find Andreasson gaping at the far wall, on the other side of which lay the ballroom. The piano in that room had fallen silent several minutes ago, yielding to the heated tones of an argument.

Another shriek now penetrated. The wondering look Andreasson turned on Simon bespoke an imagination running wild.

It did rather sound as though the woman in the next room was being tortured.

Simon tapped his nail against a key. While Nell claimed to understand the importance of appearing presentable and mannerly, she was not taking well to the instructors hired to tutor her. Simon gathered that the lessons came as unwelcome interruptions to her routine of reading and feasting and . . . costume changes. Every time he caught sight of her, she was sporting a different gown. She strutted about as proudly and loudly as a peacock.

Her jaunty defiance made a peculiar sort of sense to him. He knew how unpleasant it was, how dispiriting, to be disciplined and commanded. He ran his fingers over the keys now, plucking out the scale in a mindless little exercise, as familiar and comforting as the breath in his lungs. Old Rushden, for instance, had removed all the pianos from Paton Park that summer after Nell's disappearance. He'd claimed that Simon's head was addled, his health weakened, by his obsession with music. That had been the final straw, the snapping of which had severed any kinder ties that might once have existed between them.

If Rushden had left the pianos alone—if only he'd been willing to let Simon have this one pleasure—then perhaps things might have gone differently between them. But it was as if he had seen Simon's absorption at the keyboard as a threat to his own authority as the earl, the rightful giver—and denier—of all joys.

Ah, well. Suffice it to say, Simon knew very well that disciplinary strategies never inspired happy cooperation among the governed. He was willing to tolerate Nell's airs; indeed, he could admire her pluck. And then there was her mouth, and the memory of what he had done with it . . .

"You can bugger off, then!"

The muffled curse caused Andreasson to flinch. His English vocabulary might be weak, but as a musician, he certainly understood tone.

Simon allowed himself a half smile. "Please forgive my cousin. A dear, young girl, new to London ways. I fear she dislikes her dancing master."

"Oh." The Swede gave an abashed tug to his waistcoat. Raw-boned and blond, he towered a full head over Simon's six feet, and was constantly adjusting and twitching his clothes: his tailors, perhaps, did not know how to accommodate such bulk. "He is . . . strict with her?"

"No. Merely French." Nell strongly disapproved of the race. She had a new, Parisian lady's maid as well. Sylvie's attempts to lace her as fashion dictated had earned Nell's suspicion that the woman was trying to squeeze her to death.

What excuse she had for mistrusting Mrs. Hemple, who had been hired to teach her deportment, Simon could not guess. The woman was as English as suet pudding. But Nell greatly resented, for instance, Mrs. Hemple's assertion that she did not know how to take her seat properly. "I've been sitting me whole life," Nell had snapped to Simon over breakfast this morning. "Hasn't been a chair yet to complain of me. The bint's daft."

Now came through the wall a distinctly French, masculine voice: *"I 'ave 'ad enough!"*

The piano groaned out a dark chord. Simon removed his hand from the keyboard. Nell had a specific goal in working with these tutors, and he saw no sign that she was taking it seriously. Indeed, he'd arrived home from the symphony last night to discover Mrs. Hemple weeping in his entry hall, determined to give notice. It had taken an hour or more to calm her.

The last thing he needed was Nell's own tutors running about town wailing of her savagery—or, worse yet, taking the stand in court, at Grimston's behest, to testify to her character.

"We'll work on this piece later," he said. He'd given Nell a week to adjust. He was not like Rushden before him; he had no interest in crushing her spirit. But her spirit needed to conform to the main aim: becoming Lady Cornelia. Otherwise he had no use for her.

"Yes," Andreasson murmured. "Of course, your lordship. At your convenience."

He was everything amenable, was the Swede: he knew whom to thank for his current popularity. As Simon saw him out, he found himself wishing that Nell might prove so wise. She was sabotaging her chances with these tantrums. If she did not intend to cooperate, he would overcome his interest in her and put her back on the street so he could look for a rich woman to marry.

He would not feel a moment's guilt over it, either. Where Nell misunderstood him was in her apparent belief that he took his wealth for granted; that this whole exploit was a lark to him. How wrong she was. No day was brighter than those in which he discovered some new aspect of his power. The House of Lords was largely toothless these days, but he'd taken his seat at the first opportunity. He belonged to all the best clubs, though he had no interest in the company. Various corporations asked him onto their boards, not for his nonexistent business acumen but for the honor of having his name on the charter, and he always immediately agreed. The fawning adulation of shareholders did not interest him, but he simply liked that he *could* have it, should the mood ever seize him.

Wealth gave one so many choices. If she imagined he would risk losing them, she was badly mistaken.

As he neared the ballroom, he realized that his irritation had sharpened into something nearer to anger. Knowing that rash words would not serve him in the coming confrontation, he paused in the doorway to collect himself.

Inside, Palmier stood, fists on hips, his tufted white brows raised in affront. Nell paced a tight circle in front of him. She'd changed since breakfast, and her pale pink gown—designed no doubt with a banker's daughter in mind, some girl who spent afternoons watering flower boxes in a bourgeois bungalow in Hampstead—did not suit her aggressive strides. She put Simon in mind of a feral cat dressed up in a ruff.

Or of Kitty, upon discovering a rip in her hem. Another tantrum was coming.

"You turn too fast," she was saying. "And if I can't lift my blooming skirts, it's hardly *my* fault if they get in the way, now, is it?"

"Ha! The train of a ball gown—"

She spun toward him. "I'm not at a ball, am I? And if I were, sure and I wouldn't be dancing with the likes of *you*!"

"You would not dance at all," Monsieur Palmier snapped. "No gentleman would dare to partner you. An elephant has lighter feet!"

Nell's spine snapped straight. An ominous silence descended as codger and guttersnipe glared.

Nell loathed this little elf. She'd met with him six days in a row, and they'd started out well enough; the movements of the quadrilles and polka and gavot were familiar and didn't challenge her. But once leaping had left the picture and gliding entered it, she'd faltered. She'd never waltzed before or danced any form like it; there wasn't room for sweeping turns in the pubs where she'd danced.

"You must be graceful," he told her now—sternly, as though she were deliberately trying to lurch and stumble. His scowl shouldn't have looked so fearsome on a man of his small height, but he was wizened as a gnome, with the most peculiar white eyebrows, tufted into points. He looked so close to a fey creature that had he gone walking down Peacock Alley to pick up the dishes of milk left out by the Irishwomen, not a soul would have dared to stop him.

"I'm trying," she said. "You can't fault me for putting weight on my feet! Ladies have legs, too, don't they?"

From the piano in the corner of the ballroom came the sound of a throat being cleared. "One doesn't refer to legs in the company of gentlemen, Lady Cornelia."

Nell grimaced. Mrs. Hemple was yet another of the lot St. Maur had inflicted on her—one of those plump, self-satisfied, older women with opinions on every-bloody-thing. She was serving as the pianist right now but her main specialty was manners. She followed Nell about the house, from dancing lessons to elocution to the dining table, commenting on every single thing Nell did wrong.

Apparently ladies weren't meant to eat cheese at dinner. No savories, either. They took at least a minute to strip off their gloves lest they appear fast. They didn't comment on their own bodies. Perhaps they weren't meant to know they *had* bodies. That probably helped them avoid mentioning their own legs. What legs? They floated, Nell supposed. Maybe they imagined they had wings.

She had a sudden flash of herself, flapping her arms as she whirled across the slippery oak floor. A giggle slipped out.

Palmier visibly bridled. "If you laugh once more, I will have no choice—"

"But what?" She was tired of being judged and found wanting. Wasn't a soul on the staff who didn't gawp at her like a creature from the zoo. But she wasn't an idiot or incompetent, either. She'd made her way by far more difficult means than sweeping floors or teaching ladies how to *twirl* and *sit* properly. "What'll you do to me?" She stepped toward him. "I'd like to see you try!"

A lazy voice came from the doorway. "What an intriguing pedagogy."

Palmier whirled as St. Maur strolled in. "Your lordship! Ah—we'd paused for a brief respite."

Nell felt her mood brighten. St. Maur looked properly rich in his dove-gray suit, and how absurd was it that she felt glad to see him? At least he spoke to her like a fellow human being.

As well he should, she reminded herself. It had been *his* idea to keep her here and put on this farce. She hadn't asked for any of this.

He paused before her to make a short bow. "Lady Cornelia."

"So they tell me."

He locked her in a look that took on an edge of challenge as the silence extended.

With a roll of her eyes, she put out her hand as Hemple had instructed. "Good morning to you," she said, sing-song.

He took her hand and gave it a light press. "And to you." He released her, the warmth of his fingers seeming to linger as he said to Palmier, "You may continue, sir."

Palmier made a swift advance. "Chin up," he said in an undertone. "Recall your arms."

As if she could forget them! They were attached, weren't they? She bit her tongue but didn't bother to check her scowl. She could do this stupid waltz. Even Mum had admired her skill at dancing—grudgingly, of course; Mum had always said that the dances in Bethnal Green were naught but excuses for sinner's mischief.

She shoved the thought away. She couldn't think of Mum. Otherwise grief would find her again, that blue ache that stabbed at the spot where the corset boning dug in sharpest. She put her fist there and took as deep a breath as she could manage. "All right," she said to Palmier, who was shifting impatiently. No point in feeling stupid or foolish at her clumsiness. Mum had told her to come to Rushden for help. As long as she left this place with a nice collection of things to sell, she'd count herself successful.

She stepped forward and gave the Frenchie her hand. Mrs. Hemple launched into the song.

The first few turns went well enough, but at the far corner, she tripped and then somehow took control of the dance: all of a sudden she was guiding instead of following, and the next she knew the music had died and Palmier was pulling free of her.

He turned toward St. Maur as reluctantly as a man facing the firing squad. "She is making progress, but . . ."

"Yes, so I see." St. Maur's mouth thinned as he studied her, his disappointment so clear that she felt herself biting back a nasty remark. It wasn't *her* fault if he'd been fool enough to think he could convince people that she'd been born to this world. And God help her if she had been! The rules here were rotten.

"That will be all for today," he added, and as though he'd pressed a button on one of those mechanical dioramas they displayed at the fairs, Hemple popped up from the piano bench and Palmier spun for the door. Not an inch of spine in either of them.

She didn't wait for their exit to defend herself. "It's not *my* legs that are the problem. That Frenchie—"

"As Mrs. Hemple said, your legs are not an appropriate subject for discussion."

The cold rebuttal startled her. The door shut softly behind the servants, closing her into silence with him. He put his hands behind his back and set his jaw, doubtless waiting for an apology from her, some groveling plea for failing his bloody expectations. Well, he could think again! "If you're to lecture me on manners," she said, "you might try them out yourself. Shooing people away like flies, not sparing them a word of farewell— "

St. Maur lifted his brows. "No. One doesn't owe the staff such courtesy."

"Then it's not courtesy," she said. "If it's only to be used around certain people, it's *hypocrisy*."

"An interesting perspective," he said calmly, "but

irrelevant for our purposes. Manners are merely a game, Nell. As with all games, one applies the rules in particular situations, but not in others."

She'd heard similar logic before. "That sounds like the rules of a cheater."

"Goodness." He pulled out his gold pocket watch and flipped it open to regard the time. "A moralist, are you?"

"I don't like hypocrisy," she said flatly. "Showing a different face to different people." She'd always known the world was unjust, but she'd not been prepared for firsthand evidence of how easily the fortunate ignored the injustice. Let them dress up their blindness as *good manners,* if they liked, but she wanted none of it.

He snapped the watch shut and tucked it away again. "How far will this dislike guide you?" he asked. "Would you be a hypocrite, for instance, for learning to alter your speech?"

"I expect I would, if I actually cared to try."

"Yet I notice you're already capable of speaking more genteelly when you choose to do so. Were you always a hypocrite, then?" He smiled. "Or do I inspire you?"

She pulled a face. Over their conversations at breakfast this last week, she'd grown to recognize the patterns of his slippery logic. He liked to turn an argument back on a person. Just this morning, they'd had a healthy debate about Caliban from *The Tempest.* In her view, Caliban's ignorance didn't excuse him: he was a clear villain who should have been killed for trying to ravish Miranda. St. Maur hadn't disagreed, but he'd asked her if she thought a crime ever could be mitigated by the circumstances in which it was committed. Had she, for instance, ever been tempted for selfish reasons to steal from someone who'd done her a good turn? If so, why?

"Is this about that bleeding handkerchief?" she'd demanded.

"Not the handkerchief," he'd said.

He obviously knew she'd taken his silverware.

"I'm not ashamed of the way I grew up speaking," she answered now. "If I know two different ways of speaking"—if she could do a fair brilliant imitation of Mum's accent—"that doesn't mean that I agree that one's better than the other."

"Your agreement isn't required," he said briskly. "All I ask is your compliance. In the circles you're about to join, your . . . accustomed accent will send an inconvenient message. To aim for a performance better suited to those circles is not hypocrisy but good strategy. With servants, however, such performances are unnecessary: the staff will judge its employers by different standards, their expectations being primarily financial."

"Fine," she muttered. "If that works for you, so be it. This is your show, not mine."

"Of course it's your show," said St. Maur. His voice suddenly sounded clipped. "It's always a show, Nell—for all of us. 'All the world's a stage,' as the bard wrote."

"He also said life was 'a tale told by an idiot, signifying nothing,'" Nell shot back. "If that's the case, I might as well find a grave to go lie down in."

"But *why*? Why must any of this be justified through some greater, noble meaning?" His mouth pulled, a quick, sideways grimace of frustration. "Bear in mind the point of this whole exercise is nothing more arcane than to become *rich*. Money is your aim—nothing noble. But certainly it will guarantee a good deal of pleasure, once you have it. Isn't that enough?"

She stared at him. "No," she said. "It's not." Until coming here, until learning what it meant to be privileged, she'd not understood how far down St. Maur's kind had to look in order to see hers. But here, in his own words, was the philosophy that made his lot comfortable with never bothering to look down at all. "Money's no virtue. It shouldn't be an end in itself." She gave a dry little laugh. "And neither should pleasure. If you knew any gin addicts, you'd realize that."

He put his hands in his pockets. "You have strident opinions. It must be very tiring for you."

"It's only tiring because nobody thinks I should have any."

"I hope I don't give you that impression," he said after a pause. "You're very sharp."

"I know I am." But against her will, the compliment mollified her. When being prodded and trained and scolded like a thickheaded child, it was too easy to start feeling like the whole world thought her a dunce.

He gave her a slight smile. "I take it you have specific intentions for the money?"

She hadn't given it much thought. No point in dreaming of miracles that had no chance of coming true. But the question brought to mind an answer. She knew exactly what she'd do if given a fortune. "I'd buy the factory where I worked."

His smile grew. "Will you, now? A sweet species of revenge."

She frowned. "Not for revenge. To change it. The workers need windows."

"You're a reformer?" He lifted a single brow. "You,

the denouncer of do-gooders? Why, this is quite deliciously ironic."

"I denounce do-gooders who don't *do* anything." The sharpness of her own voice caught her off guard. She took a long breath. "Maybe I do feel out of sorts," she said by way of apology. "This corset is squeezing the life from me. *Blast* it," she added. "I'm not supposed to mention undergarments, either, I'd wager."

"Indeed not," he replied, laughter edging into his words. "Manners, you see, come down to a single principle: talk of nothing that might actually prove interesting." He paused, looking immodestly impressed by his own wisdom. But when he continued, his mischievous tone punctured the effect. "Perhaps I'm noble for sparing my servants the bore."

"Boring's the rule, it seems. Even this dance is tedious."

"Indeed? I always enjoyed the waltz."

She shrugged. "Seems like the reason to dance is to enjoy the music, not spend the entire time worrying about how far apart you're supposed to stay from the person who's touching you."

"Ah. Then it's not your technique which is the problem," said St. Maur, "but your attitude. The dance is a prolonged flirtation—a sort of ritual form of it, anyway."

She snorted. "A peculiar way to go about it, then, paying more mind to staying away than getting near."

"I wonder. It seems to me that the heart of flirtation is all about distance, and the possibility of closing it."

"Maybe," she said. "We do things differently, where I come from. But I shouldn't be surprised if *you* lot even do your flirting topsy-turvy."

He looked amused. "What do . . . you lot do, then, when you decide to flirt?"

For some reason, his teasing riled her. "I don't know how to explain it."

"Then demonstrate, if you please."

She cast him a disbelieving glance. "You must be joking."

"Not at all." He stepped back against the wall, propping a shoulder against it as he crossed one boot over the other. It was actually a very proper attitude for his suggestion; she'd seen a dozen boys a day loitering by the factory like this, waiting for the whistle to blow and a chance to eye the girls.

But he wasn't a lad. He was a man, with a man's shoulders and a man's knowing eyes, and a mouth that could tempt any woman under ninety. He'd made it easy to avoid him, these past days, but the thought of demonstrating *anything* for him was enough to make her blush. "I can't," she muttered.

"So you didn't flirt, then."

He sounded mildly disappointed. Her eyes narrowed. She knew when she was being poked like a rooster in a ring. "You're trying to trick me into showing you."

"Am I trying?" he asked with a grin. "Or am I succeeding?"

The grin did it. Felt silly to be nervous when he was acting so companionable. And how much she'd been longing for a bit of friendly conversation! She hadn't realized until this moment just how lonely she'd been feeling. Wasn't much point to pretty clothes without a chance to try them out on a man.

"All right, then," she said on a breath. "First thing we do is, we give a man a saucy look. And then we—"

"I thought you were going to demonstrate," he cut in. "If I wanted a lecture, I'd go to the Academy."

She rolled her eyes. "You think you're quite clever, don't you?"

"I know I am," he said, dimple flashing.

She laughed as she recognized the echo of her earlier remark. All right, he was a charmer. And he was about to get more than he'd asked for, if he but knew it. "Very well, your lordship." She bobbed a mocking curtsy. "Let the guttersnipe demonstrate."

She turned away, then glanced back at him out of the corner of her eye. It wasn't an effort to look admiring. Nothing more mouthwatering than a tall, long-legged man with a narrow waist and a nice, lean set of hips on him.

She tossed her head and sashayed onward. Counted to three, and then came to a stop. "There you go," she said as she pivoted back.

He lifted a brow. "That's all?"

"That's the first stage. Flirting isn't over in a minute, St. Maur; it takes a few days to get started."

"A few days!"

"Sometimes a week or two." She stared at him, mildly scandalized. "What sort of ladies do *you* keep company with? Never say these girls in their lily-white dresses go from A to zed in an hour!"

He laughed. "Oh, it depends entirely on your definition of zed. We can exchange those, too, if you like." More speculatively, he added, "I'd be happy to demonstrate."

Her face went hot. "I just bet you would. No, I don't think so."

His smile took its time to spread. "Quite right. One thing at a time, with proper concentration. That's my philosophy as well."

She eyed him. "Are you demonstrating, now?"

"Indeed not," he said, his expression comically in-nocent. "So, Nell, saucy looks. What next?"

"Well, after a few days of giving a lad the eye—and mind, if he starts to approach, you don't let him; you take off real quick with your friends, and make sure to throw a few more looks at him as you're leaving—"

"No doubt whilst giggling amongst yourselves," St. Maur said ruefully. "Yes, I begin to feel sympathy for the lads of Bethnal Green."

"Oh, don't feel too bad. They enjoy it."

"I've no doubt of that."

"And the next stage, you let them approach you. Say a lad you've been looking at finally finds the courage to walk up, nice and easy. Well, you don't give him a saucy look anymore, not at that point. But you don't run, either."

He nodded. Slow learner, this one. She crooked a finger at him. With a visible start, he straightened off the wall.

"If I'm demonstrating," she said, "I need somebody to demonstrate on."

"Right," he said, and walked toward her.

Here was the problem with demonstrating East End ways in Mayfair: she couldn't remember any lad who walked like St. Maur did. Nobody in the Green had the *time* to walk like this—a long, fluid sort of prowl that put her in mind of a hunting cat who'd had his fill to eat and now was just playing about for fun.

Still, she'd set herself a task, and she would see it through. Rounding her eyes, she backed up toward the wall. "See? I'm being coy here."

His mouth quirked. "So you are," he said, and ran an appreciative look down her body.

"Very good," she said warmly. "Now you come on

up and I'm going to pretend to ignore you until the very last—"

But the words dropped right out of her brain as he stepped up and set a hand on the wall over her head.

"Go on," he said, too close for comfort. So close she could make out the strands of green and gold and gray in his eyes.

Nobody in the Green smelled like him. Nobody had lips like his, either. They were purely a wonder, full and soft looking, such a contrast to the sharp square of his jaw. She regretted that he shaved so regularly. That first night she'd seen him, he'd sported the handsome beginnings of a beard.

"What happens now," he murmured—and then, after a pause that lasted a moment too long—"in Bethnal Green?"

She cleared her throat. "They don't do this in the Green."

"Don't do what?"

He was large. Truly large. His stomach was flat and she wanted to run her hand down it because she remembered how it had looked, ridged with muscle; she wanted to see if she could feel the separate bands of muscle, how they moved beneath his taut, hot skin when he leaned closer toward her, now, his breath fanning across her face. A hot current leapt between their flesh, reminding her of what nature had designed men and women's bodies to do, pressed together.

Swallowing hard, she forced her brain to work. "They don't . . . they don't crowd a girl at this stage. Otherwise the girl might decide to get away."

And then she ducked out from beneath his arm, sidling down the wall away from him, a giddy laugh twisting up in her throat. Long time since she'd felt like this, gay and light and laughter-prone, and how queer that she should be feeling it here, in this grand, empty, gorgeous hall, with gilt on the walls and a man turning to follow her with eyes like the sea. He looked so rich and decadent that if she took a bite, she swore he would taste like chocolate, dark and complex and addictive.

"Very bad of me," he said, and his voice was pure sin, deep enough for a girl to fall into it and never see the light of day again. "Generally I take a great deal of pleasure in following every step a lady requires."

She wasn't the only one giving a flirting lesson. "Well, you've skipped one," she said, unable to resist.

"I await your instruction," he purred.

The wicked impulse worked through her too quickly for good sense to catch up to it. "There's a bit of touching required," she said with an offhand shrug. "Accidental-like, only of course it isn't."

His eyes narrowed. He took a deliberate step toward her. "And teasing as well, I think."

Her breath was coming shorter. "The teasing is all on the girl's part," she said. "Well, the talk, anyway. It's the lad's part to tease with his . . ." *Body*, she wanted to say, as her eyes took on a will of their own and skimmed down the length of him. When they reached his face again, her throat tightened at the look he was fixing on her. "Maybe it doesn't matter," she said hastily. "It's not like you need to know how to flirt with a Bethnal Green girl—"

"Oh, I think I do." Suddenly he was right in front of her again, and his palm was cupping her cheek, his thumb brushing lightly across her lower lip. "I'd like very much," he said huskily, "to know how to please a girl from Bethnal Green."

"You're doing fine," she whispered.

"I aim for better than fine." His eyes dropped to her lips and his expression darkened. "But you," he said, "do not."

It took a moment to realize the comment wasn't kind. "Beg pardon?"

His hand fell away. He took a measured step back. "You are making no effort," he said. "You are wasting my time. You are wasting my money. If you don't mean to take this project seriously, then . . . leave."

"Leave?" It took a moment to reassemble her wits. "You—you're changing your mind about all this?"

"I've not changed my mind," he said. "I never expressed an interest in supporting you for your own amusement. I wanted an heiress to wed. If you have no interest in becoming Lady Cornelia, then I have no interest in you."

Panic leapt up inside her, tangling with sudden, smarting anger. His judgment wasn't worth two farthings to her! She had enough fancy goods squirreled away by now; she'd be happy to leave! But she'd thought she'd have more time before having to risk facing Michael again—and she hadn't yet laid plans to find a new job—and how dare he break their agreement so easily!

"Go back to Bethnal Green," he said. "Waste the rest of your undoubtedly short life by slaving for pennies in a factory that you otherwise might have bought. Or stay here and put in the work necessary to reclaim your birthright." He shrugged. "The decision is yours. But make it quickly. If you're not willing to become a lady, I need to make other plans for myself."

He turned on his heel and started to walk out.

"Wait," she blurted.

Impatience marked every line of his body as he turned back.

She took an unsteady breath. She'd known he could take all of this away, but she'd thought—foolishly, she was a damnable fool—that maybe he liked her. Besides, he had so *much*. Couldn't he spare a bit of his good fortune without making her grovel for it?

But she'd misjudged him. Now the fairy tale was ending. Her stomach shuddered at the thought of returning to the Green before she'd laid plans for a job—and for handling Michael. It *couldn't* end like this. How terrible it would be to look back on this moment and have to put the blame for it not on St. Maur's arrogance but on her own stupidity.

How *terr*-ible. That was one of the harder words for her to say properly; Mr. Aubrey, the elocutionist, always chided her for letting the *e* slip into a *u*. It was *terr*-ible to feel slow and cloddish. In school, she'd always been the quickest in class. Numbers, letters, geography, shapes—not one of them had given her pause. She'd always thought herself clever, not just for a girl from Bethnal Green but for a girl from anywhere. She couldn't bear to think she might be wrong about that.

Maybe that fear had kept her from trying as hard as she might have done.

She opened her mouth to say all of this—or to say, "I'm sorry." But nothing came out. Her tongue felt as stiff and useless and stubborn as her pride.

St. Maur's sigh sounded loud in the silence. "Come," he said. "Before you decide, I want to show you something."

9

A quick, calculated decision prompted Simon to take Nell to the gallery. Perhaps he hadn't done a good enough job of showing her the advantages that cooperation would afford her. The gallery would advertise them effectively.

When they rounded the corner, she came to a stop—amazed, as he'd guessed she would be, by the arched cathedral roof and the long wall fronted with stained-glass panels. "Stars," she said softly. Her hands burrowed like small, frightened creatures into the folds of her gown as she looked around.

While he found himself staring only at her—and remembering, with sudden vividness, how she'd looked that first morning in the library. Exhausted, bedraggled, she had gazed up at the skylights and glowed in just this way, a glow so bright that it had drowned out every ragged detail.

That glow now worked a different magic. Paired with her demure, pink gown, it recast the significance of her features, leading a man to misread the shine in her large blue eyes as innocence—or vapidity, he told himself. That was Kitty's vacant gaze on her face.

But he couldn't hold on to the idea. The tight roll of her coffee-brown hair was no mode Kitty would favor. It conjured—ludicrously—a lack of vanity, the style of a girl who ducked her head when walking to church. Only someone who knew her better would guess that those small pink lips, parted now in admiration, concealed a hot tongue that bandied insults like a sailor.

He knew her better.

The thought sent a strange shock through him. That her disguise was so transparent to him suddenly felt profound, an intimacy next to which his irritation seemed trivial.

"It's like a palace," she said.

He caught his breath as her eyes found his, shining in a face alight with interest.

Her guttural intonations were not the only thing that distinguished her from her look-alike sister. Despite their unfriendly exchange minutes ago, Nell made no attempt now to hide her admiration. In her sister's world, in his world, people strove to appear unimpressed.

For the first time, he wondered why that was. Gratification so transparent as this only made a man long to witness it anew. To impress her all over again. He would like to be the focus of such wondering looks at all hours of the day.

The direction of his own thoughts began to unnerve him.

"It's not at all like a palace," he said. "I'll have to show you Buckingham sometime."

Her glow dimmed. Perhaps she didn't believe he meant the offer. "Every newly married couple must be presented to the Queen," he said to clarify. "She'll not hold another levee until next May, but"—he paused only the barest moment—"if you decide to stay here, we'll attend."

Her mouth screwed into a little smile. She did not take his bait. "You're daft," she said. "You want to take me to meet the Queen?"

The amusement in her voice caught him off guard. For a moment, and no doubt in tandem with her prudish outfit, it actually chastened him.

Perhaps he was daft. If, come next May, they remained married—if the law had acknowledged her as Cornelia; if wedlock proved financially fruitful—then it still did not follow that they would socialize together. No matter how rich she became, she'd remain a product of the East End, a girl who'd grown up in filth while working for her living. He could not imagine her enjoying his circles.

In fact, he could not imagine her finding anything to admire in them.

The thought unsettled him. But why should it? What did it signify if her upbringing limited her ability to appreciate his world? His friends would see nothing to esteem in her, either. The fashionable set admired his tastes; he could persuade them to believe nearly anything about art that they did not understand. But about poverty, they believed they knew everything. They had maids and coachmen; they each had an amusing tale of encountering some aggressive street Arab. They saw dirt and filth daily, out the glass windows of their coaches. They would see no novelty in Nell, no beauty in her. They would find her terribly uncomfortable, in fact: proof that beneath the dirt lay human beings. She would be, to them, no more than a reproach in human form.

Changing their minds would be a challenge, the greatest he'd ever undertaken.

But he did so love to make people change their minds despite themselves.

"Court is terribly tedious," he said. "Hot. Dull. You'll loathe it. But we'll go, if you stay."

She eyed him. One moment he saw Kitty's face, and wondered why he minded so much the thought of her leaving. The next he saw a woman with darker eyes, a blue so close to navy that they put him in mind of the sea five hundred miles from shore. These eyes were an invitation to drown.

He took a sharp breath even as she spoke. "Dull to rub elbows with the Queen, is it? You're a hard man to impress, you are."

And then she gave him her back as she turned to look at the paintings.

Bewildered, he studied her slim shoulders. Once again, as in that disorienting moment in front of the staff last week, he felt himself unbalanced by her, adrift in a sea of broken expectations, with no near handhold to cling to. She had something that no amount of money could purchase: an outsized presence.

He wasn't sure he liked it. She needed to come off the lady, but only grand dames drew admiration for their talents at discomposing a man.

What did she see when she looked at him? Did he even want to know?

Well, in regard to this moment, the answer seemed clear. She thought he'd been bragging.

Good God. Perhaps he had been.

To his disgust and amazement, he felt himself flush.

This business of charming her was idiotic. She needed to cooperate of her own free will. "We could skip the formality," he said.

She made no reply, turning a little to behold the length of the row of portraits. Her weight shifted to one leg, causing her hip to jut.

She was ignoring him. He realized the novelty of

it in the depth of his astonishment. It took effort to check a childish remark: her posture was unladylike in the extreme.

He stepped up beside her, deliberately crowding her. On an intuitive level he understood her show of indifference. After the gauntlet he'd thrown, she salved her pride by demonstrating that it would not be regard for *him* that kept her here.

But she was too intelligent to let this opportunity for betterment pass her by. *Pride got you nowhere,* he thought. *Use your brain, Nell.* This arrangement required concessions from her. She would need to be guided by him. She would need, he thought, to recognize her debts. "You like the clothing I've provided you," he said. "That much is obvious."

She did not so much glance at him as present a three-quarters profile. Her nose, Kitty's nose, had been fashioned to support condescension. "It's good, strong stuff." She sounded grudging. "I need a better-fitted corset, though. And a bit of lace wouldn't do any harm."

Now he did laugh. He *was* a hard man to impress. But so, it seemed, was she. And he wanted to impress her. He had no bloody idea why he hadn't managed it yet.

God help him, he was losing his mind.

He cleared his throat. "As I said, this wardrobe is—or would be—a temporary measure, only."

She nodded. "That seamstress—"

"Modiste."

She slanted him an unreadable glance. "That *mow-deest* said it would take ten days for the first gowns to be ready."

He nodded. A pity that he'd missed that fitting a

few days ago. He suddenly envisioned how he might
have interrupted it at an opportune moment, discovering her only in her chemise, corded by measuring tape,
her pretty lips rounding into an *O* as she trembled and
blushed beneath his inspection.

But he was an idiot. She'd not have trembled; she'd
have chucked a stool at his head for spying.

"Who are these people?" she asked.

Right. Here was the main reason he'd brought her
to the gallery. He followed her regard to the glowering
old man in front of her. "These are your parents," he
said. "The late Lord Rushden, before you. And to the
right, your mother."

Nell's belly gave a queer little leap. She walked closer
to the paintings. The last earl was posing on a horse in
front of a long lawn that led up to the building she'd
seen in the painting in the library. Paton Park, St.
Maur had called it.

The house was too pretty to be believed—a palace
of rosy brick set amid low hills greener than St. James
in the spring. This was her second view of it. The
sight raised a flutter in her breast, a curious feeling that threatened to grow stronger the longer she
looked.

She wrapped her arms around herself. These queer
notions were the work of her imagination, no doubt.
Dazzled by the clothes and the fine surroundings,
rattled by St. Maur's ultimatum, she was inventing lies:
You remember. You belong here. You deserve this.

How easy it would be to delude herself! Mum
had deluded herself over any number of things. She'd
thought herself better, more saintly, too good for
everything. Look what it had gotten her! The scorn of

the Green, the resentment of the labor-mistress, and the worst job in the factory—a quick road to a painful death.

But for all her foolish airs, Mum hadn't been cruel. If Nell decided she knew this place, that would mean that some countess had been her mother, and Mum had been more than cruel—she'd done an unspeakably wicked thing.

She swallowed down the weird urge to laugh. It wasn't funny, not at all. Mum had loved her. She was sure of that. Mum had been touched, but she'd never been dangerous.

"My mum wasn't bad." It came out choppily. She shouldn't have to say such things.

"I'm glad to hear it." St. Maur put his hands into his pockets, watchful. Waiting. No judgment in his face, no concern.

No concern: that summed him up, it did. That was the phrase she should have used to describe him to Hannah. He seemed wholly unburdened, albeit not in the way of idiots: Nell gathered that he saw the world as cynics did, not looking for false hope.

But he didn't let the world worry him, either. He had the air of a man who knew that when it came to a struggle, he'd always have the upper hand.

He certainly had the upper hand on her. His offer was devilish, wasn't it? *Become somebody else.* Ordinary men bargained only for a woman's body. His bid was higher, and so was his demand. He was asking her to betray the memory of someone she'd loved.

Nell gave her lip a chew. She'd vowed never to sell herself. But nobody had ever offered her so much. And for whatever it meant . . . she did know that place in the painting.

On a Bible, she would have said that she remembered it.

She forced herself to look back to the portrait. She'd never backed away from a fear and she wouldn't do so now. "There's a bridge. An arched bridge over a river." She remembered—had dreamed of—dropping pennies into it. Copper flashing in the sunlight.

"A stream," he said. "Behind the house. Yes."

His voice was neutral. Unsurprised. Temper lashed through her. She wished something *would* surprise him. He was the definition of high and mighty, immune to the scrapes and bumps that other people suffered as part of life's course. He'd probably never been rattled in his life. "Would it matter to you if there wasn't a bridge? Do you even care if I really *am* this Cornelia?"

His glance dropped briefly to where she hugged herself. "No, not particularly."

She straightened her arms, lest he mistake her posture for a sign of fear. "How convenient for you. It's not *your* mum they'll call a lunatic. And if I did remember this place . . ." Then the names they would call her mum would be true.

What sort of woman stole a child? What could drive a woman to that?

She felt an inkling, dim but unsettling. Mum had called Rushden a lewd devil. She'd always been so convinced that she could tell wrong from right better than anyone else could.

St. Maur took her hand. It startled her, but she didn't pull away: his grip was firm and he was looking at her squarely, no mischief on his face. "If you remember that house," he said, "I don't think you harm your mum by admitting it. What's done is done. All you do

now is gain a new view on what already happened—
long ago, mind you. Almost two decades."

Smooth logic. "And if somebody called *your* mother
a criminal? Would it matter to you?"

"Ha." An exhalation of breath, distinctly amused.
He let go of her hand, put his own into his pocket. "I
cannot begin to imagine," he said. "But her reaction
would be spectacular. She guards her good name quite
jealously." His smile was wry. "She got on well with
your father in that regard."

Nell looked to the father in question. He sat atop
a horse, Paton Park looming in the distance. She had
an idea of what a dad should look like. Her stepfather
hadn't lived long but he'd been sweet, funny, always
smiling. He'd bought her fried oysters on Sundays
after church and set her atop his shoulders at the
penny gaffs.

This man didn't look like he'd ever let a little girl
climb on him. Beneath his heavy, dark brows, his brown
eyes glowered. Bushy muttonchops. She knew that look
he was giving her. Fancy folks in their carriages who
caught her eye by accident, they got just this smirk on
their lips, amused, disbelieving.

What sort of man asked to be painted in a way that
ensured he'd spend eternity looking down on people?

Still. Somebody might say that she'd gotten her
cleft chin from him.

They'd say she'd gotten her eyes and nose from his
wife.

She drew a breath and fixed her attention on the
countess. Pretty lady. She sat in a light-filled drawing
room, one long-fingered hand poised atop the book in
her lap. Lovely white shoulders. Kind eyes.

"Was he mean to her?" she whispered.

A slight pause. "He was cold by nature, I think."

"No, but was he *rough* with her? Did he knock her about?" Mum hadn't scrupled to lay on the paddle when she felt Nell's soul was in peril, but as long as she'd had the strength, she'd never let Michael raise his hand. If Rushden had been a violent type, perhaps Mum had thought it best . . .

"Not that I saw." St. Maur paused. "Many men manage their tempers without the use of their fists, Nell."

She gave a dismissive shrug. That wasn't news to her. "How did she die, then?"

"Heartbreak, they said. Some two years after you were taken."

Nell twisted her mouth. "Heartbreak—now there's a rich woman's disease. The rest of us can't afford but to die of a real sickness."

He glanced at her, the line of his mouth grave. "A clever aphorism. Do you believe it?"

His soberness caught her off guard. He wasn't behaving as she'd expected. He was actually *talking* to her, asking her questions as if her answers might be of interest.

How queer. She'd almost prefer it if he remained a haughty, high-handed nob. "I think if a person could die of heartbreak, there'd be a lot fewer of us in the world," she said slowly.

"You've had your heart broken, then?"

"No."

"You're fortunate."

"Or smart." Not some empty-headed girl like Suzie, to let a handsome face fool her into forgetting her own best interests.

St. Maur studied her a moment longer than felt comfortable. "You're very young, aren't you?"

His condescension irked her. "Why? Did somebody break yours?"

"Oh, yes." He said it easily, without hesitation. "One of the risks of being a wastrel, I'm afraid."

She stared at him. "Who?" What kind of woman had managed to get under the skin of this one?

"Simply a woman."

"What sort of woman?"

He shrugged, one-shouldered. "The wrong one, I suppose." He turned back toward the painting. "The countess wasn't dull-witted or weak. Too generous on occasion, certainly. Compassionate, caring—everything her husband was not."

She recognized how neatly he'd sidestepped the issue of this mysterious heartbreaker, but something else struck her more sharply. A warmth entered his voice when he talked of the countess. This wasn't gossip speaking. "You knew her?"

"Yes."

Of course—he'd been the old earl's ward. This woman would have helped to raise him.

She frowned. Something didn't make sense here. "Your mother—you talk as though she's still alive."

"Yes. She is."

"Why were you the earl's ward, then?"

An unpleasant smile edged onto his mouth. "Your father thought me inappropriately prepared for the honor to be bestowed on me."

She hesitated. "So your mum simply . . . let him take you?"

A muscle ticked in his jaw. She'd hit on a nerve. Good to know he had one. "He had a talent for convincing others of his own importance. I don't suppose it ever crossed my parents' minds to protest."

How awful. "We have something in common," she said, amazed. "If you're right, we both got taken from our parents."

He met her eyes. "I suppose we do. Of course, yours wanted you back."

Not a trace of self-pity colored his words. But their very impassivity revealed an effort to speak without emotion.

All at once, she felt ashamed. She'd been poking at him for her own satisfaction. Now he held her look and forced her to confront the evidence that he had feelings, after all. His parents' betrayal had rankled.

Something in her softened. She laid her hand on his arm. "I'm sorry, St. Maur."

He glanced toward the spot where she touched him. "Don't be. As I said, what's done is done."

She felt even more strongly now that he was wrong about that. "Are you close with them, then?"

"My parents?" At her nod, he looked mildly incredulous. "Does that signify? My father is dead. As for my mother, I suppose we're cordial. We acknowledge one another when our paths cross."

She didn't see him move, but suddenly his arm was out of reach. She pushed her hand into her pocket, balling it into a fist, feeling awkward. Where she was from, a friendly touch was welcome. "I gather that's a fancy way of saying no."

He gave her an unreadable look, then nodded toward the painting. "Do you see the book on her lap? Lovely illustrated copy of Dante's *Inferno*. Your love of reading comes from her, I expect."

She went along with his change of subject. "Do you have it? I'd like to read it."

"No." His voice turned dark. "Her books were sold."

"Oh." Feeling off balance entirely now, she scouted for a topic that couldn't rub him wrong. "I want some dresses like that one," she said. The countess's gown was frilled and flounced in tiers of blond lace. Must have cost a fortune. Take it apart piecemeal so the pieces could be sold one by one: it would make a nice sort of insurance for a girl.

"Bit old-fashioned, I'm afraid. But why not? Have one, if you like." He laughed. "Yes, create your own style. Set a new fashion."

He was joking, of course. "Right-o," she said.

His smile faded into a more thoughtful look. "But you do realize that's what I'm offering you. Not simply money, but the power and position to use it in whichever way you please."

She didn't see much difference between money and power, but she nodded politely.

It didn't fool him. "Oh, Nell." He sighed. "Darling, I know you have an imagination. Is it that you simply don't know how to use it?"

She frowned at the endearment. She got it regularly from the Irish blokes, but it sounded different in his creamy drawl. Unsettling. Men like him, they called girls like her *darling* only as a joke. *Darling, be a love and bring me another glass. Darling, I'm not paying you to talk.* "I don't follow you."

He stepped closer to her—and then closer yet. "Dear girl," he said softly. He lifted his hand and ran his fingertip down the rim of her ear, his touch as soft and warm as a breath.

She took a step back, her stomach knotting. Unlike her brain, her fool body had not an ounce of good sense in it. Her heart began to pound. "Not until we're married."

"A touch," he murmured. He caught her lobe, stroking it with his thumb. "Nothing like sexual congress." His hand turned, his knuckles brushing down her throat.

Even a touch was too much when he paired it with that smile. It made her pulse beat harder. She remembered again, with visceral warmth, how his kiss made parts of her dissolve. She couldn't feel that way and keep her wits straight. "Hands off, I said."

"But you're irresistible. As proper as a vicar's wife, scrubbed clean, tamed. I can't tell if it's a pity or a terribly effective provocation."

She pushed away his hand and retreated another pace. "Neither. That's not my doing." She wasn't trying to tempt him into anything. She had no blame in this.

He looked into her eyes. "Are you afraid of me?"

She nearly laughed. Of course she was afraid of him. It would take a newborn not to be afraid of him. He was a bloody *peer of the realm*. Did he not realize that all his talk of her birth and her fortune were for naught as long as he was the only one who knew it? He could tell her sweet tales of being an empress if he liked; none of it would mean a thing unless he put cash in her hand as he spoke.

"Don't flatter yourself," she said.

"There's no need, you know." Still he was watching her, his damned eyes too sharp, seeing too much. She had a bad habit of underestimating him, of forgetting how quick he was, even if he'd been coddled in silk his whole life. "Your best interests happen to coincide with mine. That should comfort you, if nothing else does."

"You're right, I'm comforted. Show me more of my family, why don't you?"

He didn't take the bait. "In a minute," he said, still studying her. Why was he so interested? There wasn't anything in her to hold the attention of a man like him. If he wanted somebody like her, he could go out and buy ten, twenty girls for a night.

But not her. She wasn't his plaything. She'd be his wife or nothing.

He stepped toward her again and she betrayed herself with a quick step back.

"There we go," he said on a nod, a man whose peculiar notion had been confirmed. "But it makes no sense. What could account for your skittishness? You don't seem timid by nature."

"I'm not." She resented, bitterly, how breathy those two words sounded.

His gaze dropped, lazily tracing her neckline, trailing down her bosom. He looked her over with a frank, sexual appreciation. Not a drop of shame in the smile he gave her tits, her hips, her mouth—which went dry beneath his look. A girl with any self-respect wouldn't welcome this survey. He sized her up like a man with a boughten whore.

But she couldn't lie to herself. To have a man like this stand before her, wanting her, brought out the stupider side. If he were an animal he'd be the prize in every competition, his long, elegant bones strapped by muscle, straight and tall, the prime specimen of his kind. Humans were animals, too, and never before had she realized it so strongly as now, with this heat stirring in her stomach.

Her breath restarted with a gasp that he didn't even pretend to miss. His gaze lifted, hot, calling to mind dirty words, bodies pressing together in darkness, while his tone contradicted the message in his eyes, growing light, almost playful: "Would it be so bad to marry me?" he asked.

A flush burned through her. She knew what he was asking. *Marry* had become their little word to stand in for other things. "I don't know you," she said through her teeth. "Maybe it wouldn't. I can't say."

"I'm an open book." He stepped forward once more, and this time she held her ground. To the devil with his hot eyes and his bullying!

He noticed the victory; the smile on his lips assumed a roguish angle. "And you *are* skittish," he said. A challenge in those words: he was about to prove it to her. "I promise, lovely Nell, that I have no intention of seducing you before supper."

She watched in a private agony as he reached out to stroke her neckline. If she backed away again, her reluctance would grow painfully conspicuous.

Normal, she told her pounding heart. He only thought to handle the woman he meant to wed, and that was normal.

But there was nothing normal about the way his touch seemed to burn through the wool, straight to her skin. She was wicked, wanton at heart, and self-destructive as a gin addict on payday. Nothing wise or good could come of wanting a man with the power to grind her to dust, but he touched her like a man bent on more delicate operations, his finger skimming lightly across her collarbone to her shoulder. His hand turned, stroked open-palmed down her arm, slow and firm, feeling the lines of her, and everything in her wanted to incline toward him.

Such a stupid, simple touch! Why couldn't she hold herself away from it?

He wasn't unaffected, either. A pulse beat at the

base of his throat. His eyes, when they rose to hers, were knowing. "Say it," he murmured. "You feel this."

Her throat tightened. "I feel your hand."

He made a little *tsk,* a chiding click of his tongue. "Obtuse," he said, but his tone told her that he wasn't put off by it. He liked a challenge; it *lured* him. "I can do so much for you, you know." Casually, conversationally, he spoke to her, as he handled her flesh. "I'm the last to give you lessons in being a lady, but I could teach you very well about other things. About pleasure, and beauty, art and glamour—all the worthwhile entertainments. Lessons in scandal"—his laughter was soft, an invitation: *Think of the possibilities,* it invited—"yes, I could teach those very well. And in . . . power?" He laced his fingers through hers, his thumb stroking across her palm. "You want money; I know that much. But what of power, Nell?"

The word sent a frisson down her spine. *Power:* what he was exercising right now, holding her riveted with only his words and the light press of his wicked fingers. What a terrible power, too—what a terrible context in which to discover such a power existed. Better for her sake if he'd exercised the clumsier forms: raw strength, muscle, a shout. Brute force she knew well enough.

But no, nothing so simple would appeal to St. Maur. Power, the idea, the very word, assumed new dimensions when purred by the man who owned this house, who'd paid for these clothes on her skin, who'd walked into a jail and thrown over the lawmen in a quarter hour, without breaking a sweat or—Hannah had claimed—even lifting his voice. He looked as cool as the moon now, the devil's minion who made her skin flame with just the stroke of his thumb. He worked magic with just that one finger, rubbing slowly, intimately, down the center of her palm.

This way was more deadly than the strike of a fist. First he lured her body into colluding with him, and then he asked her imagination to join the plot against her. Her desire, her ambition, and him: she couldn't fight all of them. He'd make her into her own enemy.

The thought stabbed into her. She met his eyes. She wouldn't feel this. She'd stay quick. "I'm not weak. You're wrong if you think I am."

"Not weak," he murmured. "But these calluses on your palms tell their own story. Your time and labor haven't been your own. Imagine what it would be like to set your own course, Nell. To answer to no one's bidding. I can make that possible for you."

It wasn't a promise many could offer. But she didn't doubt that he could keep it.

He lifted her hand to his mouth, his lips closing on her knuckles, and she felt them everywhere, a liquid warmth that weakened her.

"To ignore the world's opinions," he said against her skin. "Or to create their opinions for them." He lifted her hand to his face, pressing her palm along his cheek. "That's a heady drug," he said, and for a confused moment, she thought he meant the sensation of his skin, freshly shaved, hot and smooth.

What an odd thing to do, to make a woman touch your cheek. She stared at her hand where he held it against him. A woman might touch her lover like this to express true and tender affection.

The thought panicked her. He was seducing her not only with his body but with false hopes besides. *Look at yourself,* his gesture said, *touching me as though we might care for one another*. What a cruel possibility to tempt her with. What a malicious, wicked strategy. She knew herself and she knew his type, too: when they met, it was usually in a back alley right after coin was exchanged.

She yanked her hand free. "You know I was a thief?"

He might have been deaf for all the effect her angry words had on his smile. "So I gathered," he said, "when my handkerchief ended up in your friend's possession."

"The handkerchief wasn't anything! I would have stolen more than that if I could have managed it. I would take the rings off your fingers!"

"But now you won't have to." He paused. "Does that frighten you?"

"No," she whispered. Theft didn't frighten her. She understood well enough what the risks were, there. *He* frightened her. These feelings he called up inside her . . . and the dreams he tempted her to entertain . . .

"If something frightens you," he said, "that means it's the best place to start."

A startled sense of recognition prickled over her. Aye, that was right. If you ran from your fears, they only chased you faster.

She made herself look back to the painting of the last earl, with Paton Park in the background.

Cowards ran from fear, but only a proper fool ran from the truth.

She took a large breath, feeling dizzy, like she hovered on the edge of a fall. "Tell me honestly. Do you really think I'm that girl?"

"Yes," he said. "And so do you."

❖ ❖ ❖ ❖

That evening, in the hour before Polly brought up the dinner tray, Nell sent Sylvie to the library to find a book that didn't exist and locked the door.

The sun was well into setting, casting the bedroom into a gloomy blue haze. The murky light suited her mood. She struck a match and set it to a single candle before going to her knees beside the bed.

Prayer wasn't her intention, but the posture reminded her body of a hundred Sundays spent kneeling under Mum's sharp regard. She hesitated only briefly before setting the candlestick onto the carpet. Her hands shook as she folded them together at her breast. In the dimness, fragrant with candle smoke and the carpet's soft perfume, she bowed her head and prayed.

Let her forgive me, she thought. *I can't understand it, but I do love her still.*

And then, fingers tightening, she swallowed and added, *And please forgive her. She loved me, too.*

On a long breath, she pried up the mattress and pulled out her loot.

By the light of the candle she arranged the items on the carpet: candlesticks; doilies; a slim, illustrated volume of Regency-era fashions; a silver spoon; an enameled bowl the color of the summer sky. The bowl fit perfectly into her cupped palm. It was small enough to be ignored and dismissed. But a canny pawnshop broker would recognize its weight and fine glaze as proof of its value. It might easily fetch money for five months of food.

She rose and carried it to the hearth, her hands steady as she replaced it on the small shelf above the mantel where she'd found it.

The handsome book of illustrations—a month's

rent, easy—went to the little tea table in her boudoir. Polly would find it there and return it to the library.

The spoon she put on the seat of the tea chair. Two weeks' worth of food. The doilies, worth fine tea and hot rolls for six weeks, she strewed across the dressing table in her bedroom. The candlestick holders, silver, heavy, half a year's surety, she placed by the door to the hall, where someone would be sure to trip over them.

Blowing out her candle, she sat down on the bed and stared at the candlesticks, now veiled by shadows. The gentle tick of the clock measured out her dwindling opportunity to take them back.

This shivering sensation in her stomach was like the feeling of falling.

She remembered pennies dropping over a bridge, flashing in the sunlight. She remembered the sweet floral scent of a woman holding her close, while across the room light slanted through impossibly large windows framed by pale, transparent curtains.

Witches' dreams, Mum had called them. *The devil's whispers.* The dreams had upset her so badly that Nell had learned never to speak of them. She'd stopped asking to hear certain lullabies. She'd ceased to cry for a doll with red hair and blue eyes. She'd come close to forgetting the great staircase she'd once slid down on her belly, a staircase broader than any in Bethnal Green.

She'd thought them dreams.

They hadn't been dreams.

So she wouldn't take back those candlesticks. She needn't feel like a thief in this house. This house had been hers, once upon a time, and so had Paton Park.

She exhaled, long and slow. This is my place, she thought.

Your birthright, St. Maur called it.

Amazement prickled over her, sharp like fear, but so much sweeter. She had not only a fortune and a place to belong, but a person to call her own: him. Simon St. Maur, Earl of Rushden, meant to marry her. The quickest, handsomest, most frightening man she'd ever known wanted to make her his wife.

Who do you think you are? Michael had liked to scream at her. It had only taken one look for St. Maur to know. He'd seen the truth the moment he laid eyes on her.

Feelings knotted in her throat, hot, thick, too many to name. She thought of the way he had touched her and suddenly it took her breath away though he was nowhere in the room. She could have him if she wanted. That magical creature.

God above, but she wanted him. She would admit it now, a secret to keep to herself.

She crossed her arms, hugging tight, holding close these wild ideas. *He wants the money,* she reminded herself. She couldn't embroider too many fancies on *that* pillow. She wouldn't let herself. She would think of somebody else who was also hers, and not for anything to do with a fortune. She had a *sister*. Lady Katherine Aubyn had known that bridge, that staircase, that same soft embrace. Flesh of Nell's flesh, whose bones had formed and grown alongside her own.

So wondrous: somewhere in London, her sister was sleeping.

The hot track of a tear startled her from her thoughts. She pushed it off her cheek with the back of her hand—pushed away, too, the hard-won habit of doubting, scrupling, scorning. This strange turn of events only seemed miraculous because it *was* miraculous. Anything was possible for her now.

A hitching laugh escaped her. As she fell back onto the sheets, she laughed again, just for the feeling of it, the sheer joyous sensation of *believing*.

Anything was possible now . . . even, God help her, learning to waltz.

10

The Faculty Office had a gossip in its ranks. Simon had been forced to divulge the name of his bride in his application for the license, and it seemed somebody had let slip the news. Not four hours after he received the license, a threat arrived—traveling quietly, in an unsealed letter delivered by an urchin. It found Simon at a restaurant in the Strand, where he was sharing a bottle of port with Harcourt.

You're a madman. I am warning you: these shenanigans will not be tolerated. You are long past due for your comeuppance.

The author was too much of a coward to sign his name, but Simon recognized the penmanship. Over the years, he had received countless letters from his guardian recorded in Grimston's cramped hand. At first, he'd even read some of them. Later, he'd discovered what an excellent substitute they made for kindling.

He smiled as he refolded the note. Of all the many advantages that would accrue through marriage to Nell Aubyn, Grimston's displeasure would be one of the sweetest.

"I can't get over it."

Simon glanced across the table at Harcourt. "I can see that." Harcourt was doing a very poor job of recovering from the news. "His compositions are quite shocking," he added, straight-faced. "I suppose I can't blame you."

Harcourt blinked. "The . . . oh, yes. Quite." On the

way to the Strand, he'd accompanied Simon on a brief stop at the studio of a promising, if unconventional, young violinist by the name of Gardner. "Those, too," Harcourt said with a tentative nod. "Very . . . vigorous."

"Crude, you mean." Gardner sawed his bow as though trying to break his instrument in half.

Harcourt hesitated. "I don't . . . really care, to tell you the truth. I'm still stuck on the other matter."

"Goodness. It's been nearly an hour since I broke the happy news."

Harcourt shook his head and rubbed a hand over his face. He was a blue-eyed redhead with the coloring to match, but at present, he looked even paler than usual. "Look here, you've had almost five weeks to come to terms with the idea that she isn't dead. *I* recall the girl tumbling about in her pinafore on our lawn at Hatby. My mother took to bed for a fortnight after she disappeared." He grimaced. "I believe she made my father interrogate the entire staff, lest he discover one of them harboring hidden intentions with regard to the nursery."

"The great servant purge of 1872," said Simon. "I believe an entire generation of nannies was scarred by it."

Harcourt frowned. "But you must remember her, too. You were at Paton Park that summer, weren't you?"

"No," Simon said. "Not that summer."

"But I recall letters from you. That was the summer you were thrown from a horse during a steeplechase, broke your collarbone. Am I imagining this?"

Simon sighed. That summer he'd come up with a hundred lies in his letters to friends. Rushden, infuriated with him for some reason Simon could no longer recall, had exiled him to some gloomy estate in Scotland. He'd escaped his escorts at the train station in York and managed to get to his parents' home. When they'd promptly plotted to return him to the earl, he'd fled yet again, to London.

The paltry sum in his pockets hadn't lasted four days.

It had been a lonely and bitter journey back to Paton Park, where Rushden and the countess had awaited him. Adolescent boys could muster a great deal of angst, and the realization that he was incapable of fending for himself—that no choice remained but to run back to Rushden with his tail tucked between his legs—had felt at the time like the blackest blow life could deliver.

It occurred to him now that at the same age, Nell had been working half-days at a box factory. Or so she'd claimed during one of their breakfasts together. In his shoes, she would have known exactly how to fend for herself.

The thought absorbed him. When Harcourt cleared his throat, it took Simon a considerable effort to muster his wits for a reply. "Yes, the steeplechase. I must have forgotten about that." He remembered very little of that summer but the depth of his rage. It had driven him to a variety of stupid things—including an impossible jump for which he'd not forgiven himself for years. He'd suffered a broken collarbone, but his horse, Jupiter, had not been so lucky.

Rushden had insisted that Simon fire the bullet that ended Jupiter's suffering. It was one of his only decisions that Simon, looking back, could respect.

"But you must have met her at some point," Harcourt said.

He ran his fingers down the side of the bottle that

sat between them. "A few times. Very briefly." He'd first met the twins while visiting Paton Park on a holiday from school. He recalled being unable to figure out which was Cornelia and which was Katherine. In retrospect, he had a good guess. Nell had been the one who demanded candy from him. Kitty had been the one who'd thrown her doll at his head when he'd admitted he didn't have any.

"Is she much changed, then?"

"She was five years old at the time," Simon said dryly. "Put your mind to it."

"No, but what I mean is . . ." Harcourt shifted in his seat. "You say she was lodged in the rookeries. Does it show?"

"Do you imagine that it wouldn't?"

"I simply—" Harcourt fumbled. "I wonder if she managed to retain any of her upbringing. Surely she can't be . . . like the rest of them?"

Simon found himself wordless. It wasn't the absurdity of the question that gave him pause as much as the revelation it forced on him. Though Harcourt had been raised in privilege, he was well traveled and broad-minded. If *he* imagined that Nell's high origins might have allowed her to float through her upbringing unaffected, then the majority of their peers would not only imagine but *expect* it of her.

What a pity. Over the last few weeks, her attitude toward her tutors had transformed. The results of her enthusiastic efforts were awkward; from Bethnal Green to Mayfair was a very large leap. But Simon had calculated that all she required was a rudimentary ability to avoid offending those persons who might be tasked to judge her fitness as Lady Cornelia.

Harcourt's questions now forced him to reconsider

the matter. Reclaiming her inheritance would not guarantee restitution of all the privileges her birth should have safeguarded. Kitty Aubyn moved through the world assured of her welcome in it. Nell, on the other hand, would never find it easy to belong.

Surely she can't be like the rest of them?

Of course she could.

He tried to reason with his own uneasiness. Her fortune would go far to soothing any troubles her new life might cause her. She had no interest in the social circles that might disdain her want of savoir faire. Why should she? He'd learned at a young age that some men's approval was not worth the price it required.

His silence was causing Harcourt to squirm. "Dash it, Rushden, you know what I mean. Bethnal Green! It's the wretchedest fever den in London, I expect!"

"Surely not," he said flatly. "I believe that honor must go to Whitechapel."

The waiter appeared, clearing his throat to discreetly draw their attention. Simon took the bill, ignoring his friend's complaint as he reached into his jacket for his billfold.

"I was meant to get this!"

"Be at ease," Simon said. "My fever-den bride will soon put my worries to rest." He laid down a note and looked up into Harcourt's wide-eyed regard.

"You mean to do this, then? Truly?"

Good God. "I assure you, I will not invite you to make Lady Cornelia's acquaintance until I'm convinced that she carries no contagions."

Harcourt hissed out a breath and sat back. "Ho, old fellow—I didn't intend—"

"No, of course not." He paused, feeling uneasier

yet. How absurd to take offense. Harcourt spoke of Nell Aubyn as a dreaded last resort because she *was* the last resort. "Forgive me. My mood is uncertain."

Harcourt hesitated. "Dare I ask why?"

He picked up the letter from Grimston, giving it an indicative flick with his thumb before tucking it into his jacket pocket. "Minor irritations," he said. "Nothing more."

The stairs loomed before Nell, promising a long and winding descent toward the checkerboard floor of the lobby.

"Harmonic poise!" Mrs. Hemple called up. She was waiting at the base of the stairs beside St. Maur, and the low neckline of her fine, dark gown revealed two extraordinarily large surprises. Strange society, this, in which a girl couldn't flash her ankles but a woman of sixty prepared for polite company by donning a dress that bared half her bosom.

"We're waiting," St. Maur said dryly. "Breathless, etcetera."

A smile twitched Nell's lips. She'd wager he was breathless with boredom. This was the fifth time she'd come down the stairs toward him, and she was determined to do it without tripping this time. Dinner was waiting and her stomach had started to growl.

She straightened her shoulders and placed one gloved hand on the banister. The heavy knot of her hair weighed down her skull, pulling her chin up to the proper angle. With her free hand, she hooked up a loop that unobtrusively shortened the skirts of gold silk. The unforgiving boning of the corset held her spine straight, and the tight sleeves ensured her arms maintained a pleasing bend as she descended.

As she reached the first landing, Hemple chirped, "Attention to the turn! Gracefully, now!"

"All I ask is that she doesn't break her neck," St. Maur said in an undertone.

"She must master it," Mrs. Hemple said cheerfully. "Monsieur Delsarte considers stairs an excellent test of harmonic poise." Every day this week, she'd put Nell through various exercises from Delsarte's *System of Expression:* first the *serpentine movement,* then the *sinking wrist* and the *rotation of head in various attitudes.*

Descending a staircase was more complicated than Nell had ever known.

But as she glided around the turn and reached the safety of the final descent, she finally felt light on her feet—untroubled, at long last, by the yards of silk. Since a lady wasn't meant to look too pleased with herself, she directed her smile toward St. Maur. In a close-fitting black coat and starched white cravat, he made a very convincing object for a girl's admiration.

He smiled back at her, while in the periphery of her vision, Mrs. Hemple's frown became apparent. "Gravity," she warned. "Do not grow overconfident."

Just this once, Nell ignored the instruction. St. Maur's expression told her how well she was doing. His own smile was fading but his eyes did not leave her face. Smart lad; Nell knew she looked smashing: this shining gold gown was lovely. What cause for gravity? She was mastering the stairs, a gorgeous man was ogling her, and the dinner ahead was bound to be delicious.

As she reached the lobby, she laughed, and so did St. Maur. "Neck intact," he said as he held out his arm. "Well done."

Mrs. Hemple sniffed. "Your lordship, you agreed that practice would benefit Lady Cornelia. Please do not skip the formalities now she has reached the lobby. You might have asked for the pleasure of her escort, in reply to which she would have made a verbal acceptance before taking your arm. That's how it's done, you know."

Nell met St. Maur's eye again. "Oh yes," he said. "I do know." He gave Nell a quick smile as he released her. Taking a precise step backward, he sketched a lithe bow. "My lady," he said. "May I have the pleasure?"

He was only following the script, but the rich timber of his voice on that single word—*pleasure*—made Nell's mind go briefly blank. What a wicked smile he had.

"My lady," Mrs. Hemple prompted.

She blinked. "By all means," she said, and took St. Maur's arm.

The table looked like a miniature hothouse, so many bowls of flowers and ferns that a girl couldn't reach for her wineglass without encountering foliage. At intervals, small lamps covered by colorful shades cast a rosy glow over the snow-white tablecloth. Tonight's formal dinner was an exercise to prepare her for debuting into society. Nell had doubted the necessity until she'd caught sight of the place settings: seven pieces of silverware flanked each plate.

"You've not touched your oysters," observed St. Maur. He sat at the head of the table, Nell at his right, Hemple at his left.

"They're raw," she said. Everybody knew oysters were tastiest—and safest –fried to a crisp.

"That wasn't by oversight," he said.

"Vulgar," Mrs. Hemple sang. "It is not your place to make observations on your host's menu. Now, do have an oyster. Once one has accepted a course, one must take at least three bites; otherwise, one casts doubt on the dish."

Nell looked at the quivering lumps on her plate. She'd no wish to spend the night hanging over a chamber pot. She braced herself with a sip of wine, white and sweet, and then another—muttering a silent prayer of thanks when the footman came by to collect her plate.

"Saved," St. Maur said, too softly for Mrs. Hemple to catch.

"Fry them," Nell muttered. "I beg you."

Mrs. Hemple clapped her hands together. "Small talk? Excellent! His lordship and I will demonstrate its proper substance and nature for you." Clearing her throat, she turned toward St. Maur. "My lord, do you enjoy the theater?"

St. Maur gave Nell a wink before turning to Hemple. "Why, yes, I attend quite regularly. And you?"

"I fancy myself an enthusiast," Mrs. Hemple said with a girlish bat of her lashes. "To wit, I recently enjoyed Mr. Pinero's newest play. Perhaps you saw it? *Sweet Lavender* is the name."

"Indeed," said St. Maur. "A work of great wit. Who can forget the immortal line: 'Where there is tea, there is hope'?"

Mrs. Hemple turned expectantly toward her. "You see how it is done."

Nell rolled her lips inward. "Oh, aye," she said. "I'm agape with interest."

St. Maur snorted.

"Mind you don't come off as pert," Mrs. Hemple said sharply. "And please be mindful of your diction! Now if you will please attempt an exchange with his lordship."

Nell nodded and turned toward St. Maur. He sat back in his chair, a smile playing on his lips. "Do you like the theater?" she asked.

"Not the theater!" Mrs. Hemple cried. "You must never ask a question which may expose your . . . lack of experience. Avoid questions of the theater until you have attended it. The weather, my lady, is always a wise choice. Or . . . let me see . . ."

"Literature," St. Maur said. "Lady Cornelia can speak marvelously on Shakespeare." He lifted his glass to her.

A flush of pleasure spread through her—intensified by Mrs. Hemple's evident surprise. With a smile at the old lady, she said to St. Maur, "Have you read—"

"I do not recommend literature," Mrs. Hemple cut in. "In this day and age, all manner of rubbish is printed."

"The weather, then," Nell said through her teeth. "How pleasant the weather is today, don't you agree?"

"It rained," Mrs. Hemple said.

Nell felt herself begin to scowl. "And what if I like the rain?"

The opening door saved her from Mrs. Hemple's reply. A footman came around to serve a creamy soup that smelled of mushrooms and divinity. But he dispensed the portions so stingily that Nell could almost see through the bisque to the bottom of her bowl. "A bit"—*more*, she was going to say, but from the corner of her eye she saw St. Maur shake his head.

Once the soup was dispensed, another footman distributed glasses of sherry. After his exit, Mrs. Hemple spoke. "One does not ask for more soup," she said as Nell lifted her spoon. "Or more of anything, for that matter, but *particularly* not for soup. A full bowl would be *very* vulgar."

One taste and Nell knew this was the stupidest rule she'd heard yet. The soup tasted of heaven, of rich cream and cunning, savory spices and the tenderest mushrooms ever grown on God's green earth. "Maybe," she said after swallowing, "since this is only practice, we *could* ask for more—"

"Absolutely not."

Nell glanced at St. Maur, but with a slight shrug, he ceded the ground to Mrs. Hemple. Smart man: he wasn't wasting time talking with soup like this in front of him.

Nell went for another mouthful.

"My lady! Do not place the spoon into your mouth!" Mrs. Hemple looked shocked. "You sip from the side of the spoon, never from the tip!"

The best food in the world couldn't hold up under all these pointless rules. "The spoon does its job either way, I expect!"

"Practice," St. Maur murmured. "Practice and patience. She's correct. One drinks soup from the side of the spoon, though God knows why."

She normally drank soup by picking up the bowl and setting it to her mouth. The technique had the happy effect of warming one's hands to boot.

But she saw in St. Maur's level gaze a reminder of her own goal, and her determination to succeed at it. On a deep breath, she forced herself to make her dainty way through the thin inch of ambrosia. Once finished, she reached for a large swallow of sherry.

"Don't drink that until the soup is removed," Mrs. Hemple hissed.

Nell set the glass down with a thump. What nonsense was *this*? "Why did they bring it out if it's not meant to be drunk?"

"These rules have no logic to them," St. Maur said. "Were they logical, anyone might deduce them, and then how could we know whom to invite to our parties, and whom to shun?"

The trace of irony in his voice placated her. She sat back, eyeing the service door, willing the footman to reappear.

St. Maur leaned forward. "For our next discussion of the weather, I may introduce the topic of thunderstorms—but only because I like you, you understand."

She managed a thin smile.

"Your *lordship*," Mrs. Hemple began in aggrieved tones, just as the door swung open again.

Seeing her chance, Nell lifted her glass—saying, as her tutor fixed her with a frown, "They've come to clear the course!"

"Only a *sip*," Mrs. Hemple said. "With a new glass for every course, you will *not* wish to become tipsy."

Good God. Nell couldn't think of a better state in which to pass this dinner. But by sheer dint of effort, she kept the smile on her face and returned her glass to the table after a single—very large—sip.

Next came the fish course. "The fork," Mrs. Hemple instructed when Nell picked up the knife to debone her fillet. "When in doubt, *whenever* possible, one uses a fork. The spoon is somewhat vulgar, the knife *definitely* so."

Then what in bloody hell was it doing on the table? Gritting her teeth, now, Nell picked up the fork and began to pluck out the tiny bones. One popped off her fork and went flying away. Neither St. Maur nor Hemple seemed to notice—although when she took another peek to be sure, the corner of St. Maur's mouth twitched suspiciously.

The beef course—little round patties cooked in a buttery sherry sauce—restored her good cheer. By God, she'd do and say anything if she could eat like *this* every night. Spoons were vulgar? She'd swear never to touch one again, as long as *this* stuff—*lay-ree-doo-vo,* Mrs. Hemple called it—appeared nightly on the table.

Her plate nearly clean, Nell had moved on to the accompanying vegetables when Mrs. Hemple struck again. "No, my lady! That is *asparagus*!"

Nell looked up. "Aye—yes," she amended, "so it is." And she meant to eat it. It was slathered in butter and cream sauce. The kitchen wouldn't be having it back.

"One doesn't eat the stalk," said Mrs. Hemple.

Still giddy on the flavor of the tenderest meat she'd ever tasted, Nell stared across the candlelit table at a woman who'd clearly eaten more than her fair share in this life. "That's . . . nonsense."

Mrs. Hemple's large bosom swelled. "It is good ton. One eats the *tips* of the asparagus, no more."

Nell turned toward St. Maur. "I want the stalks."

He lowered his fork back to his plate and considered her squarely. "Go ahead," he said. "I'll never tell."

A sharp breath gusted out of her. She wasn't a child to be humored. But she supposed that was how she was acting. These lessons were for her benefit, not theirs. Heart sinking, she cast her own fork to her plate.

It clattered, causing Hemple to perk up like a dog on the scent of rubbish. "One doesn't—"

"Make a noise," Nell sighed. "I know. Quiet as mice, we lot."

Mrs. Hemple sat back, visibly mollified.

And so it went for the next half hour. One did not butter her bread. One did not use a spoon save when one simply did *not* use a fork, as in the case of pastry;

then, *of course* one used a spoon, otherwise how would one capture the sauce?

"Do not eat the cheese," Mrs. Hemple instructed. "Only the fruit."

"With a fork," Nell predicted wearily. "Or—no, a spoon."

"Indeed not. Use your fingers! Really, my lady, did you not read the books I provided? No, not like that— your hand should not close completely around the grape. Yes, very good. Now return the seed to the plate very discreetly."

One didn't fold one's napkin at the conclusion of the meal. "Lay it beside your plate as it falls," said Mrs. Hemple. "And now we shall leave his lordship to his port and cigars, and withdraw to the drawing room for coffee and pleasant conversation."

Nell, having just let go of her napkin and turned away, stopped dead in her tracks. No, no, *no.* She'd surrendered the asparagus stalks. She'd resigned herself to a fifth of a bowl of soup. She'd looked longingly on but not touched the fine, creamy cheeses. She'd managed to restrain herself from eating her peas with a knife; she'd not even tipped the pastry bowl to her lips to capture the last sips of raspberry liqueur. Another minute of this and she'd—she'd—

"I think that's enough for one night," said St. Maur. He'd risen as they had and now, suddenly, was taking her arm. "That will be all, Mrs. Hemple. Thank you."

Nell found herself overcome with gratitude at the sight of Hemple's exit. She laid her hand over St. Maur's where it cupped her elbow. "Thank you," she said fervently. "*Thank* you."

He laughed down at her. "Believe it or not, you did well."

She let go. "And pigs are flying. No matter. So long as your cook keeps making that beef, I'll gladly practice till I'm the Queen of the World."

"How very good to know," he said. "For such diligence, I think you require a reward."

"Oh?" Interested, she tipped her head. "So long as it's not another etiquette manual . . ."

"You tell me," he said. "What would *you* like to do?"

The white ball cracked into the red, sending it spinning into the top pocket. Nell straightened with a broad grin. She had an unlighted cigar clamped between her teeth, and as she cast down her cue, her hand went to the glass of whisky she'd balanced on the table's edge. "Three more strokes to me," she said. She plucked the cigar from her mouth and pointed it at his eye. "How's that feel, laddie?"

"I'm trembling," Simon drawled.

"As you should be." She winked at him, then tipped back her glass for a long, unfeminine swig. Simon's gaze wandered down the line of her throat to the low neckline of her golden gown. The lean, graceful tension of her bare upper arms fascinated him. He regretted the long white gloves that disguised the tender curve of her inner elbow. Uncreative schoolboys might dream of orgies featuring nuns, but the truly precocious dreamed of a woman like this: bohemian and endlessly surprising. Self-possessed and quick-witted enough to keep any man on his toes.

Generally boys grew up to realize that such women existed only in dreams. Finding one in his billiards room somewhat took his breath away.

Her swallow was noisy. She smacked her lips as she set down the glass. He'd invited her to behave without a care for propriety, and she'd spent the last half hour testing the sincerity of his offer. "A dead heat," she said gleefully.

He retrieved his cue, grabbing a length of sandpaper to roughen the leather tip. "Not for long, of course. But by all means, enjoy it while it lasts."

"Oh, I expect it won't be long," she said comfortably. "You'll be fouling, this next strike."

He snorted. "My dear, misguided twit, you're playing the top scorer in the Oxford-Cambridge matches of seventy-five and seventy-six. I never left St. James's Hall that I wasn't carried out shoulder-high."

"Oh ho, a sharper!" She retrieved her glass to make him a toast. "My sympathies on your coming defeat, then, boy-o. Bound to be bitterer than your whisky."

He laughed as he exchanged sandpaper for chalk. She was a sharp-toothed tiger wrapped up in silk. "I think I'll make you pay for that taunt."

"Will you, now! And what price for *your* arrogance, me pretty lad?"

He looked up from the chalk, smiling slowly. "I am pretty, aren't I? High time you noticed."

Color rose in her face, but she did not look away—not even as she returned the glass to the small shelf behind her and placed her cigar beside it. Eyes remaining on his, she came padding around the billiards table in her stocking feet.

It was he who broke the gaze to look downward, to the white silk stockings that revealed glimpses of the slim shape of her toes. Her small feet flexed gracefully, the arches deep, her ankles trim—she was lifting her skirts higher than her short steps required.

He felt his smile deepen. Oh, he knew what she was on about, here.

As she arrived at his side, the delicate scent of lilies reached him. Somebody, the French maid, had put perfume on her, and it seemed to spread tendrils that twined into his brain and tightened around it, strangling his good sense.

Her breasts brushed his arm as she leaned past him to set the red ball at the billiards spot. "You're going to lose," she purred, glancing up at him from beneath her long, dark lashes. "In that dining room, you may know what's what, but this is *my* sort of table."

"Hmm." He held her eyes, arrested by the glint in them. That glint invited him to commit mischief: she wasn't the only one intending to misbehave. "Perhaps we should make a wager on it."

11

Nell did not look impressed by the idea of a wager. Lifting a brow, she said, "Sure and we could bet on it. But I'd feel bad taking advantage of a duffer like you."

Simon laughed. "Darling, you may take advantage of me whenever you like."

Her lashes lowered, concealing her thoughts. "You remember you said that, St. Maur."

"Simon," he murmured. "If you mean to be bold, you might as well go the distance."

"Simon," she said. "You're the striker." Her head tipped toward the table.

"Growing impatient, are you? Or perhaps nervous," he teased. "Very well. We agreed to play to a hundred strokes. Let's add twenty to it. What are the terms?"

She set her cue to the ground with a thump, leaning into it as she looked him up and down. A smile began to play at the corners of her mouth. "What a world of possibilities," she said. "All right: I'll play for . . . the right to send one of my dresses to a friend."

Her proposal served a neat blow to his growing intentions. He'd had in mind a wager far less noble. "Agreed," he said. "But do add something to sweeten the deal."

"That's pretty sweet in itself," she muttered. "But if you insist on being a victim—I'll take a trip to a bookshop and the chance to spend twenty pounds from your pocket."

Good God. "What a depressingly virtuous standard you set."

Her smile sharpened into a taunt. "Oh, don't mind me, *Simon*. Set any terms you like. You're not going to win, so it makes no difference, you see."

"Excellent," he said briskly. "Then I'll demand five minutes of your virtue."

Her eyes narrowed. She pressed her cheek to her upright cue and scowled at him. "What does that mean?"

"Since I'm apparently bound to lose, it doesn't matter, does it? I'll decide what I mean during those five minutes."

"Those five minutes you won't have," she retorted.

"That's right." With a grin, he turned his back on her, bracing his cue on the bridge of his hand to test his aim on the white-spot ball.

No challenge came in reply. It seemed she meant to accept the bargain. After a brief moment of amazement, he felt, all at once, very determined to win. He bent lower to the table. If he could hole the red by striking his ball off the white-spot—

"Sad to watch you," came Nell's idle voice from behind him. "I hope you won't weep when you lose. This dress hasn't the pockets for hankies."

He didn't look up. "My, such confidence. Didn't Mrs. Hemple teach you of modesty? A very ladylike quality." Perhaps the canon was overreaching. A losing hazard, to the middle pocket—

"I never was very good at modesty."

His hand seized on the cue. She'd purred the words directly into his ear. He could feel the heat of her breath on his nape. It lifted the small hairs there.

Slowly he turned his head. She didn't retreat an inch. A sly half smile curled her mouth. It shot through him like an electric current, arrowing straight to his groin.

"Am I distracting you?" she asked.

"Not in the least," he said, but the huskiness in his voice betrayed him. She laughed and glanced toward his cue.

"You're about to commit a foul," she said.

With a silent oath, he withdrew his cue, which had wandered dangerously close to her ball. "And how, pray tell, how did *you* grow so skilled? I didn't imagine Bethnal Green would be home to many tables."

"Not like this one," she said promptly. "This here is a fine setup, indeed. Slate and India rubber, aye? But we've got tables thereabouts, if none so flash."

"And you were able to play at them?" He could not imagine women were welcomed into billiard clubs, even in the East End.

She mistook his meaning. "It ain't all work in the Green. My friends and I, we always knew how to spend a half day properly. Down at O'Malley's pub, there's a table and some card games, too. Poker was always my favorite. You going to shoot anytime soon, or do you give up?"

He laughed and bent back over the table, sighting quickly.

She leaned near again. "That's a Long Jenny you're thinking to try. Don't know as I'd advise that to a man with a weakness for the screw."

He gave her a sharp look. The brightness of her smile announced that she was well aware of the double meaning. She all but danced backward, laughter glinting in her eyes. "The screw," she said. "You know, that spin you put on the ball when you strike it below the center."

"I do have a particular talent for the screw," he agreed. "I'd be glad to demonstrate it. Now, or shall we wait for my five minutes?"

"Ha!" Her laughter sounded giddy.

He shook his head at her, then took his shot, sending his ball rebounding off hers and into the top pocket. "Three to me," he said, turning so rapidly that she had no time to dance away again; suddenly they were standing chest to breast, and the sudden dilation of her pupils suggested she was no more immune to this current between them than he.

He reached out and brushed his knuckle along her satiny cheek. A pulse beat at the base of her throat. He moved his thumb to it, pressing lightly. "I am looking forward to those five minutes," he said quietly.

Her throat moved beneath his thumb as she swallowed. Her dark blue eyes were fathoms deep, brilliant in the light shed by the electrolier overhead. She did not look so much like Kitty after all. She looked nothing at all like Kitty.

"You're cocky as a rooster," she whispered.

"Yes," he said. "You'll have to tell me if my confidence is justified."

"Seems unwise to count on victory when you haven't seen anything from *me* yet."

She started to step away and he closed his hand on her upright cue, effectively trapping her. "I cannot tell you how eager I am to remedy that." He ran his palm down the stick, pausing a bare inch from her hand, brushing her knuckles with the tip of his littlest finger. "Indeed, I can think of no one I'd rather play games with."

A visible shudder moved through her. "You play games with a lot of people?"

"Not lately," he said quietly.

Her chest rose on a long breath. "Oh. Why is that?"

"I seem to have lost interest in them."

A flush stained her face. The smile she gave him trembled a little before disappearing. "You're good company," she said. Then she shook her head and laughed. "When you're not going on about the weather."

He let go of her cue and stepped back, strangely exhilarated. "Thank you," he said. "Then you'll be glad to know that I also play poker, now and then. I confess you're the first lady I know to do so. How did you learn?"

As she looked away toward the table, the brightness faded from her face. "Oh, Michael has a knack for it. My stepbrother," she added with a shrug.

Now she appeared as stiff as she had in the dining room. "You've never mentioned a stepbrother before," he said.

She remained silent for a passing moment. "Well. Hannah, the girls from the factory . . . Some people are worth missing. Some aren't."

"You lived with him, though?"

The look she flashed him seemed resentful. "Where else was I to live?"

The odd reply triggered an intuition. "He was the one who hit you."

Her face became impassive as she turned to take up the chalk. "Aye, well. They say you can't choose your family."

He watched her closely as she scrubbed the chalk across the tip of her cue. "But now you know that he isn't your family. Although I suppose he was chosen, by your supposed mum."

Her eyes narrowed as she looked over her shoulder at him. She was still quite tetchy on the subject of Jane Whitby. But after a moment's study of his face—she was deciding, he gathered, whether or not he'd meant the remark as a jibe—she decided to relax. Turning to lean against the table, she said conversationally, "She'd no idea what she was bargaining for with that marriage."

This remarkable moment—this decision to trust him, even if only in a matter so small that she probably had not consciously debated it—gave Simon a thrill of satisfaction. He found himself smiling, and realized how thoroughly inappropriate it was only when she frowned at him. Forcing his expression to straighten, he said, "Tell me. What bargain did she end up with?"

She shrugged as she set aside the chalk. "Jack Whitby was a good man. But he died within a year of the match. All we got for it was his wretched, no-good son. And a flat," she added thoughtfully. "That is—" She rotated the cue in her hands. "We got the right to rent his flat after he passed. Mum might have had a hard time finding one for us, otherwise." She pulled a face. "Nobody likes to rent to a woman. Can't depend on her for the money, they say."

"Because women are paid less," he ventured.

Her look suggested he'd said something very obvious. She reached for his glass, not asking before she took a long drink. "They're always the first to be sacked if times are hard. Or if they fall pregnant. And they're worth less on the lines than a man, anyway. People think they're not dependable tenants."

He accepted the correction with equanimity. To her, these things *were* obvious. To him, the rules of poverty—and of honest moneymaking, for that matter—seemed fairly obscure. "And when did he take up hitting you, then?"

For a long moment it seemed she wouldn't answer. Then she sighed and finished the last of his drink. "Well, he always had a bad temper. But"—her glance was sharp, daring him to object—"my *mum* stood in the way, more often than not. And when he was younger, he obeyed her. Scared of her, no doubt." A breath of a laugh slipped from her. "Mum could be properly fierce."

He made some noise of agreement, although his thoughts were blacker. Indeed, a woman capable of snatching a six-year-old in the night might be willing to do any number of things to put fear into someone. "What changed, then?"

"He got put in jail." She pushed off the table and surveyed the spread on the baize. Then she leaned over and took the shot in one smooth move, knocking out a canon that potted the red ball and netted her five strokes.

Simon felt a flicker of dismay. A lucky shot, no doubt.

She did not remark on the victory as she turned back to him. "That riot last year in Hyde Park— Michael got taken up by the bobbies. Wasn't the same afterward."

The hint of sympathy in her voice shocked him. She could feel for a man who had blackened her eye— more than once, Simon suspected. "I would hope that you don't feel sisterly toward him."

"No," she said after a moment. "But he's a pitiful creature, you'll agree."

Pitiful creature. As Simon lined up his shot, the description put him in mind of a fatally lamed horse. He knew how to deal with those. It required a bullet.

He knocked out a winning hazard, then turned to catch her attention. "You needn't worry about him now," he said. "He'll never come near you again."

Hearing Simon talk of Michael made her feel queasy. God forbid they ever met. Michael would loathe everything about this man: his handsome clothing, his untroubled laughter, even the hew of his broad shoulders and the easy, muscled grace of his well-tended body. He had arrogance bred into him, and Michael had been nursed on rage. If ever they met, somebody's blood would spill.

A shiver broke over her and left behind an ache that felt like foreboding. She shoved the thought away as she leaned over the table. It didn't take but a moment to spot her target. She made another canon and pocketed her ball, causing the lord of the manor to groan.

Good Lord, maybe he really imagined he'd win. The thought made her grin. He couldn't complain later that she hadn't warned him.

As she straightened, all this talk of family stirred a thought that had been preying on her for days now. "I want to meet my sister."

"Ah." A brief silence. Simon glanced toward the tip of his cue, where his thumb was testing the grain of the leather. "I called on her this afternoon, but she wasn't at home. I left a note."

"She knows I'm here, now."

"So I assume."

She took a quick breath against the sinking feeling in her stomach. "You think she doesn't want to see me?"

His light eyes met hers squarely. "She *hasn't* seen

you, yet. Once she does, her opinion of my tidings will change."

"Or maybe she didn't get your letter." She couldn't believe that Katherine wouldn't even be curious. "Who'd you leave it with? Could somebody have taken it? To protect her, you know. If her guardian thought me a fraud—"

His long mouth twisted in a grimace that said it was possible. "If he did intercept your letter, I suspect it wouldn't be the first time he'd done so. You did try to write to your father, didn't you?"

Nell's cue slipped from her grasp, the butt thumping hard against the floor before she caught it up again. "He was the one who got old Rushden's letters? The guardian—Grimston, aye?"

He gave a single nod.

"Well." She wet her lips. "Grimston." The name felt unhealthy on her tongue, slippery and sour, like the skin on spoiling milk. "Now I know who I should have saved my bullets for. He's a bad 'un, is he?"

"He likes money," he said. "Your sister has it. I believe he has designs to wed her—preferably as the sole heiress, you understand. Whether or not she knows his intentions, I can't say."

"Maybe somebody should tell her."

"Kitty has never been known to take advice."

"*I* could tell her."

He slanted her a cynical smile. "By all means. But do keep in mind that family is . . . often not as one would hope. And you were raised very differently, of course. Katherine Aubyn is very much her father's daughter."

A nervous flutter stirred in her stomach. "Was old Rushden so bad, then?"

"To her?" He shrugged. "I suppose she wouldn't think so."

"But to you, he was."

"Ah. Old business, long finished. Too tedious for a night such as this."

"It's all right if you don't want to talk about it," Nell said. "But I admit I'm curious." She cleared her throat, feeling a touch awkward. Reaching out to run her finger along the edge of the baize, she added, "I grew up thinking my father a farmer from Leicestershire, you see. But I supposed you aren't the best man to ask about the late earl."

Simon laid down his cue across the corner of the table. "It is a bit of a tall order, to ask me to speak of him in any measured way." He turned away to the liquor cabinet, glass clinking as he refilled his whisky and poured another for her. She accepted it with a murmur of thanks.

They leaned against the table and drank, their eyes on the fire burning low in the hearth. Woodsmoke and the scent of oiled leather blended with the rich fumes of the drink in her hand; the silence felt companionable. She'd almost forgotten her curiosity when Simon finally continued.

"I will say this: he was learned. He liked the trappings that came with his station. Ritual, tradition, meant a great deal to him. Manliness," he said after a brief pause. "Honor, courage. He would have flourished as a soldier—a general, mind you, someone who gave orders rather than took them. But he would have put himself at the front lines, no doubt, and cursed any bullets that dared to strike him." He hesitated. "I suppose you have that quality from him: very little cows you."

The compliment startled her, since it was delivered at some price to him: it had required him, in a backhanded sort of way, to compliment her father as well. "Thanks," she mumbled—fighting a losing battle with a foolish smile, which she directed first toward the malachite mantel, then to the tall brass dogs that guarded the fire screen.

"Your courage is not exactly like his, of course." Simon spoke in a slow, low voice. "His was—inflexible, you see." She stole a quick glance at him and saw that he wore a slight frown, a look of concentration. "He had no patience for any way but his own."

She gathered that he was feeling his way out of the previous moment—trying to retreat from any appearance of kindness toward old Rushden. But he was proceeding carefully in the attempt, lest he wound her by accident in the process.

He was kinder, she saw suddenly, than she'd ever imagined a man like him could be.

She put the glass to her lips but didn't drink.

She *liked* this man.

The idea required a long, bracing swallow. *Like* wasn't a feeling most people held in high value, but when paired with all else Simon St. Maur kindled in her—attraction, interest, admiration, gratitude—kindness tipped the balance of feeling into something hotter. It kindled a greedy longing that flamed through her body and left her unable to remove her attention from his sharp-boned profile.

All she said was: "Go on."

Simon nodded absently, his eyes on the glass in his hand. "Cowardice rather fixated him. He was terrified, I think, of being seen as . . . weak? I've no idea why, but, yes, that was his devil. And so he saw weakness everywhere, in the most peculiar places." He gave her a brief look of significance. "In harmless inclinations. An eye for beauty. An interest in art, in music."

She nodded to show she understood. "I hear you playing the piano sometimes." Next to the ballroom was a small room filled with a variety of instruments, one of them a glossy black piano. During her lessons with Palmier, she sometimes heard him playing, a low, melodic counterpoint to Mrs. Hemple's choppy tunes.

"Yes," he said. "Your mother, in fact, was my first teacher. She was very talented."

"Was she?" She gave him a chance to speak, then added tentatively, "You play really nicely."

He smiled slightly. "Thank you."

He deserved better. "You play . . . beautifully."

His smile turned into a grin as he turned toward her. "Do go on."

She laughed. "But I mean it," she said, then hesitated. She didn't want him to think she'd been spying on him. "A few nights ago, just after I'd had my dinner tray, I heard you. You were playing a piece so sad, it nearly made me weep." She'd been thinking of Mum, and the music had seemed to reach in her soul and squeeze every part of her that hurt. "It went from very high to very low, all at once—like a heart sinking, breaking."

As soon as the words were out her mouth, she regretted them, her face turning hot. What claptrap. *A heart breaking.*

But all he said was: "Ah." And then he held quiet so long that she thought he'd say no more on it. Their eyes locked; inexplicably, she couldn't tear her gaze away from his.

"You describe it well," he said. "I was heartbroken when I wrote it."

The admission—so unforeseen, so bloody honest—pierced her like a hook. She stared at him.

He'd *written* that?

An instant later, she realized what it meant. "That woman you said you loved?"

"Yes." His smile made her decide never to trust his expressions again; this one looked easy and charming, mismatched entirely to what he said next: "She was the daughter of a composer I studied with in Italy. Rushden had cut me off when I went abroad, and I'd assumed him to have washed his hands of me. I learned differently after we became engaged to marry. He—or rather, Grimston, as his henchman—approached the lady with an offer, a tidy sum for ending our connection. Which she accepted." He shrugged. "I was very young—twenty-one, the age for melodrama. The étude is not particularly good, you understand, but it's certainly flamboyant. I was thinking of letting . . ." He gave her a quick smile, and she had the impression that he'd just decided against saying something. "I'm sorry if it made you cry."

She shook her head. Not important, apology unnecessary. "That's awful. No wonder you hated the man."

"Indeed. Although I suppose he thought he was only doing right by the title."

It seemed out of character for him to make allowances like that. Because she feared it was for her sake, she said, "A title is just a name. Worth nothing against a person's love."

He lifted a brow. "Are you an idealist, then?"

What a question for him to ask—and of her, of all

people. They were two people thinking to marry on the cold hopes of a fortune. She might have laughed at him if he weren't regarding her so soberly: as though he was waiting for an answer that would mean something important.

It made her search herself for the truth. "I suppose it depends on what you mean by the word," she said slowly. "I've always been a hand at wanting the impossible." Windows in the factory workroom. Respect from the labor-mistress and lads on the street. A home of her own, a bit of security. Someplace to be safe. Somebody to love.

Somebody to love *her*.

"What's impossible?" he countered. "If we succeed, Nell, what will be impossible for you?"

Gripped by revelation, she stared at him. In one moment, with one small question, he inadvertently had laid it bare: so little of what she wanted could be bought, no matter the size of the fortune coming to her.

A shadow passed over his face. "What?" he asked. "What did I say?"

She shook her head and looked away from his concern. When he laid a gentle hand on her arm, she closed her eyes, torn by twin impulses: to knock his hand away, or to clutch it in her own.

She'd thought it safe to keep company with him as long as they stayed out of a bedroom, but this friendly companionship was just as dangerous—more so, even. He thought he was offering her everything she needed, while in his kind words, his conversation, his laughter, he tempted her with everything she *wanted*—none of which he'd offered to give. Why would he? No matter where she'd been born, life had led her far from the places where a man like this looked for love.

God above. How stupid, how unforgivably idiotic, to be suddenly and burningly jealous of a woman whose name she didn't even know.

She opened her eyes. "Do you think—"

Do you think you could ever love a girl like me?

Only a fool asked such a question when she knew she wouldn't like the answer.

On a deep breath, she called up a smile. "I could beat you blindfolded," she said as she put aside her glass. "You should have asked for a handicap."

And then, retrieving her cue and bending over the table, she knocked off a shot: striking the red ball into his, she sent them both into the top left pocket, while her own went careening into the right. The ten strokes she netted for it gave her the victory.

When she faced him, his amazed expression held none of the disappointment it ought to show. Slowly he set down his glass. "Well *done*," he said, and then, shaking his head, he began to laugh. "My God! Nell, I've never seen anything to match that!"

She broke into a grin. "Aye, well," she said, scuffing her foot against the carpet, making a mocking little show of false modesty for him, but only because she knew he'd see through it. "I've never been carried out on shoulders, but I've been bought a few rounds, let's just say."

"I'll wager you have! Or, no." He pulled a face, mocking himself, now. "No more wagers with you."

"Aye, right you are. You're lucky I only asked for the dress and twenty pounds. With your nonsense about terms, I might have asked for anything. This house, say!"

His smile faded, but his regard did not waver. "Ask for it," he said. "It's yours."

A queer excitement rippled through her stomach. The way he was looking at her . . .

She cleared her throat. "Enough wagering for the night. I beat you soundly. I reckon you've learned your lesson."

"And yet, as you once observed, I'm a bit of a cheater." He took up her cue, which she'd laid between them, and put it behind him, the movement precise and deliberate. "You see, I'm going to insist on my five minutes anyway."

Her body understood before her mind did. It pulsed from head to toe. *Yes,* she thought, and stepped toward him; and then: *No, no, no,* and stepped back again. After the mad thoughts she'd just been entertaining, it would be the height of recklessness to put her body to his. If a woman could win love with her body, the world would have no bastards.

But oh, he was so beautiful. As he took the step that closed the distance between them, his slow smile might have lured the angels from heaven, flocking noisily, arms outstretched, happy to burn for him.

"We had an agreement." She didn't sound convincing even to herself. "You said you wouldn't do—"

He laid his fingers over her lips. As easy as that, everything in her—breath, heart, brain—froze. The next second, her senses awoke again, telescoping on that single delicious inch where his skin touched hers. She stood immobile, the table at her back, small shocks radiating from the pit of her stomach.

He leaned forward to press his cheek against her own. In her ear, he whispered, "What mustn't I do?"

Her mouth went dry. She had no honest answer to give. *Do anything,* she thought.

With one finger still laid across her lips, he used his other hand to delicately cup the back of her neck. She sucked in a breath as his lips, soft and hot, pressed against the tender skin beneath her ear. "Is this what I shouldn't do?" he breathed.

The gentle press of his fingertips at her nape, her lips, burned like brands. It wasn't fear that made her shudder. Everywhere she felt the heat of him, and he was melting her, like flame to pliant wax. "No," she managed. *Do this all you like.*

His finger slipped from her mouth. He pulled back to look into her face, his own so close that she could see the shadow cast by his lashes along his cheeks. With a curious, one-sided smile, he returned his finger to her lips, and then, steadily, his eyes daring her to protest, he pushed one finger against the seam, breaching her mouth.

His finger slid in to touch her tongue.

Shock scattered her thoughts. The taste of him sent a pang through her, close to hunger but more frantic, more needy. In all her life, she had never been so hungry for food. Caught in the spell of his eyes, she held very still. Slowly he pushed the finger in to the middle knuckle; as he withdrew, her teeth scraped over his skin. He did it again, invading her with steady, gentle pressure; retreating with grave-eyed concentration. And all she could do was lean against the table—stunned, thrumming with tension. Men did such things? *He* did such things.

She felt his breath on her cheek, and then, with the tip of his finger still in her mouth, he placed his lips against her chin, sliding them up to nip at her lower lip, and then up yet again, so his tongue licked gently at her upper lip. He traced the underside, played delicately at the corner of her mouth. She inhaled, an involuntarily moan, and he withdrew his finger. The rasp of his breathing filled her ears; and then he cupped her cheek firmly and laid his mouth over her own, angling her head back so his tongue fully penetrated her mouth.

Something snapped in her. Clean and simple. *This* was simple. Want, and the solution for it: him. She grabbed at his shirtsleeves, then the backs of his arms, desperate to pull him against her. He stepped between her legs, and dimly she felt the cool air as he gathered her skirts up, higher and higher yet. His thigh parted her legs and he moved into the space between them, unyielding in his advance. His hands hooked under her thighs to lift her to the tabletop. With his mouth on hers, she closed her thighs around his narrow hips, so the solid, hardening length of him nudged up against the spot where she was softest.

His kiss offered no mercy. She didn't want it. She arched upward to the force of his kiss, craving more of the pressure, the grind and thrust as he rolled his hips against her. His hand slipped down to her breast; his thumb drew a light circle around her nipple, once, twice, and her hands, somehow now on his back, dug in to demand more. His fingers firmed, pulling, tugging, rubbing her nipple as his arm slipped up her back, making a long, steady brace for her spine as he lowered her backward, slowly, laying her almost tenderly against the baize tabletop.

A soft click sounded: in the periphery of her vision, she saw a cue fall against the table, then slide slowly out of sight to thump onto the carpet.

Irrelevant, unimportant. Her hands scratched across his nape into his hair, her fingers twining through the thick, soft strands. A low noise came from him. He moved against her sinuously, his hips arching and pressing, making her gasp as their lips met again. She could no longer govern herself; she twisted up against him without conscious intention, shuddering as his hand found her ankle, slid open-palmed up her calf, over her knee, his hot skin burning through the thin layer of silk until it found the gap between garter and combination and closed in a firm grip on her thigh.

Harder, she thought. Being gripped, being held, being directed—he nudged her thigh, opened her wider to him—felt good, right, in a way that she had never imagined. She made a noise of protest when his body withdrew from hers, but then his hand came between them, down low, brushing against her. A grunt burst from her. Her body wasn't hers; it bucked up against the heel of his palm to show its approval.

"Yes," he said, his voice hot, rough. His mouth moved down her neck, her chest, and his hands seemed to be everywhere, sliding and molding and shaping and stroking, now her tits, and now, sliding along the baize beneath her, to cup her arse, to squeeze and lift. Then he took hold of her neckline, pulling it down; she heard fabric rip, felt his clever fingers freeing her breast of the corset. His head slipped down farther yet, the hot, hot wetness of his mouth closing over her nipple. His teeth, God above, he was like a devil above her, a dark-haired demon who knew exactly where to touch, how to suck and lick her; there was no part of her not throbbing for him.

His hand delved below again, probing, testing; a high sound broke from her throat as he found the spot where her pleasure concentrated. As he stroked, hidden parts of her opened and clutched for hope of him, for hope of that long, hard erection she'd felt against her before. It wasn't enough, or it was too much, this torment he worked with his hand. She twisted and his mouth returned to hers, his hand hooking in her hair, tightening to the edge of pain. His kiss grew ferocious, his hand between her legs moving insistently, issuing a demand that grew harder and faster, drawing her out, tighter, higher, to the edge of—

The sensation burst over her, rippled and purled through her, pleasure so intense that she cried out. With the flat of his palm he cupped her until she eased, and then his kiss grew gentler, and his mouth broke from hers to wander her face, to trace the line of her jaw, until she put her arms around him tightly, and he turned his face into her hair, his ragged breath loud in her ear.

Her hand traced the long line of his back, skated the curve of his spine, reached the hard muscle of his buttocks, which tightened beneath her fingers. The feel of him stirred her anew.

This wasn't like hunger at all, not if it could be roused again so quickly after being fully satisfied. She shifted beneath him, pushed up against him, amazed at herself as she issued the silent demand.

His hoarse laugh warmed her ear. That laughter made her go still. She heard in it a wealth of knowledge she didn't yet share.

"Tomorrow," he said as he lifted his head to look into her face. The curve of his mouth bespoke satisfaction—and a promise he underscored by the

light touch he traced over her bottom lip. "I have the
license," he said, his slumberous gaze intent on hers.
"We'll be wed, and then . . ." His smile tipped into a
lazy angle. "You'll decide which you like better: this
table, or my bed."

12

Simon's way to the wedding led through a house that appeared deserted. Rushden's ghost was no doubt raging about the rafters: the coming ceremony would, in most respects, seem a perfect specimen of revenge on him. Had it not been for his shenanigans, Simon would have married long ago, and been unavailable to missing daughters who turned up in the night.

Alas, Rushden had offered a bribe and Maria had taken it, removing herself from Simon's reach.

His steps slowed as he turned through the entry hall. He hadn't given real thought to Maria in years, but after speaking of her last night, her face seemed newly vivid. Turning a profit off love was a trickier endeavor in a parlor than on a street corner, but she'd managed it.

She'd managed, also, to make a fool of him. Naturally he hadn't thought of her in years. Thinking of her entailed remembering how he'd chased after her, demanded and then begged her to reconsider her decision—heedless of his own pride, careless of the humiliation. He'd spent years building his immunity to Rushden's jibes, but one sneer from her and he'd been flattened.

Well. Long ago. That boy—for he'd been very young—seemed a stranger to him, now. Yet in letting go of Maria and of the part of himself that had loved her, Simon also had abandoned—forever, he'd imagined—a certain vision of himself: as someone's husband, a man obligated. Only natural, then, that this coming moment should seem surreal.

Not that he'd be *obligated* to Nell, precisely. He made himself smile as he turned down the corridor toward the formal drawing room. These sober reflections were ludicrously inappropriate. If the courts denied Nell her birthright, he would break the connection, easily as snapping a twig. He'd have no other choice.

Nevertheless, as he caught sight through the open door of the waiting deacon—and beside him, Nell, her eyes on the carpet, her back rigidly straight—he came to a stop, struck by something that he hadn't been prepared to feel. He drew a sharp breath and stepped behind the doorjamb, out of sight, where a laugh escaped him: What on earth? Why was he hiding like a guilty schoolboy?

He looked down at himself, dressed in a morning coat of dove gray, freshly brushed, with diamond cuff links at his wrists. An uninformed observer would have called him the very picture of the well-dressed groom.

Perhaps he should have told Nell that this marriage need not be permanent. It had been Rushden's way to bully a person with lies and threats, but his own specialty was different: he pushed unpalatable truths on people and made them like it. Marrying her without telling her the whole of it felt like . . . poor sport.

But she was skittish. Oh, underneath him on a billiards table, she was . . . the most perfect picture of soft, scented, willing compliance that any man could imagine. But when on her feet, she still examined his claims skeptically, from every angle available. Her trust was new, fragile, and undependable.

Meanwhile, whether permanent or not, this

marriage would serve her best interests. If everything worked out, they *would* remain wed. And if everything . . . did not work out, he'd find some happy settlement to send her into a rosier future than the past she'd left behind.

A factory girl, for God's sake.

No, he'd find some way—somehow—to give her a sum that would see her well settled.

On credit, perhaps, he'd raise that sum.

But no doubt it would work out. Daughtry's men were on the case. Now it was his turn to take the crucial next step. And if he'd gambled correctly—well, then despite the informal setting, this ceremony would be binding. A momentous occasion. Twenty years from now, he would look back on this moment in the hallway as the last of his bachelorhood.

He reached up to tug at his ascot. His valet had knotted it too tightly.

The marriage would change nothing, of course. Both bride and groom entered into it with dreams of pounds and pennies, nothing lofty or noble. Pounds, pennies, and pleasure. Nell was a sensible woman; it would never occur to her to demand more of him than that. What else could a cynic desire?

And he *was* a cynic, he reminded himself.

He tugged down his long coattails—feeling foolish, suddenly, to have dressed so formally—and entered the room.

The hush that greeted his appearance felt not so much suspenseful as weary: it had started out as puzzlement, perhaps, but had since collapsed into boredom. Along one wall, a line of neatly starched mobcaps disguised the down-turned faces of the six upstairs maids, who bobbed in unison for him. His butler bowed staidly. Mrs. Collins's creaking knees popped as she straightened.

Not for the first time, he wondered why he had so many damned servants. He could have raised a fortune simply by firing them, but decency continued to impede that temptation.

By the window, Nell looked up from her study of the carpet. The afternoon light cast her in gold. Madame Debordes had delivered the new gowns four days ago, and for this occasion, his bride had chosen to don what must be the soberest of the lot: a steel-gray silk walking dress shot through with black.

The dress was darker than his coat by several shades, and to his distracted mind, the choice seemed significant. A darker gray, a paler face, her expression impassive, her square jaw set. The lady's maid had trammeled her bangs, sleeking her hair straight back from her brow. She looked calmer than he felt; she was outdoing him somehow.

The thought made no sense. He let it go as he walked to her side. "My lady."

She bent her knee in reply. "Lord Rushden."

The slight curtsy was appropriate and perfectly accomplished. He saw not a single sign that she remembered where he'd put his hands and mouth last night, although memories of it had kept him up almost until dawn.

The absurd sense of inadequacy deepened. He had the fleeting idea that her ragged clothing and gutter accents had been a disguise, and the face she presented now, serene and composed, was her true demeanor. That perhaps this, too, was another bad joke pulled off at his expense, and designed by her late, unlamented father.

What a singular, nonsensical idea. He dismissed it, but its effect continued to register in the sudden tightness in his throat. He had a premonition, real and unshakable: complications, unforeseen consequences, a cost to himself . . .

The next second, he was marveling at the misfiring of his brain. He nodded to the Reverend Dawkins, who stood a few paces away, Bible in hand. When they had spoken earlier in Simon's study, Dawkins had done a poor job of disguising his curiosity. This made him well suited to the task at hand: within an hour, despite Grimston's best efforts to trammel it, word would spread that Lord Rushden had married.

The notion settled the last of Simon's nerves. It would be an interesting night at the dinner tables in Mayfair. The game, as they said, was afoot.

Dawkins cleared his throat. "Your lordship, if you would take the bride's hands."

Her small fingers were cold and steady. Not by a flicker of her lashes did she react to his touch. Simon fought back the impulse to squeeze, to tighten his grip until she reacted. She should be more nervous than he. She thought this marriage was unbreakable.

Ridiculous, this sudden guilt.

She lifted her brow now. Questioning his stare. He mustered a smile, which she readily returned. He focused on that glimpse of tooth where her lips did not quite meet—that gap that had seemed such a provocation when he'd first spied it, a baring of something unmeant to be seen.

But almost immediately, her smile changed, her lips tightening, shutting her teeth away. She deliberately restrained her smile. No doubt someone had told her that ladies were not meant to grin so broadly. And she'd believed this advice, as of course she should, since it was true.

The thought drove a pang through him. What a pity it would be if her uniqueness was flattened into the regular ways of the herd.

But wasn't that the aim?

"Marriage is not to be entered into unadvisedly or lightly, but reverently, deliberately," Dawkins intoned. The right words, nothing in them to mark that this marriage ultimately might be a sham.

Nell's smile yet lingered, very slight, the look of a woman lost in private thoughts. She had ideas and Simon could not guess at what they might be. Was she envisioning a happy future for them? He hadn't bothered to discuss with her what their marriage of convenience might entail. He'd never imagined it would be necessary to enlighten her: her cynicism, after all, seemed a match for his own.

The liturgy unfolded. As she spoke her vow in a clear, strong voice, he felt a frown creeping over his brow. He felt restless, suddenly, as though her grip were the only thing holding him in this room. Marrying a woman in rags would have rendered this occasion more transparent. But an onlooker, right now, might mistake this for something other than it was. They might mistake it as a romance.

They might think he actually cared for this woman.

"I will," Simon had just said. That meant they were married. The fat man was about to pronounce them husband and wife. Nell cut another wary look toward the deacon: a fraud, perhaps? And yet . . . all these witnesses: the entire staff lined up against the wall. The lawyer, Daughtry, stood beside the butler, straight-faced, earnestly observant. Would a man of the law show up to witness a fraud's ceremony? Maybe if Simon paid him enough.

For himself, Simon looked genuinely puzzled as the deacon spoke the conclusion: "Those whom God has joined together let no one put asunder," he said, and Simon's frown deepened, as no doubt did her own: this shared look between them was taking on the flavor of mutual confusion, as though each of them had been waiting for the other to break first—*All right, you got me, I didn't mean it*—and now found themselves baffled, stunned: had this really just happened?

As the deacon began the closing prayer, a hysterical feeling tickled her throat, the beginning of a lunatic laugh. After the dreams she'd had last night—one nightmare right after another, in all of which Simon had mocked her, scorned her as a slum rat—she'd woken convinced that something awful was going to happen today. Simon was kind but not an idiot. He wouldn't marry her before her inheritance was guaranteed. They'd all but tupped last night on his billiards table—and afterward, she'd been ready and willing for *more*. No peer of the realm took such a woman to wife! Since she'd walked into this room, she'd been braced for the joke: he would pull away, shake his head, wave everybody out, simply flick them away like flies off a pastry, as went his usual style. *Changed my mind. Let's call it off.*

But he hadn't. She could barely comprehend it. They were *married*.

"You may kiss the bride," said the reverend—to confirm her thoughts or maybe to prompt them both to action: they were staring at each other like proper dolts.

She heard a cough from the servants' side. A murmur ran through the room.

Simon blinked. "Yes," he said. "Of course." His face cleared; kissing, he was not confused about. "By all means." He leaned down. She waited, watching him, slack-mouthed still with surprise.

His lips brushed hers. Instantly, he retreated.

A snort escaped her. *Oops.* She put her fingers to her lips. His frown returned. He scowled down at her, the master of the house, his dignity offended.

She laughed. She couldn't help it. Lord High and Mighty had just *pecked* her like a fussy aunt.

"There you go," she said, all but brimming with hilarity. He looked so bloody disgruntled, glaring down at her. At least the servants were getting a good show! Her laughter sounded giddy, drunk.

The murmur behind her rose to a mutter. Yes, she thought, that's right: the new countess, she's off her rocker.

The deacon cleared his throat. Dutiful, godly, he attempted to recall her to the audience. "Your ladyship, your lordship, allow me to convey my best wishes."

Simon's lips pressed together; he took an audible breath through his nose. "Our thanks," he said. Perhaps a bit of a tremble on that last syllable.

"Yes," she said, locking eyes with her new husband. Lifting her brow. "Our thanks."

His cheek hollowed, as though he were biting the inside of it. "Lady Rushden, then." Definitely a tremble. And then suddenly he was grinning at her. "My *lady.*"

She pressed her knuckles to her mouth. Nodded. "Apparently," she said.

"So it seems," he agreed, and then laughed, a

short, somewhat wild sound. "It suits you," he said. "Countess."

Her breath caught. *Countess.* Had a choir of angels appeared to sing it, the word couldn't have amazed her more.

He'd done it.

He'd married her.

This man, this beautiful, charming, maddening man, was her *husband* now.

His smile slowly faded. Her face must be speaking something strange. Peck her like an auntie, would he? The beautiful dolt.

She stepped toward him, heedless of the servants, of the reverend, of Mrs. Hemple, who doubtless waited to scold her for some mistake. She was a countess now; what was *this* lot going to do if she misbehaved? She took hold of her husband's broad, warm shoulder—smiled into his blinking surprise—and went up on her tiptoes to plant her mouth squarely on his.

Mine, she thought. Her hand slid up into his hair. She didn't want fussy pecks from him; a husband should be bolder. With her free hand, she caught his elbow and tugged him right up against her. *Mine.*

For the space of a heartbeat his surprise held him motionless. And then, with a smothered laugh, he took her by the waist and pulled her into him harder yet, returning in equal measure the kiss she gave him: a deep, hot tangling of tongue and teeth, her breasts crushed into his chest, his knees in her skirts, the heat leaping wildly between them.

When she pulled away, she was breathless and he was grinning. "Right," he said.

"Right," she said fiercely.

His hand closed around her arm. He tugged her

around so sharply that she almost lost her balance. "May I present the Countess of Rushden?" he asked the room, which was gaping at her as though she'd stripped to her knickers and done a little dance.

But the room, knowing Lord Rushden had no use for its permission to do anything, understood his question for the order it was. Collecting their jaws from the floor, they bowed and bobbed, while Nell clutched Simon's large, lovely hand and smiled back at them all. "God bless you," she said to the company.

God bless the whole bloody world!

Like any girl, Nell had dreamed of a marriage for herself: some shy lad waiting in the rough wood hall of the parish church, a body of guests turning to smile at her in their patched Sunday finest. A dance at the pub afterward. Rollicking fiddle music and tankards of ale. No more than half an hour into this merriment, her groom would urge her to steal away, the two of them slipping out the back door to avoid the hooting of the lads. They'd fall into each other's arms in the first dark, private room they could find.

But the nobs did it differently. First came a stiff celebration in the morning room, in which the servants toasted their master and new mistress and cheered the news of a half holiday. Then came a formal meal in the dining room, during which Simon seemed distracted and overly polite, as if she were some stranger whom he'd just met at the altar. After dinner, he retired to his study, a thing he'd never done before, leaving Nell to mount the stairs alone.

She wasn't nervous, not even when she found Sylvie waiting in her bedroom with a costume of scandalous dimensions—a robe and nightgown of white silk, the neckline cut so low that a girl couldn't stand too quickly for fear of shaking herself out of it. "Stop blushing," she told Sylvie as she slipped it on. Aye, this was a costume for tupping, but what of it? Every mother in the world had managed the act.

The maid finally excused herself, leaving Nell alone in the deep, thick silence peculiar to this house. She spent a minute at the mirror looking at herself. Her face had grown a bit rounder in the last weeks; her arms had fleshed out and the yellow tobacco stains had faded from her fingers. Soon her body would show no signs of her former life. She was decked out like a harlot bride, dressed all in white but barely clad.

Growing restless, she walked into the sitting room, took up a book, and curled into an armchair. But the sentences on the page—a bit of fanciful history about the ancient Persians—made no sense, though the English was plain.

She laid down the book and breathed for a while. Her eyes knew where they wanted to go, but she made them watch the fire, burning so merrily in the blue-tiled hearth, in this soft, luxurious room, amid walls molded in gilt, beneath a ceiling painted to resemble a summer sky. She wasn't worried at all.

The door across the room—the door (Polly had told her in passing) which opened into his lordship's apartments—remained shut.

She forced herself back to the book. It wasn't until the muffled chimes of the clock in the hallway struck eleven that a knock finally came at that door.

She'd been waiting but it still struck her as a shock. Her fingers tightened over the book and wouldn't loosen. No point in being nervous, but her vocal chords didn't realize that.

The knock came again.

She pinched herself, a sharp little pain. Stupid to be nervous! "It's open," she croaked.

The door swung inward. "Took you long enough," said St. Maur.

How romantic. She measured him up. No special outfit for the man, it seemed. He looked half disassembled, his fine neck cloth gone, his charcoal vest hanging open. The open collar of his snow-white shirt exposed the length of his throat and a small glimpse of sparse black chest hair. No jacket.

She glanced beyond him into the darker furnishings of his sitting room, an Oriental carpet of bronze and green, a low chaise longue covered in chestnut velvet. Masculine colors. He had a fire going in there, too.

She looked down to the book. Back up to him. Her body seemed to have forgotten the natural rhythm of breathing. She put aside the book as her mood clarified: she was annoyed. "I was waiting," she said. "You're the one who's late."

He smiled a little. Put his hands into his pockets and dropped his shoulder against the doorjamb. He looked so utterly at home in this rich house, so casually in possession of its wealth.

A dark feeling swelled through her. He stood only feet away, but there was a subtler distance between them that would never be spanned. No matter how he tried, he would never know the whole of her. Never guess that more than once, she'd knocked a rat away from a loaf of bread before eating it. That she'd gone on her knees in the mud to grab up coins tossed by men and women like him, while they'd laughed from the windows of their fine coaches.

He'd never guess these things because imagination wasn't enough to compass the distance between his world and Bethnal Green. Nothing could span that distance. Had any bridge existed between the two worlds, one or the other would have burned already.

He said, "My apologies for keeping you waiting, milady"—speaking lightly, playfully.

"That's all right," she said hoarsely. She felt herself balanced precariously on the edge of something. At the next step, the step onto new territory, that bridge behind her would collapse.

His head tipped, his temple coming to rest against the door frame. He tested the title against the sight before him: "Lady Rushden," he murmured.

She wanted to take the step. It scared her and it drew her. They were married now—before God and man, as the saying went. She wanted to stay on his side of the bridge. She wanted to be done with hunger, with cold, with fear. He was as beautiful as the world in which he lived. She wanted to stay with him forever.

She took a bracing breath and rose. Her limbs felt stiff. He need never know what the other side was like. He need never learn of the rats, of the bitter nights and begging. He was hers now and tonight would make it official. Nobody was taking him away from her.

Only he hadn't moved an inch from the door.

She squared her shoulders and raised her chin. He wouldn't be backing out now. They would see this through. "May we get on with it?"

He laughed at her. "Goodness. Will it be so bad as all that?"

That laugh lit her temper. To have waited in this chair all night for him, ill with worry—she realized now, in an instant—that he regretted the marriage, that he was out conferring with lawyers on how to undo it—only to have him *laugh* at her? And all the time she'd waited, like a worried, faithful dog. What right had *he* to keep her waiting?

Every right.

She caught her breath. Aye, now that they were married, she had no choice in anything, did she? For the rest of her life, whenever the mood struck him, he'd do with her as he liked, would require her to walk through that door in which he lounged right now and bare herself to him.

Or to wait. It would be his choice, not hers.

But *one* choice did remain to her. A small one, but a choice all the same.

She walked toward him. He straightened off the door frame, interested, alert. She focused on the spot where his hair brushed his collar, inky black curls that lay this way and that over the crisp white cloth. Her hand slid through those curls, soft and warm, and felt the heat of his skin as her palm closed over his nape. She pulled his head to hers.

It was the second time today that she'd kissed him, and this time he was ready for her: his hands came around her waist, his lips firm. She stepped into him and forced him back a step. She would be a different kind of wife. She wouldn't wait on his decision. *She* was deciding.

Simon had been trying to decide on his approach— absurd exercise; he'd put more time into thinking of how to seduce his own wife (his wife, he was married) than he'd ever given to seductions rightfully more complex, of wives whose husbands kept unpredictable schedules, of women with jealous lovers and important political connections. He'd nearly had her last night on his billiards table but today, it had seemed so important to show restraint. To prove to himself that he could be restrained.

He'd kept himself away from his apartments (mindful, constantly and despite himself, of the door that joined his sitting room to hers) through the postdinner brandy, through an hour or more of staring sightlessly at piano scores sent to him by somebodies or others in search of a patron; and then, having advanced up the stairs, somehow (he didn't recall his passage) he'd found himself in his sitting room waiting for the strike of the clock. Hanging on the silence, waiting for the chimes to puncture it, like a trembling child on Christmas morning, congratulating himself for this fine show of self-control: eleven o'clock, a fine hour to bed one's wife. A very respectable specimen of restraint, those three hours he'd passed in chaste absentia.

But now his efforts looked less noble than ludicrous. Seduction? He was being seduced. She came at him like a storm, her mouth hungry and hot, her small hands gripping tightly as an animal creature's, her body writhing up against him.

He was willing, delighted . . . puzzled, for a fleeting moment. Very fleeting.

He cupped her by the elbows and drew her into his rooms, away from that chair where she'd been cuddled up with Herodotus—God save him, he'd taken a guttersnipe bluestocking to wife; what were the odds of that? Guided her into the safety of his less scholarly confines, where behind him a fire crackled and every preparation—champagne, wine, a pot of chocolate, she liked chocolate—had been laid to woo her. Only she did not require wooing. Of course she didn't. Whom had he imagined he'd married? She'd kissed him today in front of his entire staff; it had been all he could do not to push her against the wall at that moment, before everyone.

No restraint now. He wanted to devour her. He turned her around, slouching a little to prevent their separation; she was not short, but he was tall—too tall, perhaps. He had vague intentions of steering her through the next door, into the bedroom; these small questions of height could be neatly resolved once they both were horizontal.

But then her hands found his shirt and gave it a yank, and the ripping sound—a button flew off, the tab broken—seemed to startle her. She froze. All at once, he was holding a block of wood.

He pulled back, torn between a snort and a laugh when he beheld her expression: rounded eyes, rounded pink lips. She was shocked by herself.

"Only a button," he murmured, reaching out to hook a finger around her little ear, her hair falling in wisps over his knuckles.

She blinked. A delicate blush spread through her cheeks. "I'm sorry about that," she said.

"I can afford a new button."

She bit her lip, chastened, childlike in her guilt, in the confession that followed: "I think I ripped your trousers, too."

He laughed, delighted by this. "I have others." In fact, he felt grateful for the interruption, for the way it had slowed them. There were wonders here to attend to. Her skin was warm and resilient, her cheek soft beneath his stroking fingers. He watched his knuckles chart the side of her throat, knocking away the robe. The gown beneath it was sleeveless, light: a gown for a bridal night.

He traced the smooth curve of her shoulder. "Bend your arm," he murmured.

She blinked at him, puzzled and wary, but obeyed: her hand rose to grip his elbow. So finely muscled, her limbs: he rubbed his thumb along the small bulge of her bicep, then bent down to take it in his teeth, as he'd longed to do from the moment he'd seen it bared. Her inhalation was soft but distinct. Her muscle contracted further as she tensed.

He flicked his tongue along her skin, then pressed a kiss there. Whoever had decided that muscles were not beautiful on a woman had been a fool, ignorant of the variations in nature's genius. He felt down to the sharp point of her elbow. Amazing how his palm covered her so completely, cupped her so wholly. Her presence was so outsized that one easily forgot how narrow, how finely fashioned were her bones. How fragile in the flesh she was.

It came to him that she was trembling, her breath coming faster. He straightened. Her flush was deepening, her lips parted.

He watched those lips as he slid his hand down to her waist, then around to the curve of her lower back. What peculiar pleasure there was in charting someone's, no, this woman's angles and curves and planes, she who'd resisted him so stridently now watching open-eyed, breathless, as he made himself free with her body. It had been sweet to touch her before, but now her consent was wholly his, and her willingness worked its own power on him, lending even the brush of his skin against hers a carnal complexity: *she* was going to be his. There was no question any longer where these touches would lead.

He stroked her spine with his thumb as he leaned

down. Her eyes drifted shut; she lifted her face to his. Her cheeks were rosy, her lashes long, sable. A trembling bride, awaiting her husband's first kiss. He did not even want to mock the thought.

He took her lower lip gently in his. She tasted of chocolate. She drank chocolate as a child would, delighted, gleeful, as if each sip tasted better than the last. He could feed her pots of it, perhaps, before she grew tired of it, or failed to glow at the taste. As he tasted it on her lips, he could understand her enthusiasm. He licked into her mouth, looking for more of the flavor. Her tongue met his, shyly; he felt her hands slip around his waist.

He smiled against her mouth, delighted with himself, with how unexpected this moment was becoming: a hundred clichés came to mind as their tongues tangled, clichés made vibrant by the wondrous truths they suddenly appeared to contain. He closed his eyes, fighting the urge to gather her to him, to push himself up against her, into her, to crush her beneath him. *My God, she is sweet.*

Her body came against his anyway, of her accord. The kiss deepened. He cupped her nape and walked her backward; she followed his lead pliantly, elegantly, graceful as a woman raised to complex dances. Together they crossed the threshold into the bedroom, sat onto the bed, still kissing, so earnestly, yes, this was earnest; he would have kissed this woman for hours no matter where he found her. He swept his hand up her back, into her hair, and realized his hand was trembling. Hot and desperate and gluttonous and hesitant and uncertain and tentative as a boy with his first woman: this moment, this simple bedding, was turning into something strange.

He broke the kiss, sitting back, breathing deeply, uneasy suddenly. The scent of her was lilies and lavender. Her eyes met his. Dark blue, ageless in their depths, they swallowed his attention. She reached out to touch his face, silent, her expression solemn, and parts of him, his skin, his lungs, expanded, prickling with sensation. He felt her touch low in his gut, like the contraction before a sharp blow.

He opened his mouth to speak, then bit his tongue, battling some sudden, low urge to break the moment with a comment he would not be able to take back. The silence felt too weighty. Her eyes pressed too keenly on his.

"It's all right," she said softly.

A knot formed in his throat. He spoke from old, defensive reflex, dry and sharp. "Yes. I've done this before."

He regretted it instantly. He sucked in a breath and she started to pull away. *You goddamned fool.* He caught her hand beneath his and turned his lips into it in apology, shutting his eyes, wrestling with a peculiar sensation of embarrassment. In the darkness behind his eyes, sitting here with his thigh pressed to hers, she did not feel like a stranger to him; she did not feel merely convenient. She did not feel convenient in the least.

Silk rustled. He felt the heat of her skin, smelled the lilies more strongly, before her lips touched his throat. Some soft noise escaped him. He folded his lips together to prevent another, wondering at himself, unnerved.

Her foot came atop his, a warm, slight weight, as though to pin him in place. She moved against him, a languorous undulation that brought her breasts into his chest and made his breath catch. Her tongue flicked lightly along the bare skin where his throat and shoulder joined.

He felt his balls tighten. The heaviness, the lift and contraction, was all it took: animal hunger simplified his view. His uncertainty now a dimming memory, ludicrous, he knew what he wanted: to cover her, hold her down, and penetrate her as she moaned.

Simple.

He took her beneath her arms and lifted her across the bed. She lay back, her dark hair streaming around her, as he came over her on hands and knees. He drew his open mouth from her lips to her throat, setting his teeth, very lightly, against the tender skin there. Her sigh lifted the hairs on his nape. A woman like this, so yielding, her skin silk-soft, her hands clever and unpredictable, her nails turning into his back as her hips lifted beneath him, was a rare gift: a dream to lead a man home from the dark.

He brushed aside the neckline of her chemise. To think he'd not even seen her breasts fully bared until now, that imagination could never have compassed their beauty, when all the time they'd been waiting for his attentions: small but perfectly shaped, sweet now beneath his tongue. He put his mouth to her stiffening nipple and she gasped.

He suckled, taking her between his teeth, flicking his tongue to draw, like magic, another sound from her throat—higher, almost desperate as she writhed beneath him. His hand skated down the uneven landscape of her ribs, the sharp curve where her waist indented. Her belly's smooth slope carried his palm farther yet, until he touched the soft curls between her legs, a slick, hot delta cradled, protected, by the tensile strength of her thighs. She bucked harder, the audible rasp of her breath sharpening to almost a keen. She was hot, so hot. He lifted his fingers to his mouth to taste her.

Nell dragged in a breath. He was bent over her like some mythical creature, a succubus, a vampire, feasting on her. His mouth released her and he looked up the line of her body, his eyes finding hers, glittering. A cloud slipped free of the moon and cold light poured through the windows, bathing in silver the hard set of his features, the flaring of his nostrils. He was breathing hard, long deep rasps like a man who'd been running.

He did not smile at her. Their eyes locked and he stared, his mouth a flat, fixed line, his expression so intense, so dark, that for a single moment she felt a flutter of fear. Spread out before him, helpless—

His hand closed over her wrist, holding it to the bed. Stopping her before she even recognized the intention to push herself up. "It's me," he said.

She froze, panting herself, helpless in his regard, trapped in it.

"Only me," he said. He came up over her and rolled his hips against her and the breath escaped her, catching on her vocal chords, a low, startled moan that made her flush all over.

She sounded like an animal. She felt like an animal, pinned beneath him. Her body knew what to do. She bucked against him and his hand loosened on her wrist, his thumb tracing a firm line. "Yes," he said, very low.

His other hand closed on her ankle, sliding slowly upward, turning so the edge of his nail drew a whispering line up her calf. She laid her head back to the pillow, staring up at the blurring ceiling. Pulses beat everywhere, behind her knees, in the tips of her breasts, most intensely, most deliciously, between her legs, at the spot his slow hand now, finally, reached, as he eased his hips away just enough to permit himself access: he cupped her very lightly, too lightly, and then, all at once, firmly, possessively, the heel of his palm rolling against her.

A guttural sound burst from her throat. Now she didn't care. Her consciousness was too heated and swollen for delicacies such as words.

His thumb prodded, finding the source of her throbbing, circling it once. He leaned down, his long body lowering against hers everywhere, his hand trapped between them, his mouth finding her ear, hot breath, low voice: "I am going to put my mouth here." He drew back, giving her the devil's own smile. It faded, replaced by a dark, concentrated look as he studied her, devoured her with his eyes. Then, silently, he moved down her body.

And oh sweet God in heaven, he did put his mouth there. First the briefest touch of his tongue, teasing, just the lightest flick—a notice to her: *this is where I will touch you*—and then a long, hungry stroke that made the top of her head lift off. She lay back, helpless to do anything else, and clutched his head as he made good on his promise: as the pleasure built within her, pulsing, pulsing harder, spiking and splintering her into hard, fierce contractions, she did not think of anything at all; she simply gloried.

Her eyes closed, panting, she heard the soft sound of cloth sliding. For a moment he withdrew from her. She was limp, too drained almost to open her eyes, but when he lay back down over her, the shock of heat from his skin against hers jarred her back into a building tide of want.

"Yes?" he said softly.

He made some slight adjustment of his hips and she felt him come up against her, a solid, blunt pressure, poised to invade her. But he was asking, and if she said no . . . *he would listen.*

The idea moved through her like electricity, this piece of faith in him she hadn't known she possessed. But he deserved such faith. He'd never misused his power with her.

She lifted her head to kiss him, the contact hard, almost bruising, the feeling in her almost violent. "Yes," she said against his mouth. "*Yes.*"

He cupped her head in his broad palm, cradling her for his kiss as he pressed his hips into hers. She tensed at the discomfort, sharp, not pleasant; then he filled her, pressed into her, the burn fading. She was full beyond measure, pinned beneath him, penetrated, her head still encompassed in his cradling grip. Her own hands skated down the broad, strong plane of his back, slipping down to the flex of his buttocks as he moved inside her. The sensation took her breath. He thrust steadily at first, such a curious feeling. She felt . . . possessed.

She lifted her hips and his mouth broke from hers to coast down her throat, softly biting the crook of her neck. His groan made a shiver run through her. With their bodies joined, his flesh communicated directly with hers. She turned her lips into his hair. The smell of his skin was like the woods on a moonlit night; it made the wild parts of her waken.

"Harder." That hoarse voice was hers; her nails sank into the solid flex of his pumping buttocks, directing that power, those muscles, into his use of her body; he rolled his hips against hers and thrust harder, and she felt it coming again, the pleasure: she would melt into the bed or leave him raked bloody.

The pleasure of being human, of being vulnerable: as her muscles contracted around him, he lifted his head to look into her eyes, and something passed between them. She fell into him as though into a dark, soft silence, everything in her going still. She wrapped her arms tightly around him, unsure for a dizzying moment where she ended and he began; boneless, liquid against him, so much at home that her own body seemed superfluous.

His expression hardened. Briefly, it puzzled her; his look seemed so close to pain. And then his eyes closed and he shuddered, a soft moan announcing that he felt the furthest thing from pain—that he was lost in pleasure as overpowering as what she had felt.

She watched, fascinated, as his tension slowly eased, his mouth softening, the grip of his hands gentling. How young he looked, suddenly—his lower lip as full as a child's.

His head now dropped to her breast, his forehead settling into the crook of her neck. She pushed a hand through his hair as his ragged breath slowed. Another, smaller shiver moved through him, and wonder touched her. She could never have guessed that a man might seem so vulnerable at this moment— or that, lying beneath him, she might feel so curiously strong. Her body bore Simon's weight so easily. She did not feel used at all. She felt ferociously, vibrantly alive.

That night Nell lay awake long after Simon had fallen into sleep. With his arms around her, she found the whispering of the rain at the windows didn't sound melancholy as much as . . . peaceful. Noises in the night didn't make her flinch; they gave her an excuse to move closer to him, more deeply into his embrace.

But after long minutes or hours in the silence—she no longer had any grasp of how time was passing—a strange excitement crept over her. She was lying next to *him*, and he wore not a lick of clothing. Sleep seemed positively wasteful.

She inched out of his grasp. Several slow tugs on the sheet bared him to the scope of the moonlight. The air across his bare skin caused him to shift in his dreams, and her breath caught as the bands of muscle across his abdomen contracted with his movement.

So much to see: a dark line of hair arrowed down to his cock, which slept cradled between hard thighs dusted with more black hair.

His thighs narrowed in sharp vees into neat, square kneecaps. Earlier, when he had padded away to fetch water, she had noticed the sharp shelves of his calf muscles, how they flexed as he walked. His bum had looked taut, with twin dimples above each cheek.

As his wife, was it her right to pinch them?

She bit down on her fingers to keep them from misbehaving, then looked up his body again. His shoulders were broad and thick, his biceps bunched in the arm tossed over his head.

He'd mentioned, once or twice, swimming: he liked to swim in the early mornings, she gathered, at some gymnasium in Kensington. She supposed that explained his body.

Never stop swimming, she thought.

It came to her that she was grinning like a loon. She yanked the sheets back over him and then squirmed into his side, putting her arse against his groin.

His arm came around her waist and tightened. For a second she thought she'd awakened him. "Simon?" she whispered.

He murmured something unintelligible—*goose pastry*, it sounded like—and put his face into her hair.

She swallowed a giggle and forced her eyes to close. *Sleep*, she told herself. *No reason not to sleep. You're happy, is all.*

Which seemed miraculous in itself.

This *was* happiness, she thought. And this was her *husband*. Both of them—*both* of them—were really, truly hers.

13

ℕell St. Maur was not a creature of the morning
hours. Simon woke her with a kiss only to watch her
fall back asleep. He nibbled on her ear for a bit, which
coaxed out an appreciative noise that collapsed into a
snore. He sat beside her, at a loss for a moment, and
then lost for a long minute in simply admiring how
frankly her face advertised her spirit: the stubborn
square of her jaw, the saucy point of her chin, the bold
lines of her dark brows.

He ran a finger down her cheek. No response. She
was dead to the world.

Whimsical thought: he wanted her awake because
he missed her.

He leapt off the bed and opened the curtains, then
watched in amusement as she rejected the daylight
with a hand tossed—more accurately, flopped—across
her eyes. When he returned to the bed and blew on her
cheek, she made a small noise of irritation and rolled
away from him.

An idea struck. He turned and padded from his
own rooms into hers, where her blushing maid sat
waiting beside a cooling pot of chocolate. No, he told
the girl, he did not require her help to carry the tray.

Her smothered giggles followed him back into his
apartment.

One wave of the cup beneath his wife's nose brought
her to scowling, rumpled life. The fingers shielding her
face widened, allowing him a glimpse of lashes rising,

falling, then rising again. With an audible sniff, she pushed herself up by an elbow. "Chocolate," she said hoarsely, and seized the cup.

He sat back, smiling as she shoved a handful of chestnut hair out of her face. At the first sip, her eyes closed again and the look on her face made his body tighten. They'd enjoyed each other three times last night, but another day brought with it new opportunities. And they were, after all, in a bed together already.

"I do believe you prefer chocolate to me," he said teasingly.

She lowered the cup and met his eyes. "No." She cleared her throat. "I do not."

The color rising on her cheeks riveted him. "Blushes?" She'd been so magnificently uninhibited last night.

"Not for shame," she said softly.

"No," he agreed, just as quiet. "That would be foolish indeed."

Their look held, becoming magnetic somehow: comfortable yet all-consuming; he felt no need to look away and she did not lower her eyes. Perhaps this was what obsession felt like. Yes, he thought: he had a full-blown and still growing obsession with this woman he'd married.

Should it unnerve him? It had, in the past. He could no longer remember why. This blush, so lovely . . . Every moment he looked at her, she seemed to offer something new. "Drink," he said.

She lifted a brow, then took his suggestion with enthusiasm. Once upon a time, she had slurped. No longer. The grime was gone; her accent was smoothing out; she no longer fell on her food as though she feared it might be taken from her. Often he found himself for-getting her roots entirely.

Or, no—he hadn't forgotten whence she came. But lately he found himself marveling at her for reasons that had nothing to do with her history. He did not admire a guttersnipe's quick wit or a guttersnipe's grasp of sophisticated literary techniques; he admired, simply, *her*: a woman of unusual insight, unafraid of disagreement, but also generous in her concessions when he made a sound point; intelligent, quick-witted, delightful company.

Delicious company. She yawned, showing a small pink tongue, covering her mouth with one hand, kit-tenish, impossible not to touch. He caught a lock of her hair, rubbing the silken strands. How demure she looked, how small in his bed. Such a deceptive appear-ance of fragility. When the mood struck, she could deal a set-down as sharp as any her father ever authored.

The thought gave him pause. Perhaps it wasn't a coincidence that the first woman to truly capture his interest in years also happened to be the first to dis-approve of him so sternly. He wasn't in the business of sticking his head into the sand: he could see that his feelings for her might contain an echo of his old, quixotic quest. In her disapproval, she bore more than a passing resemblance to Rushden—whom he'd tried to please, time and again, until it had become clear that his own spirit would be the cost for it.

He smoothed her hair back behind her ear and she gave him a frowning little look. Ironic that her disap-proval should wreak the opposite effect of her father's. It filled him with a frustrated, hungry, unnervingly intense desire to discover how to please her. How to locate, or fashion, the key that would unlock her trust—or, failing that, the spot to hit with a hammer to crack her open.

"What?" she asked. He'd been staring too intently. "Do I have chocolate somewhere?" She reached up to pat the corners of her mouth, looking flustered and entirely feminine.

"No," he said. "No chocolate. Only you." And that, he feared, was enough.

Her flush was spreading down her throat, into smooth terrain concealed by the sheet hiked beneath her arms. It occurred to him that he'd wondered about that blush. He reached for the sheet and she squealed, leaning away from him. "Hey! What's this?" she demanded.

"A husbandly inquiry. I believe I once expressed a need to know how far your blushes extend."

"Oh." She eyed him for a moment before breaking into an impish smile. "Well, then," she said, setting aside the cup of chocolate. "Why don't you come find out?"

Some two hours after they awoke, Simon escorted his new wife from his apartment toward the breakfast room. "I am quite serious," he said, speaking over her laughter. "I'm going to carry you over some threshold or another. It's quite scandalous that I didn't even lift you into my rooms. I can't imagine what I was thinking last night."

With a sparkling look from under her lashes, she said, "Oh, I can think of one or two things that were on your mind." She lowered her voice, mocking his own: "*Took you long enough,*" she said gruffly.

He laughed back at her. He was in charity with the world, too amazed with his good luck, with the wondrous kindness that fate had performed in presenting him this woman. "Take care," he said. "I might have hauled you over my shoulder long before this: to the magistrate, that first night." The memory of it now amazed him. How fortunate for him that he hadn't. So easily she might have been lost to him.

"You're lucky I didn't get away," she replied promptly. "If I hadn't been kind enough to tarry and chat with you, I'd have made a neat job of it, too."

"I'd like to hear how," he said. "One shout from me and the entire house would have been up in arms."

She snorted. "Right here," she said, waving in front of him; they had reached the top of the staircase. "I would have slid down this banister, past all your gawping servants, and shimmied on out the door."

"The balustrade?" He ran a skeptical eye down its length. "A happy thing you decided to tarry, then. You'd have broken your neck."

She snorted. "This here is a prime prospect for sliding, St. Maur."

He opened his mouth but was startled by a dim recollection that caused him instead to laugh. "You're right." As a boy he'd had these exact thoughts: it *was* the perfect banister for sliding. He'd never done it, of course; it hadn't taken long to realize that banisters in this house were not meant even for gripping: a proper gentleman should make his way down the stairs straight and stern and untroubled by any obstacle, even a missed step.

A devil seized hold of him. "Let's do it," he said. Why not?

Disbelief deepened her smile. "You can't be serious."

"God help us, but that's a phrase nobody should have taught you," he said. "Now you sound like every stuffed-up lady I've ever known."

Her eyes narrowed. "Stuffed up, am I? I'll wager you can't keep your seat past the curve."

He eyed the drop from the aforementioned curve. A good ten feet to the marble flagstones below. It could crack a man's head. "For the sake of the St. Maur line, one hopes otherwise. But I suppose there's only one way to find out." He leapt up to sit on the rail.

She shrieked. "No! I wasn't—"

"Serious?" he finished for her, and then let go.

Like flight. No friction: his staff was too well trained; they oiled this banister morning and night. Nell continued to shriek above him. He laughed as he leaned into the curve, exhilarated and also aware of how absurd this was, to laugh his head off at a boy's game. Such a simple pleasure. Such joy.

The bend flew by; he was home free now, bound at startling speeds for the bottom of the staircase. He remembered this skill at the level of muscle and sinew; he pushed himself off the rail and landed on his feet at the base of the stairs.

He turned around. She stood at the top of the stairs, hands cupped over her mouth.

"Graceful as the breeze," he called up.

She dropped her hands to her hips. "More like a lunatic!"

"And you're a braggart. All talk. No follow-through."

He could see from here the sudden tilt of her chin. Another laugh welled in him as she stalked over to the banister, her movements jerky with spite. She was too easy.

But she didn't hop up on the railing quite as easily as he had. Of course. Her skirts would impede her.

Concern overlaid his amusement. "Don't," he said. "I was only jesting. You're not dressed for—"

She launched herself down.

He made an aborted movement to mount the stairs. But she was moving too quickly; he would be as likely to knock her off as catch her. His mind began to calculate the best place to position himself on the ground floor, so that when she fell backward and came tumbling down, he could break the fall—

And she whooped. "Here I come," she cried, and he realized she was going to make it.

Laughing himself—from relief as much as from delight—he stepped backward to provide her space to land.

She made nearly a perfect dismount. But the speed caught up to her, so that she came stumbling forward, right into his arms.

No, he thought—a perfect dismount all around.

She was breathing hard, flushed, her eyes sparkling. "Told you," she said. "I would have gotten away."

"And I would have caught you then, too." As his attention fixed on her mouth, he remembered, with a pleasant shock, that they were married. He could kiss her wherever in his house he liked.

He leaned down. Her eyes widened, then her soft hands were covering his elbows, drawing him closer as she went up on her tiptoes. Their lips brushed, a hot reminder, too sweet not to be a prelude to something more.

"Upstairs," he murmured into her mouth, and felt her soundless laughter warm his lips. He was physically turning her, goading her to mount the stairs again, when a throat was pointedly cleared behind them.

Hemple. Blast the woman. Simon would have ignored her on any day but this one. Sighing, he transferred his hand from Nell's hip to the more decorous perch of her muscled upper arm. "Mrs. Hemple," he said in greeting. Nell's instructor looked pink. "I was just fetching your charge for you."

"How fortuitous," said the matron, looking between them anxiously. "It's an important day for her ladyship. A very momentous day, indeed. We cannot waste a minute."

He felt his bride tense. "What happens today?" she asked.

Christ, had he forgotten to tell her? He caught her hand and kissed it in apology. "Tonight," he said, "you make your debut into society."

Nell moved through the day like a drunkard, silly with thoughts of Simon. Hemple put her through her paces, demanding that she mime all manner of situations—being introduced to a fellow countess (a *fellow* countess!); to a marquess; to a princess; to some sorry baron who barely merited even a curtsy (and what an idea *that* was—that there were nobs now who ranked beneath her!). Nell bobbed as directed, her body barely registering the indignities. Her flesh no longer seemed her own. At the very thought of her husband, it throbbed.

Dressing for society was no small task. It began immediately after a late tea, when Sylvie, nervous as a fluttering bird, drew her upstairs to choose a gown. Apparently Simon had set her into a tizzy by informing her that the party would be small but exclusive.

Exclusive was the word over which Sylvie fretted. The heliotrope satin was cunning but its flounces, she argued, were too bold for elegance. The sapphire velvet would look lurid beneath the Allentons' electric lights; best save it for gas. The lavender-tinted taffeta—was it not too girlish? But the emerald silk shot through with threads of peacock blue, over which floated an overskirt of green tulle—this gown was sprightly yet mysterious in a feminine way, sure to strike a most elegant picture.

Nell, who hadn't known dresses had personalities, felt relieved to be offered the chance to approve. She rose to don a chemisette of fine silk in preparation to being strapped into her corset.

As she stripped off her woolen combination, Sylvie hastily averted her eyes. Nell looked down for the cause and found a love bite on the upper slope of her breast.

She felt her face catch fire. The high color still lingered when she sat down at the toilet table a quarter hour later so Sylvie could dress her hair. Could this feverish, bright-eyed girl in the mirror—this girl whose knees were quivering with thoughts of the night past—really be herself? For so long she'd believed that the only safe way to enjoy a man was to enjoy him less than he did her. But this giddiness that had seized her didn't allow for caution.

They were *married*. Surely she was safe now to feel as much as she liked?

Sylvie turned her hair into a high roll at the crown of her skull, then threaded the roll with a fine chain of emeralds that glimmered like green stars. "Very elegant," she pronounced.

"Half naked," Nell suggested. The gown had long, tight sleeves but it dipped very low in the front. Her breasts popped up like fresh-baked muffins.

"Elegant," Sylvie said adamantly. "Like a countess."

"Beautiful," came a low voice from the doorway.

Simon came forward, long and lean in a black evening suit, a leather box in his hand. He circled her once, a smile playing on his lips. "Elegant as well, of course—but the word is too bloodless to suit you."

His mouth was so beautifully shaped. Full, well-chiseled lips. She wished he wouldn't waste them on flattery. They had such better uses.

Her next words sounded hoarse. "Thank you; that's very kind." Mrs. Hemple had told her that a lady never argued with a compliment.

His smile widened briefly before disappearing. "This is for you," he said in a different, more formal voice.

She felt a flicker of unease as he opened the box—something in his manner put her on the alert. But the contents within the velvet-lined compartment robbed her of her wariness.

The necklace sported emeralds the size of robin's eggs. Those on the bracelet were not much smaller. The stones seemed alive in the light, casting a sparkle so vivid that she hesitated to touch them for some irrational fear they would singe her.

These jewels were fit for a queen.

"These have always belonged to the Countess of Rushden," Simon said. "Your mother wore them. She particularly loved the bracelet. In many of my memories of her . . ."

She looked up as he trailed off. His expression was impassive but she wasn't fooled. He had a knack for making his face unreadable at those moments when he felt the most.

"I loved her, of course," he said lightly. "Now they're yours."

She had no idea why tears suddenly stung her eyes. She reached up to touch his face. His eyes held hers, deeper and graver than she'd ever seen them. "Thank you," she said.

Her throat felt thick as she turned to face the mirror. She watched as he laid the necklace around her throat. His mouth touched her nape, a light, warm brush that made her shiver. His fingers slid along hers as he coaxed the bracelet onto her wrist, promises in the slow stroke of his fingertips.

The woman in the mirror colored. She took a large breath, then smiled—a strange and wise smile that sent a shock of recognition through Nell.

It was not a factory girl she saw in the glass, but a woman with jewels at her throat, with assurance in her proud carriage, with serene confidence in her eyes.

She had seen this lady before, in a photograph that hung in a shop window.

The Allentons' drawing room was candlelit. From the high ceiling, rosy Grecian gods looked down on guests who gleamed in silk and satin. The gold brocade of the damask upholstery winked in the low, inconstant light; gems flashed on throats and wrists. Some sweet, subtle spice scented the air. The soft bowing of a violinist hidden by a screen of ferns vied with the pleasant, steady murmur of conversation.

Nell's stomach cramped as she hesitated on the threshold. Here was a perfect dream of wealth. Right and left, luxury and smiles and gentle, understated laughter flourished. These people had no idea that they were about to meet a factory girl—about to curtsy to her, even.

Simon leaned near. "You belong here," he murmured.

She forced a smile to her lips. "I'm not nervous," she lied. She knew she wasn't a coward. On a deep breath, she took the step across the threshold.

"Lord Rushden!"

Simon steered her gently around to greet their approaching hostess, a short, plump, auburn-haired matron with the unremarkable but pleasant features of a Madonna.

The woman laid eyes on Nell and her serene smile collapsed. "I . . ." As Lady Allenton drew up, she looked rapidly between them. "Lady Katherine, good evening to you."

"Ah, I fear you misunderstand," said Simon courteously. "Lady Rushden, may I present Lady Richard Allenton? Lady Allenton, my wife, the Countess of Rushden."

Hearing her cue, Nell watched her own arm pop out like the stiff limb of a cranked automaton. *Harmonic poise,* Mrs. Hemple's voice silently chided.

But their hostess was too startled to note the finer points of the performance. "My goodness," said the lady. Bright color bloomed on her cheeks as she took Nell's fingers. She gave them a light press and bent her knee slightly.

There: the first curtsy. It triggered in Nell a rising tide of hilarity. Somebody with a *Lady* before her name had just *curtsied* to her.

Simon's shoulder brushed hers—a subtle nudge. *Right.* She wet her lips. "How do you do," she said.

"Very well," Lady Allenton said breathlessly. "But I had no idea—that is, my very best wishes to you, Kitty." Pursing her lips, she corrected herself: "Lady Rushden."

Nell's breath briefly stopped. "Lady Allenton," Simon said gently. "I fear you mistake my wife for her sister."

The lady's hand clamped around Nell's, then just

as quickly let go. She retreated a pace, her eyes huge. "I—" She swallowed. Shook her head. Then managed a little laugh. "Did I mishear you? I don't quite . . ."

"Forgive me," Simon said, "for breaking the news so suddenly."

Nell dared a brief look at him. His eyes met hers, the smallest smile curling the corner of his mouth. Didn't he look bloody jolly! She tried to smile back but her lips wouldn't do it.

"Well!" Lady Allenton shook her head once, then fell silent, as pop-eyed as a reverend at the devil. A pulse was beating visibly in her throat. Was she going to throw them out? Would she call for a guard? Would she—"You naughty, clever boy," she said, a look of humor entering her face as she turned to Simon.

Nell exhaled. Simon's dimple was flashing. "What can I say?" he replied.

"I can't even begin to imagine." Lady Allenton's eyes turned back to Nell. "I—what a pleasure! I don't expect you recall—" Her words now picked up speed, tumbling breathily over one another. "I knew your mother, of course, but you were so small—no, you wouldn't—but how devastated we were, afterward, how hopeless—" Her lips clamped shut, but her wondering gaze continued to rove over Nell's face. "I must ask," she burst out. "Where have you *been*?"

"And here you are!" A strapping, ginger-haired man bounded up to clap Simon on the shoulder. He sent a quizzical glance toward his frozen hostess, then looked onward to Nell. "Oh," he said, swallowing noisily. "Quite—quite right. Lady Rushden, then?"

"Lady Rushden," Simon said equably. "My lady, Lord Reginald Harcourt, a friend of old."

Nell gamely extended a hand, but the redhead had

bowed too quickly for her. "Terribly glad to meet you," he said as he popped up again, the grin on his face putting her in mind of a jack-in-the-box. She recognized his type. Sporting, jolly: he'd be comfortable down at the pub, singing sailor songs at the bar with the lads who liked to brawl after their fifth or sixth glass. "Expect you've come to set the crowd on its ear, eh?" He cocked an eyebrow at Lady Allenton. "The first victim."

"I am quite well," Lady Allenton murmured.

"No doubt of that," the man agreed. "Soiree of the season, what? A hard title to come by, once June rolls around, but I expect Rushden has clinched it for you."

The words seemed to rouse Lady Allenton. She looked around her as though coming awake. Her eyes narrowed as they returned to Nell, and then she smiled, suddenly and perfectly delighted.

"But what an honor," she said. "What an honor, that you should choose my little party to announce this—this miracle!" Her trilling laugh steadied, edging into robust glee. "Oh, yes. Lady Rushden, you *must* allow me to introduce you."

And so, at their hostess's direction, they walked from group to group, the first and second knots of guests greeting Nell with confusion—and then shock, much as Lady Allenton had done. But as their progress continued, leaving astonished exclamations in its wake, the entire room began to catch on. The genteel atmosphere dissolved into a sharp, increasingly frenetic babble that drowned out the violins. Only two words leapt clearly out of the hubbub: *Cornelia Aubyn*.

To her own surprise, Nell relaxed; she actually began to enjoy herself. Mrs. Hemple had framed this evening as a test, but Simon had been more correct: it wasn't a test as much as a spectacle, and her part in it barely required words. With each new person, she extended her hand, made a shallow curtsy, and then settled back to let them gawp and ogle her. Simon managed all the rest: he guided the stunned guests through their disbelief and into excitement; dexterously deflected their more complex inquiries about her former whereabouts; laughed often, generously, until his interlocutors laughed, too; accepted compliments on her behalf; and smoothed over those moments in which a question was put to her that she had no idea how to answer. "No, she's not so fond of hunting, but what a lovely invitation; and, yes, I'm working to change her mind"; "The gown is Worth, I believe, but altered by Madame Poitiers; you know she has a gift for muting the harsh French angles"; "Why, no, we were discussing it just last night; she hasn't chosen a favorite yet, but I'm wagering on Hunsdown's filly to take the race."

Nonsense, clever nonsense, all spun in Simon's low, smooth voice. He was a bloody genius with these people, slicker than any confidence artist, more popular than whisky in a room full of Irishmen. People doted on his remarks. They courted him and he rewarded them for it, lavishing his charm on anyone who wanted it, using his free hand to flirt, to deliver glancing brushes over ladies' wrists and solid, manly claps to gentlemen's shoulders. He radiated approval, amusement, *belonging*, and people gathered to him like stars around the moon. Under his influence, their avid curiosity about her shifted into simpler warmth; they looked at her anew, seeing not a grotesque surprise but a delightful discovery, *Rushden's* discovery.

When somebody pressed a glass of champagne into her hand, Nell lifted it to him in a silent toast, congratulating his cleverness. His eyes laughed back at her; in the pretext of inclining to speak in her ear, his lips brushed her temple. "Steady on," he said. "You're doing brilliantly."

She flushed at the compliment, though she hardly deserved it. In this hullabaloo, nobody noticed if her vowels occasionally collapsed on certain syllables; if, once, she slipped up and called a marquess *your lordship,* like a servant. But oh, sweet irony! Her tutors would have despaired at how this richly dressed crowd stared and stammered. As Lady Somebody-or-Other gabbled at her about the glorious righting of terrible injustices, she nodded and patted the woman's hand and thought, *Mind your E's, there, duck, and don't step so close when you speak to a girl: it ain't polite.*

When that lady finally stepped away, another took her place: a scarlet-gowned woman whose pale, heart-shaped face might have blurred with all the others had the sight of it not caused Simon to hesitate briefly before issuing a greeting.

The Viscountess Swanby was tall and dramatically curved, with pale blue eyes as sharp in their sparkle as glass. She received news of Nell's resurrection with unusual serenity, nodding through the introduction and then immediately inquiring whether or not Simon had received her invitation to a performance by some Hungarian pianist.

"Thank you, I did," he said.

Mrs. Hemple had told Nell one wasn't meant to allude to invitations in public, lest one's companions realize they'd been omitted from the guest list. But the blonde did not seem to realize her faux pas. "You can't miss the performance," she said. "I believe his *piano* is another man's *pianissimo*."

The Hungarian bloke had taken somebody else's . . . piano? Was a *pianissimo* a fancy brand of piano? Nell glanced uncertainly to Simon, who was nodding. "Certainly he has an unrivaled grasp of the counterpoint," he said.

Counterpoint. Now there was a word that *sounded* plain enough, but Nell couldn't imagine the meaning.

The viscountess, however, seemed clear on it. "Oh, yes," she enthused. "He makes me look with new wonder on the connection between musician and instrument. Why . . ." Her voice lowered. "I've never encountered a softer, more skillful touch."

Touch. In the viscountess's purring voice, the word seemed suggestive. Nell looked sharply toward Simon and saw that he was not smiling. For the first time all night, he made no effort to appear entertained. "Is that so?" he asked.

"Well, I've experienced it only once, of course," the viscountess replied. With a cold start, Nell realized that she was inching closer to Simon. "But I've never managed to forget it." Her ice-blue gaze trailed down Simon's body to the vicinity of his . . . hands. "Ever since, I've been longing to have him perform again."

Comprehension iced through Nell's stomach. This conversation might have been in Chinese and she still would have sensed the undercurrent here. "I suppose it might be more complicated than you expect," she said flatly. She could send her own message; she understood the idea of a *performance,* at least. "For you to arrange another show, I mean."

Simon's arm tensed beneath her hand. *Yes,* she thought blackly, *I'm not an idiot.*

The viscountess flicked her a dismissive glance. "Does Lady Rushden take a real interest in the arts, then?"

"She has a remarkable instinct for them," Simon said, his voice unreadable. "I should trust her opinion on any question touching on such matters."

For a second, faced with this bloodless exchange, Nell doubted her own suspicions. But then the viscountess lifted her brows, and her thin lips took on a superior, sneering curve as she said directly to Nell, "How lovely! Of course, when it comes to the arts, one must wish for a variety of diverse opinions, the better to invigorate the debate. Don't you think?"

The sneer in her voice dispelled all doubt. In Nell, this woman saw a rival.

Nell took a hard breath. In Bethnal Green, a wife would be lifting her fist about now. A wise husband would be retreating. Nobody would tolerate this odd, elliptical sparring. "I expect the right opinion is the only one you need," she said.

"If you'll excuse us," Simon said, but Nell resisted the pressure he was exerting on her arm, for the viscountess was opening her mouth to speak and you didn't turn your back on a snake.

"I must solicit your opinion, then," the viscountess said to her. "The last time I spoke with Lord Rushden, we had a very passionate discussion of Andreasson's tone-color effects. *I* feel that Bach's fugues tolerate it very well, but perhaps you do not." Her tone was pleasant, but her eyes nailed into Nell's, steady and hard, as though she saw straight to the truth and knew Nell had not an inkling of such matters. "Such a hot debate under way! May I know where you stand?"

"I doubt she has ever contemplated the question,"

said Simon. "I confess I never gave it much thought myself after our discussion. Neither I nor my wife pay much attention to these passing salon styles."

Whatever Simon meant, it looked to be the equivalent of a slap, for the woman reddened and retreated a pace. "Yes, I see your point. My goodness, is that Marconi I spot on the other side of the room? If you'll forgive me—"

"Oh, we would never keep you," Simon murmured.

The viscountess turned on her heel and stalked away. Watching her retreat, Nell felt sick. Maybe the champagne was souring in her stomach. "What's a salon style?"

"A musical term," said Simon. "That's all."

No, it wasn't. Her husband might as well have been speaking a foreign language with that woman—some cozy, secret talk that Nell couldn't hope to understand. Like adults around a child, she thought, spelling the words to keep the nipper from catching on.

"You're some sort of musical expert?" she asked. How important did he account this business?

He shrugged. "I'm considered a reliable critic by circles who don't know very much about it."

"But you write music. You play the piano every day." Those weren't the signs of a man only mildly engaged by a passion.

"Yes." A line appeared between his brows. "Does that trouble you?"

She shook her head and looked blindly across the room. Lady Swanby was in close conference with a lady in sapphires, both of them smiling, creamily satisfied with themselves. Her pale blue eyes flashed in the light, finding Nell's briefly, her smile never faltering as she glanced onward.

What if Simon came to long for somebody with whom he could discuss such matters as—as *tone color*?

"Nell," he said softly, insistently, until she had no choice but to look at him. "There is no cause on earth to let any woman here trouble you."

Her throat thickened. Sure and he felt that way now, but in three months, or six, when this current between them dimmed, her ignorance might start to trouble him.

A balding, rotund baron staggered up with three glasses of champagne. "A toast," he chortled. "A toast to Rushden's newest find! Ain't you the clever one, Rush! Should've known if anyone would find her, you would."

Nell took the glass with an effortful smile, the liquid sloshing as people pressed in to join the cheer. Simon lifted his flute, making some joke that set everyone to laughing.

A queer chill ran through her. Simon was a man at a party that had started without him but now revolved entirely around him—Nell herself perhaps only the excuse for what was the natural order of things: people crowding forward to bask in her husband's attention.

She looked down at her glass, at the bubbles popping and disappearing. He'd told her his reputation was too black to win a more conventional heiress—that fathers wouldn't approve of him, that people talked poorly of him. She didn't think he'd been lying to her, but obviously he had been lying to himself.

She wondered what had given him such a black view of his own prospects.

She wondered if that black view explained why he'd looked no higher for a bride than a guttersnipe.

She drowned the wicked thought in a long swig of champagne.

An hour later, the company was still buzzing when a man walked into the room and made directly for the vacant piano, where he flipped out his coattails and took possession of the bench.

"Ah," said Lady Allenton, returning to Nell's elbow. "Andreasson has deigned to appear!" She directed a delighted look toward Simon, clearly pleased with her party; were she to glow any more brightly, there'd be no need for all the candles. "Your discovery continues to enchant," she said to him. "I find his music quite . . . transcendent!"

Nell sighed. Her spirits had started to lift again—the occasion was too merry, the scene too beautiful, to sulk for long. But if everyone was going to start talking music again, she'd need another few glasses of the bubbly to brace herself.

The pianist picked out a few notes, testing his instrument. A hush descended—gradually, incompletely, stray voices still leaping out here and there. Simon took the opportunity to draw Nell back against the wall, putting a foot or two between themselves and the hostess. "Are you all right?" he asked.

"I'm fine," she said, and with his hand on her arm, she meant it.

He returned her smile with one of his own. "What do you think of the crowd tonight?"

She felt as though she'd been walking through a cloud of butterflies, all of them flapping in her face, angling to be noticed. Mostly harmless. Mostly amusing. "They're friendly," she said. *But not because of me.*

A thunderclap of chords split the air. The remaining

chatterers fell silent. Anticipation sharpened the pause that opened. And then Andreasson filled it, slamming his hands onto the keyboard and launching forth a dark, vigorous sort of . . . marching tune, Nell thought. Violent and jangling. The sort bound to give a girl a headache.

But the crowd seemed to like it. Half of the eyes that had pressed upon her a moment ago now turned toward the piano. Nods of approval spread right and left, looks of appreciation on thoughtful faces.

She bit her lip. Didn't take Mrs. Hemple to guess that laughing would be rude.

Simon leaned down. "What do you think?"

"I think he can't play nearly as well as you."

"You'd be wrong," he said. "Technique aside, though—he's quite innovative in his compositions."

The snooty tone rubbed her wrong. He wasn't talking to Viscountess Swanby. "I can bang on some tin pots for you," she offered. "I guess that would be original if I did it in a drawing room."

He snorted. Heads turned and he smiled down at her. "You'll ruin my reputation with such talk."

Now he was teasing. "If this pianist didn't harm it, I'd say you're ironclad."

His smile faded a little, growing softer, more intimate, like the look he'd showed her in bed this morning. "You haven't learned yet when to lie." Slowly, as if the words were being dragged from him, he added: "I confess, Nell, I hope you never learn."

She found herself staring at him. Unsteadying thought: there was something hot in his eyes that wasn't purely want. It was too tender, too . . . affectionate.

Under that look, secret places in her fluttered to life. *Look at me that way forever,* she thought. She'd learn everything there was to know about music as long as he always looked at her so.

A dark thought intruded: he might be looking at her, but if he thought she didn't know when to lie, then he was watching a woman who only existed in his imagination. Nell could lie through her teeth all the day long. *Sorry, Michael, only fourteen shillings this week. Hannah, the gloves are lovely. Simon, I don't care what you've done with that viscountess; this marriage is only for money, after all. I could leave you and never regret the loss . . .*

The piece segued into another—and Simon's expression went blank at the same moment she recognized the music: the piece he'd written when heartbroken.

Lady Allenton approached, evidently deciding that the bride and groom had enjoyed enough privacy. "Have you had many opportunities to enjoy Mr. Andreasson, my dear? I hope Lord Rushden is not selfish in sharing his coterie's talents!"

"Not yet," said Simon, speaking before she could open her mouth. "But I've an artist in mind for our wedding portrait. A very unusual talent. There's a deceptive simplicity to his palette, but his brushwork is extraordinary. The results are astoundingly rich."

"You *must* give me his name," Lady Allenton said.

Nell tried to tune out their banter. The music continued to unroll, aching as a bruise, blue as an autumn twilight. It was too sad for company. Listening to it was a terrible pleasure, like putting a frozen hand too close to the fire after a trek through the bitter cold.

But Lady Allenton wanted more of her attention. Inching closer, she said, "Argos. My favorite piece of his. Remarkable, isn't it?"

"Yes," Nell said softly.

"Some people say he's a misanthrope," the woman continued. "But I fancy there must be some other reason for his seclusion. Illness, perhaps. A man who could write such music—he must have a very large heart, don't you think? I can't imagine he would scorn the world."

"Who?"

"Argos," Lady Allenton said. "The composer of this piece."

"But this is—"

"Your taste," Simon said, shooting Nell a look that made her clap her mouth shut, "is superior, Lady Allenton."

Lady Allenton preened. "Yes, well, I spend a good deal of the winter in Paris, as you know. In such a city, one receives an incomparable education from a mere willingness to listen."

Nell gaped at him. He let people think this was someone else's music? He'd never struck her as a modest man, much less a shy one.

The piece drew to a halt. Stunned silence settled—to be punctured, hesitantly at first and then with building, resounding, enthusiasm, by applause. *Click click click* went the ladies' fans, tapping against rings and jeweled bracelets. Andreasson stood, making his bows, a scowl still fixed firmly on his brow.

"Oh, have we missed the performance?" came a sweet voice—one that caused Simon to catch hold of Nell's upper arm as though to keep her upright. She glanced up, startled, and then followed the direction of his grim, instructional nod.

The first thing she saw beyond her hostess's swiveling head was a tall, string-thin man gaping at her in open horror.

And then she saw the girl beside him, one hand frozen where it had lifted in greeting to Lady Allenton. Lady Katherine's smile was crumbling from her mouth as she locked eyes with Nell.

"Oh, splendid! I was *hoping* you'd join us," said Lady Allenton.

She was real. Nell could have watched Katherine Aubyn forever: moving, talking, hands waving, voice a bit shrill as she spoke.

"This can't be happening," Lady Katherine said. "What sort of trick is this?" She was kicking up her russet-brown skirts, furiously pacing the carpet in Lady Allenton's library. The hostess had been creamily solicitous, deliciously glad to offer a private room for their *historical reunion,* as she'd put it.

For her part, Nell stood stiffly beside a chair. She felt as though somebody had brained her with a cast-iron pan. Try as she might she couldn't muster a coherent thought other than: *she's real*. Which was stupid. Of course she was real. Had there ever been any doubt?

But a photograph hadn't captured the vividness of the living woman.

This woman pacing the carpet might have been Nell's double.

She felt as though she were watching *herself*.

She couldn't look away, although she was the object of stares of her own: a portly lady, Katherine's chaperone, gawked; Katherine's guardian—the balding, nasal-voiced man called Grimston, glared from the corner, where he was exchanging terse words with Simon.

Lady Katherine suddenly pivoted. Her hands were locked together at her waist, an angry grip by the livid color of her fingers. "Who *are* you?" she burst out.

"Katherine," came the low, oily admonition from the corner. Sir Grimston stepped forward. "Perhaps we should go—"

"No." Katherine came toward Nell, elegant in a collar of diamonds, her hair piled high, her face pale, her eyes a touch wild. "You can't—I can't—" Her hand lifted, trembling, as though to touch Nell's cheek, but at the last second, her fingers curled away as if from a flame. "You're . . ."

"Yes," Nell managed. "I think so."

"Enough," said Grimston. "This is a very clever sham, Kitty, but you mustn't—"

"A sham," Katherine whispered, staring at her. "You're wearing my mother's bracelet. Her necklace. Are you a sham?"

Nell took a breath and looked down at the emeralds on her wrist, at the pristine white elbow gloves that disguised the hands beneath them, the rough calluses on her palms, the freckles that spotted the backs of her knuckles. "No," she said softly. She looked up. "I don't think so."

Katherine opened her mouth. Shook her head as if the words wouldn't come.

Nell knew how she felt. She felt the empathy quicken her heartbeat and draw her forward. Her own hand unsteady, she reached out to take Katherine's.

They stared at each other. It just . . . didn't seem possible that they were so much alike. That this gorgeous creature, who'd walked into the drawing room so casually, who faced her now in a fortune of diamonds, whose face had looked down at her rags in Bethnal Green, could be related to her.

Blood.

Her *twin*.

Katherine blinked, tears threatening to fall. "Where have you been all these years? Why didn't you come back to me?"

"I didn't know. I didn't remember. I couldn't."

"Oh!" A soft, shaky syllable. The hand in Nell's turned, gripped her fingers hard. "Was she very cruel to you?"

"No," Nell said softly. "She was . . . I thought she was my mother."

Katherine let go, physically recoiled a step. "That monster! Your *mother*!"

"I didn't *know*," Nell said. "How could I know?"

"But you must have felt it!" The girl's voice turned pleading. "Didn't you—miss me? Didn't you long for your sister? Not a night passed that I didn't wish for you, pray for you to come back—"

Nell shook her head, mute, miserable. "I'm sorry," she whispered. "I just didn't . . ." *Know.*

How hadn't she known? Seeing this girl before her, she found her own ignorance astonishing. Hideous. Shouldn't she have known she was missing the other half of her?

"But *where* were you?" Katherine took a sobbing breath. "Father looked and looked—did she take you from the country?"

"No. I was right here in London. So close. Only in Bethnal Green."

"Bethnal Green . . ." Katherine frowned. "But that's . . . the East End? Dear Lord," she gasped. "And you . . . you lived in such filth? How did you—" She looked Nell up and down, as if searching for proof of the tale on Nell's body. "How did you survive it?"

"I worked," Nell said—and realized too late that the question had been rhetorical: the shock, the *horror* on her sister's face, gave that away. "Respectably," she stammered. "Proper jobs, at factories." It didn't seem to penetrate; Katherine's mouth had fallen agape. "Not anything—low," she said. "First I made boxes and then I rolled cigars."

"Cigars!" The girl laughed: a high, hysterical sound. Trembling fingers covered her mouth. "Oh, my God." She turned toward Grimston. "A *factory girl*?"

"Ludicrous," he said flatly.

"Can you imagine—" Katherine wheeled back to her. "What people will say—"

"Calm yourself," said Grimston. "Nothing has been proved yet."

"You look so like me," Katherine said slowly. "But . . ." Her eyes narrowed. "You say you didn't remember me? I remembered you—I remembered my sister every day of my life!"

Nell swallowed. "I can't explain it. But—"

"How could you forget?"

"I don't—"

"You were in the same city, so close, but you never once tried to come home?" Katherine retreated another step. "You can't be her," she said hoarsely. "Cornelia would have tried—" She shook her head. "You're not Cornelia," she hissed. "I never forgot. *Never.* My sister *never* would have forgotten me!"

Nell sucked in a breath. The words scraped over her like razors. Caused her ears to burn. To be turned on so quickly—did this girl not have eyes? Did she not *see*?

Oh, yes. Katherine saw, all right. She was looking at Nell now like a bug that had just crawled out from under the carpet.

Anger felt good. Like a cure. What right had *this*

girl to judge her? Of course Lady Katherine had remembered: she'd had the whole world reminding her of what she'd lost. Probably had been pitied and coddled every time she'd wept. She'd never had to lift a finger her whole bloody life. How *dare* she judge?

Nell spoke hard and sharp, with scorn—aimed at this girl and at herself for letting such a creature wound her. "Sure and I'm not your sister," she said. "Funny how quickly your mind changed once you found out that I'd done a bit of honest labor. I suppose you'd be happier if I'd been locked in a box all these years."

"How *dare* you." The girl turned to Grimston, lifting her chin, announcing it: "This is not my sister." Her voice suddenly trembled. "My sister is dead."

"Curious," Simon said. He was suddenly beside Nell, his hand a warm, steady pressure on her back. "You felt so strongly to the contrary in the courtroom last autumn."

"Enough," Grimston harrumphed. "This was wicked of you, St. Maur—"

"Rushden," Simon said mildly.

"—bringing her here, imposing her on these unsuspecting people! And you—" Grimston faced Nell, his face purpling. "You, young lady, are either a very clever confidence artist—"

"Aye," Nell said sarcastically, "it took an awful lot of work to end up with this face I'm sporting. I do confess, I wonder why I didn't choose a prettier one." She sent a pointed look toward Katherine, who bridled.

"A natural daughter of the late earl," Grimston said curtly. "Of that, I've no doubt. But whether you are a deliberate fraud or the innocent, ignorant victim of Lord Rushden's evil games, I cannot say. Nevertheless, you should know that you are testing dangerous waters with this stunt. We will prosecute you for fraud and extortion—"

"And isn't that the Aubyn way," Simon said. "So warm, so familial."

"You mustn't think you can simply swan into a room of your betters and find welcome. The insult!" The man glowered. "The *effrontery*! Your claim will be easily disproved. There are distinguishing marks, evidence of which you"—Grimston directed a venomous look at Simon—"have never been made aware of."

"Nor Lady Katherine, apparently," Simon said.

The girl in question wiped the puzzlement from her face. "You know nothing of me," she snapped at him. "You're a boor and a blackguard and a—the *worst* sort of gentleman—not a gentleman at all, but a wolf in sheep's clothing! You drove my poor father into an early grave—"

"Save it for the stage," Nell cut in.

"We've endured enough of this." Grimston straightened and turned to Katherine's chaperone, snapping his fingers at her as though to call a dog. "We will speak through our lawyers. Rushden, you may depend on hearing from me."

"Oh, I do," said Simon. "You owe my wife a considerable sum of money, I believe. Something near to . . . nine hundred thousand pounds?"

A strangled noise burst from Katherine. "Beyond vulgar! To see my father's station reduced to this—to *you*—who would play such a cruel and tasteless joke—when I have *longed* to see—oh, I cannot bear it!" She spun on her heel and fled from the room—Grimston and the older woman following.

As the door slammed behind them, Nell stood stock-still, gripped by astonishment, dumb with it.

A gentle hand closed on her shoulder. "I'm so sorry," Simon said quietly. "I thought—" His laugh was brief, humorless. "I didn't think," he corrected. "I didn't expect to see them here tonight, but no matter— it was terribly sloppy not to plan for it."

She shook her head. What difference did it make how she'd run into them? "No wonder Mum took me," she said. "My . . . other mum, I mean."

"Yes," Simon said after a moment. "Or what a pity that she did." His fingers traced her cheek, and to her shock, she realized she was weeping. "What a terrible crime," he said. "You deserve so much better."

"Do I?" she whispered.

Not a night passed that I didn't wish for you, Katherine had said.

But then she had taken it back: those words were not, after all, for Nell.

These tears seemed to ooze like pus from a wound. She felt infected, dirty, contaminated by this knowledge she hadn't wanted or asked for. *I am that lost girl,* she thought, *and there is nobody left who wants me back.*

The landau was spacious. On the drive to Lady Allenton's, Simon had taken the opposite bench to avoid crushing her train. Now he settled down beside her, causing her silk skirts and underskirts to crunch and shush in protest.

"I should have gone about this differently," he said as the coach started forward. "Should have insisted . . ." He sighed. "Had she been prepared, it might have gone differently."

Nell shrugged. Her tongue felt dead in her mouth.

Now that her tears had dried, she felt embarrassed by them. The weeping seemed like a betrayal of herself. She'd spun such foolish dreams about what would happen when she met her sister. So much for them. Why should she care whether or not the bint acknowledged her?

Because that *bint* was her sister. Nell had looked into her face tonight and felt . . . an unspeakable wonder. *You could know me. You're one of mine.*

Only it wasn't true. Katherine Aubyn wanted nothing to do with her.

"Of course, it makes no difference either way," Simon said. "Her support would have been helpful, but sixty of London's most prominent persons acknowledged you tonight. That's a triumph by any angle. And tomorrow, every newspaper in town will be declaring your return."

There was a persuasive flavor to his voice. He was trying to hearten her, to charm her into sharing his view of things, just as he'd done with all those guests tonight.

His effort made her throat tighten. She reached blindly for his hand, lacing her fingers through his, not looking at him. This sadness rising in her seemed too large, too sharp, to manage with reason or words. Her skin would split with the effort to contain it.

Mum, what did you do?

Jane Whitby had robbed her of the chance to know the people who'd rightfully belonged to her. Her mother, her father, a sister who would have loved her.

Simon's hand turned in hers, his grip firming. "There's no cause for concern," he said.

"Right."

"Do you believe me?"

She nodded and leaned into his body. She supposed he knew more about her chances in a court of law than she did.

"You did brilliantly, you know." His knuckle skated down her cheek. "We could not have hoped for a better performance."

The words pierced her. Aye, it had all been naught but a performance. She'd enjoyed herself grandly, with the glee of a girl who felt she was getting away with something. But Katherine had seen right through her. *A factory girl,* she'd said with scorn.

Maybe the viscountess hadn't been fooled, either. Perhaps that hadn't just been jealousy jaundicing her manner. "Did you sleep with Lady Swanby?" she asked.

He tensed beneath her. After a long pause, he said, "Before I met you. Yes."

"And now?"

His hand caught her chin, lifting it so their eyes met. The shadows suited him, emphasizing the stark beauty of the bones of his face. "Now I'm married," he said.

A moment passed. His gaze remained intent, unwavering.

"All right," she said softly.

The landau lurched to a stop at an intersection. She pulled away from him on the pretext of looking out the window. Under the bright lights of the shops, dozens of pedestrians paraded in Saturday evening finery, the gents' canes flashing with fake gold plate, aigrette feathers bobbing in the ladies' long hats.

"I'll never know half of what she does," she said to the street scene.

"Katherine?"

"Her, too."

Slowly he said, "I think you misunderstand the matter of the viscountess. It wasn't . . . significant, in any regard."

She willed herself not to say anything more. But her fears wanted out. "It doesn't matter, though. I don't know anything about music, Simon. About how softly a man should touch the keys." A gulping little laugh spilled out of her. "If he touches the right ones, that's enough for me."

"And there are countless things you know that I don't," he said readily. "But we can learn from each other, Nell."

She shook her head. He knew all the right things to say. That was the gift of his charm. This voice in her gut told her that his charm wasn't empty: he meant what he said.

He meant it right now. But would he always?

She turned back toward him, putting her face into his shirtfront, inhaling the scent of starch, the citrus of his cologne, the smell of his skin. She wanted so much to believe in him. It was an ache in her, this need to believe.

His arms came around her and the feeling of them was beyond a miracle. Here was why God had made arms in the first place. Now she knew.

It came to her that guarding her heart was a fool's errand. She'd already lost it.

A tapping noise intruded into the silence. She felt his chin brush the top of her head as he looked toward the noise.

She bit her lip. She knew the cause of that tapping. Somebody was hungry outside in the night. "Give him a coin," she whispered.

His chest vibrated beneath her ear as he spoke. "I'm not carrying any."

Her eyes came open. The anger leapt up in her so quickly that she knew it had only been waiting for an opportunity. It was easier to be angry than to hope.

She withdrew from him in one jerky movement, grabbing the reticule that she'd discarded on the opposite bench. A lady was meant to carry nothing but a handkerchief, smelling salts, and perhaps a vial of scent. She jammed her hand inside, feeling for the coins Simon had handed over, laughing, when she'd collected on their billiards-game wager. She didn't meet his eyes as she yanked down the window and thrust out her hand.

The beggar woman had gray hair, a face carved by time and too many cares, a threadbare shawl around her bony shoulders. She reached up with gnarled, shaking fingers that fumbled the coin. As the coach rocked forward, her head dropped out of sight. She had gone onto her knees to recover the best luck the night would bring her.

Nell sank onto the bench where her reticule had rested, putting her opposite Simon, who was staring at her as though startled into some dark revelation.

What he said was: "You carry coin in your purse?"

Aye, and I've gone on my knees, too, she thought. *I've scrambled for a coin tossed by some pretty woman's hand. Right before she'd taken to thieving, she'd done it. I've crawled in the mud and I'll be damned now if I travel without a coin when I have one.*

There were so many things he didn't know that she'd never tell him. A hundred or more crowded into her mind, suddenly—among them that she had nothing to teach that he'd care to learn. What she knew was how to make a shilling or a pot of soup stretch further. How to use a candle flame to mend a crack in gutta-percha. The best time of day to find a likely bargain at the butcher's. The safest road home in the dark.

What came out of her mouth was: "I'm not ashamed."

He leaned forward. "You don't need to be ashamed," he said fiercely. "By God, Nell—what cause have you for shame? Katherine Aubyn is a silly, spoiled child. The viscountess is a vapid piece of fluff. Their opinions count for *nothing*."

She tried to smile. "I know," she said. She had the easier part in this marriage: she'd seen both sides of it, now, whereas he'd only ever know his own world. She couldn't teach him the feel of the mud between her fingers as she'd scrabbled, or the hard strike of the ground against her knees as she'd knelt. He had no way of guessing that even now, after glorious meals in which she filled her belly, the memory of hunger still buzzed deep in her bones.

She didn't want him to guess. She liked that he didn't see the weakness and fear in her, that small, cowardly part of her that never felt safe. If he ever managed to see it, he'd look at her differently. And oh, how she liked the way he looked at her now.

"What is it that troubles you?" he asked. Frustration edged his voice, but she didn't take it amiss: she knew it wasn't aimed at her.

"I'll never belong to your world." She spoke carefully, with all the honesty she could offer. "Even after twenty years, Simon. Or forty." The memory of hunger would still be inside her. It would prevent her from taking good fortune for granted as he did.

"But nobody belongs to that world, Nell. Nobody *feels* as if they belong, at any rate. They're all watching each other—fearful of the laughter coming from across the room, wondering to themselves, are they the target? Are they the joke?"

She bit her lip. He thought she was afraid that she'd be judged by his circles and found lacking. Evidently it had never occurred to him that she feared the lack in herself.

"They don't feel that way when they're with you," she said. "You make them comfortable."

"Not entirely," he said. "Never entirely. It's a world of pretensions, you see—not of substance. No one feels able to be fully himself."

His words reminded her of a puzzle from this evening. "Is that why you don't put your name to your music? You let people think it's somebody else's because you're afraid they'll make a joke of it?"

He frowned. "I'm not afraid," he said. "I've told you, I don't look for anyone's approval. Not in those circles."

"Don't you think you're owed some approval? For your music, I mean?"

"Perhaps. It doesn't signify to me."

She looked down at her hands. Moments like these, she felt the distance between them most keenly. He spoke of his own indifference as though it were a style he'd chosen, but she knew indifference to be a luxury that only the fortunate few could enjoy. At that moment when she'd dived to her knees for a passing coin, the whim of some glittering woman had been everything in the world to her.

He made an impatient noise and moved off the opposite bench to sit beside her. Taking her face in his hands, gripping hard, he looked at her. "Tell me," he said.

She swallowed. He was a creature designed expertly to terrify her—not her dreams come to life, but rather the sum and total of everything she'd never even allowed herself to dream. "I can't explain it."

"You can," he said. "If it's not Katherine . . . then is it the injustice that troubles you? That beggar woman, I mean? You have the power to change that, now. You realize that, don't you?"

So earnestly he spoke, trying to untangle her thoughts, to understand her. "That, too," she whispered. But she was selfish. He was what troubled her most. *This ache where my heart should be,* she thought. *That troubles me.*

It was a sweet ache, though. How amazing to recall now that second night she'd known him, and how poorly he'd painted himself as he'd tended to her eye. She'd believed every lie he'd spoken of himself: a ne'er-do-well with nary a care in the world apart from his pocketbook.

But bad lies had a way of coming quickly unraveled. She lifted her hand to his face, cupping his hard jaw, returning his searching look with one of her own. He was kind and frighteningly clever, quick-witted and funny and—though he'd probably deny it with a gun to his head—sensitive. He did care what others thought. Otherwise he'd never have worked so hard to hide his true face, and his music, from the world.

"You're a good man," she said. "Do you know that?"

He mistook her meaning. "You're right to care," he said. "It *should* bother us. And those do-gooders who do nothing—you can teach them differently. As I've told you, everything is possible for you now."

She felt herself smile and then his fingers were tracing that smile. "That's better," he whispered.

"It is," she agreed. She pulled down his head and pressed her lips to his, asking for the taste of his tongue. He gave it to her, pressing her back against the squabs to kiss her in earnest, his hard arms coming around her, scattering her fears like night creatures from light. Teeth, tongue, a dark, sweet assault. His grip was firm, declarative: he had her and so here she would stay.

She slid her hands up through his hair and dug in, hard and harder yet. He made a faint noise of surprise but kissed her even more fiercely. No attempt to loosen her grip or pull away. He wouldn't yield, wouldn't give. She loved that about him.

She was the same.

The thought sparkled through her like fireworks lighting a moonless night. Here was their common ground: this obdurate place in each of them, hard and insistent as diamond. Here was the substance to bind them. Cut from the same hard stone, they *would* be bound together; they would hold each other hard. Katherine hadn't wanted her but he did; he had married her and would keep her.

She took his tongue deep in her mouth as she reached for her skirts. Inch by inch the foaming silk and lace filled her hands, until her calves and knees were bared. Then she bucked beneath him, knocking him back, clambering over him to sit astride his thighs.

She felt his soft, hot sigh on her throat as she pressed their bodies together. He was tall, broad, light on his feet but so solid in his bones, the muscle of his spread thighs supporting her so easily, his grip on her waist sure and firm. How marvelous to be him; how marvelous to be against him. He felt like the answer to every curiosity she'd ever had, a promise of more surprises to come, always good surprises; he never disappointed her.

She wrapped her arms around him, holding him fast as she moved against him, not letting an inch open between their bodies. Her balance was unnecessary; he had her. He would hold her. The only cause for concentration was this kiss, building like a storm between them. She arched as his fingers dug into her spine; she wanted to slip inside his skin and inhabit this wondrous body of his, to know what it was to move through the world as he did. That old Irish prayer, the road rising to meet you: the world rose to meet him; it clamored for him. There was magic in him and she wanted it.

Her cloak slid from her shoulders, thumped at her feet. His teeth slid down her throat. A little scrap of lace, a fichu, lodged between her breasts; he took it away with his teeth, deliberately, intently. His hands slid down her body, and she grew aware, suddenly, of herself more than of him: with his lips pressed now to the upper curve of her breast, his soft, heated murmur was muffled, too vague to interpret but . . . worshipful in tone. This man wanted *her*—she was well worth the wanting.

She laughed softly, exultantly. Her hand between them found the thick length of him, traced his outline through his trousers. Oh, yes, this was where she wanted to be, with her skirts knocked up above her knees and him beneath her, always. She wrestled with the tab, suddenly impatient, wanting all of him, his skin against hers, his cock inside her.

He growled in her ear, the thrust of his hips

pressing his erection into the palm of her hand, thin fabric separating them for another infuriating second. And then he was free, springing into her fingers. She guided him into her, slowly sank down onto him, a long breath escaping her at the sensation rippling through her body. He filled her so certainly, as though he'd never known a moment's doubt of her. His hair brushed against her skin, the strong, hot pull of his mouth on hers now echoing how he penetrated her below.

She closed her thighs around his lean hips, squeezing hard, and moved over him, her nails digging into his muscled shoulders as she rose and fell. *Mine,* she thought. *Mine.*

He was hers and she was not letting him go.

In the days that followed, something shifted inside Nell, so she felt as though she walked slightly off-balance. Aslant, the world appeared at new angles to her, revealing all kinds of joys she'd never guessed at.

She spent the mornings abed with Simon. Afternoons they passed reading to each other in the library or walking in the park. They toured the British Museum and debated the paintings. They returned to the house through the mews to avoid the newspaper reporters who'd taken to congregating on the pavement, despite the bobbies' best attempts to drive them away.

Inside, they rarely took their hands off each other.

In the evenings, Simon played the piano. His music dazzled her, and then, afterward, he translated its mystery into words, explaining to her how music might be a science as well as an art. She came to understand what Lady Swanby had meant by one man's *piano* being another man's *pianissimo.* She laid her own hands on the keys and laughed as he guided her through simple scales. He kissed her where her neck met her shoulder and told her she had magic in her fingers.

She turned on the bench and drew him down beside her and showed him exactly what sort of magic she could work with her hands.

They dined together. They read side by side before the fire. They acted . . . domestically, as husband and wife. She spoke to him honestly, and only moments or minutes afterward did she remember, as though part of an irrelevant past, that she might have cause for caution.

But one sunny morning after breakfast, a note arrived that made her realize the fragile foundations of her happiness. Scrawled in Hannah's unsteady hand, it mysteriously promised some news to do with Michael. Despite mention of her stepbrother, the invitation to visit should have overjoyed her, for she missed Hannah terribly.

The invitation did not overjoy her. It raised a bolt of panic sharp enough to steal her breath.

She looked up, through the bright light of the morning room, at the footman who'd brought the note. He was young, slim, with a smooth, hard face that revealed nothing as he said, "Shall I wait to take my lady's reply?" But in his pale eyes she saw a shrewd glint that said he'd missed none of it: the broken penmanship; the misspelling of Simon's direction; the lack of a seal; the cheapness of the thin, brown envelope.

"No," she said. "That will be all."

When he left, she followed him into the hallway, the note crumpling in her sweaty palm, bleeding ink across her skin. Five steps down the hall, she realized her intention: she was going in search of a place to burn this note—as though Hannah's friendship was something sordid, to be denied and rebuffed.

The thought shamed her into stopping. She loved Hannah. She longed to see her. But if she accepted this invitation, Simon would want to go with her. He was so curious to know how she'd grown up. He'd asked a hundred questions about her youth, but she saw only now—in a blinding instant—that she answered him so freely because she knew it would never occur to him to ask the questions she truly dreaded to answer.

She took a long breath. So what if he saw her comfortable in the rookeries? What did she care if he was disgusted? Aye, she'd lived over a pig slop most of her life, with fever in the flat next door nine months out of the twelve. So what? What did *she* care for his judgments?

But these questions, which once might have stirred a healthy, solid anger, no longer worked to insulate her. She did care. She cared for his opinion more than anything. And once he saw how it was in Bethnal Green, his imagination would begin to wander down darker, truer paths. Instead of asking about her responsibilities at the factory, he might ask instead, *How did you travel safely at night? How did you keep clean without running water?*

It was easier to care for a woman when you did not have to imagine her being grabbed and groped by drunkards on the road, or scratching at the pricks of nits and lice.

Once he saw her in Bethnal Green, he'd realize that beneath these fine clothes still breathed the sort of girl a man like him would pass in the street without a backward look, were circumstances different.

She closed her eyes, hating to think such a thing of him. Hating herself, even, for thinking him capable of such small-hearted snobbery.

A sound caught her ears: his voice, coming dimly through a doorway down the hall. The low timbre triggered some dumb reflex that pulled her lips into a smile—and the smile, in turn, acted like a medicine. As her eyes opened, she suddenly could not doubt him.

Let him come with her. She trusted him not to judge her. And once he saw her in Bethnal Green and did not treat her differently for it, then she would have no cause in the world to doubt him.

His voice was coming from the study. She started forward, smoothing out the note, her heart drumming faster. *Hannah has some news for me concerning Michael,* she would say. *No, I'm not sure what it might concern, but I thought to pay a visit. Perhaps, since you've seemed curious about the Green, you might wish to come along—*

She was lifting her hand to knock when the conversation inside registered.

"—look so very bad," someone was saying. Not Simon. That was Daughtry's voice, she thought—the lawyer. "We guessed that Grimston might go to one of the newspapers, so we mustn't be too surprised."

Since her appearance at Lady Allenton's, the newspapers had been full of speculation about Lord Rushden's new countess. Only this morning, she had discussed with Simon the possibility of giving an interview to a friendly reporter.

"I'm aware of that," came Simon's sharp voice. "But the rest of these pieces speak of her fairly. Surely there's no harm in making a public remark on yellow journalism."

"I understand that you wish to decry the article,"

Daughtry said. "However, I'll say it again: I strongly urge you to ignore the whole business. Acknowledging these allegations may endanger your claim to ignorance in the case that the countess is ruled a fraud. It would become much more difficult to end the marriage."

End the marriage.

"But that's no longer a concern," Simon said—distantly, dimly, through the pulses suddenly thundering in her ears. "I've no interest in an annulment."

"Of course," replied the lawyer. "Nevertheless, it would be wisest to proceed in a manner that keeps every option available for you. Surely we can agree on that."

Every option?

She turned away from the door, staring blindly across this fine, quiet hallway, the handsome wood and morocco paneling, the stone busts with their haughty noses: it all looked unfamiliar suddenly. Nothing to do with her. And she could not catch her breath. She was panting like an animal, cornered, tricked into a cage.

End the marriage.

That ceremony—she'd feared the minister a fraud. But all along, it had been the groom playing the trick on her. All the while, Simon had known that the marriage could be undone.

She found herself walking toward the lobby. Where was she going? *Fool,* her footsteps clipped as she stepped onto the checkerboard tile. *Fool, fool, fool.*

The stairs. She put her palm on the balustrade. He had been planning all along to put her aside if she was ruled a fraud. *My God,* she thought. The steps towered before her, an endless climb; her bones felt brittle and rusting; her joints ached. *I hurt.*

She climbed slowly, too slowly: the conversation

had come to a quick end, and now, below, in the entry hall, Simon and Daughtry spotted her. She heard Simon call after her. It took all her effort, with one hand on the banister, to keep moving. It seemed important not to stop. She throbbed as though she'd been slammed into a wall. Why should she hurt like this? The banister was so smooth; he'd slid down it laughing like a boy, carefree, untroubled by his lies. She'd followed him down, so happy that it had felt as though she were flying.

This bloody house! The first night she'd entered it, she'd known it would end her.

The tears came all at once, a hot flood of grief that leaked from her slowly, steadily. She shouldered them away. Such a fool, she was, with no eye for reality, only stupid hopes. She'd trusted her mum. She'd trusted *him*. Clear enough, now, that she couldn't trust herself.

Good God. Take him to the East End to dispel her last doubts, would she? A strange laugh ripped from her throat.

"Nell." His arm hooked around her waist, firm, startlingly hot. He caught her, and with her momentum broken, she could do nothing but stand frozen, wobbling a little as he physically turned her to face him.

When he looked into her face, his own went pale. "What is it?"

She wet her lips. *I heard you.*

But when her lips moved, no sound came out. Some instinct demanded she keep quiet. He could get rid of her whenever he liked. Better not to displease him.

My God, she thought. *Once again, I must keep a master happy for my keep.*

His grip tightened. "Are you all right? What's happened?" He looked down, but her body, of course, showed no injuries; her innards were shredded but he saw nothing amiss.

His eyes locked onto her hand; he took the note from her fingers, reading it quickly before looking up. "Has something happened to Hannah? I don't understand. The mention of your stepbrother is ominous, but the note seems calm enough—"

God forgive her, that she'd scrupled to welcome Hannah's invitation for fear of what *he* might think. Hannah was worth ten of him. Hannah always had stood by her, whereas *he* had always planned to leave her if his plot didn't go as planned.

She saw the puzzlement come over his face and felt a spiteful, horrible pleasure at causing it. How easily his life had been laid out for him. He'd planned all the while to knock her out of it if she made it more difficult.

She didn't owe him a word of explanation. She owed him *nothing*. She couldn't bear to look at him right now, much less speak to him.

"I'm going to see her," she told the space over his shoulder. Her voice wasn't her own. Low and choked. Why did this hurt so much? If she had lost her heart, she could take it back. She would not let herself hurt like this.

"Of course," he said. "I'll have the vehicle brought around. Wait here."

She watched as though from a great distance while he turned and bounded back down the stairs, athletic, so damnably *concerned*. He always knew the right face to wear, the best attitude with which to charm a girl. But it was a thin mask indeed, for it covered the face of a liar.

Why had he lied to her? They'd married on the

cold hopes of a fortune. He might have told her that he planned to end the marriage if she was not found to be Cornelia Aubyn. He'd have lost nothing by being honest.

She put her fist to her chest, where it seemed a great weight was slowly crushing her. What profit had he hoped to gain by lying?

Had he told her the truth, she'd never have gone to his bed.

Knowing the marriage might end, she would never have risked getting with child by him.

She swallowed hard against the urge to vomit. God save her if she was pregnant. God *save* her if she'd bring another creature into this world to tremble and dance at a rich man's whim!

"All right," he called. Climbing back to her, he said, "Five minutes."

Her sluggish brain pointed out that he was pulling gloves out of his pocket, putting them on. "You're coming?"

He gave her a look of surprise. "Of course," he said. "I wouldn't let you go alone."

"Of course," she echoed. Aye, he knew how to play the attentive husband. He was a hand at crafting appearances. Why not? He could order the world to conform to his wishes. He would lie when it suited him, as long as it guaranteed his comfort. She'd never seen him less than confident.

But not in the Green. The Green was *her* world. He'd not be comfortable there. "Good," she said.

Some note in her voice caused him to frown. "Is it the mention of Michael that troubles you? You needn't worry—"

"No. It's nothing." Nothing troubled her but him,

and he wouldn't do so for long. She'd not cater to his good opinions a moment longer. She'd learned her lesson now. It had seemed like a fairy tale because it had never been true. Now she saw the truth. His judgments were as rotten as his word, and just as useless.

Her anger sharpened into resolve, spiteful and hot. Let him see the truth, then. Let him see her as she truly was.

Let him try to charm away the disease and poverty, too. Let him try to stay comfortable in a lane filled with sewage. In the East End, his brand of charm got you *nothing*.

Aloud, she said, "You'll want to change your clothing. Put on your shabbiest if you're coming to the Green."

$\mathscr{I}$n the thoroughfare, the sun was blazing brightly. But here, in a muddy lane too narrow for Simon's brougham to negotiate, the light barely penetrated. On either side, sagging buildings showed crumbling faces. Windows stuffed with rags and newspaper emitted sounds of life: a squalling child; a man's hoarse groans; the raucous laughter of a woman. Occasionally the sweet strains of a fiddle wisped past, fading like ghosts into the shadows.

Simon noted these details absently, his focus trained on the woman who walked beside him. She stumbled now, but when he reached for her arm, she evaded his touch and walked faster.

His hand curled into a fist, which he returned to the pocket of his coat. What ailed her? On the drive, she'd denied aught was amiss, but the invitation from Hannah Crowley had thrown her into a darker mood than he'd ever witnessed.

Perhaps she was only nervous to show him her old world. He wouldn't press her now. But once they were back in the brougham, he meant to know the cause of her temper.

"Mind your feet," she said over her shoulder, her face shadowed by the plain, hooded cloak she wore. "Here and there the gutter runs open."

He didn't need eyes to know that. The smell of sewage, of pig offal and rotting vegetables, clogged the smoky air. Broken glass crunched beneath his boots.

The mud puzzled him most of all. "It didn't rain in the West End last night," he said.

"Broken pipe."

He glanced up the lane, seeing no end to the mud. "A very large pipe, then."

"Does that surprise you?"

The anger in her voice baffled him. "The size, do you mean? Or the fact that it's broken?"

She made some impatient noise. "No matter. The mud serves its purpose. Makes kneeling a touch easier on the knees, I reckon."

He frowned. Was he meant to understand why kneeling should be required? Her stony profile yielded no clue to her thoughts.

"A problem down Mile End way, too," she went on. "Puts me in mind of the time one of your lot was kind enough to throw me a coin thereabouts. I was up to my knees in the muck, scrambling to find it where it had fallen."

Ah. "I see," he said quietly. This explained, no doubt, her reaction to the beggar woman they'd encountered after Lady Allenton's party.

"Reckon I should be grateful that *some* fancy folks carry cash with them," she said. "Otherwise I'd have been crawling for naught."

Her eyes flashed at him as though he'd been the one to throw the coin. "And then you met me," he said slowly. "No need to think on such things any longer."

She flushed. "Asking for gratitude, are you?"

"No," he said, but his own temper was beginning to stir. If he'd committed some sin against her he'd be glad to learn of it. As far as he was aware, *he* was not her enemy.

"I expect you think I should be grateful, though!

Such a far leap I took to wed you. Why, before you were kind enough to take a notice, I had to fight off the rats for my bread! Thought about cooking one, once, only Suzie said I could take plague from it. How do you like that?"

He came to a stop, staring at her through the scant beams of sunlight that penetrated the stinking gloom. "What in God's name is this about, Nell?"

Her laugh sounded high and wild. "What's it about? I reckon you would be asking yourself that—I'll wager you never thought to wed a woman who might have eaten rat stew! Well, there are more stories where that came from, *your lordship*. How about the winter me stepbrother took to pissing himself to keep warm? I was right jealous of his aim! How do you feel about your wife now?"

His bafflement was briefly too large to compass. She gave him no opportunity to muster a reply, bounding past him up a stair and striking her shoulder into the door to open it.

"Nell," he said as he followed her—but found himself alone inside a shabby little entry hall built to house a sagging staircase that he would, in the normal order of things, have hesitated to test with his weight.

She'd already started up it and so he followed. At the first landing, he made the mistake of placing his hand on the banister. The whole thing wobbled in his hand, and a laugh—of astonishment, of unhappiness— slipped from him.

He stepped around the corner to find her glaring down at him.

"If you fall," she said, "no doctor will be coming for you. It took a month's hard thieving to earn the money that bribed *one* of them to meet my mum at a church."

To hell with this treatment. He did not deserve her scorn. He'd done nothing to merit such a manner. "They would come," he said through his teeth. "For the Earl of Rushden, they would come anywhere in the goddamned world. That makes it all the more galling for you, I suppose."

Her face whitened. She whirled and continued up the stairs. At the next landing she threw her fist against the first door, which opened immediately.

A short, spare, silver-haired woman stepped out, smiling. "Nell!" she exclaimed. "Now here's a lovely sight for sore eyes."

He paused on the last step as his wife moved into the woman's arms. The sight of her strained face turning into the older woman's bosom—the ferocity with which she wrapped her thin arms around the woman's waist—touched off a cold foreboding in him. She looked . . . crushed.

Whatever troubled her had nothing to do with coming to Bethnal Green. His gut informed him that it had everything to do with him.

He stepped onto the landing. The older woman glanced up with a frown. "Who's this?" she asked as she pulled free of Nell.

Nell also turned to look at him, and in her expression, he saw something dark and tight and ungiving. His throat tightened.

It had been years since he had felt a shadow of his old awkwardness, of his inability to satisfy or charm— but in this rickety, pathetic hallway, he suddenly remembered with visceral force what it had meant to be judged and found miserably wanting.

He racked his brain. What had he done?

"That's my husband," Nell said, and then walked past the woman into the Crowleys' flat.

Hannah cast down her knitting and rose from the rocking chair to give Nell a hug. As Nell let go, her eyes fixed on the chair. Not eight or ten weeks ago, she had sat in that same seat (had sat there as still as possible: the chair lacked for one rocker, always had done) and felt so easy in her skin. Now she felt the last thing from easy. Her skin didn't seem to fit her anymore. Her misery had caused it to shrink around her.

Simon was taking Hannah's hand, murmuring some empty flattery over her knuckles. Nell wrapped her arms around herself. She'd never let herself want the things she couldn't have, and now that she knew that she couldn't depend on having him, the very sight of him hurt. If only he weren't so beautiful—dark and lean and graceful, even in his oldest togs.

Mrs. Crowley had known with one glance that he didn't belong here. Arrogance was stamped in his bones. For eyes bred in the Green, it was obvious he was somebody to fear.

She sat heavily into a Windsor chair. Her idiocy burned in her chest. God help her, she'd imagined them *equals*. She'd thought him bound by the law as completely as she was. Her rotting, broken brain! How had she forgotten the lessons of the world? Everything worked differently for his kind.

She'd *known* it was too good to be true.

She had nobody to blame for her breaking heart but herself.

Hannah was trying to give the rocking chair to

Simon. "Keep it for yourself," Nell said—too shortly; everybody gave her a look of surprise.

"But it's the largest we've got," Hannah said. "And he saved me from jail, didn't he?"

Mrs. Crowley brightened at these tidings. "Why—of course he did! Sure and I'm a fool for not putting two and two together. I'll insist on another hug from you, lad."

Over the woman's shoulders, Simon met Nell's eye and winked. He didn't understand that he might have been winking at a stone. He'd never faced anyone who didn't bend to him in the end.

My father didn't bend.

The thought gave Nell strength. Aye, she would be like stone to him. Let him do as he will. Let him think what he liked. Let him sneer, even.

The vision rose up sudden and vivid: his chiseled lips curling in contempt as he looked her over.

She'd told him she'd begged on her knees. God above . . .

She gritted her teeth and made her hands into fists, hidden in her skirts. Yes, she had told him that, and if he sneered, she wouldn't care. She'd sneer back at him.

He took a seat in the rocker and looked around the room, inspecting it like one of the do-gooders on their home visits. But the Crowleys didn't require his pity. Their flat had three well-ventilated rooms, the largest of which faced the Green itself. The fresh breeze that passed through the window carried the scent of growing things in the park, clean and pleasant. Nell had always loved passing the time here—a safe and spacious place, blessed by a family that cared for each other.

But as she followed Simon's regard, his presence twisted her view. She noticed for the first time the shabbiness of the rough lath-and-plaster walls, chipping in some places, yellowed in others from the damp. The crude wooden floorboards didn't fit together as much as they battled each other in a hopeless bid to lie flat. The crockery on which Mrs. Crowley now produced biscuits and cake had a substantial piece missing from the rim.

In the world she'd just left, this was wretched living, and no doubt of it.

She turned her eyes back to Simon. He could judge her all he liked. But if by word or look he made her friends feel bad, she'd carve out his heart with a spoon.

Evidently he'd decided to ignore her. With a smile, he took a biscuit from Mrs. Crowley. His thanks made the woman blush. Then he settled back, somehow making himself comfortable in Hannah's seat—occupying it with a look of ease, for all that his knees rose higher than his thighs—and made some friendly remark to Hannah, who laughed.

When Nell relaxed slightly, he sensed it—glancing toward her, his brow lifting. Was that a question on his face? Or did he think he should be congratulated for daring to eat with the laborers?

"Mum used to have a chair like the one you're using," she told him. "We had to burn it one winter to keep the fire going. Would have frozen to death, otherwise."

Out of the corner of her eye, she caught Hannah's startled look. Simon said neutrally, "Was that the same year Michael pissed himself to stay warm?"

Mrs. Crowley made a choking noise. "D-dear me," she sputtered, as Nell felt her face catch fire. "Tea went down the wrong way."

"Michael pissed himself to stay warm?" Hannah asked, her eyes very round.

"Why don't you tell Nell and his lordship your news?" Mrs. Crowley said hastily.

"Oh! Your stepbrother came by," Hannah exclaimed. "Nell, he left you something!"

Nell ripped her eyes from Simon's, hesitating a moment before taking the small bundle of cloth that Hannah had plucked off the table. Michael was not a gift giver by nature. "Poison, I reckon?" she muttered. "What did he say?"

"Open it," Hannah urged. "We thought the same, but then he showed us—oh, just open it, Nell!"

"But perhaps hold your breath while doing so," Simon said.

She surprised herself with a short, hard laugh. "Aye, that's a bright idea." Her hands trembled a little as she unrolled the cloth.

A fine silver spoon winked up at her.

"What on God's green earth?" She lifted the spoon. Turned it around in her hand. The handle was engraved with scrolling initials: *CRA*.

Simon held out his hand. Arrogant cheek, she almost called it, but then he said, "May I?"

Reluctantly she passed it to him. "It looks like a christening spoon," he said immediately. "CRA: Cornelia Rose Aubyn." He lifted a brow. "Well," he said softly. "How interesting."

A bit too interesting, Nell thought. "Why on earth would *he* have had it?"

"He said it was your mum's," Hannah offered. "He found it tucked under a floorboard along with a Bible." She grimaced. "Which I'm sure he didn't know *what* to do with. Probably moldering in the rubbish right now."

He'd probably sold the Bible. "Why didn't he pawn the spoon? Did he have a story for that?"

Hannah shifted in her seat. "Well, he didn't hand it over, precisely. That ten pounds you left me—"

"You gave that to him?" Nell slammed her palm onto the arm of her chair. "That was meant for you! I told you if I didn't come back—"

"But it *was* yours," Hannah said. "Calm down, then, Nellie! I didn't have a choice in it. He came by wanting me to speak to you about buying it—I reckon he thought you'd be willing to buy it at a better rate than Brennan would. And you know Michael; if I'd waited for you, he'd have gone off and gotten blind drunk and been robbed of it—or gamed the spoon away, maybe. And I couldn't let that happen, could I? It's proof! Ain't it? That spoon must have been yours!"

"You did very well," Simon said, as gracious as a lord of the manor with his peasants. "And we'll recompense you for what you spent. With interest," he added, ignoring Hannah's protest as he continued: "This is a very fortunate development, as you say."

"Which I still don't trust an inch," Nell said to Hannah. "If that spoon belonged to Mum, he'd know what it meant. He could have bullied and bribed me for a good deal more."

Hannah's lips parted but for a moment she didn't speak. Then, hesitantly, she said, "Ten pounds, Nellie. It's no small amount."

Nell felt her skin crawl. "Of course." She cast a quick, abashed glance toward Simon, expecting to see smugness: he'd said much the same to her once.

But what she saw on his face was something else entirely.

She looked quickly away, down to her hands in her lap, the blood pounding through her face. The sympathy in his expression felt harder to bear than a smirk. She felt exposed by it—and caught up in the strange idea that he understood her better than she'd guessed.

But it made no difference. If he'd truly understood her, he'd never have lied to her. He would have dealt with her plainly instead of cozening her into his bed.

"Well," Simon said. He tucked the spoon into his jacket pocket, asking, as an afterthought, "May I keep this for you?"

Nell realized the question was for her. Highhanded, even on his best behavior. "Go ahead," she said.

His tentative smile struck her like a knife. Her traitorous heart trembled. How beautiful the world had seemed when she'd thought they were going to walk through it together.

God save her but she was weak! The idea of getting back in that coach with him suddenly terrified her. He'd ask again what ailed her; he'd start in with his questions and she had no faith in herself not to bend, not to give, not to yield again. She'd come so close to loving him completely; her feelings for him felt like a fatal crack running through the core of her. If she let him close now, if he hit on that crack, he'd break her clean apart.

The matter of the spoon settled, the ladies took up their drinks and chattered on, trading the easy gossip of women reuniting after an absence. Meanwhile, Simon found himself listening with a sense of increasing disbelief.

Harry Connor had lost a finger to the cutting machine. David O'Riordan had been picked up by the coppers for lying dead drunk in the road; his wife had come down to the pub and struck deals with three separate men, out in the alley, to get the money to post him. A weaver had caught one of his apprentices thieving, and had chased him into the lane with a whip; nobody would have objected to a thrashing, but he'd not laid off at the sight of blood. It had taken all the women coming into the lane to pry him off, and he'd still not apologized, which didn't seem right, did it? And so Peggy Hart and the Miller twins had decided to box his ears for good measure.

Crises and solutions, street justice and casual cruelty, heartbreaking, told in the cheerful voice of harmless gossip.

He looked at his wife, who was smiling faintly, nodding to show that she listened, and steadfastly avoiding his regard. She had grown up in this rough place, ducking her stepbrother's fist, working at a place where men lost their fingers to feed their families. And somehow, in the midst of all this, she had fashioned herself into a strong, honest, intelligent woman.

His temper slipped away from him. Its loss left him altogether flat.

A half hour later, as the conversation wound down, his wife finally seemed to recall his presence. She stood, and he followed suit, only to hear her say: "I'm staying here for the night."

The words seemed to startle her as much as they did him—and her friends, who exchanged a speaking look.

"No," he said. He was not leaving her in this godforsaken neighborhood.

Her expression darkened. "Just for the night," she said.

He was across the room at her side in three steps, where he took her by the elbow and said to their wide-eyed hostesses, "Thank you for your hospitality," before leading his wife straight to the door.

She yanked free of him as soon as the door closed behind them. In silence they descended the stairs. As they stepped into the lane again, he said, "If you wish to spend more time with them, you are welcome to invite them to the house."

"Of course," she said tonelessly. "Until my money's in your accounts, I reckon I'm too valuable to be risked in the rookery."

He pushed out a breath. God knew the denizens of this street would find nothing novel in the sight of a public argument. Indeed, it might be educational to them to learn that a whip was not required to settle their differences. But he did not quarrel in the road.

The mocking look she gave him said she knew he was biting back words. "Imagine your fine friends seeing you now," she said. "Strolling with a guttersnipe in the filth."

"With my *wife*," he said.

The smile that curled her lips was slow and unpleasant. "For how long?"

He walked faster, longing ferociously for the bend in the lane that would yield the first glimpse of his carriage.

Her voice came softly behind him. "I heard you," she said.

He swung back. "You heard me," he repeated. "What does that mean?"

She fixed him with a clear-eyed look, then stepped around him, taking the lead around the turn.

The carriage stood where they'd left it, and the sight of it in the open sunshine—the sight of his footman moving to open the door, to take them both away from this place—made him feel as though he were finally waking from a nasty, senseless dream.

Her next words, however, made it clear that the nastiness was just beginning.

"I heard you with the lawyer," she said over her shoulder as the servant handed her into the vehicle.

For a moment, one foot poised on the step, Simon did not understand. He'd met with Daughtry this morning to discuss an egregious piece of libel masquerading as journalism, a piece no doubt paid for by Grimston, which claimed that Nell was a clever imposter who, in cooperation with her new husband, was scheming to steal a fortune. Simon had wanted to take action against the newspaper. A woman might be grateful for such husbandly urges.

And then, all at once, he recalled Daughtry's exact objections to these urges.

He leapt into the landau.

She sat tucked into the corner. "Well?" she asked.

"Before I knew you," he said rapidly, grabbing onto the strap and taking his seat as the coach lurched forward, "before I really knew you, I asked for Daughtry's advice—"

"Yes," she said. "You knew you could end the marriage whenever you wished."

"I don't wish," he said fiercely. The very idea now seemed ludicrous. She was his *wife*. "Did you hear my reply to Daughtry? Did you hear me say that I had no interest in an annulment?"

"I heard it," she said. The serenity of her manner struck him as ominous: she had the air about her of a woman who had survived, and now was recovering from, an illness that would not kill her after all. She no longer looked troubled in the slightest. "Tell me, am

I meant to be grateful that today, your mood favored me? But what if our plan goes bad? What if a judge isn't convinced by my face and a silver spoon?"

"Even then," he bit out. "We are married."

"Even then?" Her smile looked gentle. "You would consign yourself to poverty for my sake, you say?"

"Yes." He was astonished by the readiness of his reply—and by the fact he felt no doubt of it. "Yes, I would."

The afternoon light flooding through the window lit vividly the look of uncertainty that crossed her face, chased by a flicker of . . . fear?

Then her face hardened. "You talk a pretty game," she said. "I've never doubted that."

"But you doubt me," he said.

"You've no idea what it means to be poor. Without a penny to your name—your *affection* for me would be the first thing to go, I warrant." A little noise escaped her, poisonous. "For all that it's worth."

He sat back, briefly speechless. "I suppose you're right," he said at length. "I've no idea what poverty means." God knew he liked wealth very well, though. His mind shied at any thought of how he might support them—the notion of teaching music to the whey-faced daughters of the middling classes was laughable.

"But I would find a way," he continued slowly. "God help me, but if it came to that, I would figure out something." A million uncertainties could be balanced, couldn't they, by a single certainty? "You and I . . ." he said, and then trailed off, unable quite to find the words to persuade her that he saw a hundred reasons for hope in her, and a thousand more for his future with her. These thoughts were new to him; they surprised him as much as they would have done her.

But now that they were unfurling, he found himself riveted by the revelation. Alone, before, he'd never had cause to think ahead, or taken any joy in imagining what the coming years might hold. It had all been today or tonight, the sick rush of immediate pleasures, the empty mornings afterward.

But she had brought a new temporality into his life. Now he thought about tomorrows.

Now, when he sat at the piano, he did not play music for the company the notes provided him. He played the music so she might hear it, and come a little closer to him as she listened.

With dawning amazement, he looked at her and realized that since she had come into his life, he had never once felt alone.

"I would figure out a way," he said. "But it won't come to that, Nell. Daughtry feels certain we'll prevail. The christening spoon only aids us further."

She looked away from him. Evidently this made no difference to her. Or perhaps it weakened his argument to admit that he'd no belief they would need to face impoverishment together.

He tried a different tack. "An annulment is a legal device. Not a secret plot I fomented against you. *Think* on it, Nell. When we met, you threatened to kill me. You spoke like a criminal. I knew nothing of you apart from your willingness to commit murder and your miraculous resemblance to a woman I very much dislike. Of course I inquired about ways to safeguard my future, in the event that you and I should fail to deal well together. I thought you—"

The glance she sent him glittered suspiciously. His breath caught. Were those tears in her eyes? "You thought me an animal," she hissed. "Yes, that was very clear."

The urge to take her in his arms was nearly undeniable. Only the suspicion of how little she would welcome it held him in his seat. "*Listen* to me," he said. "I should have made clear to you that the marriage could be dissolved. I admit that my reasons were cowardly, and I beg your forgiveness for it. But you cannot behave as though my past actions tar the present."

"You tell me," she said, "why I should believe your words now, when I was wrong to believe them before." She tipped up her chin, looking down her nose. "Tell me," she said, "why I should put my faith in the claims of a man who takes pride in advertising that he cares for nobody's good opinion. Such an accomplishment, St. Maur—tell me why it should recommend you!"

Her aim was true and her scorn sliced through him like a blade. "What do you think, then?" he said hoarsely. "That I would cast you back into the rookery? Is *that* what you think of me?"

She gave a one-shouldered shrug. "I think you lied because it was convenient for you. Because you knew that otherwise, I'd refuse to share your bed."

He took a sharp breath. "That is the most *insulting* piece of vitriol I've ever—"

"What other explanation do you have?"

"You were skittish." Christ, that did not sound convincing even to his own ears. He raked a hand through his hair, helpless, frustrated.

The coach slowed, the wheels thumping in a more regular pattern as they entered the flagstone paving of his mews.

"I'll have my money," she said at length. "And then"—a hitching breath interrupted her—"we'll see who wants to end this marriage. An annulment can work for a woman, too. Perhaps Daughtry will advise me on how to be rid of *you*!"

A cold laugh escaped him. Brilliant. This was bloody brilliant. Not six hours ago, she'd been giggling into his neck, and now she was plotting to leave him. "He'll advise you of no such thing."

She slammed her hand onto the seat. "Who are *you* to stop me!"

He leaned toward her. Anger he could match. Anger was far easier. *"Your husband, the Earl of Rushden."*

She stared at him. "And I am the countess," she said faintly.

"Quite so," he said. "No matter whom the court decides you to be, that will not change. I'll still be Rushden, and you will be my wife. And if you think that does not give me every advantage in the world over you, then you're more naïve than I ever imagined."

A pulse became visible in her throat. "I'm the last thing from naïve," she said. "I see you for what you are, now."

"Oh? And so you think you cannot trust me? And yet," he said, "from the moment you first stepped foot into my house, I might have done a thousand things to you far worse than ask you to marry me. So easily, Nell, *so easily* I could have misused you. You were nobody—nameless—threatening to kill a peer of the realm. My staff would not have helped you. The law would not have aided you. You *knew* this, once upon a time. You were not so naïve then. But you stayed anyway—and why is that? Because you *did* trust me. You had faith that I wouldn't abuse you. Did I betray that faith? Did I ever lift a hand to you or make you feel my power?"

Her face was losing color, her eyes widening. "What? I'm meant to admire you for not playing the devil?"

"No," he said sharply. "You never admired me. But you counted on your faith in me, and you still do— even at this very moment, though you refuse to admit it. This coach in which you ride—this house to which you return—the locks on your bedroom doors—the very clothing on your body—they are *mine*. I could take them all away, or I could turn them against you; I could turn the locks and order the servants to forget your existence; I could do *anything I liked*. And yet I do not see you trembling for fear!"

"Maybe I should be," she whispered.

"Then decide," he bit out. "Which is it? Will you tremble? Am I a villain who deserves none of your trust? Or are you the villain, here—a coward grown too afraid to own your own feelings, though I have proved to you that I deserve your faith?"

The vehicle rocked to a stop. Silence pressed down between them.

He said, *"Which is it?"*

Her lips parted, then folded into a mutinous line.

"Fine." He sat back. "Very well. Let me remove the burden of cowardice from you. I'm glad to play the villain. You will *not* be leaving me, Cornelia St. Maur. I am going to keep you, whether you wish it or no."

The door opened. Her eyes remained locked on his, her face a blank mask. She made no move to rise.

"Go ahead," he said curtly. "Go into the house. You know now that I mean to keep you there. You have no choice in it."

A shudder moved through her. Then she burst to her feet and slipped down the stairs. Simon waved

off the footman waiting to help him out and stared
blankly at the spot where she'd sat.

The rage evaporated. It yielding on a sickening jolt
to disgust. *The Earl of Rushden.* Quite right, he thought
blackly. Never until this moment had he felt so akin to
his predecessor. His own words might have come from
old Rushden's mouth. *You have no choice in it.*

Was this tyrannical act what she required from
him? Did her long familiarity with bullies lead her to
trust his threats more than his apologies? Would he do
better never to mention love, and to speak instead of
lust and possessiveness only?

God help him. He *did* love her. If she'd listened
carefully enough, she would know that. He liked his
wealth too well to give it up for anything less.

The humorless smile slipped away as he shut his
eyes. After all, he was *not* like Rushden before him. He
would never use his power to bend someone's will.

But Nell was his *wife*. Whether or not she believed
he meant to keep her made no difference. He *did* mean
to keep her.

And if that made him like old Rushden, so be it. He
was not letting her go.

That night, Nell woke to the sound of piano music—
some soft, delicate melody so muffled by the walls that
at first she thought she was still dreaming. Fairy music,
she thought muzzily. Achingly sad, like the dirges old
sailors sang when remembering the sea.

She lay adrift on it for minutes, grief seeping
through her, until she had to know. To see his face as
he played. She slipped off the bed and into the hallway.

Through the window at the end of the corridor she
saw the full moon against a sky mottled with midnight

clouds. Down the wall, the stone profiles of busts froze in three-quarters profile, their bony noses and sculpted wigs casting strange shadows along the carpet.

The strains of music flitted down the hall like ghosts, drawing her toward the atrium.

In the eyes of the law, she was the mistress of this household. Tonight, it made no difference. She felt as though she were stealing through someone else's home, breathless, terrified. Every shape in the dark caused her to flinch.

Nearly to the broad balcony, at the very last door, she found the music. Peering around the doorjamb, she saw Simon seated at the piano, his hands, pale in the moonlight, moving fluidly over the keys.

His back was to her. He hadn't lit lamps or the candlestand at his elbow. She couldn't see his face. But his posture as he played bespoke a man lost in music sad enough to poison a soul.

She'd never heard this piece before.

It made the other étude sound like a lullaby.

She lingered there a long minute, speared by the notes, riven by impulses she couldn't obey: to walk over and touch him. To curl up and weep.

The music explained something to her that she didn't wish to know. Deeper than the level of words, it told her of his pain. If he was lost in it, then he must be hurting as much as she.

What was she to do with such knowledge? It could not help her. It only made her ache more sharply. She'd come so near to giving him everything in her; to trusting him as she'd never trusted anybody—maybe not even herself. And all of it had been based on a promise that was false. He'd always known he could leave her if plans didn't go as predicted. He'd even planned for it.

Now he said he wouldn't leave her, but why not? Katherine's enmity had made plain that they couldn't count on an easy road to reclaiming her birthright. She might never have what was owed to Cornelia—in which case, nobody would blame Simon St. Maur for ridding himself of a penniless, gutter-bred wife.

The thoughts laid bare a hollow inside her blacker than any hunger she'd ever endured.

I deserve your faith, he'd said.

But she was the one with everything to lose.

To stand here and long for him . . . to keep hoping for him when he'd already laid plans to arrange for her loss . . . It might truly kill her.

When the first tear fell, she took a long breath and gathered her skirts for the lonely walk back down the hall.

16

She next morning, Nell woke with a headache that only sharpened as the light grew stronger. She ordered her breakfast to be brought to her room, then picked at it listlessly as the clock in the hallway counted out the painfully slow march onward into the day.

Sylvie offered to accompany her for a walk. But the thought of being chased by journalists did not appeal. She did not want company at all. She felt too inclined to burst into tears.

Finally she took herself down to the library in search of distraction—braced, at every turn, to run into Simon. But the hallways were empty and so, too, the library. Inside, in the murky light shed by the cloudy sky without, the still air smelled of paper and old leather. She walked along the shelves, through a silence that seemed to thicken with every footstep. She grew strangely conscious of the accumulated words in the volumes all around her, the restless thoughts of men long dead, each soundlessly begging for attention.

"Any of them will do."

She gasped and turned. Simon sat in a wing chair in the far corner, the white cravat at his throat catching what little light the room retained, cutting a precise and ghostly shape in the shadows.

Her mouth went dry. She made herself attend to his remark. "Am I disturbing you?"

He placed a bookmark in the volume in his lap and

retrieved a glass from the table beside him. Some quality in his movement—a cold, unhurried efficiency—set her heart to drumming. "My wife asks if she disturbs me," he murmured. "How remarkable."

"Is it?" When he spoke so coolly, it felt like talking to a stranger—a glossy, handsome stranger with no use for her. "I thought it was polite."

"Oh, it is. Very proper, I assure you. We husbands and wives of the aristocracy must ensure that we never speak in an unmannerly fashion to our spouses."

Something dark was edging into his voice—sharp and soft and more cutting than simple irony. Abruptly she decided to come back later, once he'd left.

But as she turned away, a book on the long reading table caught her eye: very old, she could tell at first glance. She brushed the cover with her fingers, feeling how worn and soft the leather was. There were two categories of old things, she'd gathered: for the poor, old meant worn-out, useless. For the rich, a thing just got more valuable the more it aged, because that meant that somebody with enough money to buy a new one had kept the old one for a reason. She'd gathered this logic from the mere fact that so many carpets in this place were worn to threads. "From the seventeenth century," Polly had told her of one of them—although a sensible person might take that as a good reason to buy a new rug already.

At any rate, this book clearly belonged to the rich and worn-out category. But when she opened it, she realized she was wrong to compare it to a threadbare carpet.

It was gorgeous. Illustrations of saints' martyrdoms in vivid, shocking colors. As she turned the page, Simon spoke.

"It was your mother's."

She stiffened. "I thought they all got sold."

He shrugged and took a sip of his drink.

"Did you buy this back?" she asked.

"Yes."

She absorbed this silently as she flipped a page. "Any others?"

"All of them, if I can."

Her hand stilled. She felt a sting at that admission, a sting that spread out into a broad ache and made her entire body throb like a bruise.

He'd told her enough of his own history for her to gather that the countess's kindness must have been very important to him. Rare and precious. Now he was repaying it by buying back her mother's books from the hands of strangers.

The thought caused something to untwist inside her. He knew what it meant to be hurt, just as she did. His family had cast him out, turned him over to an unfeeling stranger. She'd been lost to her family, and then shoved away when she found them. They'd both lost something a person shouldn't have to lose. They both had been marked by it.

"You may take it, if you like," he said.

She clutched the book to her chest and walked quickly out of the room, back down the hall and up the stairs. Once in the safety of her apartments, she threw herself into a chair and stared at the book.

He'd hunted this down because it had been her mother's. Reclaiming it could not have profited him. But he'd done it anyway, because he'd loved the countess.

She took a choking breath. The thought seemed very important. He'd loved her mother and he'd kept loving her even after she died. He hadn't let go of love when it had become more convenient to do so.

She tried to push the idea away. But when she set herself to reading, the words blurred, and her hand shook as she turned the pages.

Yesterday, her rage had been clear and strong and insulating. But in the night, the sound of that piano had cracked the shield that protected her from the murky turmoil of these other feelings for him. These longings, this desperate need for him, now felt as strong as her anger.

She told herself that she couldn't trust her judgment of him. But perhaps she had it wrong. Perhaps her fears kept her from trusting her judgment.

Maybe he was right, and she was a coward.

When the door opened, the leaping of her heart—her anticipation of seeing him—brought her to her feet.

But it was Polly who was bobbing a curtsy in the doorway. "Lady Katherine Aubyn to see you, milady. Shall I say you're at home?"

Her mind went blank. "What—what does his lordship say?"

"His lordship just stepped out," Polly replied. "But Lady Katherine, she asked after you, ma'am."

Lady Katherine waited in the rose drawing room, staring out the window into the damp street. As Nell entered, she jumped and pivoted as if fearing to be caught at some mischief. Her gloved hands locked tightly at her waist. "Good morning," she said stiffly. She wore a dark blue walking dress and a matching hat with a narrow brim, atop which two little stuffed quails lifted their wings at a very unlikely, vertical angle.

Had it not been for Mrs. Hemple's so-thorough instruction, Nell wouldn't have caught the insult in Katherine's decision to keep her gloves on. This call wouldn't be social, and it wasn't intended to last long.

Nell took a breath and closed the door. "Good morning," she said.

Katherine moved toward a brocade chair, then appeared to think better of her presumption and decided to hover beside it. "I . . . had hoped to speak with you," she said.

A passive way of telling Nell to sit down so she could do the same. For a moment longer, Nell held on to the doorknob, the darkest corner of her heart tempting her to turn around and leave.

But returning upstairs would mean returning to this terrible inner battle over thoughts of Simon. She was glad to be supplied a distraction from it. And now that she'd laid eyes on Katherine, her curiosity was stirring. Katherine was shifting her weight like a nervous schoolgirl, and the pallor of her face suggested that the situation already was costing her something. Why was she here?

Nell told herself to stay wary. She let go of the door and took a seat.

"This is awkward," Lady Katherine acknowledged as she sat down opposite. "I had thought perhaps to run into you at a social event—but you've made no appearances since the Allentons' rout."

Nell shrugged. "You're here now," she said, "and I'm listening."

"Yes." Katherine took a visible breath. "Sir Grimston met with Rushden's solicitors this morning. Some matter of new evidence? At any rate, he tells me that he has decided not to challenge your claim. He will recognize you as my sister, he says."

Nell nodded slowly. They weren't entirely identical, she observed. Katherine was built on a slightly larger scale—taller by an inch and a bit broader through the shoulders and hips. Her slimness had disguised that at first. "And you? Will you recognize me?"

The other woman glanced down to her hands, which had been twisting in her lap but now fell still. "I am led by my guardian."

That string-thin man who snapped and barked? "From what I've seen, that looks like an unpleasant position for you."

Katherine gave her a startled look. After a brief pause, the girl said, "He is only concerned with my best interests."

How convenient that those interests also put money into his pocket. Nell contented herself with another shrug. It wasn't her business, after all.

Katherine cleared her throat. "More to the point: I was . . . wrong . . . to speak to you so coldly, before. You must understand how shocked I was—I fear my emotions got the better of me."

"I understand." But Katherine had them under a tight control now. Maybe she still thought Nell a fraud and only felt bullied by the circumstances into hiding her doubts.

"Well—that is kind of you. Generous." Katherine's lips rolled inward, making a flat line of her mouth. No, she didn't believe it. The christening spoon hadn't made a whit of difference to her. But now Nell's claim looked ripe to be accepted, she had no choice but to put a polite face on her anger.

Not a happy girl, Lady Katherine, not at all pleased

to speak her next words: "Nevertheless, I feel compelled to make amends. I wonder if . . . if you would do me the kindness of joining me for a drive in the park?"

Nell stared at her. "Why?"

"Why . . . it's a fine day," she said, making an awkward little wave toward the window.

Nell followed that gesture and lifted her brows. The window showed a cloudy sky and leaves still damp with drizzle.

Katherine gave a little laugh. "All right, it's a dreadful day. But—well—there will always be people in the park at this hour. And I—I might as well be honest with you. If we're to share social circles, I think we might as well make a public appearance together as soon as possible. It would be terribly uncomfortable, don't you think, to have the whole world speculating on our opinion of each other—watching us and whispering behind our backs? But if they see us together, behaving in a cordial fashion, the question of our feelings might be laid to rest. I cannot wish to be the subject of wagging tongues, you know. Nor can you, of course," she added hastily.

Nell smiled despite herself. "I don't seem to have much choice in it. I don't suppose you missed the flock of reporters on the pavement."

"No," Katherine murmured. "Perhaps we could—have my driver meet us in the mews?"

Nell hesitated. The memory of their last meeting recommended against this invitation. But maybe . . . forgiveness wasn't always unwise. In difficult situations, people could make mistakes, could act to protect themselves without thinking through the consequences.

Simon hadn't known her when he'd plotted the grounds for an annulment.

Katherine hadn't been prepared to meet a long-lost sister that night at Lady Allenton's.

Nell lifted her eyes to her sister's face—this face so like her own. Of course she wanted to know the woman behind it. Katherine must feel the same.

"All right," she said. Perhaps this could be a new beginning for them.

Inside the safety of the coach, they sat in silence as the driver navigated slowly onto the road. The clop of the horses' hooves was nearly drowned out by the yelling from outside:

"Lady Rushden—just one question—"

"Is it true what Mr. Norton says, that you worked as a common hand in his factory in Bethnal Green—"

"Is she your sister, Lady Katherine? Do you confirm it?"

Katherine reached up to give a dainty pat to her ridiculous hat—taking care, Nell noted, to avoid poking the hapless quails. "One of them was pointing his camera through the railing," she said with a grimace. "I believe they photographed me."

"You look well," Nell said without thinking, as if this were Hannah or somebody she felt able to reassure, instead of a girl who looked hard-pressed to sit across from her without spitting. "The hat's on straight."

Katherine eyed her. "The toque is not meant to sit straight. At a slight angle, in fact, over the brow."

"Oh." Hannah would have known that. "Well, um—should I—just—" She leaned forward and gave the hat a slight tug, tipping it down a bit to shadow Katherine's forehead.

Katherine did not move or protest, but when Nell sat back, she found the girl staring at her, wide-eyed, looking stricken.

Nell found herself caught in that look, returning it with a rising sense of helplessness, of confusion—that dizzying sensation of looking into herself. "Do you really not believe it?" she asked softly.

Katherine took a sharp breath and looked away. The coach was picking up speed, beginning to rattle and thump properly now. "It must be safe now," she muttered, and reached for the shade, drawing it up with jerky, staccato yanks.

"I'm sorry I don't remember," Nell whispered. "I wish I did."

A brief glance was all she got in reply. Katherine seemed determined not to look at her too long.

Nell bit down hard on her cheek. It was her natural instinct, or perhaps a habit formed through hard practice over long years, not to offer more than she was offered in turn.

But she owed it to herself now to try. She wanted to know her sister. "I was . . . gutted," she said, "after I saw you at the Allentons'."

Katherine spoke in a choked voice: "Don't. Just—please, don't."

"Why not?" Frustration pulled Nell forward in her seat. "That's what you came for, isn't it? To speak to me? To settle this question in your mind? This is a closed coach, Katherine. If you wanted to show us off at the park, you'd have come in a barouche." Simon had made a joke of it, one day when they'd driven in Rotten Row: a brougham was for business; a barouche was for seeing and being seen.

Katherine shook her head. She was biting her lip,

a frown cramping her brow. All at once she twisted to knock on the back window. "You're right," she said rapidly, "this weather is wretched. Hardly an opportune occasion." When the footman popped his head down, she spoke quickly: "Return us to Rushden House at once."

A lump hardened in Nell's throat. She spoke around it, hoarsely. "You're taking back the invitation, then?"

"It was wrong to ask you. I would not wish to discomfort you. You are not ready to make a public appearance—your husband did not grant permission—"

"I don't need his permission. If Grimston makes you take *his,* then he's not a guardian so much as a jailer!"

Katherine squinted at her, as though looking into a light too bright to be viewed comfortably. "You understand nothing. You—" Her voice broke. She wet her lips, leaning forward a little, and the urgency in her expression, the white-knuckled tension in her hands gripping the edge of the bench, communicated an alarm that suddenly became contagious: Nell found herself holding her breath. "In the future," Katherine said, "please, *please* don't leave the house without your husband."

The carriage slowed. Rocked to a halt. They looked out the window as one. "Stopped too soon," Nell muttered, just as a rattling came at the door.

"Oh, my God," Katherine said in a low voice. She threw herself toward the handle, seizing it, bracing herself against the paneling to hold the door shut. "Go away!" she cried.

Shock prickled through Nell. "What are you doing?"

A muffled voice from without shouted, "Katherine, are you all right?"

"Go away," Katherine said shrilly. "I've changed my mind! Go away!"

Dread pulled Nell off the bench, put her into a crouch so she could see out the window. Two bobbies stepped into view and her heart banged into her ribs. "What have you done?" she whispered.

White-faced, still holding the door closed, Katherine stared at her. "I didn't know," she said. "Or I didn't—I was so confused—"

The door burst open, and Katherine fell directly into Grimston's arms.

His dark eyes found Nell's. "That's her," he said crisply.

A policeman stepped into the doorway. He had a mean look to him, one familiar to Nell: lantern-jawed, heavy-browed, satisfied-looking, smug on his own authority. His beady eyes fixed on her as his thick lips formed a smirk.

"Come down then like a good girl," he said.

Katherine twisted in Grimston's grasp. "Leave her alone!" she screamed.

Nell stepped back but there was nowhere to go. "You can't take me," she said as the bobby started into the coach after her. "You can't." The words tumbled from her in a rush. "I'm married now. I'm the Countess of Rushden. You can't do this."

The bobby's partner appeared below, a heavy baton in hand. As his thick hand closed on her wrist, the bobby said, "All I know is, you're to come with us."

The inspector, Mr. Hunslow, was a slight, bald man whose sallow face shone in the gaslight as though he'd been dipped in oil. Every few seconds, he paused to lick his lips, which were badly chapped, cracking at the corners. "The police-magistrate does not sit again until ten tomorrow morning," he said. "It would be better for you to speak frankly, while you remain comfortable."

Nell understood that for the threat it was. This room was small, the air stale, only a single high window to prove the outside world existed. But it was private. It wasn't the usual prisoner's lodgings.

"I have told you," she said, her voice flat. She felt somehow removed from this scene, disbelieving of it, disbelieving of her own stupidity. "I didn't steal the spoon. I had it from a man named Michael Whitby." She would not call him her stepbrother any longer. She would not think of Katherine as her sister, either. She would never spare a thought for either of them again.

Hunslow's jaw ticked side to side. Through the bare, whitewashed walls came the sound of ordinary justice being done: somebody wailed; a baby cried; two voices lifted in argument. He was in a quandary, the inspector. He believed her a pretender and a thief; he knew—and had mentioned straightaway—that she came from the part of town where people properly feared his kind. He'd read the newspaper accounts, he'd informed her with a thin smile.

But he also knew she was married to a lord. He couldn't lay a hand on her, and evidently he didn't dare to raise his voice, either. Without the usual tactics, he had no idea how to browbeat her.

She stared up at him, not blinking, until he hissed out a breath and said, "We'll look for this man. Mind, though—should we happen not to find him, this story will do you more harm than good."

"Then go look for him," she said. "I can't do a thing but tell you the truth."

A knock came at the door. Hunslow tugged down his dark jacket and went to answer the summons.

Nell returned her attention to the crack in the bare, whitewashed wall opposite. It seemed important to focus on that crack. That panic in the first moments after they'd nabbed her—that sick tide of betrayal as she'd looked into Katherine's tear-stained face—had transmuted into a more comfortable numbness that she didn't want to fade. She wouldn't think about herself, about the circumstances, about the fact that Simon could have no idea where she was. She'd only focus on that crack in the wall.

"Very good," she heard Hunslow say, and the note of triumph in his voice made her stomach tremble. She swallowed hard. The walls needed a new coat of whitewash. Flakes of paint dusted the wooden floorboards where they met the walls. These sorts of walls, they rubbed off on your clothing when you leaned against them. A terrible pain, washing out those powdery white smears.

The door closed. The hollow thump of footsteps announced Hunslow's return. Only when she looked up, it wasn't Hunslow before her but Sir Grimston, cadaverous in a black suit, the slightest smile on his thin lips.

"Yes," he said thoughtfully, taking up the chair last occupied by the inspector, folding himself into it as stiffly as though his gawky limbs had never bent before. "You do look at home here," he said.

She'd never seen a man so emaciated still able to walk. There was something fascinating and terrible about how clearly the bones of his face stood out beneath his sunken skin. His Adam's apple protruded too distinctly; it looked like a ball stuck onto his throat.

To imagine himself as Katherine's husband, a man with these ugly looks would need to be possessed of a terrible arrogance—the sort that could excuse any manner of sin. "I reckon you gave Michael that spoon," she said.

"Conjecture," he murmured. "Very difficult to prove. Nearly impossible, in fact." He crossed his legs, his trousers whispering. His long fingers, clad in black leather, drummed once atop his knee. "Yon soldiers of the law will discover that he was on a holiday in Ramsgate the day the theft occurred. His friends, an innkeeper, and a barmaid will vouch for his alibi."

She kept breathing. She looked him right in his dark, cold eyes, set deep into his face like holes in a skull. You didn't look away from fear; you didn't back down. "You made a mistake," she said. "You put your cards on a greedy drunk. That spoon came through somebody else, who will vouch for his possession of it before I ever saw it."

Grimston's laugh sounded like the rustling of dry leaves. It raised goose bumps on her flesh; it seemed to skitter off to scrape along the walls. "You refer, I suppose, to Miss Crowley? Oh, yes, I do invite you to tell the inspector of her role in it. A woman who should be in Newgate for thieving—whose freedom was won not through the lawful channels of the courts, but a bribe. How interested they should be to learn of her collusion in yet another theft. Do tell them, Miss Whitby."

Her throat was closing. He'd done his research, all right. He'd seen the angles before she'd even thought

to look for them. He was right: she'd never bring
Hannah's name into this. "What do you want?" she
whispered.

"Ah. Nothing too dreadful," he said. "I wish you to
go away, Miss Whitby. It needn't be jail, however. You
understand, with this new mark against your reputation . . ." He paused, looking struck. "Which, come
to think of it, is not the first time you've committed a
crime, is it? Why, my men have turned up not a few
accounts of a certain meeting at some ladies' society.
I understand you ardently proclaimed your larcenous
tendencies before company. Can that be?" He gave her
a benign smile. "Tell me, what could have driven you
to commit such a marvelous indiscretion?"

She set her jaw hard. He'd talked to the ladies at
the GFS. They'd told him of the day Hannah had been
arrested, when she'd tried so loudly to draw the blame
back where it belonged: on herself.

She'd called those bints every nasty name she'd
ever heard. Sure and certain they'd be glad to speak
against her to a judge.

"Well," Grimston said, studying her curiously. "I
see you have no defense at hand. Which is fitting: the
witnesses to your earlier confession will not help your
defense in court, should I choose to prosecute you for
theft of the spoon."

"Get to the point," she said through her teeth.

"The point is merely this: your most recent crime
surely ends all hope you may have had for claiming
Lady Cornelia's inheritance. If I do not choose to withdraw my accusation against you, you will be tried as
a thief and most likely convicted. Once that verdict is
issued, I cannot think of a judge in the land who will
be kindly disposed to call you Lady Katherine's equal.

"An imposter and a confidence artist," he continued smoothly. "Those are the more likely names for you, and they carry heavy punishments of their own. Your lodgings"—he flicked a speaking glance around the small, rude room—"will make these look quite magnificent by comparison."

She took hold of the bench beneath her hard enough to draw a splinter. It was a very convincing picture he painted. She'd always known the courts would be set against elevating a girl from her background. They didn't like to give poor folks ideas. And Michael's wretched state on his release from prison showed clearly enough how the law dealt with people who dared reach above their station.

But Simon wouldn't let them jail her.

Where was he?

He *would* come. Her doubts were nothing compared to her trust in him in *this* matter. He'd free her. He'd do it very easily, just as he'd done for Hannah.

But Hannah hadn't had a fellow as powerful as Grimston angling to prosecute her.

She couldn't draw a full breath suddenly. Simon wouldn't be able to make this problem disappear as easily as he'd done before. All the lessons, the deportment and speech, the fancy clothing, would be for nothing. On the dock nobody would see a countess. They'd see a factory girl who'd stolen a bloody spoon.

She spoke slowly, her voice seeming to come from outside herself. "And if you choose to withdraw your accusation?"

"Quick-witted," Grimston said pleasantly. "Or perhaps only animal instinct: you scent the blood in this proposition. I am not a hard-hearted man, Miss Whitby. I understand your background is humble, your prospects—until recently—pitifully dim. I could hardly ask you to surrender your only chance at betterment, no matter how slim it now seems.

"However," he went on, "it is not your only chance. I am glad to offer you another path. I would be willing to gift you a not-inconsiderable sum with which you might return to your old haunts and live very comfortably. But you would have to return there. You would never set foot among your betters again, and you would admit, publicly, that you are only Nell Whitby, no one more. You would repudiate your claim to being the Aubyns' lost daughter."

She let go of a breath. "That would be all but admitting to fraud."

"Or perhaps only confusion," he said with a shrug. "You are female. Ignorant, uneducated, easily misled. Perhaps you were unduly influenced by the lies of an evil man who whispered in your ear for his own gain." He smiled thinly. "Lord Rushden has been known to influence the opinions of those far more sophisticated than a factory girl. I do not think anyone would be too surprised if it transpired that he had swayed you."

Everything in her rebelled. "I will not do it," she said. "Look elsewhere if you want to hurt him."

His lips flattened; for a moment, he visibly battled irritation. "You can't be so foolish," he said. "Never say you *care* for the man."

"I won't do it," she repeated.

He expelled a hard breath through his nose, then shrugged again, less fluidly this time. "As you wish. Tell the world you had an episode of madness. Whatever you want, so long as you admit that you are nobody: only Nell Whitby, the daughter of a yeoman from Leicestershire. Do you follow me? I will ensure you aren't prosecuted for fraud or any other matter. And for your pains, you'll be granted your liberty and a thousand pounds to spend as you please. What do you say?"

A thousand pounds.

She'd not imagined he'd offer so substantial a sum. She wet her lips, unable to speak.

He saw her amazement and leaned toward her slightly, as though the sight gratified him so intently that it merited closer inspection. "Exactly so," he said softly. "A thousand pounds at no risk whatsoever. On the other hand: prison and penury. I should think your choice is clear."

She struggled to think clearly. He spoke as persuasively as the devil, but everything in her cried out against it. Her heart said, *Simon will solve this*.

Her heart! What sound decision had ever been made by a heart? If there was one thing she'd learned in life, it was the danger of romantic notions, the poisonous work wrought by wishful thinking. She'd always looked for the brighter way, but every effort to hold out for hope had ultimately led to disaster. Instead of whoring she'd thieved, and Hannah had suffered for it and Mum had died anyway. Instead of keeping her mouth shut at the factory, she'd asked for improvements and been sacked. Simon had come along like a miracle and for a short, blissful time it had seemed that all her secret desires were coming true. Then she'd overheard Daughtry.

History taught lessons to those who attended to it: why should she be surprised now to learn that all her hopes, once again, had been in vain?

She searched herself for a solid objection that did not center around foolish dreams. She couldn't bank on hope, on faith, on . . . on whatever she felt in her heart for her husband.

But he *was* her husband. "I am married," she said hoarsely—unspeakably relieved to realize that there *was* an objection. "Even if . . . you are right, and I will never be recognized as Cornelia, I cannot simply go back whence I came."

Grimston burst into a laugh. The surprise in his face struck her as the first genuine emotion she'd glimpsed since his entrance, and the sight closed around her heart like a cold fist. "You poor girl," he said. "Marriages can be undone very easily these days." She tried not to react, but his laughter trailed off as he leaned closer to her. "Oh yes," he said, his voice oily. "I can see you *do* know this fact."

She stared at him. He poked squarely at a bruise that didn't heal, that only seemed to grow sharper with each passing hour. She wouldn't give him the satisfaction of knowing it. "You should go," she said.

"Five thousand pounds." He sighed. "But that is my final offer, Miss Whitby. You have a minute to decide."

Five thousand pounds.

She swallowed a surge of bile and looked away from Grimston, fearful of what he might read in her expression. The small window set high into the far wall showed a patch of sky that grew steadily darker. Night was falling and Simon hadn't come yet.

If he knew what had happened, he must be horrified. It was the end of his hopes for the inheritance.

Oh, of course he'd know she was innocent, but what difference would that make? He'd said the money didn't matter . . . that he'd keep her, regardless . . . but if she truly wasn't to be an heiress, she'd be naught to him but a terrible mistake—one he'd spend the rest of his life regretting.

And now she'd be in prison to boot.

She closed her eyes and pushed down the despair. She had to deal in facts. Simon would no more wish to have a wife in prison—a poor wife, like a millstone around his neck—than she'd wish to live and die there.

It would mean his freedom to take this money Grimston offered. And her own, as well. Walk away free and clear of this mess. No courts or judges to concern her. No more agonizing nights pretending to be somebody she wasn't, fearing of how she might disappoint somebody. How she might drive a man— her husband—to turn away from her, or worse yet, to regret his decision to stay by her side.

Taking Grimston's offer would be a favor to Simon, really. He needed money. He needed to profit by marriage.

But taking Grimston's money and walking away from Simon . . . Hadn't another woman done the very same?

Her stomach cramped; her eyes began to burn. She bit down on her cheek, dragging in a hard breath, resisting the tears. The woman he'd loved once—she had done this to him. She'd broken his heart. He hadn't said much on the subject, but that song, that achingly sad song, had told her everything.

"Time is up, Miss Whitby."

She opened her eyes and looked Grimston in the face. She'd be a fool not to take his five thousand pounds. If she turned down his offer and her future fell to tatters, she'd never be able to blame anyone but herself. This moment, in retrospect, would have been her doom.

"All right." She managed a single nod. "I'll accept your offer if it means I can leave this place right now."

He broke into a wide smile. "But of course. I'm very glad to hear that wisdom has prevailed." He rose, flipping out the tails of his jacket, and then turned on his heel, snapping his fingers at her. "Follow me," he said.

She understood her part well enough. Head bowed, she trailed him into the hall, where he announced that there had been some mistake; the spoon had not been stolen, only lent unwisely. Dismissing the inspector's blustering protest with cool efficiency, Grimston then took her by the elbow and escorted her in a hard grip out the door and into his coach.

Increasingly she felt sick. Five thousand pounds: a bloody fortune and her freedom to boot.

On the other hand . . . Simon.

He'd lied to her, yes.

But then he'd told her he'd never let her go.

Could it be that she believed him? Now that her fears and doubts in him were put to the test, she couldn't hold on to them. All she could think was how gravely this betrayal would strike him. The devil might have designed it. To do to him exactly what that other woman had done . . . even if the gain to her would be immeasurably great, her freedom and a fortune . . .

God help her. God *damn* her. She couldn't bear to lose her freedom but she couldn't bear to buy it if her soul was the price.

"Where are we going?" she asked, once they were closed into the dark little compartment and bouncing down the road. Her voice sounded properly shaky, as well it might. One moment she felt numb, the next, inclined to hysterical laughter. She couldn't believe what she was about to do. She was a thrice-damned idiot.

"I am taking you to my lawyers," Grimston said, "where you will sign a document disavowing your former claim, and receive a bank check to reward your good sense."

She nodded and settled back against the squabs. Tears pricked her eyes—tears born of disbelief, of dumb amazement. Simon had been right; she loved him, there was no other explanation for this, yet she'd mistrusted him, reviled him, because it was easier by far to hate him. Of course it was easier to mistrust than to love. She'd seen firsthand the hells into which a heart could lead. She'd seen where love had taken Michael's wife.

Yet here she went, tripping down the same path for Simon's sake! Twenty years from now, no doubt, she'd still be cursing herself for this unforgivable stupidity.

When the coach took a sudden, sharp turn, she manufactured a choking noise.

"What is it?" Grimston asked.

"Nothing," she whispered.

A brief silence fell.

She took a deep breath, willing all this pain, this confusion and despair, into her stomach. If only she could rid herself of them and feel nothing at all—not even love. Especially not love.

She retched.

"Good Lord!" Grimston snapped straight. "Are you going to be sick?"

"Think it's—the nerves," she mumbled.

He banged on the roof. "Do not vomit in this vehicle," he said sharply.

"No, no—" She clutched her stomach and heaved again as the coach slowed.

"Open the door!" he shouted, and then the cool

night air was flooding in, and strong hands wrapped around Nell's waist to lower her to the ground.

She bent double as though to puke, and then straightened with her elbow aimed straight for the footman's groin.

The man howled as the blow connected. She hiked up her skirts and started to run.

Grimston's roar echoed after her down the street: "You are making a grievous mistake!"

She didn't waste her breath on a reply.

Simon spotted Nell in the road, stumbling to a stop, her hand lifting, waving tentatively at his vehicle, as though she feared he wouldn't stop. His rage was an animate, living creature that had overtaken any part of him that he recognized. He banged the roof and did not wait for the vehicle to slow; he opened the door and leapt down onto the pavement, catching her by the elbows as she sagged against him.

Her warmth, her cheek beneath his, was the first clear and clean sensation he'd felt for an eternity it seemed. "Are you all right?" he demanded.

She was breathless, her body shaking with exertion, her skin damp with sweat. He pressed his lips against her brow, his hands flexing on her arms, straining not to tighten too fiercely, not to hurt her.

"I'm—fine," she gasped. "Please—let's go—he was turning the coach—to—follow me."

"Grimston," he said.

She nodded against his chest.

He would rip the man limb from limb. He would cut that bastard's heart out and feed it to the crows. He lifted her, ignoring the way she jerked, her startled exclamation, and installed her in the vehicle. "Take her home," he said to the staring coachman, who had twisted from the waist to peer at these curious events.

"What—" Nell leaned forward, the light from the streetlamp on the pavement behind him lending her face a bluish hue, rendering in chiaroscuro her panicked expression. "You come with me!"

"You said he is coming," Simon said flatly. "I need to—speak with him."

Her eyes rounded. "Not now! Simon, please—"

Please. Her voice broke on that syllable. He sucked in a long breath. *Please.* She'd been arrested. Katherine had sent a goddamned *note.* A note to break these tidings, a slip of paper that had lain in the entry hall hidden amid a pile of bloody *invitations* for—he knew not how long.

"Please," she repeated, and her voice snapped him back from red reverie: he looked at her, exhaled, and bounded into the vehicle, slamming the door shut himself.

As he sat down on the bench beside her, the vehicle launched forward, jolting her into him. He felt the contact like a shock, a blow to the brain; his intentions shifted, resettled; he drew her to him so fast and forcefully that she made a small sound of protest.

On a long breath, he forced his grip to loosen. His fingers threaded through her hair; he stared unseeing at the window as her breath puffed against his throat in ragged, uneven pants.

"How long?" he asked.

"What?"

"How long were you there?"

"Oh. A . . . few hours?"

He gritted his teeth. What to do with this emotion: he held very still, not even daring to breathe for a long moment, because his muscles were knotting and balking and she leaned against him, fragile, shaking, he was going to kill Grimston subtly; the man did not deserve a trial or a notorious death; he deserved to be stamped out, exterminated like a rat, in some back alley execution.

She tried to pull away. He stopped her, and then caught himself and let her go. She would be angry at him, no doubt. She had every right to rage. She was his wife. She was . . . *Nell,* he had let her spend hours alone, surrounded by enemies—"I didn't know," he said hoarsely. "I promise you—the moment I found out, I came. The carriage was already readied—I was going to look for you—my God, had I not thought to look at those letters, I'd have gone in the opposite direction, to Bethnal Green—"

His throat closed. The prospect of her running alone in the dark—not encountering him—fleeing from Grimston—caught by him—

"It's all right," she said softly. She shoved a hand across her nose and blinked at him. The curves of her face, the wideness of her dark blue eyes—he was not going to recover from this: the agony of helplessness in which he'd sat right here, not minutes ago.

He exhaled. Marshaled his thoughts. "Why did they take you?"

Her breathy laughter hitched. "You didn't know? The spoon. Grimston says I stole it."

He nodded. He could not take his eyes off her. "Are you all right? Did anyone lay a hand on you?"

She blinked. "No. I'm . . . fine."

Of course. She was always fine. "Are you *all right*?"

"Yes," she said after a pause. "Yes, Simon: I mean it." A frown dawned on her brow. "Come here," she whispered, and then contradicted herself by moving back into his arms.

He closed his eyes as he held her. His pulse was finally slowing. "When I read Katherine's note—" He swallowed. "Nell, I might have—" He felt a shudder move through him. Words defied the experience.

"I can guess," she murmured. Her face turned, her nose pushing hard into his chest. "He offered me money to leave you," she whispered.

Fleeting surprise flattened into black humor. Of course Grimston had offered her money. He'd been the messenger sent to Maria, too, so many years ago.

But unlike Maria, Nell had refused his bribe.

He turned his face into her hair, breathing deeply. Nothing in the world had ever felt so right as her in his arms.

"What will we do?" she asked.

We. Never had a word sounded so sweet. "It's a lunatic charge," he said. "We'll put them on Michael." And he would deal with Grimston.

She shook her head. "Michael was in Ramsgate when the spoon went missing. And I can't have the Crowleys involved."

None of this interested him. He wanted her home, upstairs, as far from the exits as possible, with every door between her and them locked, bolted; he wanted to have her squarely, securely, ensconced. Miracles were to be guarded. He would guard her with his life.

"Not right now," he said. "Later, we'll discuss it."

"But—" She sat up, pushed away from him. "I *can't* involve the Crowleys. There's no way to disprove it."

"I'll make it go away."

"But what if you can't?" Her wide eyes searched his.

"I can." If he could do anything, put his mind and all his energies to anything, it would be this.

She stared at him a moment longer. Opened her mouth as if to reply—then seemed to think better of it. With a sigh, she rested her head again on his shoulder, exactly where it belonged.

17

This time, Nell didn't let him keep her out of his conference with Daughtry. When the lawyer arrived and Simon tried to dispatch her upstairs, she stood firm. She kept her composure when Daughtry said, "Plainly speaking, this looks very bad." When he said, "It would be irresponsible of me to suggest that these charges do not deserve your grave concern," she received the words calmly.

Simon did not.

He lost his temper, though the lawyer wasn't the man who deserved his abuse. She listened to his anger, so different from Michael's, words without fists, the cold beneath it harder and more dangerous than Michael's fire—but not to her. It was clear to her suddenly that he'd never be a danger to her.

The lawyer tried to defend himself. She could see in his uneasy, sidelong glances toward her that he was censoring what he really wanted to say. He wanted to urge Simon toward that annulment, no doubt. "I must remind you," he finally said, red with frustration, "of the provision we once discussed. If your financial concerns are paramount, then you must consider . . . that discussion."

Simon cursed. "Absolutely not."

Well, yes, she thought. It had come to that, now.

She slipped out. Simon caught her on the stairs. His hand closed on her arm to commandeer her progress, to direct her, to make it seem, maybe, as though she moved at *his* bidding. He was, after all, the Earl of Rushden.

She didn't fight. She came to a stop. "He's right," she said. "Nothing good can come of it now."

"You cannot mean to give up," he said.

"It's not giving up. It's sound strategy."

His voice came in her ear, a raw whisper. "God damn you, Nell. Do you not understand that I'm in love with you?"

She stared unseeing, straight ahead. Those words. "I wish you weren't," she said. It made everything so much harder.

Abruptly his arm was beneath her knees; he was scooping her up, lifting her. As he looked down at her he showed her the face of a savage. "You're not running away," he said.

She turned her own face away. As he carried her, stone busts marched by, eyeing her from their comfortable pedestals. *In love,* he'd said.

He shifted her in his arms, his biceps flexing as he angled himself to strike the door with his shoulder. She could feel him vibrating, the muscles in his chest and abdomen contracting, turning into stone. A clever trick, a handy ability for his kind. In death they became immortalized in stone busts; in life they turned to stone when events opposed them. He stalked onward, immovable against her squirming.

She twisted out of his arms in his sitting room, turning to face him.

He stared at her. Not stone, after all. He looked . . . ravaged. Exhausted. "I would never let you go," he said slowly. "Do you believe me, now?"

"Yes," she said. She wanted to weep for them both.

He pushed his hand slowly up his face, through his

hair, knocking it into disorder. Beautiful, weary, and all at once, visibly disgusted: with her, or himself, or both of them, who'd made a simple business deal into something so dreadfully messy.

He turned away, pacing toward a cabinet; pulled out a decanter of brown liquid, making violent splashes into two glasses with a hand that shook.

Her numbness evaporated so suddenly and completely that she keened silently for its loss. Without its substance to cushion her, she felt hollow, ripe to shatter. He'd decided love was a part of it now. The money had always and ever been his explicit aim, but now he felt differently—now, when she'd be a criminal, not an heiress at all.

"You wanted the money," she said. The reminder felt like a favor she was doing to him at her own expense; the words lacerated her throat.

He loved her. They loved *each other*. She loved him, too, and that was now the secret she was keeping. Because tomorrow, or the day after, or the day after that—what was to hold him when they had nothing? What was to hold him when he woke up to poverty?

He knew so little of being poor. He couldn't understand what it meant. He traded on credit, but credit could not last forever. Then life would grow bitterer than he could imagine. There would be no piano for him to play. Had his thoughts gone that far yet?

He turned back. At first she thought he meant to hand her one of the glasses—and perhaps so did he. But he bolted the first one directly, and then, looking at her, he lifted the other and drank it down, too.

He sat into a wing chair. "Yes," he said dully. "I did want the money. And so did you."

She sank down across from him, unable now to

remove her eyes from his face. Complex, important things moved across it, tightening his mouth, narrowing his eyes as he looked blindly around him, from her to the fire to the glasses in his hands, the sight of which abruptly caused him to grimace. He set them onto the table and locked his hands together, his fingers threading, folding at his mouth as he drew a long breath.

"This will be difficult," he said. "More difficult than we imagined."

He sounded dazed. A sharp little laugh caught in her throat. Defeat, the world's refusal to bend to him, had stunned him.

"But that doesn't mean—" He locked eyes with her and she felt as though she'd been pierced, blinded by a sudden bright light. She looked down, blinking back tears.

"That doesn't mean," he said hoarsely, "that we turn back now."

He sounded desperate, as well he might. If he wanted reassurance, she could give him none. His lawyer knew better. Grimston knew better than both of them. Even she herself had always known it was a gamble. But a good gambler knew when to withdraw.

She exhaled, twining her own hands together, squeezing hard. He would hold her here and watch her be jailed. She would go to jail for *him,* because he was the only reason she'd not taken Grimston's offer tonight. She would rot in prison and he'd be left bankrupt—rotting more slowly, but rotting all the same.

He believed that keeping her here was love. They both would suffer for it.

Only natural that she saw it more clearly than he did. His arrogance was finally blinding him to facts. She could not wait, for love of him, to be captured in

Grimston's trap. One of them needed to be sensible, and she, the one with the most to lose, would have to play that role.

She'd planned for this once. It seemed hard to remember that conversation with Hannah in the coach. So long ago, it seemed now. The . . . dresses, she thought. Her brain moved sluggishly. She'd promised she would take the dresses when she went.

"Nell," he said. "Look at me."

She lifted her head and fixed on a point just to the right of him. She didn't want to look at him like this, with his desire plain on his face, more vulnerable than she'd ever wished to see him. She couldn't wish to hurt him. But he himself had planned to leave her once, and he would hurt her if she stayed—hurt not just her but also himself.

He had such faith that life would turn out right in the end. Maybe it was his gift to believe that in spite of all that her father had done to him. Maybe that was why he'd hidden himself from the world: so it couldn't correct these romantic notions.

She would have liked to live in his private world. To keep this precious confederacy of two, their bold, intoxicating alliance. But love wasn't enough—not in a world where her history in Bethnal Green could become a weapon to be wielded against her. Not when both their futures were at stake.

He spoke flatly. "You *are* a coward." He saw in her face, perhaps, the path her thoughts had turned down.

She shrugged. Maybe she was cowardly. She couldn't live here on a knife's edge, her heart growing ever softer, sprouting countless tendrils that would wrap around him so tightly that she'd never recover her own independent shape—knowing, all the while, that the day might come when they would be yanked apart, and the sudden distance would rip her heart from her chest.

The law would take her from him. And as she sat alone in jail, Daughtry would come whispering in his ear. He might reconsider his love. He might not. She and he would both be doomed, regardless.

She rose slowly. She had the dresses to gather.

In the next second he was in front of her. She didn't see him move; she didn't realize he had until his broad palm cupped her head, his fingers pushing through her hair, pulling her face up, his mouth coming down onto hers.

A hitching little sound escaped her. She leaned into the kiss, let her arms twine around him. She ached, and when he touched her, the ache did not lessen; rather, it strengthened, it grew unbearable—but sweeter, all the same. This dark, consuming kiss assured her that there was cause to ache, that something great and magnificent would be lost tonight: the sweetness of him, the perfection of him, the strength and the skill and the force of *life* in him, were worth aching for. It was like holding her hand to a flame, but she put herself to him and reveled in the pain.

Somehow they were moving now; somehow she was lying back on the bed as he came over her. Feverishly they kissed; their hands coursed over each other's bodies as though not touching this curve or that surface would consign parts of them to the ether; as if only their touch made this real. In the back of her brain, that pulsating, terrified part of her so concerned with survival, with tomorrow, warned her, screaming, that she should not take this risk. Carrying his bastard, she would find the path ahead even steeper to climb.

She didn't care. Life had denied her a million things, the chance to know her true family not least among them. Now it was denying her *him*. Life was cruel, not a fairy tale; one took one's happiness long before the ending, because the ending never came prettily or well.

She struck his shoulder, sharply, the blow itself reviving her anger. Nothing was ever fair. He understood; he caught her hand and held it to him as he rolled, putting her on top of him—for once, in these brief moments, in control.

She wanted him beneath her; but then she didn't. She did not want to look at him. She shook her head as their eyes met, furious, furious as she took him by the hair and pulled up his head, pulled him halfway off the bed and shoved his jacket from his body. Off with the waistcoat and the braces and the shirt and the vest beneath it; she fell back over him like a ravening creature, sinking her teeth in the solid muscle of his shoulder, glad, violently so, when he shuddered beneath her.

He needed scars. His polished skin required wounds, bruises, signs of what had happened here and would be over tomorrow. She turned her nails into him as her teeth moved down his chest, closed on the flexing muscle that banded his waist. He made a guttural noise but it spoke no protest; he arched beneath her as his fingers made quick work of her gown. The fabric sloughed from her like the skin of a snake, leaving her stronger, more resilient beneath: she was a creature who made her own protection, who carried it in her very skin. She pressed herself against him, naked, exulting in the heat of his flesh.

They rolled again, limbs tangling. He caught her

ands, placing them above her head, pinning them within the circle of his fingers as he reached down to bring his cock against her. His eyes seemed lit from behind, his expression fierce, feral, as he thrust into her.

She bucked beneath him, wanting more. She wanted that small pain she'd felt that first time—or, no, something worse, something awful to balance out the perfection of this moment. It was too much; it was enough to keep her from sleep for the rest of her life. He released her hands and gripped her jaw as he thrust into her slowly, steadily, his eyes pinning hers, daring her to look away as he took her. The slap of their bodies grew louder, an excuse if she wanted it, but she held his gaze, not even blinking.

Only when he lowered his head and took her mouth did she shut her eyes. She wrapped her hands, her arms, around his head and pulled him down to her, then rolled and came atop him. It should have been her victory, to put him beneath her and take him inside, but his hands at her hips directed her, urged her faster, and when the contractions seized her, it was with nothing like joy. The pleasure hurt; it spiraled beyond her ability to bear; at last, her courage snapped, and she hid her face in his chest as he shuddered inside her, hoping, praying, he did not feel her tears.

When he woke in the morning, she was gone.

It took Simon less than a quarter hour to understand it. He'd slept so lightly, waking twice in the night, the last time in the hour just before dawn; he remembered viscerally his relief at finding her still wrapped around him, at how pliantly her limbs had entangled with his as he'd drawn her closer. How had he gone back to sleep? When had she slipped out of his bed?

He didn't find her in her rooms.

The dining room was empty, though the breakfast dishes sat ready, covered, awaiting her usual appearance.

She was not in the library.

It was the little blond maid who put to rest the growing suspicion in him. As he turned to mount the stairs again—thinking, still, that he had missed her, telling himself that she would be upstairs—he found the maid standing helplessly above him, her hands twisting at her waist.

"The d-dresses are gone," she stammered. "My lady's dresses!"

He nodded once and turned on his heel, not knowing where in damnation he was going.

He found himself back in the library. Staring sightlessly at rows of books. One still sat open on the table, marking the spot where Nell had abandoned it. She'd found another of her mother's books. *The Tempest.* Some weeks ago, they'd had a discussion—some vigorous, miraculous debate—about this play. Had she come down here at dawn to dwell on that conversation? He recalled little of it but his own astonishment, his growing wonder, at discovering the woman across from him to be so much more than he'd imagined—a world unto herself, begging to be explored.

A passage on the page leapt out at him.

You taught me language, and my profit on't
Is, I know how to curse. The red plague rid you,
For learning me your language!

Words spoken by Caliban, the poor, savage monster whom Prospero had sought to tame. Nell had reviled him, refused to grant him an ounce of pity. At the time, Simon had found her opinion diverting. He'd wondered smugly if she gathered the irony of a woman from the slums, come to convert herself into a lady, sneering at a spirit who had resisted being enslaved by the hypocrisies and strictures of Prospero's civilization.

He touched the page with a hand that trembled. The memory of his amusement sickened him now. Caliban had nothing to do with her. It was not she, but rather he, Simon, the bloody Earl of Rushden, who had learned a new language during her time here. He'd rediscovered it, maybe, gained a better understanding of it, a new fluency.

He had no doubt where she had gone. It was not the first time a woman he loved had measured her prospects and chosen a better offer. He couldn't blame her. Their situation had looked dire last night. Grimston's payment was a wise choice by any view.

His hand made a fist. The page ripped, a long, tearing, ugly sound. He exhaled slowly.

He picked up the book and threw it.

It slammed into the dead fireplace. Pages flew, flapping like the wings of mourning doves.

He waited for the lash of humiliation, the deep burning breaking feeling that had driven him after Maria's desertion, that had hounded him for years afterward: *Not good enough. Not worthy.*

But it didn't come. What filled him was a wild, unmanageable grief. He couldn't blame her for leaving. He'd seen enough to understand what drove her. Perhaps she even returned his love, but his love was no guarantee in her eyes. From the moment she'd discovered the option of the annulment, she'd known how little his words had meant when he'd vowed to take care of her, in good fortune and bad. What was love next to the guarantee Grimston had offered?

But she was wrong to trust that bastard. She was smart, savvy, shrewd, but her heart was not black enough to lead her imagination down all the possible avenues that Grimston would have charted.

He leaned heavily into the table, staring at the book where it had fallen.

She'd gone to his worst enemy, and it made no whit of difference.

He still had to find her.

Some commotion in the hallway brought his head up. The door flew open. Paralyzed for an instant—joy, relief, anger, love swelling in him—he stood there staring at her, her face tear-stained, her lips trembling.

"I was going to look for you," he said hoarsely, then came to a stop, the words tangling in his head: it would have made no difference had she gone to Grimston; he wanted her to know that, to know he was done with pride: he would have gone to find her all the same.

And then she blinked, swallowed, and that small movement was enough to break his daze, to shatter it into shards that spread through him as a prickling, rippling, ripping realization.

"Katherine," he said slowly. "What are you doing here?"

She made a panicked noise and came toward him. "Listen to me," she said. "I was—I was wrong to deny her. But he—you cannot understand, for so long he has hounded me—I did not want to marry him, he only wanted my money, he told me I could choose where I liked so long as I denied her—and I didn't know!" Her voice was high, frightened. "I couldn't be sure of her until—until—"

"Don't concern yourself," he said softly. "I have plans for your guardian."

"Oh." She went paler yet. "But I think—I think he has plans for *her*. I told him, you see, that I mean to acknowledge her as Cornelia. And he thinks it is *his* fortune that will be halved in the process. I think— she's in very great danger."

Nell left the two plainest dresses at Hannah's and bundled the rest into a ruder carpetbag, borrowed; the one she'd taken from Mayfair would attract too many eyes. Brennan's was a long walk down the broken pavements, and Hannah had wanted to accompany her, but she couldn't bear talk right now. It was enough simply to keep moving; she did not have the strength to explain anything, to put into words what she'd just done: gutted herself, used a knife to slice through her life, putting herself squarely on this, the bleaker and bleeding side of the rest of her days on earth.

She would never see him again.

Never touch him.

Never hear his voice.

She took a deep breath as she crossed the street. Her mind was dull but her body remembered the way, bolting to safety around the onward charge of a coach, the driver throwing a curse at her in passing. She stepped through a muddy puddle without feeling the damp soaking through her kid shoes.

Better the shoes be sullied. Bright, new shoes advertised to curious eyes certain comforts that she no longer had to spare. She was back where she belonged, on the narrow road between crouched buildings, where broken glass littered the ground and people leaned against buildings, talking in loud voices, eyeing passersby curiously, nodding to acquaintances.

But nobody nodded to her. Familiar faces fell silent as she looked into them. The greengrocer lifted his brows and turned away, whistling in astonishment as his shop boy gawked.

The back of her neck began to prickle. Eyes were following her, prodding into the back of her skull. She forced a smirk onto her lips and held it there as she walked. "Nellie," she heard someone mutter. "That's Nellie."

"What on earth? Do you think—"

"Don't look so flush now, does she—"

"—bloke left her flat?"

"God save her," someone whispered.

A shiver passed through her. For a moment, in dumb reflex, her thoughts flew toward Peacock Alley, the only place here that she'd ever called her own. Before Mum had taken ill, that flat had been her safety.

She thought of Mum's grave, of the rough wood marker on which had been painted "Dearly beloved. Forever missed."

Here, in this narrow lane, lined by broken windows and stares, she thought for the first time in weeks of Jane Whitby without feeling pain. They had something in common. They'd both fled that scented, plush world for these streets. Desperation had driven both of them; nothing else would have done it.

Whether or not it was right, she would forever miss Mum. Love didn't have to be pure or blameless or free of anger to be true. You could blame somebody and love her anyway. You could blame him but love him none the less for it.

She pushed Simon's face from her mind.

In the dark confines of Brennan's, the proprietor nearly dropped his pipe for shock.

"You're back!" Brennan's rheumy blue eyes narrowed as they took in the bag she clutched. He missed nothing, the old codger. He glanced beyond her, toward one of the cracked mirrors he'd set around the shop to catch thieves: they gave him every angle.

He removed his pipe and tapped it thoughtfully against the counter. Ash floated down, landing lightly on her dark wool gown. She'd donned it herself, in the hour before dawn, wrestling with the laces on her corset, weeping as her fingers fumbled over the buttons.

"Tossed you out, did he?" Brennan asked.

She hauled the bag up onto the ledge. "I've got quite a load for you."

"I read of it in the papers, you know."

Her hands paused on the bag ties. His thick Irish voice held no glee for her comeuppance. "Did you?"

"Oh, aye, and who didn't?" He put the pipe back into his mouth, squinting at her as smoke roiled up around his head. "Came here alone, did you? Best take care, Nellie. Been too much talk for you to traipse about as you please."

She nodded once, her jaw tight. It was a warning, but not one she needed. She'd known what it signified when people failed to greet her.

The knot that closed the bag resisted her fingers. "This load should fetch a fine price," she said. The words felt stilted. She listened to herself go on. "Only worn once or twice, each of them. So don't be thinking to cheat me, old man."

"Oh, I wouldn't," he said, his manner too kind, absent of the blarney he'd usually muster for such a charge. Leaning onto one bony elbow, he dropped his voice: "What happened, Nellie? I thought we'd never see a hair of you again. Wasn't you that girl, then?"

Her hands stilled. She looked up into his face, so familiar to her—more familiar suddenly than her own in the glass behind him. Dizziness rocked her, a sense of being removed from her own skin. That pale girl with circles beneath her eyes: who was she now? Not Cornelia. Not the Nell she'd once been, either. She'd changed. Her very lungs had altered. The fumes from Brennan's pipe felt unbearable, thick and toxic. Another minute in this shop and she'd be puking all over her wares.

She shook her head and shoved the bag toward him. "I trust you," she said quickly. "And I've counted them to a stitch. You send a note to the Crowleys with your bid, aye? I'll be back to let you know what I think of it."

"Not alone," he said softly. "You bring Garod Crowley with you, you hear me?"

She stared at him. "Aye," she said. "Aye, I will."

Back in the street, the clouds were thinning, shedding a clearer view of the sun, causing her eyes to sting. She stumbled over a chunk of pavement and slammed up against someone. Muttering an apology, she pushed past—and was caught and hauled back.

She blinked up.

"I was looking for you," Michael said with a smile.

ell tested the ropes again, flexing her fingers, trying to recover sensation. "Just fetch me a knife," she urged. "Please, Suzie."

Across the room, huddled against the wall, knees pulled to her chest, Suzie stared back, blank-eyed, as though she no longer understood language. In a bad way, was Suzie, bruised and battered, shaking like a leaf. "You shouldn't have come back," she said again, her voice barely audible. "You should've known, Nellie."

"Should've known?" Nell's laughter scraped her throat. It made Suzie shrink back into the wall. "Should've known what?" She was trussed to this chair, corded like a game hen—a solid, proper chair, a new acquisition, no doubt purchased with the coin Hannah had given Michael for the spoon. "That Michael's a bloody lunatic? You're right, no news there!"

Suzie folded her arms over her knees and set her head down atop them. "It's not just Michael," she whispered.

Nell stared at the crown of Suzie's head, the crooked parting in her dark hair. Not just Michael? She gritted her teeth and gave the rope a hard yank, then hissed at the pain. For her efforts she was only wearing herself bloody. "Who else is it, then?" She had an idea. Where else would Michael have found the money for that cab he'd bundled her into?

Suzie didn't look up as she shook her head. "I don't

know his name." She drew a shuddering breath, then peeked up over her arms. "Posh bloke. Tall, thin—" She broke off on a gasp as footsteps thumped in the corridor outside.

Michael's voice came through the door, sharp and angry. He wasn't drunk, more was the pity. Sobriety, height, and muscle had worked to his advantage on the street. A few people had called out in protest as he'd knocked her around; Brennan had even come out of his shop for the first time in probably a decade. But when Michael had flashed the gun, not a single person had dared lift a hand to help.

"—better deal than you can offer," Michael was biting out in the hall. "Maybe I should ask Rushden how much *he'd* be willing to pay for her."

The reply was too low to decipher, but Nell recognized the voice all the same. Grimston. What in God's name did he want with her? He was sharp enough to have put two and two together. He'd know that if she was back here in Bethnal Green, then she'd left Simon. He should be grateful; he'd gotten what he wanted without spending a penny.

The door opened. Michael stalked through, cursing. On his heels came Grimston, dressed from head to toe in black, his top hat crushed beneath his arm. He fixed Nell with a sour smile—which disappeared at the sound of Suzie's whimper.

Pivoting, he glared. "What is this?" he demanded. "Who is this woman?"

Michael's jaw jutted. Belligerent as a mule, he was; it was Grimston's mistake to have taken him as a partner in this dirty business. "She's none of your concern," he said.

Grimston's laugh cracked like dry twigs. "My

God. What do you think we're about? You invite *witnesses*?"

Nell went cold. Witnesses to what? What sort of occasion did they have in mind? Suzie was gazing upward at Grimston, her tear-stained face, her slack jaw, lending her a strange look of awe, as though the tall man in his fine clothes had dazzled her beyond her senses.

And as Grimston looked back down at her, his expression shifted. For a moment, he looked mildly disgusted, as though viewing something unwholesome that he'd just knocked from his shoe. Then his face smoothed. A cold smile curved his mouth as he turned away; his hand moved into his jacket. "Very well," he said. "Let her stay. No matter."

Every hair on Nell's body stood straight. *My God,* she thought. Her brain scrambled to deny it but her instincts insisted: he hadn't come here bent on intimidation.

He meant nobody to leave this room save himself.

"Michael," she said. "Michael, make Suzie go."

Michael gave her a curious look. Grimston, his smile widening, gave her a wink.

"Get her *out* of here," Nell said, pulling again, so uselessly, at the ropes, as Michael decided to enjoy the moment, the *fool,* grinning at her, his lips already moving to shape some gloating remark as Grimston pulled the pistol from his jacket and she threw herself sideways and he fired.

The explosion rang out and kept ringing, drowning out the world, flattening all other sound, setting up residence in her brain, ringing and ringing. There was blood; she could see the pool spreading but it wasn't hers; she couldn't tell whose it was; her cheek was flat against these rough floorboards where Mum had died.

A crash. Michael and Grimston rolled past her, tangling, Michael's hand gripped hard over Grimston's, holding the pistol up, away from the both of them. Michael was bleeding. She saw the stain spreading across his side, soiling his shirt.

A cold hand closed on her arm. She flinched convulsively, then cried out at a stabbing pain.

The ropes fell away from her wrists. Suzie knelt down by her feet, wielding a knife, cutting free Nell's feet. Nell clambered up as Suzie spun away, lifting the blade in the direction of the two men rolling on the ground.

Nell grabbed her shoulder. "No. Go—run! Fetch the bobbies!"

Suzie looked at her, slack-faced, understanding nothing. Nell pried the knife from her hand and pushed her forward, stumbled after her out the door. Doors were slamming up and down, but nobody came to see what was happening: a gunshot was like fever; you kept your distance if you wanted to live.

Another shot rang out behind them. Suzie screamed. "No! Michael—"

Nell pushed Suzie down the stairs, but her own feet, numb from the constriction of the ropes, failed her; she grabbed for the banister and it wobbled and broke free under her hand, sending her to her knees, tumbling headfirst down the stairs. A bright light slammed into her head.

She opened her eyes to a world gone silent. Suzie stood above, hands cupped to her mouth, staring up the stairs.

"Not an inch," came a cool instruction from above.

The stairs creaked. Grimston was coming down.

Nell wet her lips. Damn Suzie for a fool, and for not being fool enough: she knew what Grimston's appearance meant. With a wordless keen, she stumbled back against the wall and slid down to the ground.

Here where Nell lay, where they would die together.

No.

Nell's hand tightened around the knife she still clutched. Her grip felt slippery. Blood. Suzie had cut her when slicing the ropes. She stared at the top of Suzie's head and waited, counting the treads on the steps. He might not shoot her till he could look her in the eye, in which case he might make the mistake of stepping too close beforehand.

Or he might not wait. She'd lie here letting her chances slip away while Grimston took aim.

She took a deep breath and forced herself to her feet and around, staring straight into the lifting barrel of his pistol. The knife had its own intelligence; the knife and her hand understood each other; they flew toward his belly like magnets to iron, slamming—

—into bone. Hot agony spiked through her wrist, throwing her off balance again—throwing him, too, off balance, a miracle; she felt the gun press between them as he staggered and fell toward her, his shoulder clipping hers as he staggered past. He went down on his knees and bumped and tumbled down the stairs. She wheeled, catching herself, staying upright only by sheer instinct, a long-ingrained habit that snapped her hand up to clutch the edge of the next flight of stairs, over her head.

Grimston landed facedown, his head by Suzie's foot.

Suzie screamed, wordless and terrible, and gave him a boot in the skull, a heavy blow from a working woman's thick-soled shoe, no flimsy slippers here. He groaned and raised one sluggish hand to protect his head. Nell couldn't see the pistol—trapped beneath his body maybe; she didn't intend to wait and find out.

She leapt down and grabbed Suzie's wrist, yanking her onward. On the first turn of the stairs she heard him again, regaining his feet, thundering after them. The light came into view, the exit into the street. Suzie was sobbing, gabbling about Michael. Nell pulled her faster, taking the steps two by two, now, reckless, forgetting which step wobbled, which was loose and might give way—

A shot cracked by her head, plaster exploding before her. The doorway was only four more steps—three—

The light went dark, the doorway filling, a tall man stepping into it. A grim, cold look; steady eyes. He lifted his pistol and took aim. Fired.

A garbled gasp. And then, down the stairs, came the heavy thump of a body falling.

She let go of Suzie. She staggered forward, fell onto her knees in the doorway.

The man knelt, too. It was Simon kneeling before her; he looked stricken now, not cold at all. His hands shook as they framed her face, but when he pulled her to him, his embrace was hard, his grip steady and unbreakable.

Seated by the fire in Simon's dressing room, a blanket wrapped around her shoulders, Nell watched the doctor draw the final stitch through her skin. The needle flashed as it exited. The thread pulled tight. Her flesh felt like rubber. It didn't hurt at all.

The doctor glanced at her over his spectacles as he pulled out a pair of scissors. Behind him stood the open door into Simon's bedroom. On that bed with solid walnut posts, she'd become Simon's wife.

She stared at the bed, a piece of her own history, where she'd laughed and imagined such a different future for herself—a lovely one, full of light, free of blood. The memory already felt distant. For the rest of her life, it would only keep slipping further away.

Why had Polly insisted on bringing her upstairs? She could have stayed in the drawing room where the police were interviewing everyone. Michael and Grimston were dead; they needed to know how it had happened. Nell could have helped them. She could have spoken about it very clearly.

But with this view in front of her, she couldn't think clearly about anything. Facts, simple ideas, kept slipping out of her head. That bed. Why was she in Simon's rooms? She'd never thought to see this house again.

"That does it," said the doctor. He tied off the bandage at her forearm. Nell hadn't caught his name, but for a moment, under the reassuring pat of his hand, she felt a real emotion penetrate her numbness: *Mum needed a doctor like you,* she thought.

She barely registered the flavor of this feeling—sadness, bittersweet regret, or maybe only gratitude for his service now—before it faded and she felt cold again.

The doctor rose and turned away. "If she takes a fever," he said, "you'll call me at once."

"Of course," came the reply, which handily pierced

her daze. Katherine Aubyn had slipped in from the other door and now slithered up like a snake, taking a seat on the stool that the doctor had occupied. "Nell," she said. Her cool hands pressed over Nell's knuckles, a touch as light as the breeze, and then, all at once, the touch settled, pressing firmly. "I am so sorry," she whispered.

Nell thought about curiosity, how she should be feeling a healthy dose of it. Maybe she should ask, *Who asked you here?* A touch of sarcasm wouldn't go amiss. *The bobbies are downstairs. P'raps you might invite them to arrest me again.*

But Katherine spoke first. "I don't expect—I don't hope for your forgiveness."

"Good." It would take a fool to trust this Judas again.

Katherine moistened her lips. "But if you—if you should ever take pity on me and let me explain . . ."

Nell allowed herself a small smile. Explain what? *Sorry about that arrest. I was . . .* Bored? Greedy? She shrugged. "I'm not interested."

"I don't seek to excuse myself," Katherine said huskily. "I know it was unforgivable. Only—if I told you something of myself—of what Grimston said of you—and of me—and—and perhaps in the course of this conversation, I could learn something of you, too—which would be my greatest wish of all, to *know* you—" She expelled a breath, and her hands tightened before slipping away. "To know my sister," she said very softly. "Nell, I would be so grateful for that."

Nell stared at her. "Your . . . sister."

"Yes." Katherine made a fist and set it to her breast. "Here," she said. "I *know* it."

"And where did you *know* it when you plotted to have me jailed?"

Katherine paled and bowed her head.

Nell felt no urge to make the moment easier. As she waited for the girl to speak or go, she wondered how she'd ever looked into Katherine's face and confused it for her own. They'd been cast from the same mold but shaped in different forges. Katherine's smooth brow said she had not frowned as hard as Nell had. She had no lines around her eyes from squinting into the sun. The uniform darkness of her hair betrayed a life of protection from the elements.

But then she lifted her face again, and Nell did recognize something: the *look* that Katherine wore.

For the first time, Katherine was looking at her as *she* had once looked at a photograph of Katherine: with wonder and astonishment and a slowly growing fear.

"Perhaps . . ." Katherine took a gulping breath. "Perhaps I was afraid to see it. Before, I mean. I'd always felt . . . so *certain* that you would remember me. I can't tell you how—how long I prayed for you, how I felt so deeply that . . ." She shook her head. "I always knew you lived, but I felt . . ." Her lashes fluttered; to Nell's astonishment, a tear slipped free. "I felt sure you would come back," she said in a choked voice. "Only I thought you would come back for *me*."

Nell sat wordless—stunned—not so much by what this girl said but by the sudden feeling welling within her.

My God, she thought. *After all this?*

After all this, then. She could still hope.

"It was foolish, terribly stupid," Katherine said rapidly. "And what I did . . . yes, unforgivable. I can only say that I was afraid of a great many things, all of which suddenly look very . . . cowardly, when compared to what you've faced."

Nell snorted. "I'm no heroine," she said. "If somebody told you differently"—for it occurred to her that Hannah knew the whole tale of what Katherine had done, and, having encountered Katherine downstairs, would have shared her own opinion of it, loudly— "then they were lying."

"No," Katherine said. "I don't think he was lying at all." She took another breath. "Well. You are—welcome at my home. Wanted there, always." She bit her lip. "Of course you are. It is your home, too, is what I mean."

Your home. The two simple words checked Nell's urge to scorn the offer outright. *Your home, too.*

Once, she and Katherine had shared a home. A nursery. So many things. "Do you remember the doll?" she asked—and felt a blush start up. "I'm probably imagining it. But . . . red hair. Blue eyes. Button nose, shiny dress. A big collar at her throat, something lace— a ruff?"

Katherine's lips made an *O*. "Elizabeth—Elizabeth Regina, we called her."

Her throat thickened. Elizabeth Regina. "Aye." She pushed the back of her hand across her nose. "That sounds right." She'd loved that doll. She remembered, faintly but clearly, that she'd not been the only one to care for it. She'd had company in love, back then.

She'd had this girl to love alongside her.

"Do you still have her?" she asked when she felt sure of her voice.

"I can find her," Katherine whispered. "I promise you, I'll find her for you."

"I'd like that. And maybe . . . I'll come visit you." Only good sense to have a backup plan, Nell told herself. Wasn't like she was bound for the old flat, now. Blood still dripping through the floorboards.

Which reminded her. "Have you space for Suzie at your place?"

Katherine frowned a little. "The—lady downstairs?" Clearly she wasn't sure the term *lady* applied in this instance, for she hurriedly clarified, "I mean, the one whose husband . . ."

"Was my stepbrother," Nell said. "Yes."

"Oh." The word came out very high. Katherine's lips folded, her chest rising and falling on a long breath. Suzie was no doubt a sight right now, with Nell's blood on her ragged skirts and grief roughening her manner. "Yes," Katherine said finally, but her voice lilted, making a question of it.

Nell began to feel amused. How hard this girl was trying. How transparently she was failing. "Too lowborn for you, eh?"

"No!" Katherine's eyes widened. For a moment she looked plainly horrified. But then she squared her shoulders and set her jaw. "She is welcome," she said firmly. "Any of your friends are welcome. Whomever you wish. It is *your* home, as I said."

And some devil prompted Nell to reply, "How very *kiiiind* of you," in her best nasal drawl.

Katherine's eyes narrowed. Not stupid. She knew she was being mocked. But after a second, a small smile crept onto her lips. "I deserved that, of course."

"And much more," Nell agreed, but somehow, against her will, she was smiling, too.

Katherine cast a glance over Nell's shoulder, then rose. "Well," she said briskly. "I'll be downstairs." She gazed down at Nell, and then, on a quick breath, bent down—her kiss the briefest graze across Nell's cheek.

Puzzled by this abrupt retreat, Nell turned to look after her—and discovered Simon in the doorway. He stepped aside to let Katherine pass, murmuring something to her that Nell could not make out.

The sound of his voice ran through her like a line of fire. In her mind she saw his face as he'd lifted that pistol. She'd felt so much in that moment: the sudden certainty of safety, of relief so profound it had caused her knees to fold, putting her at his feet as he'd lowered the gun.

She found herself rising, seized by the urge to bolt, forcing herself to resist it by standing perfectly still.

He came toward her. "I told the inspectors they could speak to you tomorrow if they thought it necessary," he said. His voice was bland. Unreadable.

She fixed her eyes on the carpet, one of those threadbare affairs, the Oriental pattern worn down at a spot next to her feet. She scuffed her toe across it—adding a bit more wear, a bit more value, she thought. "Thanks," she said.

His voice came from much nearer. "You're not going to look at me?"

No. She'd left this place—she'd left *him*—for true and wise reasons. She'd been right to go. As matters had stood, it had been the only choice. But the act of leaving had still been an abandonment.

She'd fled in the night like a thief slipping away from a crime.

I had no choice, she thought, but he might not understand that—and she did not want to look into his face now and discover how her decision had changed his view of her.

"You don't need to be afraid any longer," he

continued. "They're both dead. They can't hurt you . . ." The rest of his words were lost in the roaring shock of that single word: *afraid*.

She lifted her head. "I'm not afraid." Leaving him had taken impossible strength. If she'd had the courage to leave him, she certainly had the courage to look at him now. "I was never afraid of *them*." They'd had nothing to do with why she'd left. Did he imagine that *Grimston* had driven her away?

Her fears, all of them, had centered around the man before her, who now blinked and tilted his head, looking at her as though she were a stranger. "I'm glad to hear that," he said.

His remote manner struck her like a slap. The next second, she felt a dread-filled recognition, as if she had lived through this scene already. In her nightmares, she *had* lived through it. She'd feared there would come a time when his illusions would wither and he would finally see her as she truly was.

Yes, she thought. *I ran away from you. You see me as a coward, a selfish woman now.*

She took a hard breath and made herself hold his eyes. "I'll be going, then."

"Going," he said slowly—as though it were a word from a foreign language.

"Aye." She swallowed and spoke faster. "Katherine has offered to take me in. Of course, I'll be giving you half the inheritance. That was our agreement. I mean to honor it."

He ran his hand through his black hair, tousling it. The weariness on his face suddenly struck her.

Why, he'd killed a man today. For her sake, he'd murdered someone.

She took a step toward him. "Are you all right?"

God above, she hadn't even made sure of that. "You're not hurt?"

He stared at her. "What do you mean?"

"I mean, did you get hurt?" She looked him up and down, panic thrumming through her. Bullets had flown. But surely she'd know—"You spoke to the doctor?"

He frowned. "Nell, I wasn't hurt. I came—" His laughter cracked, short and humorless. "I came barely in time," he said. "At the end. Another second—"

"But you're fine." Suddenly she had to sit again, so great was her relief. She was shaking. "You're fine," she repeated softly. Thank God.

"No." He crossed to her in two long strides. "No," he said emphatically, crouching down before her. "I am *not* fine." His hand gripped her chin, lifted her face so their eyes met. "Nell. You look into my eyes and hear me out. *Listen* to me when I say this. Are you listening?"

Having him so close only made this shaking worse. With inches between them he was still too far away. So hard the world tried to keep people apart. Otherwise it might have been easy to span the bridge between separate universes; human flesh, pressed together, recognized no impossibilities.

"Yes," she whispered. "I'm listening."

He nodded once, tightly. "When I woke up to find you gone, I thought you had decided to accept Grimston's offer after all."

Her fingers cramped, closing like vises on the edge of the seat cushion. She'd known when she'd walked away that she would never be able to come back. She'd abandoned him just as that other woman had. He wouldn't forgive her for it. "I didn't take his offer," she said.

"I gathered that." His eyes searched hers. "But it would have made no difference if you had."

Her throat tightened. "What?" How could that be true? "After what that other woman did to you—" Anger prickled through her. "You would have been a fool to forgive me." Or a condescending ass. Did he think he could expect no better of her than betrayal?

"Perhaps." He smiled slightly. "But this is love, I gather: I find it has no separate existence from trust, not in any way that signifies. You could not destroy the one without destroying the other. And so, when the first held strong, the second only bent slightly, for a small moment. For a moment, it mattered to me, this idea that you had taken Grimston's money. And then it simply . . . didn't."

He let go of her and took a deep breath. "I do love you," he said slowly. "I have said it before but now I say it with a better understanding of what it means. Had you died today, I would have lain down in an early grave."

Tears blurred her vision. She blinked them away, dashing her hand across her eyes. The anger slipped away, now, leaving only her view of his dark, resolute face as he said: "And for that reason alone, I tell you this—you should go."

She shook her head, uncomprehending. "What?"

"You have all the choices in the world. I was not truthful when I told you that before; I deceived you, as you realized. But now, with Katherine's acknowledgment, it *is* true—beyond dispute. Beyond my power to alter. And I mean to make sure you realize that."

He retreated a pace and linked his hands behind his back. In measured, formal tones, he said, "Daughtry can end this marriage for us. Not on the grounds that you are a fraud, of course—but that I coerced you into marriage. It would be easy for him to do so. I am willing to give him those instructions. The choice is yours."

He was putting this choice on *her*? Wasn't that the easy way! "You want to be free of me, do you?"

"*Free* of you?" His lips rolled together into a flat line. He turned away, then wheeled back with a savageness that made her flinch. "Tell me," he said, low and sharp, "why *I* am the one who must answer that question? You have left me once already. *I* came after you. *I* have said that I love you. Tell me, what maggot in your brain still insists that *I* am the one who wishes to be free?"

"I . . ." *Because I'm the factory girl, and you're the lord.*

These words, even in her mind, sounded small, pathetic. They sounded afraid. She could not speak them.

"You want to stay married?" she whispered instead. He did not blame her for abandoning him?

"Enough of what I want," he said flatly. "What do *you* want? Do you wish to spend the rest of your life with me?"

Yes.

She took a breath to say it but fear stopped her dead. A cold revelation washed through her.

She'd always known that Simon could not be for her. She'd been waiting for the unhappy ending. Only a fool, a woman weak enough to deserve the bad end coming for her, would have dared instead to believe that miracles could come true.

Sitting in jail, she had despaired, but she had not for a moment felt surprise.

She looked down to her hands, her square-tipped fingers knotted so tightly together. She squeezed them harder yet, focusing only on the ache. So Katherine would acknowledge her as Cornelia. But this wouldn't change the past. She still would be a woman who'd been raised in Bethnal Green, who could not take fine dresses for granted, who knew nothing of music— who might, like a beast trained to do tricks, grow less amusing to the audience over time.

"I love you, Simon." The hoarse words seemed to be jerked from her by some outside power. She froze, panic and dread leaping up inside her.

"Yes," he said quietly. "But do you want to stay here with me?"

She forced herself to look up. His steady gaze seemed to drill straight into her skull.

He saw her so much more clearly than she'd seen herself.

She wanted to stay with him. But to stay *here*? That bridge she'd walked across to reach this world— it supported no middle ground. But in jail, faced with that sneering inspector who had learned all about her from his daily newspapers, she had come face to face with the truth: a girl could never leave the past behind. It would follow her across the bridge.

"I'll never belong here," she said. "You know that."

"But *here* is where I live." The roughness of his voice startled her. "If you think there is a better place for you, then go look for it. I will not stop you; I have no interest any longer in playing the tyrant. But if you want me, you will have to take my world along with me."

"It's so easy for you," she choked. *He* would never have to walk that bridge. Whatever rebellions and infamies he'd committed, they were born of the world in which he already lived. In the future, he would not be tested at every turn, every day, by those who knew how little prepared he'd been for their judgments.

His jaw muscles flexed. "Yes," he said. "Very easy. Because it is *my* world—not *their* world, Nell, or *that* lot's world, or the do-gooders' world, but *my* world. And it requires you. *I* require you." He took a long breath. "However, if you doubt that we could carve a space in which we, *together,* might belong . . . then you underestimate my love, or I have overestimated yours. In either case, your decision seems clear: you must leave and be glad of your freedom."

She gaped at him. "*Glad* of it?" The idiot, the arrogant bastard; of course she would not, could never, be *glad* to leave him! "You can't be such a fool."

"Can't I?" He made an impatient noise and took her arm, pulling her to her feet. "Come, let me remind you how such decisions are made. One simply—walks out."

She tried to yank free but he propelled her toward the door in an iron grip. In the hallway, he released her, looking down into her face and snarling, "You see? One *goes.* You did it once: was it so difficult then?"

As he started to turn away, she lunged toward him and caught *his* elbow, yanking him back around. "It's *my* decision! Not yours! I'll go when I'm ready to go!"

They stared at each other. Down the hallway, from some remote reach of the house, came the faint sound of laughter, as puzzling and foreign to Nell's ears as the language of a distant land. There was nothing to laugh about.

The look that fleeted over his face—frustration, grief, resignation—made her go cold. "My God, Nell. You would stay for days . . . years, no doubt . . . if you thought that to leave me is to admit your own weakness." He shook his head. "I could goad you into staying forever—and God help me, I am tempted to do it. But I won't," he added with a shrug. "I won't do it, Nell."

That shrug paralyzed her breath. It seemed so completely . . . indifferent.

He turned on his heel and began to walk away.

She stepped back against the wall, her shoulder knocking a vase, setting it to wobbling. Her hands balled into fists as she watched his back. Damn him for a coward! He was giving up. He was already leaving but she hadn't even gone yet.

The next second, all her rage turned on herself. He said he loved her. She knew she loved him. What was *his* fault in this? It was all hers.

Why did she find despair so much easier to depend on than happiness? For love of Simon, she had turned down five thousand pounds; she had returned to the Green; she had given up all her hopes. Love had been a sound and sustaining reason to endure despair. Love had given her the strength for it.

Why was it so much harder to make love the reason for hope? Why could it not give her the strength to believe in their future joy?

"I'm a factory girl," she whispered.

He was ten paces away now.

Somehow he heard.

He turned on his heel and fixed her in a calm, grave look. "Yes," he said. "A factory girl. My wife. The Countess of Rushden."

She put her hand to her throat, because panic was swelling there. "I wouldn't be a lady like the rest of them. I . . . won't care for drives in the park." Each word grew harder to say, peeling away another strip of her skin, exposing her messy innards and ugly yellow guts. "Small talk at parties won't interest me. I'll never know how to do it. How to charm people as you do. How to care so much about music. I won't want to attend other people's concerts so often, because it . . ." The words burst from her: "It seems a waste of time and I've got other things to do."

"Such as?" He was watching her very closely, but his tone revealed nothing.

"I mean to buy that factory, but—" She wet her lips. "Only as a start. I'm going to buy as many as I can, I think; I'm going to improve all of them."

He nodded and took a step back toward her.

"And I'm going to do something about doctors for poor women, too." She hesitated, startled by how fluently these intentions spilled from her. They felt familiar, intimate, as though they had been born and molded in the sleeping parts of her mind, and now sprang free fully grown. "That doctor today . . . I mean to build a hospital where such men will tend to women like my mum."

"I see," he said slowly.

"Do you?" The world didn't want to hear that she had loved Jane Whitby. Very well. She would *show* it she had.

"I think so," he said.

They stared at each other. Dimly it surprised her that she didn't feel foolish for speaking such ideas aloud. Then, with a little shock, she wondered if it was *because* he was listening that these ideas seemed so good and true.

"You think I can do it," she said. "You do."

"Of course I do," he said.

She nodded once, carefully, because something was swelling inside her, and it felt huge and powerful and able to knock her off her feet if she moved too suddenly. Until she had met him, her dreams had been small by necessity.

"You made me think I could do it," she said. If he hadn't pushed her to dream bigger, to think about power, to ponder what wealth could do, these larger ambitions might never have occurred to her. She might have been content to give Hannah a violet dress every spring. "But the point," she went on quickly, "is that I won't hold myself away from it like the do-gooders tend to do. I'll be in the thick of it, making sure my money won't go to waste. It won't be proper at all."

"The best things rarely are," he said gently.

A choking little laugh slipped from her. "You certainly aren't," she said. "You're . . ." The kind of man that life in Bethnal Green hadn't prepared her to imagine.

Maybe, to dream these things and feel these things, she already *was* living in his world.

She saw him swallow. "So," he said. "Shall I show you to your sister, now?"

"No," she said.

He opened his mouth. Hesitated. Put his hands into his pockets and looked at her.

Loving him would not be easy. It would mean never again completely belonging anywhere—save with him.

But she *would* belong with him. He would be her home, she thought. And with him at her side, she would do—*anything*. Anything in the world would be possible.

He shifted his weight and she realized suddenly that he was not waiting calmly. He stood rigidly, biting his tongue with visible effort, his hands in his pockets clenched now.

He was not at ease in the slightest.

The astonishing prospect of Simon St. Maur at ill-ease unearthed a very odd impulse: she giggled. And then slapped her hand to her mouth, hearing the slightly hysterical note in it. "Simon," she said through her fingers. "I can't leave. I love you. I can't go."

He nodded, his lips white. "But do you *trust* me, Nell?"

She was too full of feeling to even fathom the meaning of doubt. "Down any road, as far and as long as we travel. You're mine and I'm keeping you, Simon."

She heard the long, slow breath he blew out. "You," he said as he came toward her, "are the most incredible, extraordinary, *stubborn* woman—"

A hiccup—a squawk—some curious noise came out of her. "Remind me," she said. "Remind me." She stepped forward and took hold of his shirtfront and pulled him to her.

There was nothing delicate or refined about this kiss. It was dark and rude and heedless of the world; only him beneath her hands, his hair now clutched in her fingers, his body pressing hers into the wall. She had no interest in anything but this.

"I beg your pardon," came a horrified voice from behind them. Nell recognized it: Mrs. Hemple, beholding a faux pas of unforgivable proportions.

Simon paid no heed. Nell laughed into his mouth and kissed him harder, while a disgusted snort, followed by the *clip clip clip* of heels, announced Mrs. Hemple's passage onward.

When, after a minute or more, they finally broke apart, breathing hard, she smiled into his eyes. "I am going to be a very vulgar wife," she said. "Terribly, *terribly* vulgar."

He laughed back at her. "I do hope so," he said.

Oh ho! She took him by the wrist and pulled him back toward his bedchamber, saying in his ear, "No use in hoping where his lordship can be certain."

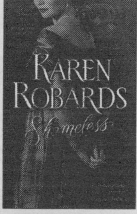

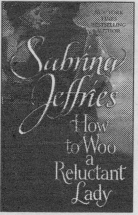